EMERALD FIRE

Cry Havoc Book Two

DONNA MAREE HANSON

Copyright Information

Emerald Fire first published by Donna Maree Hanson 2019

Copyright © Donna Maree Hanson 2019

The moral right of the author has been asserted.

ISBN (ebook) 978-0-9876381-3-7

ISBN (print on demand) 978-0-9876381-4-4

ISBN Hard cover

ISBN Large Print Hard cover

Edited by Maxine McArthur

Cover design by www.crocodesigns.com

Proofread by Jason Nahrung

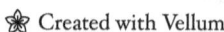 Created with Vellum

For Bridget never forgotten

PROLOGUE

T he door to the large office closed with a *thunk*. Ferdinand
tugged at the skirt of his robe and then stood straighter.

"Well, Brother Ferdinand, what news have you?" the revered leader Benedict enquired, only lifting his chin slightly when Ferdinand entered. The robed master sat at a large oak desk before a tall, stained glass window that shot diamonds of green and red around the room as the sun set.

Ferdinand cleared his throat. "Revered," he began. "Huntington has been under intensive surveillance for six months. There has been no sign of the sacred texts."

Benedict stood and Ferdinand stepped back instinctively, appalled that he had aroused his leader to movement. Not only was the master magically powerful, at the age of eighty he was still physically intimidating as well, topping six foot four and two hundred and fifty pounds. The leader of the brotherhood went to his drinks cabinet. "And this other disturbance in the warehouse district? The reports of this beast and his role in its resurrection?"

The Revered lowered thick brows over dark, glittering eyes and then leaned down to pour himself some wine from a pewter decanter.

"They are true. We intercepted a communique from an Inspector

Vickerson, reporting on Huntington's involvement. Unfortunately, the police think the incident was caused by an escaped animal of some kind."

"Animal of some kind!" The Revered let out a noise, a half-bark, half-laugh. He used the wine goblet in his hand to gesture. "They are not wrong there. This beast cannot be reasoned with as it seeks only power and blood. The carnage could increase substantially. We may be in danger."

Ferdinand started. Danger, here in Kent?

Benedict turned and his black robe swished around his ankles. He put the wine goblet down roughly, spilling some onto the desk. Then he lifted the skirt of his robe and sat.

The Revered picked up a document and scanned it. "You say we had Huntington under intense surveillance, but he was kidnapped," he said, thumping the document with a meaty finger. His voice rose in volume. "Besides that oversight, he used magical power right under your noses, has been for years. If this is not incompetence I don't know what incompetence is."

Ferdinand coloured. He felt the heat radiating from his cheeks. "His use of the art is subtle. Not easy to detect as he hides it in his machines. I believe it is not a conscious use of the art."

"As if, Brother Ferdinand, that makes any difference."

Ferdinand's ears rang with the echo of the Revered's voice. "I agree, but..." Ferdinand controlled his trembling and firmed his resolve. "It is an interesting use...perhaps even, I venture to say, revolutionary."

The Revered Benedict let out a bark of laughter. "Nonsense. Admit it. You blundered."

"I...I would not go so far..." Ferdinand stood taller. "I am willing to help rectify the situation in any way that is within my power."

Benedict snorted with laughter, though the expression in his eyes was not amused. "That is good to know." He took another sip of wine and swallowed. "You, Brother Ferdinand will be our agent. It is time for direct involvement. In addition to your reckless stupidity, you argued against killing Longhurst, which has led to catastrophic results."

Ferdinand cringed and shut his lips against further argument. It would only sink him further. Longhurst was more shrewd than magical. Who knew the insolent lout could achieve so much through his cunning alone? He had taken them all by surprise.

"As a result, you have much to do to rectify the situation." The Revered looked down at the desk and appeared to be reading.

Ferdinand considered himself dismissed and had just turned to leave when Benedict spoke again. "Did not Huntington marry the traitor Wilbur's daughter?"

Ferdinand paused and swallowed carefully before turning back. He stood calmly, hands together in front of his torso. "Yes, he did."

The smile widened, showing a gap between two front teeth. "Then you best go visiting. I believe it is time for you to renew your acquaintance with the girl child."

"As you command," Brother Ferdinand said and bowed before backing out of the room. He did not feel comfortable turning his back on the Revered at this time. There was a number of brothers he had a similar respect for. He valued his life too much to take risks. He did not wish to be another Wilbur Hardcastle.

CHAPTER 1

The morning sounds of Chelsea filtered into the room where Jemima Hardcastle Huntington reached over to pour her husband, Edward, some tea. She added two lumps of sugar and stirred before getting up to take the cup to him as he sat at the desk furiously scribbling archaic spells into his journal.

The sound of carriages rolling past distracted her as she placed the tea by Edward's bent elbow and went to cut him some fruit cake. London was indeed noisier than the country, she mused. While she was employed in this industry, he did not lift up his head from his work, and she knew better than to disturb his train of thought. Nothing nastier, she supposed, than taking down a complicated incantation and leaving out a line. She envisaged all kinds of problems occurring in such a case—explosions, discombobulation, dismemberment (quite nasty), an electrical storm or shock for those in the vicinity or just perhaps a broken neck. She wanted none of these.

With a smile, she put the plate of cake within his reach and retreated to her comfortable chair by the fire to pour herself some tea.

They were newly wed, which meant that each other's habits and moods were still a mystery to both parties. That did not mean she did not love her husband, but meant that she knew him less than she would like. Unfortunately, their honeymoon, the customary period where one became more acquainted with one's spouse, had been cut short by the appearance of a severed head in the marital bed.

Jemima shivered at the memory. After they recovered from the shock, they had come to London by the speediest conveyance. The situation with the beast, Geneck, and his daughter could no longer be ignored as those two were bent on terrorising the populace of London by drinking people's blood and ravaging their persons. Such ramshackle supernaturals had to be stopped. Unfortunately, a solution to the problem was not immediately apparent.

By taking up residence in Fulton's small Chelsea house until the situation could be resolved, they had thrown themselves into danger, for the nights on London streets had become scenes of blood, death and fear. Staying away had achieved nothing, as the severed head delivered by Geneck had proved. As Jemima's virgin blood had been used in the ritual to raise the beast, there was now a blood tie, which meant the beast could find her anywhere. She was not safe. Even now, she could remember the feel of his depraved thoughts in her mind. Whether he had the power to command her was a matter of conjecture. Edward said that the beast had succeeded before but he had been able to break her free of Geneck's control by appealing to her good nature and strong affections.

Her husband assured her that, due to the application of his magic, she could not be brought under Geneck's control again. Yet, the connection still existed for good or ill.

Swaying slightly so that her wide skirts did not overset the small tea table, Jemima bent down to throw more coals on the fire. A small amount of sunlight filtered through the lace curtain covering the little window illuminating her corner of the room. With some regret, Jemima thought of Willow Park, the extensive grounds and how the light beamed through the French doors in the morning room, the green surroundings imbuing a sense of freedom within. Another carriage rattled past, a milk maid on the corner called out and someone knocked on the neighbour's front door. The sound of foot traffic and horses' hooves created an altogether noisy backdrop to her morning tea. *Oh for the peace and quiet of the country.*

With a sigh, she stirred her cup of tea, doing her best not to let the small house and London noise oppress her spirits. Yet, even with her regret at having to leave Willow Park and having her time with Edward interrupted, she knew there was a lot for which to be thankful. She was alive, a miracle in itself. Edward's gift of her ruby heart kept her heart beating. To her that meant she was living on borrowed time and that she should use her time wisely. She was married to Edward, a very clever and handsome magician. These two things were beyond her expectations and once even her imagination. She could boast about none of these attributes to her friends. Only their close circle knew of their current trials—Ambrose Fulton, his new wife Milly and Aunt Prudence. Although with the latter it was not clear what she knew for no one had told her and if she knew that something strange was going on it was likely to be a conjuring of her imagination. The bustling, bothersome old dame would not likely cope with the truth and Jemima suspected that she conjured a kind of cosy reality in order to continue living with such overt strangeness.

Jemima sipped her tea and then adjusted the lace cuff on her sleeve and smoothed some wrinkles from her skirt. Her gaze passed over the neat array of little sandwiches and she wondered if she was hungry enough to partake. A light knock at the door and Jakes, the butler, walked in.

"Excuse me, ma'am, the master has arrived. He begs admittance."

Jemima stood up, smoothing her gown and adjusting the lace shawl covering the top of her bodice to ensure the rosy glow from her mechanical heart was hidden. Even with the hatch Edward had fashioned for it, light and the mechanism's whirring sound still leaked out. "Oh yes, please. Do let him come in."

Fulton walked in, with no sign of his previous limp, looking relaxed and slightly plumper than when they last met. He bowed solemnly. "Mrs Huntington."

"Oh fiddle, Fulton. Let me kiss your cheek." She did not wait for permission but hastened over and gave him a hug into the bargain. "I missed you, Fulton. How is dear Milly?"

"Doing very well. Not very happy with me for leaving her behind.

7

Before you ask, we are coping well with Aunt Prudence, who also asks to be remembered to her nephew and yourself."

"I cannot believe Milly is increasing already. How happy you all must be. Do accept my congratulations."

Fulton blushed a little, but looked well pleased with her well wishes. His smile died when he saw Edward scribbling away completely oblivious to his arrival. He pulled a folded newspaper from under his arm. Catching the direction of his gaze, Jemima stepped back and nodded. "I will pour you some tea, shall I?"

"Sounds excellent, Jemima. Thank you." While she busied herself at the tea tray, she saw that Edward was still immersed in his work and sighed. Edward had the capacity to block out all external distractions when he was concentrating. A trait useful in a magician, she supposed. Not so useful in a husband.

Fulton slapped a newspaper on the table in front of him, which made Edward start. "By god!" he yelped, throwing himself back in the chair. Then recognising his visitor, he stood up, stepped around the table and clasped hands.

"Fulton, so good to see you looking so well." They both looked down at the front page of the paper and read the headline. Jemima had seen the newspaper already. Blazed across the paper were the words: *Another twenty dead as mystery killer continues rampage on London streets.*

Edward's cheeks grew ruddy and he swallowed a few times before speaking. "I take it this is what brings you to town?" Edward glanced up to Fulton and then lowered his lashes. Jemima had yet to interpret this expression of Edward's. The closest she came was shame and hesitancy. He blamed himself for the death and mayhem the horrible beast Geneck was causing.

"Yes, I thought you would need my help so I came." Fulton stood with his hands behind his back, shoulders straight and chin tilted slightly up. He was all of five foot ten, stocky with a shaved head and bright almost amber eyes fringed with thick, dark lashes.

Edward shook his head. "There was no need. I do not wish to impose on you."

"Nonsense! The goal should be to rid us of this beast, not wallow in blame. Confess it. You need me."

Edward grimaced and nodded and then remembered his manners and invited Fulton to sit while he positioned himself on the arm of the large winged chair.

Fulton sat and leaned forwards in order to talk more closely with Edward. "Your letter about what happened to Vickerson, the detective, disturbed me somewhat." Fulton's gaze slid to Jemima, who was in the process of pouring his tea. Jemima had written her own letter to Fulton and she did not know what concerns Edward had outlined in his. It was news to her that he had done so.

The look from Fulton revealed that her husband was more concerned about the incident than he had intimated to her. If only he would stop treating her like a fragile flower. She still had work to do in convincing him of her general hardiness and abilities to navigate trouble.

Jemima passed Fulton his tea and offered him a plate of sandwiches, which he took. Having just arrived from Hatfield, he was likely to be tired and hungry. Jemima was able to divert the conversation from the terrible topic while Fulton ate and drank by encouraging him to talk of his domestic arrangements, which they heard consisted of Aunt Prudence's project to decorate the nursery. While Fulton spoke lightly of some of the happenings at Hatfield, Jemima sensed that there was some friction between Milly and her aunt concerning the running of the household. She deftly turned the conversation to avoid further elaboration of those finer abrasive points. Such topics were not good for the digestion and the enjoyment of tea. There was no point in dwelling on it, and the situation would come to its natural conclusion—a big hullabaloo.

Jemima's money was on Milly being the victor. She might appear meek and downtrodden, but her marriage to Fulton and his surprisingly large estate would give Milly the impetus to throw the old lady off or at least ensure she knew her place. Jemima was pleased that Edward shared her opinion of his aunt and that she would never be prevailed upon to live with the old dragon again.

Fulton replaced his cup on the saucer and then sat back and regarded them. Jemima understood that there could be no more prevaricating.

"Edward, could we perhaps discuss how we will tackle this situation? I am afraid my conscience will not let me sit idle while innocent people die," Fulton stated in his cultured voice. Jemima almost smiled at how he used to talk when they thought him Edward's hired man and not his good friend.

Edward stood and leaned on the fireplace, second cup of tea in hand. "I am equally troubled. We came, as you know, as soon as we were sure he was on the move. The incident at Willow Park was not easy to ignore." He placed the empty cup on the mantelpiece and rubbed at his temple before fixing Fulton with his intense blue eyes. "Your help is very welcome. We can discuss things now if..." He turned to Jemima and lifted an eyebrow.

Jemima met his expectant gaze with a blank, uncomprehending look. They were not so well acquainted that she should be expected to interpret a silent signal to leave the room, particularly when she had no inclination to do so. Edward waited a minute, turned the saucer of his empty teacup twice and then tried again. This time the expression was akin to a puppy awaiting a tasty morsel from the cook. Jemima lifted an eyebrow and decided that the tea things required straightening, thereby cutting off her view of that forlorn expression before she buckled. As much as she loved Edward, she was not about to become dull as dishwater and be sent from the room when some delicious bit of news might sully her ears.

His unspoken entreaty diligently ignored, Jemima awarded herself a point. With an audible sigh, Edward said to Fulton, "Perhaps we could go to my club."

Noisily rattling the tea cup in her hand, Jemima flashed an angry stare as she placed it on the tray. "Oh no you do not! You are not going to cut me out. I am one of your creations just like Fulton. I have an equal right to assist in fighting this beast." In surprise, Edward elbowed the cup off the mantelpiece and caught it just in time. "Now Jemima, you cannot expect—"

"You forget my connection to him. It could be useful."

Edward spluttered. "Now, Jemima, I will not—"

Just then the butler swung the door open, his dark eyes wide and innocent looking. Jemima flushed, realising she had raised her voice to her husband and that they were in the throes of an argument. Fulton stood up, an eyebrow lifted in query. "Yes, Jakes. Is there a problem?"

Jakes turned his gaze to his master, tilting his head to the side. "A couple of policemen to see you, sir. An Inspector Coleman and a uniformed policeman whose name was not given."

This was delivered rather deadpan to the surprised audience. When no one spoke he added, "Shall I show them in?"

Fulton ran his hand over his shaven scalp. "Yes, thank you, Jakes."

CHAPTER 2

With a slight bow, the butler snicked the door closed behind him with due efficiency. Jemima sought her chair after sharing a troubled look with the others. Fulton sat back on the settee and Edward hastily closed his journal and muttered a hiding spell before resuming his seat at the table.

By the time the policemen clumped down the hall, the assembled party was diligently munching on fruit cake while Jemima swung the kettle over the fire to make a fresh pot of tea. This morning, as Jakes had placed two full kettles of water to keep them amply supplied with tea for the day. At this rate, he would need to provide more.

As it was Fulton's house, he rose to meet them first, followed by Edward. Jemima stayed seated, surveying the new arrivals. The police inspector wore a black coat and black check pants. Her quick survey ended on the highly-polished, black shoes. His blond-grey hair was oiled and combed over his bald patch. When he smiled his teeth showed uneven and stained.

Switching her appraisal to the young policeman in uniform, she noted the pale, pimply skin and very red cheeks. Catching her eye, he acknowledged her with a nod and removed his tall hat, unlike the older man who ignored her. There was a hint of ginger in the young constable's hair as well as curls and a shine to the row of brass buttons down the front of his coat.

Inspector Coleman squared his shoulders and turned so that he could survey the whole room. "My name is Inspector Coleman, from the Detective Branch. It's Mr Huntington we came to see, Mr Fulton. Forgive the intrusion, but we heard from the magistrate near Willow Park that the Huntingtons were staying here."

"No need to apologise. How can we help you?" Fulton said. Inspector Coleman looked twice at him, suddenly understanding that Fulton was to be included in any interrogation and was not to be put off by a policeman's abrupt manner.

"I see, sir. Well, it is like this. We would like to ask Mr Huntington a few questions relating to the death of Inspector Vickerson."

Edward resumed his seat, effecting an untroubled air. Fulton invited both policemen to be seated. Inspector Coleman sat down, but the uniformed police officer stood behind him, straight as a rod, and pulled out a notebook. With his pencil in hand, he stood poised ready to record the results of the interview.

Inspector Coleman cleared his throat, his eyes flicking to Jemima. She turned her attention to the steaming kettle, pretending not to be there. "Mr Huntington, can you describe to me how Mr Vickerson's head came to be found in your bedroom?"

Edward maintained eye contact with the detective. "Well, as er...I told the magistrate we were asleep when the window pane shattered from the passage of the head through the glass. The severed head then landed on our sheets."

The inspector raised his eyebrows. "Do you know how it came to be thrown through a second-floor window?"

"No, the matter is quite puzzling to me. I hastened to the window and saw no-one or any mechanism by which it could be thrown." Edward's blue eyes met Jemima's for an instant before being directed once again to the inspector. Coleman looked at Jemima, finally taking note of her presence. "Perhaps Mrs Huntington would like to leave the room while we discuss this gruesome incident. I doubt it is fit for a lady's ears."

Jemima paused, tea pot in hand. "Nor a lady's eyes, Inspector

Coleman. You see I did see the severed head. It was my bed on which it landed. I assure you talking about it disturbs me no more than seeing it in the flesh. Tea?"

The inspector's expression twisted slightly as he attempted to mask his revulsion. "Ah, no, thank you, ma'am."

"Some cake, perhaps?"

He shook his head, slightly flushed in the cheeks. Jemima was rather pleased she unsettled him, for she did not like to be treated like a delicate flower. He turned his attention back to Edward with a quick lift of his eyebrow to Fulton. Jemima noticed this gesture, a comment on her she presumed. However, she chose to ignore the man's impertinence and refilled Fulton's cup and that of Edward and then handed around some biscuits.

"The magistrate said a search of your estate did not reveal the remainder of Inspector Vickerson's corpse or any evidence that he was murdered there."

"Yes, that is correct. That is what was reported to me in any case."

"And you can think of no reason why the head of an inspector of the London Metropolitan Police would be deposited in your home in the country."

Edward shifted position, took a sip of his tea and placed the cup on the saucer carefully. "No, only supposition."

"I see. You had met the deceased had you not?"

A shadow crossed Edward's face. "I had met him once, yes."

The inspector pulled a notebook from inside his black coat and flipped it open. "At the manufactury, not too much more than three weeks ago, where an escaped wild animal caused such havoc, is that so?"

Edward glanced at Fulton. "Yes, truth be told, it was."

Fulton sat forwards. "I brought the police to the scene to rescue Mr and Mrs Huntington. I was present when Mr Huntington met Inspector Vickerson."

He read from his notes. "Inspector Vickerson reported that you saw a beast, something you described as a vampire, a ravenous, blood-sucking creature, which was responsible for the mayhem and murder at the scene."

Edward sat up straighter, his shoulders squared. "Yes, that is true, I did say that, but Inspector Vickerson did not believe me."

"So you stand by that statement?" It was hard to tell what the inspector thought of the idea. Jemima admired his knack of keeping his thoughts hidden. A good trait in a policeman.

Edward glanced at Jemima. "I do, though you may think me mad."

The inspector's gaze fell upon the newspaper on the table. "You have seen the headlines, I see, sir." The 'sir' was enunciated with a rising inflection—a question, then.

"Yes, we have."

Coleman leaned forwards. "Do you have an explanation for them?"

Edward drew back fractionally. "Explanation? What do you mean? Are you inferring that we are in any way connected to them?"

"No." Coleman slid his notebook back inside the lapel of his coat, a slight smile touching his lips. "I was hoping you had a theory."

"I do, though you may dismiss it. The murders are connected to the incident at the manufactury."

Glints of interest kindled in the inspector's eyes. "So what you are saying is that a vampire you helped raise from the dead is now murdering Londoners at night?"

Edward stood up suddenly and walked to the fireplace, putting his back to the policemen. Jemima shared a worried look with Fulton. Edward already blamed himself too severely and she would not be surprised if he confessed to being complicit in the murders, which would put them all in a very fine pickle. Edward's mystical powers were necessary to stop the beast and he would be no use at all if he was incarcerated for crimes he had not committed. Although, Jemima recalled, he was quite capable of breaking out of confinement. Still she would rather not go to the trouble of him having to do so in the first place.

Edward swung around, his olive complexion quite pale. "I was involved in the ritual that raised the creature, but most unwillingly. My wife was tortured by members of the cult to force me to agree. I had no choice. Not if I..."

Surprisingly, the inspector nodded, his hand rubbing his chin. "I see, Mr Huntington. Imagine, if you will, that I believe what you told

Inspector Vickerson that night and what you have repeated to me. What action would you propose we take to combat this villainous creature?"

Edward started, suddenly lost for words. "I...I...do not know." He cast his gaze around the room, perhaps seeking inspiration. This was the very topic that Fulton, Jemima and he had been about to discuss. "I do not know how to kill it—to stop it." Trepidation weighed heavily in Jemima's stomach, as if she had eaten one too many portions of fruitcake that morning. Looking at the empty plate, she was not surprised if that indeed was the case. Edward was not lying. He did not know. And if he did not know what were they to do? How were they going to manage?

"The danger is most at night," Edward continued, almost to himself. "The creature avoids the light." Then, as if gaining confidence, he spoke loudly and directly to the inspector. "If you found its lair during the day, then there is a chance you could dispatch it because it would be at its most vulnerable. Cut off its head perhaps."

The detective sat forwards in his chair, eyes glittering with speculation. Obviously, Edward's information was better than his own. "Where would you start?"

"Somewhere dark. Somewhere the sunshine does not reach."

CHAPTER 3

The policemen took their leave, requesting that Edward remain in town to answer further questions if required. She thought Fulton or Edward would have volunteered the information that they were going to seek the creature themselves with a view to dispatching it. However, that they did not was enough of a signal for her to remain quiet on the subject.

Fulton showed the two policemen to the front door. As soon as the door shut, Jemima started tidying up the tea things, clattering cups and saucers, suddenly nervous. She did not want Edward taking the blame for that beast. She hated that Inspector Coleman had almost accused him of direct involvement. Already, she feared the guilt would destroy Edward and any good feeling he had for her. She could understand his sentiments, although she did not sympathise with them. Longhurst and the resurrection of the beast Geneck had marred her life forever.

Fulton returned and rubbed his gloved hands together. "Well, there is a good place to start our conversation. Brilliant, Edward—look somewhere dark. You had me worried at first, saying you did not know how to kill the creature. I almost lost hope until you said somewhere dark. That is a beginning."

Edward agreed. "Tonight, we plan as it is too late to start any daytime excursions now. Tomorrow, we go looking for Geneck in any dark place we can find."

"We shall indeed."

Seeing Fulton so eager, she recalled what he was capable of with his artificial arm and leg construct. He could reach into the beast's chest and rip out its heart. He could move faster than a normal man. Behind that gentlemanly facade was an efficient killing machine.

"Let's plan now, then. It will give us time to form a strategy." Edward waved his hand, rematerialising his journal. Jemima sensed the spell, a faint impression of movement in the air. So faint and fleeting was the sensation that she could not be sure if it was whimsy on her part in perceiving it. Shaking her head, she cleared her mind and sat down at the table with the others.

From the back of the journal, Edward pulled out a large folded sheet of paper and opened it on the table. It was a map of London. On it he had marked crosses. "These are where the bodies have been reported in the newspaper. There could be more, but there is enough information to see if there is a pattern. I could not quite figure it out." The crosses appeared on both sides of the Thames, in seemingly random groupings.

Fulton studied the map turning it this way and that. Jemima peered over his shoulder. "You said the beasts were vulnerable during the day and they are likely hiding somewhere dark," Fulton said. "What about an abandoned building with boarded up windows, or basements...underground? Or they could even hide in crypts in church yards. Are there any close by to these areas where the dead were found?"

"That is a possibility. Churches are ubiquitous in London." Edward rubbed his chin. "The crypts would be rather cramped, unless they used a large one." He tweaked his ear, then looked at them in turn. "Doubtless they would be well secured or visited regularly as those types of crypts and mausoleums are costly to build and maintain. At least, the better kept ones would be."

Jemima studied the map. "I did read in the newspapers about sewers," she said taking the opportunity to enter the conversation. "When I was at school there was a lot of construction in London. You know, after the big stink, miles and miles of sewers were constructed. The construction is still going on, I am sure." Edward and Fulton turned to her, their faces frozen in surprise. With a shrug, she added, "Then there are underground railway tunnels. I am not sure any are complete yet, but I believe some construction has commenced."

They stared at her in silence until Fulton blurted, "Of course! Jemima you are a clever woman. Sometimes that is a useful trait."

"Why thank you, Fulton. How generous of you." He was used to calling her an unnatural female and never went as far as referring to her as a lady.

"Forgive me, Jemima. I meant useful in the context of not turning your mind to things that involve convoluted plots and schemes...and...and let me see, what is the word? Ah yes—mischief."

Jemima composed her expression to one of innocence and turned to her husband and blinked a few times. Fulton had referred to her penchant for forging letters, a scheme to get Aunt Prudence, Milly and himself to London under the guise of shopping while they had searched for Edward, who had been abducted.

Edward's eyes narrowed, but he nodded. Then he put his elbows on the table and cradled his head. "I should have seen that myself. Why am I not thinking straight?"

Jemima, a bit concerned for his mood, reached out and squeezed his shoulder. "Not necessarily, Edward. You spent a lot of time in Sussex during that period absorbed in your work. It only sticks in my mind because I was here at the time. Do you recollect I was at school?"

Edward flushed. She did not wish to tease him, so slid her hand along his arm and laid her hand over his and smiled tenderly at him.

Fulton coughed, and they turned their attention to the task at hand. Fulton pivoted the map on the table, running his fingers along the roads. "The sewers run all under the city. I heard they are criss-crossing and looping around taking rain runoff from the streets as well as sewage. Why, they have even channelled a couple of rivers into them, taking them below ground. Then the waste water is taken to outlets on the Thames. I believe one is just past the Houses of Parliament."

Edward leaned over. "Unfortunately, this map does not show the sewer construction at all. Which is sensible I suppose, as they are mostly underground. We will have to search ourselves for openings above ground. I will send out enquiries to see if we can obtain a map of the sewers." He glanced up at Jemima. "And the rail line tunnels." He shuddered visibly. "How they intend to run trains under London is beyond me. How will they preserve the air for the passengers—"

"Where was the most recent attack?" Jemima asked, diverting her husband from his analysis of the modern railway. She pored over the map, considering that the addition of dates on the crosses would facilitate their planning. However, she was much too endeared to her husband to criticise his methods.

Edward picked up the newspaper Fulton had brought to study it. "Here on Westbourne Street, not far from here."

"Chelsea? So close?" Jemima shuddered at the thought that the monster lurked beneath her feet somewhere below the city. It did not escape her notice that she had slept in Fulton's house for the first time the previous night. His house was in Chelsea, near Sloane Square. Was there a connection? "Oh look see, there is still some sewer construction in Pimlico," she added, pointing at the line on the map with alacrity.

Edward frowned and shared a worried look with Fulton, then picked up the map and studied it closer. "That is close to Chelsea I suppose. Then there's Grosvenor canal. Some of that's covered up now with Victoria Station going in. And the additional storm water drainage. Plenty of places to hide."

"Worth inspecting at the very least," Fulton ventured. He peered again at the map. "Look, there's a main intersecting storm water drain running parallel to Sloane Street right down to the river. It could be that which is in the process of construction."

"Ah yes, we have to start somewhere," Edward replied with false cheerfulness.

"I will come with you to search."

"Jemima!" Edward and Fulton both exclaimed in unison and their expressions also mirrored each other.

She smiled in response and gave them the *I have made up my mind so do not bother arguing with me*: look.

Fulton shook his head. He at least understood her well enough not to argue. Edward was too caught up in love and chivalry to take the hint. Edward's neck reddened and his fingers clenched the map. Fulton jumped in before Edward could draw breath. "Your assistance will be most welcome, Jemima."

Jemima beamed at him and at Edward who was still groping for words.

"But...but..." Edward began. Then he schooled his features and pronounced, "I forbid it."

"Poo!" Jemima said and took the map from his now limp fingers and spread it on the table again. Studying the map made her spirits drop and her triumphant smile ebb. Why did the city build all those horrid sewer tunnels where these creatures were able to hide? Then she thought about what went into the sewers and screwed up her face. She had volunteered to go down there among the filth of the city to search for a beast who could kill her on a whim. Perhaps she had been too hasty. However, she was not about to back down no matter how much Edward glowered.

The thought of the damp, dark sewers gave her qualms though. With a shudder, she considered falling back on the excuse that she was a lady and could not possibly be exposed to such...oh damnation! Since when did she ever consider using such a silly excuse for anything? That she had entertained the idea, no matter how fleetingly, was a measure of how daunting their task appeared to her. If she must go down there, she would be smart about it and prepare a nosegay and ensure that they all washed well afterwards. She smiled at the thought of her face buried in a bunch of over-perfumed flowers. Perhaps no to the nosegay.

Fulton folded the map, leaving it on the table. "Very well then. Provided we pass the night without a visit from our friend, we will venture out in the morning." He tapped the map with a gloved finger. "We need to prepare first. I will see what I have here: lanterns, ropes, appropriate clothing. I will prepare a list and the footman can fetch the rest. Oh, that reminds me, Milly sent a chest with me with presents for you. I will bring it down."

He left the room swiftly and his muffled footsteps echoed from the stairs. She glanced at the closed door, wondering why Fulton felt the need to bring a chest down at this moment. How did it relate to their present discussion? She shook her head slightly, wondering what marriage had done to her reliable friend.

Edward reached over and clasped her hand. "My dear Jemima, I am sorry for arguing with you before. It is just…" He kissed her knuckles.

"I know you care for me, Edward, but you must allow me to help you. I would hate for anything to happen to you when I was not there. Indeed I would hate for anything untoward to happen at any time. You did say to me when you first put this in me—" Her finger tips brushed the ruby-powered mechanism buried in her chest, "—that my heart would beat for a long time."

"That does not make you impervious to harm." His eyes glittered with warmth.

"I am not saying that it does. However, I urge you to use this connection I have to Geneck to our advantage. Once we have him, I will gladly step back and let you and Fulton deal with him. Instead of worrying about me, you could be putting your mind to how he can be stopped."

He studied her face and she saw a range of emotions pass over: love, anger, fear, which then gave way to affection. "You are precious to me. I cannot believe what a fool I was leaving you in that school for so long. When I think I could have had you in my life years earlier."

Jemima laughed and squeezed his hand companionably. "How nonsensical you are. I was too young. We met at exactly the right time so no more of your regrets."

Her eyes fell upon the journal, which he had not hidden with a spell. "Did you find anything that will help us?"

Edward picked up the journal and flicked through the pages. "Many things, though I must be careful. Your father cautioned me not to use the texts he had hidden in the old chest. The spells within are dangerous for a start, but also because by unleashing the power in them I could bring myself to the attention of the brotherhood."

"The brotherhood? What is the brotherhood?" She sat back, bewildered.

"Your father was once part of a brotherhood of magicians. A secret society, so to speak. I do not know their name for he does not mention it. From what I can tell, he had distanced himself from them when he married your mother. Did you know how old he was?"

Jemima shrugged. "Just old. I was still young when he died."

"Well into his eighties when he married," Edward advised.

Jemima turned an incredulous expression to him. "But surely he was fifty when he died, and no more. No, Edward, you must be mistaken for he looked much younger until just before he died. Always so energetic, but a little sad." She knew her father had never recovered from his wife's early death. Although he never blamed Jemima for living when her mother died not long after her birth, he was always reclusive, even schooling her from home. Occasionally, they had visitors but they were never that friendly with the neighbours or had family to speak of.

Edward tapped the journal. "Precisely! Being a magician somehow lengthened his life, preserved him, making him appear younger. But the dates in his journals hint at a much older age still."

Jemima covered her mouth with her hands, aghast at the things Edward had revealed about her father. She had only half believed he was a magician until Edward had shown her the journals written in her father's hand discussing magic. Dropping her hands into her lap she said, "Oh, I never knew that he was like some aged wizard. How did he hide it? Why did he never confide in me?"

Edward shrugged. "I do not know for certain." His gaze met hers, his blue eyes suddenly intense. "But it seems to me that he was hiding from the brotherhood and he wanted to keep you safe. So he kept you home and taught you as best he could. I can empathise with that motivation. I, too, do not wish you in harm's way."

Jemima nodded. She didn't like being in harm's way either, but she had to balance that with who she was and she was not a stay-at-home miss, ready to faint at the first sight of blood. It saddened her that her father had kept the truth from her, but only because it meant she knew him less than she thought. On the other hand, she was grateful not to have known about magic then, because her upbringing had been odd enough as it was. For all her early childhood, her father had lived reclusively, apparently pursuing scientific endeavours. He spent his spare time teaching her about science and the natural world from early childhood. "Yes, that's true. He did do what he thought best in keeping me close to him and teaching me. I had little time to pine for a mother I did not know. How sad that I did not know then, that he was in fear of this brotherhood. How he must have ached to tell me of his magic. I could have shared his burden." She sat quietly for a bit, aware of Edward flicking through the pages of his journal.

Letting go of the melancholy that thoughts of her father had aroused, she turned her attention to her husband again. "So what is your plan?"

Edward looked up from his journal, put his pen down on the table and commenced pacing the room, once again taking up station in front of the fireplace. His fingers toyed with a china ornament, a figurine of a lady and her lamb. "If we are in danger, I will use one of the forbidden spells. If that is not sufficient for our needs, the use of one of those spells will advertise my presence to the brotherhood and they would be summoned forthwith. They should be in a position to help, I imagine."

Jemima did not like this plan but did not know how to discourage it. She did not know Edward well enough to propose a counter suggestion without upsetting his feelings. Her eyebrows drew together as she thought of an approach. "What if they do not come? What if they do and are more dangerous than Geneck?"

His brow clouded. "Both are good points." He nodded to himself. "I will think on it further before I act. I would not risk you again and, as you stubbornly refuse to stay out of the way, the use of the spell may endanger you." He stared into space, absently rubbing his chin. Then after a few moments, he asked, "Your father was a good man, was he not?"

Jemima's eyes widened. "Well...I think so—to me at least. None of the servants or tenants complained. He did not have many acquaintances, except one or two older gentlemen who came to visit, but I never saw him do ill to any living thing. You saw yourself his fascination with the natural world."

"Exactly. Then we must trust that he would not have associated with a brotherhood that was entirely evil."

She was about say something more when the sound of thumping reached them. A grunt and then a bang heralded the arrival of Fulton, who was presently struggling down the hall with a large travelling chest. Edward rushed to open the door to assist. Together, Fulton and Edward manoeuvred the chest into the middle of the room and Fulton unlocked it. "My," Jemima said. "It is terribly large. You must have travelled in that great lumbering coach of yours to bring it with you. I admire your forbearance."

Fulton grinned at her. He liked the old dreary coach. Jemima hated the thing and could not forget the trip where she was forced to travel with the blinds drawn for the whole tedious journey.

"Milly has been very busy of late. Even I do not know what is in the chest. I was required to bring it and then for all of us to be present when opening it and that I should do the honours in opening it as soon as possible on my arrival. Now seems as good as time as any."

Jemima smiled at how Fulton's eyes sparkled with excitement. With his penchant for handcrafts, she could not conceive of how Milly had made anything without his knowledge as he was always querying her about her work.

"Certainly," Jemima agreed. "Well, do please open it. I find the wait excruciating."

Fulton unlocked the chest. Within was a linen sheet covering the contents and a piece of paper folded in half on top. Fulton reached in and shook the letter open. His eyes widened before he finished silently perusing the letter.

"Well?" Edward and Jemima said in concert.

Fulton looked abashed and then leaned over to flick open the sheet, revealing some dark-coloured apparel. Jemima leaned in, catching a whiff of leather. "My word, what has she done?"

Fulton shrugged. "She says that as I will not allow her to accompany me while there is danger in London, she must do something to assist us in fighting the beast. She has made us durable clothing, fit for fighting monsters in unsavoury surroundings."

Jemima reached in and picked up the first item. It was a leather corset. A label inside confirmed it was for her. On examination the lining appeared to be reinforced and the whole garment quite heavy. Beneath that garment, she found what looked to be leather trousers. She glanced at Fulton, lifting a questioning brow. "She knows that you dress in men's clothing as needed. You do not remember, but she undressed you that time."

Jemima nodded, thinking the clothes extraordinary and quite appropriate. "Well much more suitable than a leather skirt and a steel-reinforced hoop petticoat."

"Indeed," Fulton said and grinned.

For Edward there was a leather vest and a knee-length leather coat. Inside there were many pockets. How Milly had made these garments in such a short time quite astounded her. She suspected she had help from Fulton, but he was not owning to it. Straight away Edward pushed his arms through the sleeves of the vest. It too was reinforced and when buttoned appeared to be as durable as her corset. The cut of the coat made Edward a dashing figure and Jemima found herself smiling as she admired him in it.

For her husband, Milly had also fashioned a leather vest, but no coat. Jemima wondered at this, but then remembered the artificial arm and leg. They did not need additional protection. At the very bottom of the trunk were three leather gorgets, protection for their necks. Quite appropriate given their quarry.

Edward cast Fulton a surprised look. "What have you told that poor girl?"

Fulton looked down, slightly abashed.

"You told her everything?" Jemima guessed. She could picture Milly, mouth agape, while Fulton told her of the horrible scenes he had witnessed when Geneck awoke, of the deeds he performed when fighting the newly created vampire host.

Fulton nodded. "I do not keep secrets from my wife. She knows the nature of the beast we seek and does what she can to contribute to our protection. A gorget will provide a first line of protection for our necks."

Jemima coughed to attract their attention "These are truly wonderful garments, Fulton. They make me feel very special and very safe. Please pass on our thanks."

"Yes, Fulton. Do thank Milly. I did not know she was so skilful." Edward continued to parade around in his jacket. "It is truly magnificent."

"One question though, Fulton. Are we to wear these in the daylight?" Jemima was thinking of how such a thing could be accomplished, already working out whether a redingote would be the best thing to conceal the leather clothing. She also had thoughts about what to wear underneath, a cotton shift perhaps.

"It would be wise, I think, to wear the protective clothing tomorrow. We do not know how active the creature will be in the dark spaces. Perhaps, Jemima—"

A knock sounded at the door. They quickly put the clothing back in the chest as Jakes opened the door. The butler's gaze passed over the chest, yet his expression betrayed nothing.

"Dinner is being served within the hour."

"Thank you, Jakes."

"Should I have that chest removed to your room, sir?" Jakes nodded in the direction of the chest.

"Yes, thank you." Fulton locked the chest. The butler left the room and soon returned with the footman. They sat around and watched as the chest was manhandled out the door. Jemima thought because Fulton had locked it, the butler was even more curious and working twice as hard as normal to appear unconcerned.

Fulton met her gaze and she saw a twinkle in his eye. "My, you are such a tease, Fulton. You know he is dying to know what is in there."

Fulton chuckled. It was good to see his easy humour. "That and what you are doing here and what I am doing here. However, it is good for him to be kept in the dark on occasion."

Jemima nodded. "I suppose we should retire to our rooms and dress for dinner then," Jemima said, standing up and straightening her skirts and adjusting her lace shawl over her shoulders again. She smoothed her hair, hoping that she did not have to dress it again for dinner. The maid had done a reasonable job arranging it in the morning.

She moved in front of the small wall mirror. Her blonde ringlets still had plenty of bounce and her plaited hair was still carefully secured in a bun at the back of her head. As a married woman, she should have covered it with a lace cap, but she was too vain to do so. She considered the custom very old fashioned and the last thing in the world she wanted to look like was Aunt Prudence with a doily on her head.

"Yes, an excellent plan," Edward said as he paused at the door to wait for Jemima, putting out his elbow for her hand to tuck in. Jemima walked out of the room with her husband, catching a glimpse of Fulton as he went to the table and found a paper and pen.

"I will work on that list," he said, waving them on. "I can manage quite well on my own. See you at dinner. I will deliver your new apparel to your room during dessert."

CHAPTER 4

The next morning they set out. Fulton had hired some men to carry rucksacks full of the items they would need when scouring the sewers. He paid them extra to keep quiet.

They arrived in the vicinity of Westbourne Street, not far from the Chelsea Barracks. The sky was overcast, complete with storm clouds growing dark grey as they looked on. Jemima frowned, certain it was sure to storm before the day was out, and she did not like the thought of being in the city's drainage system during a downpour. She had read that it was downright dangerous.

As her gaze ranged over the street scene, her mind was full of their current thinking on their quest to find Geneck and his ghastly daughter. The morning papers had brought no further news of savage deaths indicative of the beast's nightly forays, which was heartening. It may have signified nothing, but over breakfast they had discussed the possibility that Geneck had not moved his lair since the last attack. It was possible Geneck had sated himself for a few days at least and was content to stay put. This was mostly wishful thinking. The last attack had been in Chelsea, which meant they did not need to travel far to prove their theory. However, such close proximity did not engender restful sleep. Both Edward and she had tossed and turned all night, sitting up with the slightest noise.

The only thing working against their hopeful theory that Geneck was in Chelsea was that there had been no hint of him touching her mind or dreams. This fact only served to confuse the issue because if he was that close surely she would feel him. Unless, of course, he did not wish to be found and had the ability to shield himself from her. As the connection to him was both abhorrent and new, there was insufficient information from which to form an opinion. Too much supposition was unsavoury, like a bowl of cold, congealed porridge.

The start of their search was near the site of the most recent attacks. Jemima was searching as much as Edward and Fulton, for they had no idea where to find an entry into the sewers. There was not a door or a sign that said 'enter sewers here' with an arrow pointing down.

Rows of red-brick cottages lined one side of the street and on the other side there was a line of larger terraced houses. Dark terracotta chimneys dominated the steep-sloped roofs of all the houses. Decorative wrought-iron fences closed some of the forecourts off from the street. A lot of money was going into this area. An entry way big enough for them to climb through was not obvious.

As expected, the clouds emptied their load. They stood in the stoop of a town mansion taking shelter. Rain sheeted down, building up in the kerb and surging into the gutters. Jemima could hear the water gurgling below her feet. With her umbrella clutched in her hands, she edged out to the edge of the footpath, blinking away raindrops to observe the passage of the storm run-off. There was a large metal grating and an opening on the edge of the road. If they could lift the grating they would be able to gain access. Edward came up alongside her and saw the direction of her gaze. "Yes, that is it. That's our doorway." He looked around him. "Not safe in a storm, I expect. We will have to put it off for now."

"What about the railway tunnels?" she called through the rain. "Perhaps they intersect."

"Too much rain there, as well, I expect. Come."

Fulton offered to pay the men extra to take their equipment and meet there again after the rain had stopped. One folded his arms, saying he would stay right there. He was already drenched to the bone, his hat dark with rain. Others nodded, took their bundles and dashed off.

Edward, Fulton and Jemima hurried off dodging puddles and the mix of manure and sludge in the street, with Fulton leading them to a small, slovenly coffee house. Not the sort of place Jemima would normally patronise with her acquaintances. However, they were not dressed as fashionable people and nor did they want to be taken as such, so they blended in with the clientele as much as possible.

To her amazement and amusement, Fulton once again put some rough edges to his speech and ordered hot coffee and some scones. Jemima grinned as she took a seat, her gaze skimming over the other patrons. This was an adventure of sorts, mixing with a different class of persons, dressing in leather beneath her demure redingote and very plain straw hat secured with a hatpin. Underneath, her hair was simply styled, she hoped in a way that suited the scouring of drains in search of vampires. While she wished the adventure was over and lamented the delay, she was pleased that they had located the coffee shop as she did not fancy climbing into a drain with water pouring in from all sides and although she had eaten breakfast, she was suddenly famished.

The wind blew, rattling the shutters of the ramshackle building. The patrons grew quiet when the wind and rain made talking difficult. When there was a pause in the deluge, the patrons commented on the weather. A number hovered by the door, delaying their departure until the rain eased. Jemima and her companions sipped their hot chocolate and consumed scones still warm from the oven.

The other patrons stared at them. They tried to be circumspect but every time Jemima looked up a different set of eyes was on them. Most of the patrons knew each other it appeared, which explained why they were items of curiosity. Edward and Fulton were not attired as gentlemen. However, Jemima was the only woman on the premises, besides a cook who at times slapped plates on the counter, scowling at the patrons before returning to the kitchen.

Judging by the apparel, office workers were the main clients. Jemima kept her gaze lowered to avoid being recognised in future.

However, she listened to the conversations most near her, caught by the undercurrent of fear in the voices. As she surmised, the killings were much talked of. After an hour or so and coffees to chase the hot chocolates, they had dried out. Outside, the storm had passed, the rain lessening to a light drizzle.

Fulton looked around their table. "So shall we set out again? We have about four hours left of good daylight. After that, I think we should return to the house and try tomorrow."

"I do not think we can delay another day." Edward's expression was serious, his eyes surveying the room.

A quick glance around and Fulton nodded. "Quite right. Let's go then."

Once again, they stood on the pavement. The hired men returned and deposited their loads. Fulton paid them off. Jemima wondered about that. Fulton saw her look. "We can lower it below and use what we need. We do not need more tongues wagging than we have already."

The rain still kept people indoors, the streets being relatively quiet of foot traffic. Edward kept an eye out while Fulton quickly lifted the grating. A carriage drove past and the occupant looked out the window. Edward tipped his hat and smiled.

"What are you doing?" the passenger demanded.

"Maintenance!" Edward replied. The pile of equipment beside him lent credit to this statement.

"Act like nothing is amiss," Edward hissed to them as a man came around the corner, his step faltering. Edward tipped his cap again. "How do you do, sir? Maintenance inspection."

The passer-by walked on, looking over his shoulder once or twice before entering a house. Two more pedestrians walked up the other side of the street. They did not seem interested in what they were doing. "Now, I think."

Fulton looked into the opening and nodded. He grabbed the bundles of rope and dropped them and a rucksack or two. Then Fulton assisted Edward, grasping him by the forearm and lowering him down into the shaft. Next, it was Jemima's turn to be lowered. She quickly unbuttoned her redingote and rolled it up to stow it in Fulton's rucksack.

Fulton checked the street, his eyebrow raised as he took in her apparel. It was rather risqué. The pedestrians had their backs to them and it seemed she had a window before he reached for her and lowered her down.

Edward caught her around the waist and Fulton let go. Edward let her slide down his body, something she could not have done in skirt and petticoat. She liked the freedom of her new clothes. No wonder the men could achieve more, play sports and do other things unencumbered by their clothing.

Edward released her after giving her a peck on the forehead. He moved to a better position to assist Fulton as he passed down the lanterns and the last of the rucksacks and placed them against the wall.

Jemima stood back and into the square of light and admired her leather corset and trousers. Such freedom of movement. How lucky were men to be able to wear such apparel all the time. When she moved into the dark of the tunnel, a small amount of rose-coloured light escaped from her ruby heart. She looked down at her bare shoulders and considered that next time it would be more appropriate to wear a blouse beneath.

When all the equipment was down and after checking if anyone was watching, Fulton hoisted up the grate while at the same time managing to slide his legs and then body beneath, placing it as he dropped without assistance and landed easily next to them. The loud clang from the grate echoed around them.

The air was cool and damp, making her flesh form goose bumps. The floor was damp, rather than the wet she expected. Bars of pale grey light illuminated the vaguely oval tunnel that joined the platform they stood on.

Before they moved out into the darkness, Fulton handed each of them a lantern, lighting them with a match. They nodded to each other and stepped out with Fulton in the lead and Edward behind Jemima.

In the centre of the tunnel, the water reached up to their calves and flowed vigorously, possibly due to the storm water being funnelled into these underground tunnels. She was impressed with the construction as the tunnel appeared sturdy and was of an ample size to accommodate their height.

Luckily, all wore knee-length boots, which provided some protection from the water. Jemima had her leather trousers tucked inside the top of her boots, creating a kind of seal. Unfortunately, the boot's lacing did not appear to provide a watertight fit. Her stockinged feet squished and her toes grew cold.

With a shrug, she realised her footwear would be ruined after this excursion. She made a mental note to order a few more pairs from the boot maker. A quick glance at her clothes and she added a few more sets of her leather wear. She could not expect Milly to make a set. However, she had no qualms about having the design copied. She liked the feel of the corset and hoped to make a few improvements to the design. A place to hide throwing knives perhaps.

Fulton and Edward both wore their leather vests, though Edward's long coat was not so practical in the water. He stripped it off and quickly added it to the contents of his rucksack, leaving him in shirt sleeves and vest.

Jemima looked around lifting her lantern as Edward secured his rucksack. "It is not as smelly as I thought it would be," she observed.

"Most of the nasty stuff has been sluiced away," Fulton replied.

"It has been observed," Edward commented, "that the nose soon forgets the smell."

Jemima did not think that was quite right as a lady would never lose her sense of smell. They walked further on and Jemima sniffed, hoping to detect something odious to prove her point. Distracted by shifting shadows and splotches of water she forgot about the smell. Lost in thought, she did not realise it was quiet until she saw Fulton and Edward regarding her with an expectant air.

"What is it?" she asked, while she re-secured her hair in a simple bun. No curls for her today. She readjusted her hat, deciding to keep it on to protect the top of her head from the ceilings of the tunnels or whatever might be attached to them. They were rather mossy and something weblike hung down occasionally. She was conscious the hat looked slightly ridiculous but was beyond caring.

They had come to a junction. Edward cleared his throat. "I was wondering if you could feel Geneck, no matter how faintly, so that we could have a direction to take."

"I can but try. As I told you at breakfast, I have not felt him, not even a slight tremor of thought even though he could be close by."

Licking her lips, Jemima turned full circle. There were three large round tunnels and one smaller one, which had a stream of thick, smelly fluid oozing from it. While the tunnels converged, the water flowed in one direction towards the river down the largest tunnel.

Jemima peered into two of the tunnels, which were dark beyond a few feet. Not very inviting as far as destinations went. Where they stood at the junction light shafting down added further illumination to their lantern lights. The tunnel ahead was a continuation of the one they stood in. It was larger and followed the street a ways. This she could discern because there were discrete pockets of sunlight beaming down about the approximate distance of the next set of street grating and so on. Instinctively, she wanted to go that way, even though they had lanterns to explore the darker passages. However, she worried that her preferences did not have much to do with Geneck but rather an aversion to dark, smelly tunnels.

"Jemima?" Edward prompted.

"Please be patient. I need to relax. I have not done this before, deliberately sought him out. It is not the most pleasant of experiences touching his mind. Sort of like having a very full chamber pot emptied over one's head."

Fulton scoffed at her description. Edward, however, hastily assured her. "I understand. I beg your pardon." Jemima reached out and squeezed Edward's hand. He really was too sweet sometimes. She had volunteered that they should use her connection to Geneck. It was not really fair of her to then baulk when the opportunity came. "No need to apologise."

Closing her eyes, she tried to clear her mind. She heard the water churning around their feet and the echo of its flow in the tunnel, stretching the sounds and folding them back again. The smell appeared less. It was annoying that Edward was right about the smell going away. It was now sort of a muted-rotting water smell, overlaid with dung. With all the rain, this section of tunnel was relatively clean, she suspected. She conjured an image of Geneck as she remembered him—the sickly glow of his emerald-powered heart and the fathomless pits of his dark eyes. Then she recollected the evil taint of his mind and instead of shying away from it, she stroked it, coaxed it until she felt it strengthen somewhat.

She detected only a slight hint of him and was not able to get a direction. Either she had to learn how to determine which way to go or she needed to sink deeper and let him fill up her mind. This she was loath to do because it seemed like he left some of himself behind, making her less than she was. She was afraid it would sully her mindscape with depraved yearnings and lustful thoughts. She shrugged and opened her eyes. "Nothing. Well, no direction."

"Is he even here?" Fulton asked.

"I am not sure." She closed her eyes again and turned full circle to see if that assisted at all. She felt a slight twinge, as if the feeling was stronger in the tunnel to their right, like the tug of a fishing line when a fish nibbled but did not bite. She stepped away from it and walked a few feet in the other tunnel. Then she reversed her steps and went down the tunnel that followed the street above for a way. Once again retracing her steps, she walked into the dark tunnel from where she had detected the twinge. This time she could discern that the feeling was stronger than when she went down the other two tunnels.

It was the best lead they had.

It was the only lead they had.

She stood at the mouth of the tunnel she had chosen and pointed. "I think he is this way." She looked over her shoulder, frowning. "I cannot be sure so please do not be angry with me if I am wrong."

Edward smiled and hoisted his rucksack in one hand over his shoulder and the lantern in the other. "Jemima, how could we be angry? You give us a place to start. That is better than nothing. You were right to insist upon coming. However, I do ask that you be careful and stay out of danger when we give warning."

"Exactly," Fulton said. "You walk between us, Jemima. Let us know if you feel anything more. Anything—do you hear?"

"I shall do as you instruct," she replied with a heavy layer of sarcasm and a smile.

They continued on for about ten minutes until they came upon another junction, where they paused. The roof of the sewer arched overhead, a clever interconnection of bricks. One of the tunnels was dry with smaller pipes running through. Here she could smell sewage though it was not overpowering. There was no need to pull out a handkerchief and cover her nose.

"Jemima," Edward said in a soft voice. "Is everything all right?"

She nodded, fascinated with how his soft voice echoed around them. She tried not to think how nice it would be to be sitting at home by the fire instead of down here beneath the city—beneath the city with a deadly beast on the loose. She reached up and fingered the gorget around her throat. Its presence was comforting, even though she knew Geneck could rip her head off with one hand.

The thread she had established with Geneck had fizzled. She needed a stronger connection, something that would entice him to respond to her. It probably did not help that he was dormant during the day. Well, they assumed he was dormant, but whether that meant he slept or just hid from the light they did not know. The books they had consulted had conflicting information, they being mostly fictional.

With a shiver, she tried to concentrate again. Heaven forbid that she should try this while he was walking the night, his faculties unimpeded by daylight. Would he be drawn straight to her, would he come rushing out of the dark with fangs extended ready to devour her, drain her body dry?

She tried to picture what she was doing the last time she had tasted his mind strongly. She had been snuggled next to her husband in bed before the severed head came hurtling through the window. She turned to Edward and narrowed her eyes. To her he was very attractive and manly, with strong shoulders and olive-toned skin. She loved the feel of his skin beneath her fingers, the feel of his taut muscles as they moved. An idea came to her. "I say, Fulton. Do you mind turning away for a moment?"

Fulton lifted his lantern. "What did you say?" Fulton's cultured tones echoed around them. The surging water dampened the sound of their voices and the tunnels distorted sound.

"I need to be private with my husband for a few minutes," she said archly.

Fulton glanced between then, eyebrows slightly lowered and lips a straight line. However, he said nothing and turned away.

Edward gaped at her. "Jemima, please. What are you—"

Patting his shoulder companionably, she said, "Bear with me, Edward. You will catch on shortly." Fulton could be heard muttering, his words indistinguishable from the background noise. She edged closer to her frowning husband. Closing her eyes, she shut out her surroundings by trying to ignore the swirl of water around her ankles and the echoing effects the tunnel made as the water traversed it. She concentrated on her own breathing, the lift of her chest as she inhaled and the fall as she exhaled. Then she tried hearing Edward's respiration as she reached out to caress his face, smoothing away the worry from his wrinkled brow. At least he did not flinch. It was a little strange being so forward. Edward was always the initiator of their intimate moments and Jemima had no cause for complaint. She enjoyed being with Edward. Jemima tidied up all her qualms about being seen to be aggressive by parcelling them under the label 'in a good cause'. From caressing his face, she traced her finger along his lips with her eyes closed. Damp breath brushed up against her fingers. She snapped her eyes open. Then relaxing, she traced her fingers again. There, his eyes widened and a spark of arousal ignited in them.

At her urging, he leaned down and brushed his lips across hers. All of her senses came alive. She could feel the air going into her lungs, hear the blood rush through her veins. The tunnel above her and the water sliding past her. She tried to give herself over to the moment, to block out the smell of the sewers, now cleaned by stormwater, and devote herself to the sensual pleasures touching Edward inspired. She tried to ignore the slosh of water across her boots. She reached up, snagging Edward's mouth with hers and he relaxed, deepening the kiss. Now, she felt that deep-down stirring, that rising passion. She wanted to sink into it, have it smother her so that she was drowning in the feel of Edward around her, the scent of him, the soul of him. Once she had found that state, she let her mind wander, let it float. And there—a growing sensation of lust and blood and hunger—hovered in the darkness.

Jemima broke off the kiss with a gasp. Edward did not release her, his hand caressing her shoulder, his head leaning forwards to nuzzle at her ear, completely lost in the moment. She pulled away from him, even though he resisted at first. As soon as the contact was broken, Jemima's head cleared. Still she clung to the trace that linked her to Geneck. Edward blinked a few times. Once again he was present in the here and now.

"That way. I think this time he detected me. There was awareness there. I fear we will not be able to surprise him."

A look of irritation crossed Edward's features. "Damn that abominable creature!"

Her eyes tracked him as he turned away and conversed with Fulton. As they formed up again with Fulton in front, lantern held high, and Edward at the rear, Jemima smiled to herself. She had proven herself useful and dallying with Edward had been educational. Then the dark grimy tunnel they were heading down soured her mood and absorbed all her attention. So, too, did the thought that Geneck awaited them at the end of the tunnel.

Fulton's lantern cast out light that wavered as he walked. Edward's lantern did the same. She found it hard to see anything at all, cocooned between the two men and their lights. Her lantern was down low as they did not need three. It made her feel lost and alone, separated by two spheres of light. Neither here nor there. Her eyes rolled and she despaired at her nonsensical thoughts. They would not abandon her.

They came to another junction. Fulton stepped around, illuminating the features of the space they were standing in. A ray of light touched upon the rungs of a ladder. He lifted his lantern, revealing that the ladder continued up, presumably to street level. Although Jemima had no notion of what street or even which part of London they were in. Jemima had lost all sense of direction. Looking down she thought they were going in the opposite direction to the water and, hence, the river. The junction was different, too, with another tunnel cutting across the top like a platform, as if the level was different. Jemima closed her eyes, once again reaching out with her mind to find the beast. Geneck appeared to be straight ahead.

"Jemima?" Fulton asked.

Jemima nodded. "Yes, continue on that way." They moved to the mouth of the tunnel. Jemima looked around her with Edward moving slightly to the left of her, no longer behind.

A small culvert intersecting the adjacent tunnel at an angle caught his interest. He leaned down to inspect it as she was about to step under the ledge and into the tunnel. Hands seized her, gripping the top of her arms. Before she could react, she was hoisted up. All she could let out was a short, surprised squeak.

When she landed on the platform, more hands smothered her face, hampering her efforts to scream. For what seemed like an age, but was probably only a few seconds, she bit and scratched and fought them as they held her suspended as they tried to carry her away. But there were too many. It was dark and she worried that they would carry her off before the others could react. Desperation gave her strength. With a final wrench, she freed her face from the clinging hands and let out another piercing scream. "Edward!

Shouting erupted all around her in the confines of the tunnel. With the sounds amplified, it was hard to tell how many people were. She was still being carried, but there were grunts and changes in hold so that her leg would be dropped before being seized again. She twisted and kicked, making it harder for them to maintain their hold.

She kicked particularly hard in a soft spot. There was a high-pitched yelp and she was dropped. She landed on her derriere with foul water splashing up onto her face and into her ears. Immediately, she spat out the putrid liquid before she ingested it.

Hastily, she climbed to her feet. Shadowed shapes surrounded her. She had no idea who her attackers were. Either they were Geneck's followers or criminals who resided in the sewers. A hand grabbed for her arm. She swatted it and smiled when it retracted with an accompanying yelp of pain. Perhaps she did not know her own strength. She batted anything that came near her, and kicked, too. Her boots, though wet, were very effective, whether she kicked high or low.

"Jemima!" came Edward's anguished scream echoing along the tunnel.

"Here!" she cried. Her call caused her would-be captors to converge on her again. Hands grabbed. An arm snagged around her waist, dragging her along for a few feet. She bashed her fists against it to no avail. Her legs were lifted up. She screamed and kicked as she was hoisted between them again. Ferociously, she twisted and undulated her body to dislodge herself before they carried her too far.

The scene around her suddenly changed. More feet splashed in the water. It was suddenly crowded as if too many bodies were crammed into a small space. Sounds erupted—thumps, groans, painful cries cut off. Her legs were dropped. The arm around her waist let go. Again, she landed in the water, much more disgusting than before. Stench wafted all over her. "God, no!" she cried out.

Mortified more by her predicament than the danger the attackers posed, she tried to climb to her feet. The more she thrashed about, the stronger the smell became. Legs and bodies moved around her, creating more stench and splashing it over her. All she could think about was the leather clothing that Milly had made and how ruined it would be.

Ahead was the blurred outlines of a man. Angry, she took two steps and thumped down with her fist. When she heard him grunt, a grin of satisfaction came over her face. There was light now. The lanterns were on the ground, lighting up the legs of her attackers. She caught sight of Fulton. He long-jumped, appearing in front of one man and backhanded him, sending him unconscious against the wall. "Yes!" she yelled.

A figure loomed in front of her. She reached for the hatpin. The flimsy straw hat had been ripped away, but the pin remained. Drawing it out, she jabbed the man in front of her. A yelp confirmed she scored a hit. However, when he jerked away she lost her hold on her pin.

She was still in the thick of the fighting. A point brought home to her when someone grabbed her from behind, around the neck. To prevent her choking, she had to go along with the pressure and was thus drawn away from the fight. Her hands grasped the forearm pressed to her throat to allow her to continue breathing as her assailant dragged her along. The gorget would protect her neck from vampire bites but the pressure on it restricted her airways.

Through the confusion of shadows, light and bodies, she could see that her departure was not being noticed. Fulton and Edward were being kept busy. A faint tingle and she knew her husband was going to release a spell. She caught sight of him using a fist gesture and letting it go. The target was hit in the back of the head and sprawled into the muck. Jemima grew faint from the pressure on her neck. Both Fulton and Edward continued to fight. The attackers' numbers were thinning out quickly. More bodies littered the ground than were standing.

She noticed a change in the breathing of her attacker, felt the hesitation when he stopped dragging her back. That relaxation in tension was enough for her to bring up her knee and slam down on his foot.

The pressure on her throat lessened for a moment and she was able to let out a scream.

Edward ran towards her. Fulton dispatched another attacker and then he, too, came forwards. She was no longer being dragged along. Instead, he lifted her with his arm tightening around her throat. Edward and Fulton squared off with her captor. He turned full circle dragging her with him. He could not get far carrying her. Everywhere he turned was Fulton or Edward.

Somehow, they were able to give the impression that they were everywhere or perhaps it was her being disoriented by the movement. Blood thumped in her neck. The blackness of her surroundings invaded her vision. The threads of her consciousness were trailing away. Something was wrong.

She was losing consciousness. A chant filled the air. It was Edward preparing a spell. The shadowed hulk of Fulton stood poised and ready. Dim movement as Edward made a gesture. The pressure around her throat lessened and she fell forwards to her knees. Her head ached like something was bashing inside to get out. Her breath ripped up her throat.

Sucking in huge breaths, she massaged her bruised neck, her faintness fading. Her assailant started screaming. She turned and watched as he fought off a multitude of invisible tentacles. At least that is what she thought they were. She could hear them smacking against his flesh and the real terror in his voice as he struggled.

Still too close, she was in danger of being hit by the man's frantic movements. Lurching to her feet, she was suddenly seized and wrenched back.

"I have you," a familiar voice said in her ear.

Fulton had grabbed her and continued to move her out of harm's way while Edward faced the attacker. The man stopped fighting as if the tentacles had disappeared. With a confused expression, he looked up at Edward, who appeared in front of him. Edward's punch to the face snapped the man's head back and he continued his backwards momentum to land sprawled on the floor of the tunnel with runnels of rank liquid washing over him. He was out cold.

They stood there panting, alert for other attackers. Jemima's chest heaved and rose-coloured light haloed her shoulders. She tugged her corset a little higher and rubbed at her neck. It hurt to swallow so she did not waste her breath trying to talk. When they calmed and no further attackers appeared Edward came over, drew her to him and held her tight. Fulton went to inspect the fallen men. Jemima took comfort in her husband's embrace. That had been a close call. With her face pressed to his chest, she detected the thump of his heart. He had been anxious too. Jemima was so glad he had been there to save her. Fulton too, but Edward was her husband and he really cared for her.

"Jemima," he whispered in that soft voice he used when he talked to her in loving moments.

Fulton retrieved the lanterns and then bent over one or two of the fallen men, checking their necks and searching their pockets.

Fulton returned to them, handing Edward a lantern. "Well," Edward asked. "Can you tell who they are? Vagabonds or something more sinister?"

"They have bites on their necks." Fulton lifted his fist and dropped a pendant to let it swing in front of them. "An all-too-familiar design."

Edward let out an exasperated sound. "He has human helpers?" Edward shook his head. "That will make getting close to him difficult during the day."

Fulton extracted his fob watch and looked at it under the light. "Not long now till nightfall. I think we should backtrack and use the most recent ladder we encountered to reach the surface."

Jemima stepped free of Edward. "And then what?" Jemima asked, sensing that there was more to this plan than they were letting on. She guessed they would return at night, now that they had a location. She suspected they were planning to leave her behind.

"We must be close if his followers attacked. He knew it was me, too, for they were only interested in taking me," Jemima said, her voice scratchy and hoarse. She coughed to ease her throat but that made it hurt worse. Swallowing made her grimace.

Edward's expression turned sour. "Jemima, we will discuss this further when we are home and safe."

Jemima scoffed. "Safe? You forget he knows I am here now. How safe do you think I will be? I will be coming with you, Edward. There is no point in leaving me out of the planning and discussion and no point in leaving me behind."

"You would disobey me?" Edward asked, puffing out his chest. As if that was going to work on her.

Jemima laughed then. "Of course I would. But I meant Geneck will come fetch me wherever I am. I would be a much easier target when you and Fulton were off, leaving me alone."

Fulton rubbed his chin. "She has a point. There is safety in keeping together."

Edward groaned. "Not you as well. Let us fetch our things and be off. With cooler heads, we may think up a better plan. There are other options. Come along, Jemima."

Fulton *harrumphed*. "We may as well leave our supplies for our return."

"I am not sure. What if it rains?" Edward asked. He bent down to get his hastily discarded rucksack.

Fulton lifted the lantern and searched for his, snaffling it in a hand. "This lantern was the most useful piece of equipment. The ropes less so. I think it is safe to leave them. Now we know there are ladders up to street level in places we do not need them."

Edward held out his hand and took hers in his and together they walked along to the ledge. Fulton bounded down and caught Jemima as she jumped down after him. To her surprise, Edward jumped too. She gasped. However, Edward's fall was slow. He had used a spell. He had been practising.

"You are learning more and more, Edward," she commented.

"The more I learn the more I realise what I do not know," Edward returned.

"Here we are," Fulton exclaimed. A ladder hung down, not quite to floor level, but with a boost she was able to reach it.

Fulton went first and pushed open the grate and looked around him. He waved to them and Edward hoisted her onto the first rung. She climbed up with Edward close behind.

"Edward..." Jemima's throat hurt and her voice rasped.

"Later, Jemima." She ground her teeth.

There were many ways that Edward could prevent her from going with them. Some of them quite underhand, like spells. She remembered the odd occurrence at Primrose Manor after the murder of Lady Arbunkle. People could not enter her room. At the time she did not know about spells or Edward being a magician. Now she knew he had put a spell on the door.

Much had changed since then. She had to trust that the need to destroy Geneck outweighed Edward's protective instincts. Better still, she had to hope that he understood her abilities too. She was quite able to take care of herself. She rubbed at her throat and frowned. Maybe she was not as expert as she thought she was. Nevertheless, she was not letting Edward go into danger, not without her. She was no shrinking violet.

The opening to the street was more a hatch than a grate and bordered a square. It was dark out and they were able to slip out without too much notice. Once on the street, they hurried to an alley so Jemima could put on her redingote and button it up to disguise her outfit. She sniffed at herself and screwed up her nose. She hoped the leather clothes that Milly had made could be salvaged, for she hated to part with them.

Fulton left them to check their surroundings and make a note of the street so they could find their way back. It was better to descend into the tunnels closer to their target. They were no longer in Chelsea.

"Pimlico," Fulton observed.

When they had finished checking out the place, the men collected Jemima and headed out, searching for a main street and hoping to hire a conveyance to take them home.

"I am coming back when you try again," Jemima said as they walked together. Fulton was slightly behind, constantly checking if they were followed.

"We will discuss it later, rationally," Edward said, putting his hand on her elbow to urge her to speed up.

"I want to discuss it now."

"Well, we are not going to. So be still. There may be danger hereabouts. I want us home safe before we even think of the next course of action."

"Very well," Jemima agreed and let him guide her along.

Edward was angry, now they had escaped and he had time to take stock of the situation and how close they had been to losing her or being killed outright. Taking stock probably was the best rational choice. She decided to be smart and let his nerve be soothed before tackling the subject again. He was her husband, but she did not know him well, nor he her. This situation was a test of their mutual fortitude and love. It was also a battleground, for Jemima was not going to give in easily. Despite her vows of obedience, she was never going to be a normal wife, performing a normal role just as Edward was not a normal husband. He did have expectations though, that was clear, and the sooner she disabused him of them the better.

CHAPTER 5

The necessity of a bath precluded conversation with Edward and Fulton. After having entered the house through the rear door, startling the cook, the housekeeper and one of the scullery maids, they had hastened to their rooms to shuck their clothing and make themselves presentable once more.

Edward for some reason was the least dishevelled and managed to order her a bath and himself a jug of hot water, where upon he retreated to his small dressing room, leaving her their bed chamber. Although Beth, her maid, had been startled by her appearance, she quickly calmed and responded to the various orders Jemima rattled off.

When assisting her out of the leather corset Beth reacted. "Cor, Miss, you never wore that out in the street."

Jemima sniffed. "I wore it underneath a redingote, if you please. I do have some sense of decorum," she replied as if that was perfectly reasonable. "See if it can be cleaned without damaging it further. The trousers, though, I fear are damaged beyond repair."

Beth held them between forefinger and thumb and nodded. "I will see what can be done. The corset is not too bad if I do say so. Why you would wear such a thing is beyond me though." She weighed it in her hand. "'Tis so heavy."

"Never you mind. I am trialling a new fashion design and it is entirely secret. Can you pour some more water into the tub? I fear I might have caught a chill."

The bath was filled until the water steamed, wafting rose scent into the room. Beth added more coals to the fire, stoking it up so that the room was bathed in warmth.

After that, Beth neither batted an eyelid over the sodden boots, nor did she screw up her face at their peculiar stench. With the politest of curtseys, Beth assured Jemima that she would do her best to clean them and hastened away. Jemima was left to bathe in peace although her mind was quite disarrayed by the circumstances of the day.

Jemima dropped her robe and sank into the hot water with a contented sigh. It was a pity she could not sink right under the water, but her heart might not like it so well. The covering did a good job, but Jemima did not want to risk it.

Glancing at the closed door, Jemima thought of her maid. Of course Beth would gossip to the rest of the servants about the strange mistress she had. And they in turn would gossip about their respective masters. For surely Fulton brought his valet and Edward had certainly brought his man with him.

As she soaped up her washcloth and scrubbed at the skin of her hands she considered it was her that would be deemed the most outrageous because she was a woman. It was rather annoying that the men could get up to anything they liked without having it much talked of.

After scrubbing her feet for the third time, Jemima lay back and sulked. Once again she thought of the condition of her most treasured garments. It was the trousers that were most soiled, she thought. Luckily the corset had avoided the worst and she could wear it again. Clever Milly had oiled the leather so it was resistant to moisture. Jemima admired the other woman's foresight in making them so durable and widened her eyes at what Fulton must have told her of the dangers they faced. Fulton had been coated in blood after the battle with Geneck and his host in that warehouse. Surely he could not have told her all the details. She blinked. He must have.

Reclining into the bath, her mood softened like her skin and she thought about what she was to wear. As she catalogued the wardrobe she had hastily assembled for this London visit, she settled on a dress. There were other clothes she could use for their excursion later, breeches and the like. She was well armed for battle...a battle of wills with Edward.

❧

INSIDE HIS DRESSING ROOM, EDWARD DRIED OFF HIS FACE AND hands and checked the arrangement of his ascot, then frowned at his reflection. He did not look as powerless as he felt. He did not like feeling that circumstances were out of control, but he had to admit they had been for quite a while now. Since meeting Jemima at Primrose Manor, his life had been a whirlwind of drama and action, death and tumultuous fear. It was not her fault. It was a convergence of circumstances. Besides, he loved Jemima more than his own life. He was out of his depth before he knew. He cursed Longhurst and all the danger he had brought to those he loved. But it was not wise to dwell on the circumstances, because that was not going to make it all go away. Such reflections would only serve to divert his energy from more important tasks.

Edward hated how Jemima had to be involved. All his manly instincts told him he should protect her, keep her safe, but she was as bound up in this situation as he was. He could think of no way forwards that did not involve risking her life. She was right. Geneck would come for her if he left her alone and unprotected.

A sigh escaped him. There seemed little point in anything if he lost her. She was his life. Contemplating it made his gut churn, made the thought of the future seem bleak. The thought of losing her hit him strongly. With sudden clarity, he understood why Wilbur Hardcastle became a recluse after his wife had died. If he had loved her half as much as Edward loved Jemima then her death would have destroyed him, particularly when Wilbur enjoyed such a long life himself.

No wonder Wilbur had clung to the only thing that remained of her: Jemima. Jemima and her father had had a life that existed solely for them. Jemima had been devastated by his loss. Edward remembered how callously he had treated the then fourteen-year-old, sending her away, wrenching her from the surroundings she knew. Maybe all that was happening now was repayment for past bad deeds. Some universal retribution.

He shook his head. There was more at work here than some mystical force. Given what little he knew of this secretive brotherhood from the journals left to him, Edward suspected that Wilbur's death had not been natural. Jemima said his decline had been sudden but other accounts said he had wasted away. If the brotherhood were capable of murder then that gave him qualms about his proposed course of action to use some of the more powerful spells in the texts that Wilbur had passed to him. The mysterious brotherhood might respond by helping them or might kill them outright. They did not need more enemies. They needed help.

He studied his hands for a moment. They could use magic, could form spells. Would that make him outlive Jemima? He shuddered at the thought. The heart he had given her would keep on beating. Had she already beaten that mortal curse? What was in store for them if this current crisis was overcome? How he wished it was already dealt with.

The sound of footsteps in the hallway alerted him to Fulton making his way to the drawing room. The scent of food also reached him and he realised he was suddenly famished after their escapade and that he was already late for dinner. Putting away his morose feelings, he decided that there was no use fighting on an empty stomach and surged out of the dressing room into the hall.

Jakes was lifting the covers to two bowls of steaming soup when he entered the drawing room. They were on a little table with two chairs drawn up. "The master ordered dinner to be served in here, sir. He requested a serving be sent to Mrs Huntington in her room. I believe Mrs Huntington to be lying down for the evening. Mr Fulton expressed the wish that you eat informally in here rather than the dining room. I hope you approve of these arrangements."

"Thank you, Jakes. Most certainly, in here is fine. Our outing was a bit fatiguing so the informal surrounds are most welcome. I thought I heard Fulton about."

Jakes finished arranging the food on the table, placing bread and butter next to the soup bowls. "I believe you are correct, sir. He is speaking with the cook and will be here shortly. I will bring up the next course shortly."

"I see, thank you." No doubt Fulton was soothing the cook's nerves after they had descended on him earlier. He doubted Fulton would be able to curb the servants' gossip and news of their strange exploits would be circulating West London by the end of the week.

Jakes walked to the door, bowed once and left. Although hungry, Edward waited for Fulton before he took a seat, even though the aroma drove him quite to distraction.

No more than five minutes later, Fulton came in, his movements quick and energetic. Edward noted the overall improvement in Fulton's integration of the apparatuses, particularly how well he moved his leg, and was curious to see how healing progressed. Except for the slight hissing sound when he walked, one would never realise that Fulton had an artificial leg. The arm had always worked better. It was all that needlework that Fulton enjoyed. Helped his dexterity immensely. Edward had a sense of pride, considering Fulton would have lost his leg and probably his life without intervention. "You should have eaten while it was hot. No use in waiting for me." Fulton smiled and pulled out a chair.

Edward inclined his head. "It is your house, Fulton. I thought it best to wait for you, seeing Jakes said you were not far away. Thank you for thinking of the food and of Jemima. She is lying down?"

"Scheming more likely," Fulton said as he took a seat and lifted his spoon. "She sent me word via the maid."

"Fulton?" Edward asked, frowning and wondering what Fulton knew that he did not.

Fulton took a sip of the soup, nodded and took another. After swallowing he met Edward's slightly offended gaze. "There is no point in not including her. I know her. She will make her own arrangements. Mark my word, she is probably thinking up strategies while she pretends to rest."

"I have been through all the arguments. But Fulton, she's my wife. You do not know how hard it is..."

Fulton cut a slice of buttered bread in half and took a large bite. He nodded while he chewed. After swallowing, he replied. "I know and I pity you."

"Fulton?" Again Edward was thrown by how well Fulton knew and understood Jemima. He envied their camaraderie.

With a smile, Fulton nodded again. "No offence, Huntington. But your wife is capable of many things and manipulating you is probably chief among them. Manipulating me is probably second." He frowned as he puzzled this. "Maybe it is the other way around. Anyway, in this case, I think the best course of action is to let her have her way. It will completely disarm her and then we may act as we see fit."

Edward snatched up some bread and butter. "Really, you talk nonsense. I cannot bring myself to take her with us. I will not risk her. You understand—you left your wife at home."

Fulton lowered his spoon. "Yes, I did, and that is entirely different."

"I don't see how," Edward said hotly, then bit into the bread.

"Well, Milly is expecting, and I would be risking two lives instead of one."

Edward's eyes shot open and latched onto Fulton. "That's true. Forgive me, I did not think." He dipped another piece of bread into the soup and savoured the flavour.

"Besides, Milly is not Jemima. They are cut from very different cloth."

Edward's eyebrows rose and he inclined his head in acknowledgement. "So true. Forgive me." Edward tried not to let dark thoughts overwhelm him. "Yet, we must think of an alternative, Fulton. Between us there has to be a good strategy that doesn't involve having my wife die."

"There is. Let Jemima come with us. Use her to lure him out of the sewers and into the open, then send her into safety before he comes."

"You mean draw him out rather than seek him in his lair?" Edward stroked his chin. "That idea does have some merit." He began to think of ways he could protect Jemima provided she could be prevailed on to stay still. He could use a ward, like he had in the manufactury. Bringing Geneck above ground opened up other possibilities, too.

"It is no secret now that Jemima is here. Geneck knows she is near. When we went in the sewers today, we made her touch his mind. He sent his minions after her. If we bring her close to that square, and if she uses her connection to lure him, we can set the trap. We can be prepared."

"But he will be in the height of his power and he has the daughter with him and willing minions. We have no idea how many."

Fulton leaned forwards. "Then let us work out how we can trap him."

"Kill him." Edward was adamant. That beast should not live another day. Too many had died already.

"Yes. Let us prepare for as many contingencies as we can devise."

Edward still felt a surge of fear. It went so much against the grain, against his role as husband. "But the danger...Jemima."

Fulton met his gaze. "She does not have to die, Edward. God forbid it and I will not let her."

"Oh Amb...this is too much. I will risk all who are dear to me in this venture." Edward was shaken. Contemplating the loss of Jemima and Fulton was too much to be borne.

Fulton sighed and smiled sadly at Edward. "You have to accept that you cannot save us all. Age and disease will take us. Accidents and misadventure. By doing this I risk all for the greater good. You have made this possible. You have given my life meaning."

Edward held onto his reasons. "Jemima did not get to choose. I made the choice for her, although she never complains about my intervention."

Fulton lifted an eyebrow. "Yes, she has nerve, that one. She could take more than any other female I have met. She is happy because she has a life with you and that was all she wanted when she finally got over her misconceptions about your activities."

Edward managed to laugh softly at that comment. He recollected that she thought him some kind of libertine. "Yes, she is quite a goer is she not?"

Fulton nodded, using the last of his bread to wipe his bowl. "The most unnatural female of my acquaintance."

Jakes came in with a serving of beef casserole and frenched beans. He placed them on the table by the door and came to retrieve their empty bowls. Then he brought over the serving bowl to enable Edward and then Fulton to serve out a portion of the beef and then returned and repeated the process with the beans. "The cook apologises for the meagre fare. He was not certain who would be in to dine and when."

"Tell him it is delicious and we are both well satisfied. Mrs Huntington?" Fulton enquired.

"Eating quite heartily as I understand it."

After Jakes left them Edward still demurred. "I am not sure. I wish we could come up with another way that did not involve my wife."

"I do not think there is one."

They ate their beef in companionable silence.

After eating his fill, Edward nodded and pushed away from the table. "Although it saddens me to say it, I think you are right. I will have no peace unless I let her join us. Thank god she is stout hearted otherwise I could not ask it of her."

"Speaking of stout hearts. What about your inexplicable power? Thank heaven you thought to warn me. I would have had apoplexy to see you throw spells that deliver facers with a wave of your hand. Why it was as if you punched that man square on the mouth from right up close."

"Quite so," Edward said as he played with the ornaments on the mantelpiece. "I have been studying and learning in leaps and bounds. Secrecy around my abilities would have been my preference, but as I am fighting with magic, then it is only right that you should know the whole of it. However, there is danger in the knowing."

"The secret brotherhood you mentioned?"

Edward nodded.

"I will be ready and I will mind my tongue. None will hear of your talent from me."

AROUND TEN IN THE EVENING A HULLABALOO WOKE JEMIMA. THEY had planned to wake at midnight and head out in search of Geneck but were disturbed well before. Edward, who was holding her in his arms, jerked awake too. Her heart beat time in her chest, not seeming alarmed.

Fulton was yelling at someone. That was odd.

Edward bounded up from the bed and punched his arms into a robe. Jemima likewise pushed her feet into slippers and grabbed a shawl. "Is it Geneck?" Jemima asked.

"No. Something else." Edward lit a lantern from a flame taken from the coals.

"I hope it is not Aunt Prudence descending on us. That would be terribly cruel of Milly."

Edward swung open the door and darted out, leaving Jemima to catch up. Down the stairs she hurried.

"What in the blazes!" Fulton exclaimed.

A quiet, steady voice answered him. Jemima could not hear the words but the voice she recognised. "Milly," she breathed and with a wide smile hurried down to meet her friend.

Fulton stalked up and down the hallway. Jakes, wearing a patched dressing gown, held up a lantern, and standing next to a small trunk was Milly, looking anything but cowed.

"Jemima!" she said, opening her arms so that Jemima could embrace her.

Jemima pushed around Fulton, who stood rooted to the spot, emanating wrath, and hugged Milly to her. "Oh excellent. How wonderful you have come. I hope Aunt Prudence has not driven you out."

When Jemima released her, she saw that Milly's cheeks had reddened and she cleared her throat. "I thought it best to be with my husband at this time...and you," she added with a sparkle in her eye.

Jemima squeezed her hand and then faced Fulton, who had dark clouds brewing on his brow. He wore a white night dress and gloves.

Jemima smiled and turned to the butler. "Jakes, I think you may go to bed now. Fulton can see to Milly."

Jakes looked to his master for instruction. Fulton nodded. "Thank you for opening the door, Jakes. Mrs Fulton will share with me."

Jemima turned to Milly, noted the pale expression. Having Fulton yell at them might make anyone pale. Of course, her husband was aghast at her turning up. "You must be excessively tired, Milly. Do go on up to bed. We can talk more in the morning."

"No, not just yet, Jemima. I would like to hear what you have been doing."

Fulton shook his head. "I will fill you in as you get ready for bed." He put his hand out and she put hers in his. "I beg forgiveness for raising my voice to you."

"No need to ask forgiveness, I was expecting it. You did forbid me and I have disobeyed."

Fulton blustered. "I did not forbid you. I would never! I only strongly suggested."

Milly smiled again. "In that case, let us go up to bed. I fear the trip has taxed me somewhat."

Jemima watched Fulton, arm around Milly's waist, go up the stairs. There was no sign of the child she was carrying but it was early days. Too early for even congratulations but she had already written those. She cast a look at Edward, who was lost in thought as he stared at the couple soon out of sight. "I have not seen Fulton that livid since..." She frowned. She should not mention that instance. "I do not think I have seen him ever that out of countenance before."

Edward rubbed his chin. "I know exactly how he feels, though. You, little minx, shall go back to bed."

"And where are you going?" she asked, hesitating on the bottom riser.

"I shall check the house and then join you. We need a decent sleep if we are going ahead with our plans." He checked his watch. "Not much time left now. I will come up shortly."

Edward joined her in bed not long after.

"Fulton seeks to delay until tomorrow night on account of Milly," Edward whispered and nudged her.

"That is not surprising. I have never seen him so upset. Let us hope that...well, never mind." There was no point saying it and they would all feel the guilt if there were more killings. He blew out the candle he had brought with him and gathered Jemima into his arms. Jemima listened to Edward's breathing, not quite able to fall asleep herself. She lay there, happy and excited, because Milly had joined them. She knew it was dangerous her being there, but being a selfish creature she could only think of the advantages.

The next morning Edward was already up when Jemima woke to the smell of hot chocolate and the light filtering in through the curtains. Milly stood by the open window, peering out in the street, and noises intruded: horse hooves, hawkers calling out their wares and voices lifting up into the air and into the room.

"Milly!" Jemima exclaimed sitting up in bed. "How kind of you to come and check on me."

Milly started and a smile lit her face and then the smile disappeared and she lowered her eyes. "Do forgive the intrusion," she said softly, her voice hoarse as if she had been crying. Jemima sat up a little higher and she studied her friend to see what the problem might be. Milly came forwards to the bed and lifted a delicate hand towards the tray on the side table. "I had Beth bring you some breakfast. To accompany the hot chocolate there are hot muffins and freshly baked bread rolls, with some butter from Hatfield and a portion of bramble jam that Aunt Prudence ordered to be made."

Jemima peered eagerly into the basket of bread and flat muffins, trying hard to decide what to try first. The yeast smell of bread rolls won her over. She patted the bed for Milly to sit and proceeded to assemble the food. On her plate sat a roll oozing melted butter and a big spoonful of jam. "Will you not eat too?"

Milly shook her head, her complexion going grey. "I cannot just yet. It is early days and one feels a little queasy in the mornings. I have had some tea and that will do for now."

Jemima reached out and squeezed Milly's hands that were folded on her lap. "I was ever so pleased about your news. So quickly too."

Milly blushed. "Why yes, it was...I was...forgive such an indelicate topic. I would not have you think...My menses...they did not come after the wedding. Not long after I felt rather unwell. Aunt Prudence said that I had conceived and the doctor agreed with her. Since then the sickness has only gotten worse."

"That does not seem fair at all. Are you unhappy then because of the baby?" Jemima asked, knowing full well that it was not the issue.

"Oh no...that is not why...I..." Milly looked sideways at Jemima and then continued to study her fingers.

Puzzled, Jemima bit into the roll and waited for Milly to speak. Her friend was no longer shy and retiring but there was a hesitancy about her. "Jemima," she began. "I had to come. I just had to. Not only was I worried for Ambrose, but for you too. How were you to exist without female company?"

Jemima swallowed. "And was Aunt Prudence happy with this plan of yours to come to town on your own?"

Milly sniffed and pulled out a handkerchief from her sleeve. "I did not come on my own. I brought Susy with me."

"I see," Jemima said and then took a sip of the thick hot chocolate. "The maid." She put down the cup and smiled. "And what led you to join us without a letter of warning?" Jemima prodded.

Milly lifted her chin. "There was no point in writing as I would have arrived before any letter."

"Mmm...Milly?"

The handkerchief dabbed at her eyes. "Forgive me. I am rather emotional...Aunt Prudence..."

Jemima lifted her plate back onto the tray. "You do not need to elaborate there. I am quite up with Aunt Prudence's antics. Started bossing you about as soon as Fulton left, I expect."

Milly blushed. "I would not put it quite like that..."

Jemima barked out a laugh. She squeezed Milly's hand. "I would. Fulton said she was redecorating the nursery."

"She was..."

"And?" Jemima asked.

"It did not stop there. She was pleased to be useful but then she had a fight with the cook and the housekeeper and then she took it upon herself to start interviewing village girls as nursery maids. A bit early I thought and then there was the nursery furniture...I fear..." she said and met Jemima's gaze. "Where we...um...came to verbal blows."

Jemima lay back against her pillow. "That is Aunt Prudence's way. I hope you are not hoping to fob her onto us. We have no offspring in the offing so she would be totally fixated on our personal business and our business is most alarming right now."

"I know. I know and I would not inflict Aunt Prudence on you at all. I just had this feeling, too, that I would be needed. And you may think that I am a hopeless romantic, but I could not bear to be parted from Ambrose."

Jemima nodded and dusted crumbs from her hands. "I need to get up and dressed. But do give us a hug. I forgot to thank you for the exquisite protective clothing you made for us."

Milly stood. "Actually I only made part of it. I commissioned the rest. Have you worn them?"

"Yes, we did. I fear the trousers are ruined due to the sewer and rain water."

"The sewer?"

"Oh yes," Jemima said as she slid out of bed and went to the basin to throw water on her face. "Edward loved his coat and it was very clever and thoughtful of you Milly." She towelled dry and walked to the wardrobe to consider what dress to wear. "How did you know what was needed?"

Milly blushed. "I um...well after Ambrose told me all I could not sleep and all these plans and designs for ways to help you stay safe came to mind." She darted forwards and took Jemima's hand. "Were they truly useful?"

Jemima laughed. "Oh yes, and I plan on wearing them when we go out tonight. What do you think of this?" Jemima held up a pale-blue day dress.

Milly nodded at the dress then riveted Jemima with a dark-eyed stare. "You are going out tonight?" Milly asked.

"Yes. I believe so. They did try to dissuade me but I would not be left behind."

Milly's eyes widened and then she covered her mouth before laughing. "They really do not understand you, do they? You will get what you want and nothing they do can stand in the way. I admire you for it."

"You make me sound troublesome. But I agree they do underestimate me," Jemima said and tossed the gown onto the bed.

She rang the bell and Beth came in to help her dress and do her hair.

Milly went to the door. "I will leave you to it. I might lie down for a bit. The carriage ride yesterday was rather fatiguing."

◈◈◈

IN THE AFTERNOON WHEN JEMIMA EMERGED FROM HER ROOM THE house was rather quiet. At first she was alarmed, in case Edward and Fulton had left without her. On entry to the morning room downstairs, she found them lounging in chairs, reading the paper as if it was a lazy Sunday instead of going to attack a raging vampire.

"How now," she said, not bothering to conceal her surprise. Milly was still resting in her room apparently.

Edward lowered his paper. "It is about time. We have been waiting for you so we can set off."

"Waiting for me? But it is early yet." She swallowed and narrowed her eyes. What were they up to?

"Yes," Fulton said, folding up his paper neatly. He patted the cushion beside him. "Sit down so we can go over our strategy with you."

"Your strategy?" Jemima was suspicious but controlled herself.

Edward laughed heartily. "Why, have you changed your mind?" When her gaze met his, she saw an expectant brow and began to realise they were bamming her. She had not expected to win without a fight and was disarmed.

"Not at all." She sat down and began to arrange her skirts around her. Then she looked up and met Edward's gaze. "So do tell."

"Well—" he began.

She glanced at the clock and bounced to her feet. "What time do we leave? You must allow me some time to prepare."

Edward threw up his hands. "In two hours at sunset."

"Oh dear. Excuse me. I will be right back."

"Told you so," she heard Fulton say and then she heard laughter. "She will now take ages to get dressed. Must be fashionable in a fight."

Edward guffawed. "You know her so well," she heard Edward say.

Awful fellows, she thought, but was glad they had included her after all. She was not sure whether it was Fulton arguing for her or Milly's presence had changed Edward's mind. She tapped on Milly's door and poked her head through.

"If you are up for it, I need help getting dressed. I am going with them without argument."

Milly sat up and patted her hair. "Of course, I will be in directly. Should you not eat first? Fulton has ordered dinner."

Jemima paused. "Oh, I quite forgot about food in my excitement. I will go back downstairs. That will surprise them."

"I will come down also. It will not take long to dress you."

CHAPTER 6

The square was deserted when they walked into it around midnight. Edward scanned the green grass, which was surrounded by trees. In the lamp light the lawns looked black and the wave of tree boughs cast ominous shadows. While Edward had enjoyed teasing Jemima, the look on her face when she came into the drawing room had been priceless. She had expected to do battle, to continue to argue to join them and had been disarmed by their ready acceptance. It hurt him that she had not believed he would take her arguments seriously. His wife did not have much faith in him and her arguments had been logical. It was he who had been emotional. Now he had the desire to make her trust him above all others. He wanted to know her better too. Although they were married there was much to learn about each other.

He had to admit, though, that she had had her revenge for it had been his turn to be speechless when they assembled to begin their hunt. She had dressed in knee boots, a pair of riding breeches, and a leather corset with a soft white blouse beneath. Under a smart black bowler hat, a coil of plaits secured her hair to her head. Her pale skin almost glowed in contrast to her dark clothing, making her distracting and, somehow, dangerous. To him she was both at all times, but the danger was to his heart. Milly had helped her dress and it was good knowing that Fulton's wife would be there waiting for their return. Not that he had any doubt of Fulton's commitment, but having Milly in London while the beast was rampaging had put some extra vigour into Fulton's demeanour. Now Edward was afraid of meeting his friend in a dark alley so ferocious was he.

As no one was around, they began their preparations. Dark shadows flickered as gaslight passed through tree branches. Somewhere close a dog barked and a horse neighed, probably from a mews behind the row of houses fronting the square. The windows were either shuttered or dark, with the residents asleep.

With a nod from Edward, Jemima peeled off her outer garment, a midnight blue redingote. The sight of her in her vampire-hunting gear nearly made him choke. He had the instinct to rush to cover her up and another stronger one just to gape at her in all her loveliness. He never appreciated how lovely the female form was underneath all those skirts and petticoats.

As they moved, gaslight sent shadows dancing in the alleyway and around the doorways of the terraced houses. Fulton's eyes tracked every sound and movement. Seeing him do that gave Edward comfort. His own gaze went to Jemima who strode with confidence, taking his breath away. At her waist hung a small baton, something Fulton had given her. He had seen how she had fought off her attackers and was pleased Fulton had provided something other than her fists or hatpin. He cringed at the thought of the hatpin. It had been a deadly weapon. He was certain he could never look upon that clothing accessory again without squirming.

Shaking his head, he tried to focus on the task at hand. He needed a place that was out in the open so Jemima could be seen and approached but was also suitable for setting up the ward.

Edward walked the square and found the place where he wanted Jemima to stand. He did not think he could put a ward up to protect her until after she had called Geneck to her, for the ward might interfere with her connection to the beast or, worse, be detectable.

Their fallback plan should the ward fail was that she could leave that spot and remove to another position within the square. For this, he had given her an enchanted stone that she could throw to the ground in an emergency. It would provide her with a second line of defence—another ward—if somehow this first ward was overcome.

Fulton checked the surroundings, ensuring that that particular spot fit Edward's requirements. He took up position again, nodded once and folded his arms. There were none of Geneck's minions lying in wait. The residents of the square were asleep. Edward hoped their rest would be undisturbed but he did not think it would be likely. Hopefully, with the recent events in London, they would lock their doors and stay away from the windows. If they had been exceedingly smart they would have gone to the country for a long stay.

Edward shrank away from the light, using a spell to blend into his surroundings. Fulton took up position behind a tree trunk. Light from a nearby gaslight that cast a shadow was enough to disguise his presence.

Standing in the spot allocated to her, Jemima nodded and then closed her eyes. Jemima kept her eyes closed and Edward kept vigilant, not quite certain that Jemima would know whether Geneck would come or not. He tried not to get distracted by her lovely face and the minute changes in her expression.

Minutes went past with nothing but dark scudding clouds in the black sky and the rustle of a breeze in the leaves. He heard a moan and realised it was Jemima; her body swayed slightly, her face contorted as if in the grips of horror. She must be in contact with Geneck.

All of a sudden, she stiffened and opened her eyes, "He's here." She pivoted on the spot, raised her hands to her mouth and screamed.

Edward jerked, shocked beyond words. They were meant to have notice of his coming. He leaped forwards to meet him, but another body hurtled in his direction, blocking his attempt. The daughter!

"Ware!" he shouted.

He could not see Fulton. He ducked and threw a spell that smacked against the daughter and shoved her back as it hit her in the mouth, breaking her elongated teeth. Her screech ripped up his spine and made him hitch a breath. Dark, viscous blood dripped from her mouth and down her front.

Jemima still stood in her spot. The bulky form of Geneck circled her, the lurid green glow from his mechanical heart making her skin look as pale as death. While he stalked Jemima, Edward noticed that Geneck had changed. His skin glistened with a healthy glow, probably from the life taken from the many he had massacred. With wild eyes Jemima gaped at him, the look of terror on her face difficult to witness. The daughter had recovered herself as well, but was now being menaced by Fulton. Had these two vampires come alone or had they brought their human helpers?

Edward was drawn again to Geneck's transformation, the shifting of bones in his face. His features changed, flesh rearranged. "No!" Edward called out as the beast transformed into a semblance of himself.

Jemima put her hand to her mouth. She was not deceived despite his transformation as his mechanical heart still sat in his chest cavity. Yet Edward wondered what power the beast had used to accomplish the transformation. It was like a spell that Edward had known for a few years and somehow the beast had acquired it. But that could not be right, could it? He dared not think on the possibilities. The terrible thought that Geneck had somehow acquired his own magic.

Shaking off his fascination, Edward began an incantation, one with sufficient power to blast the beast.

Before he could complete it, a shot rang out, piercing the night. Danger!

He turned. "Fulton!"

The gaslight illuminated an uncanny sight. Human men came climbing over the roofs of the terraced houses, limber and quick, more like spiders than men. They came without fear, one standing on the ridge capping and aiming a gun at Fulton.

Fulton sprang away, dodging with preternatural speed. Edward dived for cover before the next shot rang out. Edward recommenced his incantation silently. He poked his head out from behind a tree trunk and saw that Jemima was safe and well behind the ward. It glowed blue and shimmered as Geneck ran a fingernail up and down it, teasing and taunting her.

The bullets were not aimed at her and Geneck had not breached the ward. However, Edward was not confident that the ward would resist for much longer. Something in Geneck's magic worried him. When and how had the creature gained this skill? How powerful was he?

Geneck ran a hand down the ward. The ward grew a deeper hue and rippled, warping the view behind it. Then Geneck punched it, his fist bending the substance of the ward. Jemima screamed, her voice so full of fear it nearly unmanned him.

"Fulton to me!" he called. He had to trust that Fulton would keep him safe while he drew the incantation together. He began again calling the words and adding the gestures. Ignoring what was going on around him, he focused on Geneck. This could not be happening. Jemima was not meant to be this vulnerable. Edward had miscalculated badly.

The beast remained fixed on Jemima, seeming to enjoy her fear as a kind of nectar, but as the power of Edward's incantation built, he paused and looked back over his shoulder. The illusion Geneck had built fell away like rotting meat from a corpse. His facade of a healthy body was gone. He roared, his voice making the windows of the nearby buildings rattle, and stepped in to attack.

Edward was not ready and he could not rush his spell as it was a powerful one and he had never used it before.

As if leaping from a high vantage point, Fulton landed in front of him. The daughter screeched at the minions who crawled down the outsides of the houses and swarmed in the street. It was not much but it gave Edward the time he needed.

Geneck was distracted and lunged for Fulton. He swung with claws extended and his hand came up empty. Fulton was not there. The man was quick. The daughter now approached Jemima, jagged teeth ripping at her lower lips. Eyes gleaming with menace.

Before Geneck could shift position, a minion flew through the air, propelled by Fulton's arm. The minion hit the daughter, sending them both sprawling.

Edward raised his hand, ready to release his spell. Geneck hulked there, the daughter righting herself not far behind him.

Fulton got out of the line of fire. Jemima ran from the protection of her ward to her secondary position. Edward let the spell go.

Geneck tensed, as if sensing that it was coming but knowing it was too late to avoid.

Edward watched as the spell hit. Geneck shuddered once, his flesh collapsing from the inside. He fell to his left knee, his hand touching the ground to steady himself only to have his fingers break off.

The daughter screamed in sympathy, calling to her lover with outstretched hands, hands that were diminishing to thin bones.

Edward thought the spell would do the job, speed up their disintegration. Then he detected something in the flow of forces, magic and will—a barrier of some kind.

Edward narrowed his eyes and his mind tried to understand. When the realisation hit, he denied it. It could not be. *No, no, no!*

The heart? As the thought solidified, he threw up arguments against it.

The heartbeat was loud. It kept beating, steady and strong. *Thud, thud, whir, whir.*

His spell should have worked. The most powerful spell he had ever unleashed should have undone the beast and his daughter. Yet, Geneck still held form. Worse still, some of the disintegrated flesh began to reintegrate. Geneck was able to channel the power of the spell somehow.

Edward watched with horror as Geneck stood, once again with smooth flesh covering his form. With a grin the beast continued towards him.

Jemima threw down her stone, a flash signalling her ward establishing. Fulton smashed his fist into the daughter's chest. She froze, a look of pain transforming her features, making her resemble the innocent girl she had once been. Fulton twisted his wrist and pulled. The heart came out still beating. Fulton crushed it and tossed it into the gutter. The girl collapsed lifeless onto a flower bed.

Geneck's head snapped around and he let out a ferocious howl. Edward feared he would retreat before they could finish him off. Edward's spell had failed and he had only the more powerful and dangerous spells left to try. The ones that would alert the secret brotherhood. He began to calm his thoughts and arrange the words, build the magic. They had to win this now.

Something happened with the death of the daughter. There was more than grief affecting Geneck. His power lessened. The beast lifted his hand, once again a naked array of bones, and clenched his brittle fingers.

A howl left his lips and the minions who had gathered on the street surged forwards, some with lumps of wood, others with buckets and any kind of domestic equipment they had found on their march through the sewers and the neighbourhood.

Fulton squared his shoulders and appeared unfazed as he blocked blows and slashed with his mechanical arm. Bodies flew up and back smacking and thudding against the ground. There were too many. Even enhanced as Fulton was he could not stand against so many. Jemima watched wide eyed. Edward could see she ached to help Fulton fight. Edward could not risk her.

It was his own fault. He had underestimated how many men Geneck had under his control, how much power the beast could bring to bear.

With a roar, Edward charged. He had to block his concern for Fulton and even Jemima, who was safe in her ward. Geneck was his main concern now that the daughter was dispatched. Lifting his hand to unleash a strike, he was distracted by two men materialising in the square. The ripple of their magic was like those after a stone was tossed in a pond but felt rather than seen. The effect tickled against his flesh.

Hidden by long cowls and dark robes, he did not know who or what they were. One lifted a hand.

Edward sensed the spell coming and quickly deflected it.

"Stop at once!" the smaller one commanded.

"Give us the sacred texts or die," the other one said.

Edward gaped. Were they serious? They wanted the texts now with all this chaos around them?

Before Edward could respond, Geneck moved. "Beware! Defend!" Edward shouted and then rolled out of the way. These two must be from the mysterious brotherhood, summoned by the use of a powerful spell. He had not used one of the secret ones from the texts yet, had only contemplated it. Perhaps they were watching him.

The smaller brother threw a strike at Geneck. When it bounced off him without harming the beast, the brother shook his head in disbelief before readying another strike. Edward could taste the small grabs of power the brother was compiling for the hit. The other brother, face locked in a grimace, growled out an angry spell.

Edward hoped these brothers had the power to destroy Geneck, because Edward was running out of ideas.

The human minions froze at the command of the second brother, who appeared to be thin and very lithe. The brother ran around the square, encapsulating the gathered minions in his spell. He checked his step when he came up to Fulton, who had blood sheathing one arm.

They circled each other, assessing. Fulton stepped back, lowered his hands from his attack position and gave the magician a slight bow.

"What is this thing?" the smaller magician asked, coming up to Edward and gesturing to Geneck.

Geneck writhed, fighting off the magic roped around him.

"A vampire from Moldavia, raised from the dead," Edward replied, despite the lack of introduction.

"And that contraption in its breast?" The brother pointed at the beast, revulsion obvious in the twist of his lips and furrow of his brow.

"A mechanical heart." Culpability filled Edward's chest as he admitted it.

"Truly?" the brother said, a trace of awe in his voice. He circled Geneck, feeding threads of power to keep him subdued by the spell. He studied Geneck in silence for a few minutes and pulled back his head. "Not any kind of machine that I have encountered. There is magic within."

His gaze fixed on Edward who had jerked in shock at the words. The magician could sense his magic. The cowl slipped back from the brother's head. "What have you done?"

Edward shook himself, not willing to reveal or discuss the matter. "Can you destroy the beast?"

The brother shook his head. "No. If I could it would have been done already. This thing you created is resistant. The machine that you call a heart exudes magic and the creature has tapped into that and made it part of himself."

Edward let out an explosive sound. Shaking his head, he said, "This cannot be."

The brother moved closer to Edward. "Your design, I take it."

Before Edward could respond, Geneck broke free. The backlash from the destruction of the spell threw the smaller brother back and he landed on the ground.

Geneck lunged in Jemima's direction and impacted on the ward. Edward tensed as Geneck was thrown back. He had been afraid that if Geneck now had magic that he could overcome the ward. Yet the shield of magic remained whole.

Relief filtered into his mind and muscles. The smaller brother climbed to his feet, somewhat dazed. He pointed at Jemima. "You I recognise, but there is something...."

The taller brother's figure blurred and suddenly appeared close by. "There is nothing we can do here. We must leave and warn the others."

"But..." Edward said, with outstretched hands. "We need your help."

The smaller brother inclined his head. "You will hear from us."

Together the two members of the secret brotherhood faded from view.

Angry at their departure with no resolution to the Geneck problem, Edward formed another spell in readiness. At their departure, the frozen minions reanimated and surged towards Fulton.

Fulton pushed up his sleeves in readiness and braced himself.

Edward charged, yelling at the top of his lungs at Jemima, hoping to distract the beast. Geneck stood his ground, reaching a hand through the ward. Smoke rose in tendrils from Geneck's flesh where it touched the magical barrier, but the beast did not flinch. He was able to breach it.

Without blinking, Edward dispatched the spell, hitting Geneck square on. Geneck tumbled back and over and over until he hit a wall.

"Run, Jemima!" Edward screamed to her. Lights came on in some of the houses. Edward did not care if anyone saw. It was too late for subterfuge. "Run!"

Jemima was running, already at the edge of the square.

Fulton downed more than half of the human minions, but their inert forms hindered his movements as they piled up around him. Geneck saw this. He let out another of his horrible screeches and the minions ran in all directions. Edward turned to Geneck, wondering what was happening next. The green light, the emerald fire of his heart, flared enveloping him. With a loud concussion, the beast was gone.

Edward gaped at the spot. They were in trouble indeed. Geneck had used the magic contained in the mechanical heart. But how? His spark, his own inherent magic, had started the charge in the stone that drove the machine. That was all he had thought. Now it seems that the whole device was magical. Was this his fault? No, he fought against the idea. It could not be. Yet, how was he to explain it. He was still shaking his head when Fulton came up to him. His friend was covered in blood and gore. Even his shaven head had smears of it. "Thank you, Am—"

"He got away," Fulton exclaimed, panting, before Edward could complete his thanks. His amber gaze swept the square. There was nothing but signs of battle and the dead daughter lying in the grass, half sprawled in a flower bed.

"Yes," Edward replied, sucking in deep breaths. "He is somewhat weakened now." Edward only hoped this to be true. The loss of the daughter had weakened him at least.

Fulton lifted his eyebrows, and then peeled a bloodied glove from his hand. "Only somewhat? Why do I get the feeling I am not going to like what you are going to tell me next?"

Edward bowed his head in acknowledgement. "Physically he is weakened, but somehow during tonight's encounter he was able to use magic."

Fulton's head jerked up. "Magic? How?"

"I have a theory but you are not going to like it."

Fulton's shoulders slumped. "If you think so I am pretty certain I will not. Do not let that bother you. Between you and Jemima I am constantly challenged."

"That magic may have come from me," Edward said, as he went to pick up his warding stones and put them in his rucksack. Fulton began to retrieve items as well.

"You gave him your magic?" He spluttered. "I cannot believe that."

"Not intentionally. I fear—oh pray, Fulton do not despair—I fear the magic comes from the mechanical device." He hit his chest. "The heart. Within is an emerald and I saw emerald fire issue from his hands."

Fulton frowned. "But it is a machine."

Edward hung his head. "Yes. It is a machine but there is magic in the gem that powers it. I thought it a small amount only, but I was deceived. Geneck is able to draw on that."

Fulton opened his mouth and shut it, looked at Edward sideways and then shook his head. "I am afraid I do not understand. We should discuss this later. I fear our activities may have drawn the attention of the police. I do not wish for my wife to have to bail me out of the lock up or worse."

Fulton picked up his rucksack and nodded to Edward.

"I agree. We best make ourselves scarce. Someone is bound to investigate and I would rather not be here to explain so many bodies." Edward cast a look around. Not only was the daughter lying dead, about thirty or so human bodies in various states of bloodiness and dismemberment were positioned throughout the square and on the street. "Jemima ran ahead. Let's get after her."

CHAPTER 7

E dward held Jemima tightly all through the remainder of the night. Her sleep was restless and every time she moaned in her sleep, Edward stroked her hair and kissed her forehead. He did not sleep at all. The night's events churned through his mind. More questions than answers. There was a puzzle and he could not unravel it. How did Geneck use the power of the emerald? How did he conjure the emerald fire? Surely the beast would need training. Had his own actions made a bad situation worse? The beast had been hard to kill from the outset, now it was damn near impossible. It could fight with magic and it could resist magical attempts to kill it. He pictured how Geneck bent the ward and then penetrated it. Normally, that should not have been possible.

Jemima had been frightened out of her wits, yet she had held firm. He was so proud of her, realising that her courage was an important part of her attraction. Jemima *was* courage. He shook his head and stroked her once again.

The brotherhood had appeared as he predicted but they had not acted as expected, nor had they been as useful as he hoped in dispatching the creature. They seemed more interested in what

Edward had done and in Jemima, which was very disconcerting. Could they have been to Willow Park when Jemima was young?

He reached out, caressing her shoulder and moving aside her hair. Did she have the potential for magic too? With his eyes closed, he tried to use his magical sense, the one he had learned to detect from Wilbur's exercises. He could feel his device, the cold yet hot ruby as it spun, generating the pulse that powered Jemima's heart. Was there something more? He could not tell—the ruby heart dominated the feel of her.

He must have dozed before dawn because when he awoke Jemima was not in the bed. His initial panic subsided when he saw her sitting at the dressing table arranging her hair. Her dress was very demure, with buttons right up to her throat, quite a contrast to her leather corset. A wave of desire came over him, just looking at her.

"Up so early?" he said.

She turned, her smile not quite erasing the residue of horror he could detect in her eyes. "Sorry to wake you. I did not mean to, you looked so done in."

"You look delicious. Will you not come back to bed?"

Jemima's eyes widened and a ghost of a smile played around her lips. "Do you mean come over there and cuddle with you or take off my clothes? I was going to eat breakfast with Milly."

"How quickly can you get that piece of confection off?"

She turned and faced the mirror and then looked at him sideways. "Not very long, but you will have to promise to reclothe me. I refuse to ask the maid to help me twice in one morning. The servants are already scandalised."

He sat up and grinned at her, meeting her eyes in the looking glass. "What are you waiting for?"

"Very well." She stood up and began the tedious task of disrobing. If Edward had not been so impatient he would have enjoyed her struggles. As it was he had to throw the covers aside, surprising his lady wife with his nakedness, and unclip her corset and ease her out of her petticoats. He was ravishing her mouth before the last piece of lace was stripped from her skin.

He loved the feel of her, the touch of her skin on his. When he thought he might have lost that, he gathered her close again, kissed her head, her shoulders, her mouth.

They lay together in a tangle of limbs, dozing in the light from the windows.

A loud banging sounded through the house. Edward tensed and Jemima let out a gasp. Feet hurrying up along the hall alerted them to the butler or Fulton going to the door. It was too early for polite visitors.

Jemima was up, her corset in her hands. "Please, Edward, help me dress."

Hurriedly, Jemima washed at the basin and towelled herself dry, then slipped on her long drawers and shift. Edward brought the corset over and fumbled with the catches and then tightened the cord to her instructions, pulling it so tight he thought she must not be able to breathe. Next, she stepped into her petticoats and tied them around her waist while he lifted the dress over her head.

He started doing up the buttons at the back while she did up the ones at her wrist and then throat. A knock sounded at the door. "I can manage from here," she said breathily. "You go. I will be down directly. There is only my hair left to re-arrange." He leaned down and kissed the tip of her nose and went to the door.

"Edward, the other door."

She gave him a significant downward glance and he followed the direction of her gaze. "I see what you mean." He could not hurry out the door as he was not yet dressed and she was directing him to his dressing room.

As he entered the dressing room, he heard Milly's quiet voice talking to Jemima. At least she would have some female assistance.

Fulton tapped on the door to the dressing room as Edward was doing up his shirt. "You best hurry down. We have some interesting visitors."

"The police again?" he asked as he tried to arrange his cravat. The valet came in and assisted him.

"No, though I expect them sometime today."

Edward sent the valet away and when they were alone again Fulton continued. "We did leave rather a mess in the square and some people would have described us, I am sure. Coleman did not appear to be that stupid. If I were him and half-believed your story, I would be back here asking questions in a thrice."

Edward sighed. "I thought last night was tough going. I shall be down in a minute."

Fulton stayed, an odd, rattled look on his face.

"What is it?" Edward asked as he drew on his coat.

Fulton helped him into it and smoothed the sleeves down. "Well, let us just say that Mr Brown and Mr White are very strange."

"Mr Brown and Mr White?" Edward frowned. "Who in god's name are they? Did they present cards?"

"No, but there was no refusing them entry. Jakes is beside himself, hiding out in the pantry and taking sips of brandy. They give off some kind of aura, something that makes you want to look away."

Edward checked his appearance in his looking glass. "How strange. Who do you think they are?"

Fulton opened the door and held it. "Could they be from the brotherhood you mentioned? They are dressed as ordinary men, but we both know that they cannot be and it is too much a coincidence. You used that powerful spell, knowing it would attract their attention."

Edward grumbled and followed Fulton down the hall to the top of the stairs. He had used a powerful spell, just not one from the texts but he decided not to clarify the point to Fulton. "I suppose you are right. Let us find out."

"I hope they restore Jakes to his normal, over-confident self before they leave. Having one's butler a quivering mess can quite overcome one's domestic arrangements."

Edward squeezed Fulton's shoulder. "I quite understand. I will deal with this directly. Pray do not concern yourself."

Edward exuded more confidence than he felt. Letting Fulton know that he was aghast at the audacity of these visitors would not do. It was Edward's actions that had caused this situation and he must deal with the consequences.

When Edward entered the morning room, the parlour where they usually sat, he paused on the threshold. Fulton was right, these were not ordinary men. One stood by the table where Edward had concealed his journals. He was tall and gaunt with dark hair and pale eyes. The other sat on the settee, a small glass of sherry in his hand. He was older with grey hair, shorter than his companion and considerably stouter. Fulton did not enter the room. Perhaps he had gone to get Milly and Jemima.

"Good morning, gentlemen. To what do I owe the pleasure of this visit?"

The tall, thin one stepped closer, almost menacing with his glowering look and thin, tense mouth. "There is nothing pleasurable in this visit. I am Mr Brown and this is Mr White. We have come for the texts. You will provide them now."

Edward coughed into his hand, trying to hide his apprehension. Then he walked over to stand by the fireplace, keeping the man near the table in sight. "To what texts are you referring? You could perhaps have the courtesy to tell me who you are. It is certainly not polite—a complete stranger entering a man's home and demanding things."

Mr Brown smiled and it was not pretty at all. "Technically, this is not your home but Mr Fulton's...your unfortunate dupe."

"Fulton is my dear friend," Edward replied automatically, not quite able to hide his rage at that dig against his character.

"As you say. I think you know who we are already. I met you in the early hours of this morning."

Edward nodded. "Ah, the secretive brotherhood. I have heard of you from cousin Wilbur. So how did you find me?"

The tall one moved forwards as he spoke. "Once we had the taste of you, your trail was easy to find. You have an interesting vibration."

These words both excited and appalled Edward. They could trace him? Now they knew his magic? Then there was no hiding from them. What of Jemima? Had he endangered her with his actions? He sank down into the chair, staring at nothing. Although he had to remember that they could be lying about that. They could have been watching for a long time, since he inherited Willow Park from Wilbur Hardcastle.

"You are Wilbur Hardcastle's heir and you recently married his daughter. Interesting." Mr Brown arched his eyebrows. Edward tried to brush off the man's gesture as theatrical except it chilled him.

As if from far away, Edward asked, "Did you murder Wilbur?"

The smaller man, Mr White, spoke up from where he sat. "If we said we did would that make the texts appear anytime soon?"

Edward focused his mind and regarded them both. "That depends. I need your help."

"Our help?" the older one said and then nodded.

Mr Brown's brows furrowed. "You cannot..." he said, addressing his companion.

But the seated man spoke directly to Edward. "You summoned us deliberately. How very bold and stupid."

"Yes," the taller one said. "Very stupid. We have vast resources to throw against you. We could destroy you and everything you love."

The seated man lifted a hand, silencing his companion. "What do you offer us in exchange for this help?"

Edward's eyes widened. He had intended to summon them eventually but kept quiet about that. He would have to play along. Mr Brown's attitude and demeanour were seriously disturbing. "Surely it is your duty to assist in battling this beast. It is dangerous and already many lives have been lost."

Mr Brown's tall form loomed closer. "That is not our concern or our responsibility. It was you who animated the beast—"

The older man broke in. "Yet we are not completely unsympathetic with regard to your plight. We are open—"

"What do you want?" Edward asked, sitting back, a pretence of calm. He opened his hands. "Besides the texts you seek."

The two men shared a look. "We want the designs for the device that animates the vampiric creature," Mr Brown replied.

Edward folded his arms and angled his head to stare at Mr Brown. "You do not want much. What would you do with the device if you could build it?"

There was a light tap on the door and Fulton entered. "Forgive my laxity," he said. "I would normally be able to offer you coffee, Huntington, but my domestic arrangements have been skewed by our early arrivals."

Fulton's barb had no effect. The visitors fixed him with a look and then Edward worried they would detect the devices implanted in Fulton, too, so he sat up. "No need. I am sure Mr Brown and Mr White are leaving very soon."

The men were oblivious to the snub.

"I see you have met Mr Brown," Fulton indicated the taller man. "And Mr White."

"Yes, unfortunately we have met but I doubt that is their names. You do not have to be here, Fulton. Perhaps you could take Milly and Jemima shopping while I deal with this situation."

Fulton let out an *oomph* of surprise and disappeared from the doorway.

In a heartbeat, Jemima walked in, bold as day, with Milly close behind. Edward cursed himself for not warning her to stay away. His protective feelings came to the fore. He was on his feet in a second, his chest puffed out. Fulton also hurried into the room and Milly smiled at him. Short of bundling them out against their wills, he had to address the situation now that Jemima and Milly were in immediate danger from these men of the brotherhood.

"I am prepared to negotiate," Edward blurted out.

Jemima's step faltered, realising these were the visitors who had been pounding on the door so early. "Negotiate what?" She turned to the visitors. "Not policemen? Oh, how do you do?" Jemima said and curtseyed to the guests. "We must have tea." She looked to her corner and stopped in her tracks. "Oh dear, Jakes has not set up the tea things. What am I to do?"

"Never mind, Jemima," Edward said a tad crossly. "These gentlemen are not interested in drinking tea and they will be leaving soon."

She looked up and surveyed the room. "Oh, is that so? What are they interested in?"

"A great deal of things, Mrs Huntington," Mr Brown said. "You, in particular."

"Me?" Her hand went to her chest. "Whatever for?"

Edward bristled. "Now see here. You cannot talk to my wife like that." Jemima was gaping at the taller man. She looked down and chewed her lip and her gaze went to the seated man, who had not bothered to stand.

Jemima's posture changed, from being still with surprise to excited delight.

Edward wondered what was going on. He could detect no magic so they were not trying to influence her. Milly stood close to her husband, looking on with her innocent dark eyes.

"Uncle Ferdy!" Jemima exclaimed. "Whatever are you doing here? Why, I hardly recognised you as it has been so long."

Fulton and Edward exchanged startled glances. "Uncle Ferdy?" Edward mouthed to Fulton.

"Why, yes. Do let me greet you properly." Mr White climbed to his feet and Jemima then bounded over to the settee and planted a kiss on the old magician's cheek. She obviously had no idea what the old gent was.

"How on earth did you find me out? I have not seen you since I was but a girl."

Transformed by her greeting, Mr White had a huge smile on his face. He was now a genial old man. "Now child, an old man cannot let out all his secrets. I admit I thought you had quite forgotten about me and did not wish to presume on an old acquaintance."

"Oh what nonsense!" Jemima replied with a dismissive wave of her hand. "How could I forget you? But seriously how did you find my direction for I am meant to be at Willow Park?"

Edward thought it wise to intervene. "Really, Jemima, please leave the gentlemen alone. It is quite rude to pry."

Jemima studied the two visitors and cocked her head. "But what was Uncle Ferdy doing in a cloak in the square?"

Everyone started. Milly cried out. Obviously, Fulton had filled her in. Again.

"Do come away, Jemima," Milly said coming forwards to draw her back for she was quite front and centre.

"Do not be silly, Milly dear. Could you perhaps ask Jakes to set up the tea things? And maybe to bring some hot rolls. Surely the cook has them baked by now. I think we all need to sit down and drink tea and eat something. We shall be much cheerier then and Uncle Ferdy can tell me all about it."

Edward did not know whether Jemima was playing them or she really had not put two and two together. Jemima tilted her head and regarded the other man, Mr Brown. Understanding slowly dawned on her as the pleasure in her face disappeared. "Then you must be..." She turned to Edward. "Edward?"

"Please Jemima, perhaps you should go out for a while. Fulton will take you and Milly for breakfast."

Mr White stood up and put out a hand. "There is no need for that. We are all friends here. Do come and sit by me, Jemima. You have grown into a beautiful and interesting lady. Who would have thought you had so much talent hidden in you?"

Edward was beside himself at the mention of the word talent. Talent was another word for magic. On top of that, Mr White, the so-called Uncle Ferdy, was insinuating himself with Jemima and she was unaware of the danger. Well, he thought she was. With Jemima one could not be entirely sure. He knew from experience that she had thrown herself into a trap to rescue him. He looked to Fulton for help.

"Jemima," Fulton said softly. "I am in a bit of difficulty with the servants. I really do need some help just to organise some tea for everybody."

Jemima looked up, eyebrows drawn together in displeasure. "You will find Milly quite up to the task. Do let her leave the room, Fulton. She cannot talk to Jakes from there."

"Jemima," Milly said. "Perhaps you could advise me."

Jemima's expression froze and Edward swore he could hear her brain ticking over. "Why certainly, Milly. Happy to help." She rose from the settee, smiled at her guests. "We shall return in a moment with refreshments. Do stay until I get back. Fulton's cook has made some excellent fruit cake."

Edward sagged against the mantlepiece when Jemima and Milly finally left the room.

"Now you see, Huntington, that you do not have a chance against us," Mr Brown stated, face fused into severe lines. "There is nowhere you can hide from us. I suggest you co-operate."

"I am happy to co-operate on certain conditions. I want your help to kill Geneck."

"You are in no position to bargain," Mr White said, no longer the genial uncle. The brother had walked across the room to the table where Edward's journals lay hidden. Edward was interested to see if the other magician could detect or even break the spell. Having never met another magician, he was fascinated. Longhurst was a sorcerer rather than a magician, and had thus dealt in dark arts and was not bound by the same principles of magic. Then again Edward had learnt everything from Wilbur's journals and his own experimentation. Then he recollected that Wilbur had been part of this brotherhood so perhaps they had some moral code, some ethics to guide them.

Mr White tried to break the spell. Edward saw the sweat beading on the man's upper lip. Felt the pressure he was exerting on the spell and relaxed when the older magician lowered his hand. That Mr White could sense the spell was surprising and that he could not break it a relief. Mr White shared a look with Mr Brown and then turned to Edward. Edward was not sure what the look meant, but he suspected that respect was mingled within it.

"The order does not care to get involved with beasts like your vampire. However, its presence does inconvenience us. We do not want the nature of the beast to be widely known. We do not like the threat to our secrecy that your meddling exposes us to."

"Meddling? I did not get involved willingly. I was kidnapped by Longhurst and his cult. I was forced to—"

"Do not bore me with your excuses," Mr Brown said with a sour twist to his lips. "You have been meddling where you should not. The evidence is all around us."

"Evidence?"

"Your friend with the leg and the arm. Your wife with her heart device. Do you think we cannot detect your magic?"

"But it was meant to be an application of science not magic!" Edward said plaintively. "I did not do it deliberately. I only put a spark of magic into the gems, not the machines."

"If you think that, you are a fool and dangerous."

There was a loud banging at the front door. They all froze. Mr

White and Mr Brown shared a look. Fulton ducked out of the room, but Edward was convinced given the hour and the timing that it was the police.

Fulton put his head back in. "Our friend the detective. I have asked him to wait, citing our lack of dress."

This information made Mr White's' eyes widen. "The police? What are you involved in?"

"I have been trying to tell you. The beast..."

Fulton stepped into the room, closing the door behind him. "Gentlemen, I can show you out the back door if you have no wish of being introduced to the police. I would also appreciate it if you could restore my domestic staff to their former selves."

Jemima swept back into the room. "More visitors. How interesting." She leaned back into the hall. "Milly dear. We will need more tea, perhaps a pot of coffee."

Then she came back in, casting a smiling gaze around the room as if she was having a party rather than an inquisition. "There are not enough chairs in here. Do you think we should go upstairs to the drawing room, Fulton?"

Fulton shook his head and Jemima blinked.

Mr White moved to the centre of the room. "In return for your hospitality, sir, we will oblige." He bowed his head to Jemima. "We will meet again soon, dear."

Fulton held the door for the older man and Mr Brown stalked out the door after him, his displeasure like a cloud hovering around him.

Jemima said farewell, a slightly perplexed frown between her finely arched eyebrows.

When they left, Jemima said matter-of-factly, "Edward, do you think perhaps you could answer the door?"

Just then a loud thump echoed down the hall.

Edward started. "Yes, yes, quite right." Edward hurried out. "Coming," he yelled.

Before he opened the door, Milly rattled a trolley down the hall, which was overflowing with tea, a coffee jug, a large basket of bread rolls, butter and jam.

Edward's stomach rumbled as he opened the front door. "Do come in, Inspector...Constable. I am sorry to keep you waiting."

"Took you long enough. Is that fresh bread I smell?" Coleman stepped across the threshold and inhaled deeply.

"Why, yes. Do come in. I believe we are having a spot of breakfast."

Inspector Coleman gave him a queer look. Edward found his thoughts as chaotic as the happenings around him as he followed the policemen into the morning room.

CHAPTER 8

E dward hid a smile at the scene in the drawing room. Except for the state of their minds, the players were in their original positions. He sat at the table, his journal hidden from view. Jemima was diligently making tea, politely ignoring the detective who had arranged his limbs and person on the settee. Milly stood next to her, ready to deliver refreshments. Fulton sat in the winged chair, glowering at no one in particular and the pimply young policeman stood erect, scribbling into his small notebook.

"Have you an inkling of why we are here, Mr Huntington?" Inspector Coleman enquired.

Edward smiled and shrugged innocently. "No, I have not. I have yet to see the papers this morning. Some upset with the servants and our routine is entirely thrown out. We have not even had a cup of tea. Could we offer you some refreshment? I fear I will faint if I do not indulge myself." Edward was sincere in his pronouncements. His nerve could not stand much more. Tea would serve to calm him, not the liquid itself but the ritual around it.

Inspector Coleman shifted his glance to the women "No, I thank you. But do not let my presence prevent you partaking."

Jemima nodded and poured tea. Milly took the first cup and

delivered it to Fulton. Fulton smiled as his wife, a doting look on his countenance. Edward hoped his own adoration for his wife was as obvious. After handing him tea, Milly manoeuvred herself around the room, doling out little fruit cakes and plates of freshly buttered bread rolls.

It was a little early for something so rich as the cake, but the bread rolls were most welcome. Inspector Coleman fidgeted impatiently in his seat and cast dark glances at Milly and Jemima as if they were bent on annoying him.

Milly took a seat near Jemima. A smile lit up Jemima's face, impervious to the man's silent strictures, and she daintily sipped her tea.

Fulton leaned forwards, his cup perched on his knee. "You were saying, Inspector, that we should know why you are here. Perhaps, you have news of the beast. Have you dispatched it?"

The inspector gave up the pretence of politeness and let a sneer overcome his features.

"You may pretend ignorance, sirs. If you will not send these women away I will speak openly about my business."

"We have nothing to hide from our wives," Fulton said, beating Edward to the point.

The man stroked his chin and then shook his head with an air of one who was beyond annoyance. "Unnatural! Let me inform you that there was an incident last night not far from here in Eccleston Square in Pimlico."

"I see," Edward replied, unperturbed. The policemen were not about to frighten him out of his wits. Not after a visit from the brotherhood. His wits were nowhere to be seen.

"Yes, three persons, two of whom matched your descriptions," he said, nodding to Fulton and Edward, "were seen by a number of witnesses running away from the square in the early hours of this morning."

Jemima stood up and placed her cup on the trolley. "Are you saying that people running away from some incident saw my husband and Mr Fulton, sir?"

Coleman let out a growl. "No, madam. You mistake me." He

grinned, showing teeth and it was not a nice smile. "Two men matching Mr Fulton and Mr Huntington's description were seen running from Eccleston Square."

"Really? But they were both with me."

Coleman's grin grew wider. "Indeed. Were you the third person, Mrs Huntington?"

"Did you say these people were running?" She turned to him. "Dear Edward, did you hear that? I stand accused of running. Why, I have not run since I was about fourteen years old. How delightful! How scandalous." She took a bite of cake and sat back with a smile on her face. Meanwhile Coleman's face grew red.

Edward admired Jemima's audacity. He could not find a lie so easily. He was an uncommonly bad criminal.

Coleman eased his stiff collar from his neck. "I would prefer to direct my questions to your husband. Are you saying, sir, that you are ignorant of the events of last night?"

"As I said, I do not quite rightly know of what events you are talking about. You mentioned Pimlico. I collect that London has many incidents in its streets at night. Has the beast struck again?"

"Not quite," Coleman commented dryly.

Edward beamed and took a sip of his tea. "That is good news, then. Innocent people dying upsets everyone."

"I did not say that people did not die. There are thirteen men and six women dead and their bodies are all over London."

Fulton sucked in a breath. "So many!"

Edward interrupted Fulton's next words as the policeman had turned to face him. "How shocking. Was there anything unusual about them?"

Coleman faced him again, his dark eyes glittering. Edward thought he was suspicious. "Unusual?"

"Well, yes. Was there something that united them in death or were the deaths totally unrelated?"

Coleman blinked. "They must be related, sir. They all died last night."

Edward acted surprised. "How odd. Were they residents of this square where it is alleged we were running from?"

Coleman blinked as if Edward was quite crazy. "No, of course not. The people living in the houses surrounding the square raised the alarm. There was something that connected them, beside them all being deceased. All had various tear injuries, including chests ripped open. Some had crush injuries as if hit by some unknown force."

Edward frowned, wanting to know more, but without divulging anything that would lead them further into suspicion. "Anything else beside the violent manner of their deaths? Any other link?"

"The coroner has not finished with his initial examination." He pulled a notebook from his pocket and then shut it. "Brinkley. What did the coroner say?"

The young policeman flicked a few pages and stood up straighter. "Sir, the coroner said he had noted tattoos on the bodies of a number of the deceased. Also markings on the neck that indicated they had been bitten at some time. A number wore medallions of a similar design to the tattoo."

"Members of a cult perhaps?" Fulton suggested as he crossed his legs, appearing relaxed. Edward dared not look to Jemima and Milly unless he lost his resolve.

Jakes knocked on the door and opened it. "Forgive my intrusion, sir." The normally confident butler was quite rattled still. "It has come to my attention that you have not eaten breakfast. Would you like to rectify that, sir?"

Fulton turned slightly. "I think we will be finished here soon, Jakes. Then we will come to the dining parlour. Please make everything ready. We are sorry to throw out your routine."

Jakes bowed. "Sirs, ladies."

The door shut. The room was silent.

Inspector Coleman coughed. "You have nothing to say on this matter, sir?"

Edward sat back in his chair, his feet tapping the floor to help him deal with his nervousness. He wanted to help the police. He wanted to be honest, and yet, he did not wish to hamper their own efforts. "Only questions because my curiosity is aroused. You mentioned when you first came in that there were witnesses to an event. Then you mentioned that bodies were all over London. I, myself, cannot conceive how these two events are linked. What were the reports that brought you here this morning?"

The inspector chewed his bottom lip and then a sigh puffed out his mouth. "Two men and a woman dressed like a man were seen running away from the scene of an altercation. When we arrived, we found only blood and some portions of human body parts. We were convinced that the witnesses' reports were accurate. There had been an incident there in the square. The bodies showed up later. Considering our discussion yesterday, I thought you could further assist us in our enquiries."

"I have nothing to say that would help you understand the incident, sir, and I have nothing at all to do with the disposal of bodies all over London. Indeed, I was most likely asleep when these events took place."

A knock on the front door had Edward leaping to his feet. "What the devil?" he exclaimed.

The police inspector studied him. Footsteps echoed down the hall and the sound of the door opening could be heard.

Within moments, Jakes opened the door. "Mr Fulton. Miss Prudence Wainwright is in the process of coming through the front door. She is now alighting from the carriage."

Milly stood up suddenly, upsetting her cup. Jemima swore, at least that is what Edward thought he heard. Fulton stood up, too. "She cannot see police here. We will never hear the end of it."

"She might have a stroke," Jemima chimed in.

Edward stepped up to Inspector Coleman. "I do beg your pardon. But could I prevail upon you to exit via the back door? I am afraid my aunt is rather sickly." There, he could lie after all.

"Very well. This stalling will not serve you well. I shall return, sickly aunt or no. You will answer my questions eventually, Mr Huntington."

"Of course, anything at all. Just please do hurry on before she gets here." He turned to Fulton. "If you could see to Aunt Prudence, I will see these gentlemen out."

Fulton shot Edward a look and Edward heard a hushed "coward" directed at him as he went to the door. Perhaps Fulton was right, as he was in no mood to deal with Aunt Prudence right now.

Edward hustled the policemen out while Jakes stood at the door, directing the coachman to set down two enormous travelling chests. He blocked the view of the policemen heading down the hall.

Edward rushed back in and thrust his head into his hands and groaned. Jemima hastened up to him and stroked the back of his head. "You did very well, dear. Do not be severe upon yourself."

Milly wrung her hands. "Oh dear. I do believe she has followed me. I am so sorry."

Fulton uncrossed his legs and stood up. "That Coleman is impertinent and a fool. How he expects us to answer questions when he on the one hand accuses us of wrongdoing and then tries to feel around for explanations. If I were a policeman, I would be much more effective."

Jemima interrupted. "The dining room, quickly. It will go much smoother if we are eating breakfast."

"Yes, yes. Do," Milly said with a degree of pleading in her voice.

Jemima and Milly raced upstairs to the dining parlour. Edward was tempted to join them, but could not leave Fulton to deal with Aunt Prudence alone. He did not wish to give justice to Fulton's charge of cowardice.

Aunt Prudence darkened the doorstep. "Do give me your arm, Fulton. I am fagged. What a tedious journey."

Fulton cast Edward a look and hastened over to the old termagant. "How lovely to see you, Aunt Prudence. Are you too tired for breakfast? We have a full selection in the dining parlour."

"Oh that does sound good." She placed a hand across her forehead. "I am excessively tired...and hungry. What do you suggest?"

"Breakfast while I will have your room made up. Then you can take your repose for as long as you like."

Edward bowed when his aunt saw him. "Huntington? You here?"

"Yes, aunt."

"Your wife, too, I suppose."

"Yes, Jemima is waiting for you in the dining room."

Aunt Prudence removed her weight from Fulton and stood up straighter, as if she was going into battle. "Well then. Let me at this breakfast. For I swear I am about to fall asleep as soon as I may."

Fulton escorted her up the stairs slowly. "You joining us, Huntington?" There was an edge to Fulton's voice.

"I will be up shortly."

When they were safely upstairs. Edward sat down in the morning room and put his head in his hands. "What a mess!" he exclaimed. Pulling his hair sounded like such a good idea. Chaos at home and chaos abroad on the streets of London. What wonderful symmetry. Surely, he had been cursed.

They had all the vulnerable women here: Milly and Prudence. What on earth were they to do with the old woman? She could not know the truth. Her presence complicated everything. Jemima was going to be most unhappy and Edward had learned that when Jemima was unhappy, he was unhappy, too.

CHAPTER 9

Jemima had been famished, but now she had no appetite. A quick glance at Milly and she could tell her sudden loss of appetite was shared. Milly appeared most unhappy and unhungry. They arose from the table and dutifully kissed the old aunt's cheek when she came into the room and then re-seated themselves at the other end of the table.

Fulton, the dear angel, catered to the old woman's every whim. Would she like some kippers? No? What about some freshly smoked ham? Each attempt was met with rebuttal and then reluctant acceptance. The old woman loved the attention. Jemima remembered the quiet life she had endured in Kingsfold village and sympathised... a tad.

Very soon, Aunt Prudence was seated with a plate piled high, a great beaming smile on her face. "You keep a good table, Fulton." She smiled at Milly then and there was an edge to it, like the joy had been suddenly cut off. Definitely something going on there.

Jemima tuned out as much of the conversation as possible.

Next to her, Milly sat quite still, face a mask, her fingers white as they clutched her fork. Something had happened to upset Milly and she had not come to London because she was worried about Fulton or

Jemima's lack of female company. It was the aunt! Jemima was sure about that. What exactly, she did not know.

Jemima was not too keen on the old lady's appearance herself, but could not see how she could be got rid of unless Milly went home and took the aunt with her. And Milly was not going to leave Fulton now that she was settled here. That meant they were stuck with the old lady for the duration. Unless, of course, Geneck fed on her. A smile lurked on the edge of her lips until she realised what a horrible idea that was. Jemima was appalled at the direction of her thoughts. She would not wish that beast on anyone. Now she had to be extra nice to Aunt Prudence to make up for the terrible cast of her mind.

Edward came in finally and offered Jemima some coffee. This she accepted. What on earth should she have for breakfast? Her stomach was roiling with nervous anticipation. Yet she had to eat. She needed to keep up her strength. A piece of fruit cake and some bread and butter would not take her far.

"How have you been, my dear Jemima?" Aunt Prudence asked from down the table.

Jemima's eyes widened, surprised at the enquiry. Normally all the solicitude went to Milly. This must be a severe breach in their relationship. "Quite well, thank you. And you, have you been enjoying Hatfield?"

Aunt Prudence put a shallow smile on her face. "Oh yes, a delightful property." Then she broke off the conversation and concentrated on her food. Jemima frowned and cast her eyes around the table. Fulton was frowning. He was probably thinking on the same problem that Jemima was. Something had happened at Hatfield.

Jemima stood up to get a helping of eggs and ham and sat back down, all the while musing. Technically, Milly was the mistress of this house and Aunt Prudence should have enquired after her health in precedence over Jemima and, considering her situation, increasing and all that, she was quite deserving of such an enquiry.

"Milly is well, you see, aunt," Jemima said before shovelling some scrambled egg into her mouth.

Milly half choked, on what Jemima did not know for she was eating and drinking nothing.

"Mmm, yes," the old woman replied vaguely. "That is good to hear."

Fulton and Edward exchanged glances, then as a pair shovelled the remainder of their food into their mouths and took their leave. Such cowards. Jemima reserved her best glare for them.

Alone now with the aunt and Milly, Jemima leaned over and put her hand over her young friend's. "Are you feeling poorly, Milly? Will you not eat something? A coddled egg perhaps?"

Milly looked up and Jemima saw the misery in the poor girl's face. Whatever had happened it must have been bad, for Milly had a high tolerance for the aunt's antics. "No, I cannot eat anything."

"More tea then? Tea is a cure for everything."

Milly smiled. "Yes, perhaps some tea."

Jemima got up to pour some from the pot on the sideboard. Aunt Prudence was cutting away at a slab of ham. "Some tea for you, aunt?" Jemima asked.

"No dear. Just a cup of milk for me. I am afraid I have an upset stomach."

Jemima looked at the food the woman was putting away and cocked her head. She thought Milly would enjoy the joke but the girl was staring at her lap. Jemima poured the tea and took it over to her. She had placed a slice of fresh bread on the saucer with a thick lashing of butter. It was not a lot but it would alleviate some of Milly's queasiness, she hoped.

Jemima sat back down and began to drill down into the problem, calculating the topic of conversation most likely to reveal the issue. "Milly wrote to us to say you were decorating the nursery. How is that project going along?" Jemima asked, keeping an eye on Milly. Milly lifted her head slightly, not looking at anyone.

"A difficult task indeed. Very wearing. I discovered the most delightful furniture in the attics but it appears they do not suit."

Jemima repeated that in her head. Furniture in the attics? She cast a sideways glance at Milly and saw the tension there. This was like a boil that needed to be lanced. Dare she?

"How so?" Jemima asked and tensed as she waited for an explosion.

"It appears that more modern furniture is required. Such a waste of money when there is perfectly good furniture there."

Jemima nodded slowly. "But there are some lovely furniture pieces being made these days. Lightly stained oak rather than the horrible medieval dark stuff that is all clunky and smells of ghosts."

Aunt Prudence's head shot up. "Smells of ghosts? What a ridiculous statement. Furniture does not smell of ghosts. This furniture has history and it is grand like the family used to be."

"It has bad associations for Ambrose. I told you," Milly said, speaking to the aunt directly, her voice low and tight. Her hands rested on either side of her untouched tea cup.

"Fiddle. You asked me to get the nursery ready and as soon as I make a decision you challenge me."

Milly squeezed both hands into fists. "I am not challenging you. I do want you to decorate the nursery but with new furniture. So that Ambrose can go in there and feel like his life is new and not be reminded of the old. Is that too much to ask?"

Jemima had the urge to depart and leave them to it. Milly had returned to her previous position and was turning her cup in its saucer, staring at nothing. Aunt Prudence was cutting vigorously into her second slice of ham, apparently victorious.

Milly stood up suddenly, scraping her chair. "Excuse me, I must lie down."

And with that, she ran out of the room, obviously in great distress. Jemima stared at Aunt Prudence, who then studiously ignored her by paying great attention to her food.

When she was nearing the end of her meal, Jemima rang the bell. "Beth here will show you to your room, aunt."

Jemima needed some time in repose to muse over this problem. At the same time, she needed to speak to Fulton and Edward about this morning, with the brothers, the police, and then they needed to discuss what they were going to do this evening, now they had Aunt Prudence in the house also. She finished off her breakfast and went in search of her male companions, the female ones not being much fun at the present time.

CHAPTER 10

"Well, here you are," Jemima said, finding Edward and Fulton in the morning room that they used as a day parlour.

Edward came up and kissed her cheek. "How is Aunt Prudence?"

Jemima gave him a weak grin. "Probably suffering from indigestion. In her room for now, but she will not stay there so we must be discreet in formulating our plans."

"Where is Milly?" Fulton asked.

"I believe she is also in her room, suffering from the presence of Aunt Prudence." Fulton made to get out of his chair, but Jemima put out a hand. "I will go see how she is shortly. We must use this opportunity wisely."

Fulton swallowed. "Quite right. Please let us be quick about it. I do not like the thought of my wife suffering alone."

Jemima sighed loudly, realising they would not get much planning done until the domestic situation settled down. "Fulton, do you know what the issue is? Something about the nursery furniture?"

Fulton looked down at his gloved hands and ran his right forefinger down each of the fingers of his left hand.

Jemima lost patience. "Well, come on. Please, answer me."

"Jemima, please," Edward said, a tad hotly. "It is not our business to get involved between husband and wife."

Jemima shook her head and stared at Edward as if he was a loon. "It is not a problem between Milly and Ambrose. It is Milly and Aunt Prudence. If we do not solve it quickly it will very soon become all our problem."

Edward's eyes widened and she could see he was digesting that little biscuit. Then he said, "Ahhh" and nodded, turning to Fulton. "You best tell us, then, Fulton."

Edward found Aunt Prudence difficult at the best of times and right now was the worst of times. Jemima chewed the inside of her cheek. Could it be possible that she was smarter than Edward? What a disturbing thought. He would not take it well if she advertised that notion.

Fulton bit his lip. "Yes. I said to Milly that I did not want the old furniture used. It brings back memories of a sad childhood."

Jemima nodded. "I get that. Did you tell Aunt Prudence?"

Fulton shrugged. "Why would I mention it to her? Milly is in charge of the house."

Jemima's slippered foot tapped impatiently against the carpet. Due to her skirts the gentlemen did not see, which was probably a good thing. "You do not see, do you?"

"See what?" he asked, truly perplexed if the deepening furrow between his eyebrows was any indication of his inner mood.

Jemima could not repress the roll of her eyes, but when her eyes resumed their normal position she fixed her gaze on Fulton. "That there is a battle of wills between Milly and Aunt Prudence. Aunt Prudence was invited to decorate the nursery, yes?"

"Yes, I thought it would keep her occupied and make her feel welcome." Fulton crossed his legs and gave the appearance of relaxing into blamelessness.

"A very good notion," Jemima agreed readily. She really had to be careful about this. "But then you just left Milly to deal with the details."

Fulton shrugged. "Milly agreed at first that it was a good plan."

"It was a good plan. An excellent plan," Jemima enthused and then thought better of it. The letdown might prove too much for Fulton. "The issue is the furniture. When Milly tried to explain your requirements regarding the furniture, Aunt Prudence got her back up. She thought Milly was undermining her authority." Jemima had started pacing as her thoughts rolled off her tongue.

"But Aunt Prudence has no authority," Fulton explained.

Jemima swung around, mouth agape. "You really do not understand, do you? Milly lived with Aunt Prudence for many years and Aunt Prudence was in charge. Milly did as she was bid. Now she is your wife and in charge of Hatfield's domestic arrangements. Aunt Prudence is now second to her. When Milly spoke to her about the furniture, it became a fight about who was in charge, who was leader, and Aunt Prudence instinctively reverted to the old form."

"Jemima, this is all supposition," Edward commented.

Jemima threw him a disgusted look and he shut his mouth.

Fulton screwed up his face as he was beginning to see what Jemima meant. "You mean like the pecking order?"

Jemima now needed to win her point for all their sakes. If only Edward would not interfere, she could talk Fulton round. "Yes, something like that. Consider being on a ship," Jemima said and Fulton perked up, being a former navy man. Jemima thought about an example. She had no real idea about the navy or life on a ship, but she groped for one. "Say the midshipman is used to mopping the decks and swilling the brandy. Then another officer comes along and decides it is his job to mop the decks and swill the brandy. Soon they would be arguing, would not they?"

Fulton laughed. "They would. But that would never happen on a navy vessel."

Jemima narrowed her eyes and balled her fists. Catching sight of her, Fulton added hastily, raising his hands in surrender, "All right, I get your point. How do I fix it?"

Jemima sighed. "That is the hard part. You have to let Aunt Prudence know about your preferences without letting on to Milly that you have done so."

"But I do not wish to tell Aunt Prudence about my issues," Fulton said, raising his voice.

Jemima threw up her hands. "Well, then, good luck to you for you will have a very disharmonious household for maybe the next ten years."

"Jemima, you are exaggerating," Edward commented. While her husband's face was serious, she detected some merriment in the twinkling in his eyes. Jemima put down that look for future reference because it gave her some insight into Edward's character that she had not known previously. He was enjoying this situation and he was amused by her. She let her shoulders relax and took a deep breath.

Jemima lifted her eyebrows and timed her final blow. "Perhaps I am exaggerating. Then again, maybe Aunt Prudence will come to live with us if this issue is not resolved." She endeavoured not to quirk an impertinent eyebrow because Edward drawing back with a look of horror on his face was quite enough sport.

Her husband sat on the edge of his seat. "Fulton! You must talk to Aunt Prudence immediately."

Fulton leaned back as Edward leaned forwards. They eyed each other for a moment and then Fulton raised his hands in surrender. "Very well, I will do so."

Seeing that her job was done, Jemima took a seat and gracefully arranged her skirts. "But first, can we talk about what happened this morning?" She raised her eyes to the floor above. "As the others are otherwise occupied, we have a small window of opportunity."

Edward sat back. "Certainly I was just telling Fulton here that he would make a good policeman for he has the power to scare criminals into good behaviour."

Fulton shook his head. "I am not sure that is a compliment."

Jemima chuckled. "Pity he is a gentleman. Perhaps a magistrate in his local district?"

"I wish for a quiet, retiring life. If only I did not mix with such reprobates as you two."

"Dullness," Jemima said. "You would be bored in five minutes."

"I would not. I am an expectant father. A blessing I never thought would ever be bestowed on me."

Edward lounged back in his chair. "I would not mind a little peace and quiet myself. Time for reflection and so on."

Jemima smiled beatifically at them both. Edward her sweet one and Fulton, who warmed her heart with his words. Milly was right for him and Jemima was glad she had done the match making that threw them over their shyness hurdle. Milly would give him love and a home that he would want to live in. An unpleasant thought intervened. If he could smooth things over with the aunt, that was. However, that was by no means certain.

Edward coughed and Jemima dropped the smile. She was forgetting herself in daydreams of domestic bliss.

"We best discuss our plans now," Edward said.

"Time waits for no man," Fulton replied sagely.

As that was what Jemima had been going to say, she was a tad put out.

"I think we should try same place, same method," Fulton suggested.

Edward pursed his lips and nodded as he considered this. Jemima could not hold back.

"That will not work," Jemima commented. With her face creased in thought, she held her chin in her hand. Geneck knew they had tried to trap him. He would not come back to the same place. It made no sense for him to do so. Also, they had not discovered his lair so he had nothing to worry about. They had to try somewhere else and a new method.

Edward squared his shoulders and lowered his brows. "Why won't it work? We almost had him."

Jemima counted on her fingers. "Firstly, but maybe not most importantly, because the residents will be wise to us and the police will certainly be there, waiting for us, or whatever the term is."

"Lying in wait?" Fulton ventured.

"Yes, that's it." Jemima nodded decisively and then tilted her head as she considered further. "Well, they would if they were smart and I am not convinced they are."

Edward murmured agreement and Fulton stared into space as if he was contemplating something.

"Where do you suggest we lay the next lot of bait, Jemima?" Edward asked and Jemima smiled because it sounded to her that he respected her opinion and that was something to hold dear to one's heart.

"Another street or another spot of our choosing, a park perhaps where there will be hardly anyone to witness it. The sewers run all under this part of London. We do not have to be in the sewer or next to it. You saw how those minions climbed over the houses. It was as if the buildings were not there." She had another thought about how the human minions had done that, but slapped it away. She was on a winning streak here and raising interesting and possibly diverting questions would not let them plan. She heard footsteps from upstairs and figured they had little time before Aunt Prudence descended upon them. "I am almost certain I can connect with him again."

Fulton's eyes widened. "I do not know how you do it. Unnatural female."

"Do what?" Jemima asked, wondering what she had done this time to earn such a rebuke.

"Make grown men, with more education and knowledge of the world, feel like imbeciles."

Pleasure radiated from her at this backhanded compliment. Jemima leaned over and patted his hand. "Never mind, Fulton. I admire you, too."

"Very well, we will choose a park." He picked up the map. "Here, at the public gardens of the Royal Hospital." He showed them the spot. Fulton nodded. "We will be still in Chelsea and as you say, Jemima, plenty of drainage."

"I will see to it that we have everything we need," Fulton said.

"I shall be ready. What time do we head out? Midnight perhaps? All should be in bed by then."

"Yes," Edward frowned as he replied. "Yes, they should all be in bed by then."

Jemima had other questions and at the same time was conscious that she should go talk to Milly and see to Aunt Prudence. Actually, it was Milly's role to see to Aunt Prudence because technically this was her London house. Jemima resisted the urge to roll her eyes as she thought this through. Edward spoke again and drew her notice once more.

"So who do you think moved the bodies?" Edward asked.

Jemima had been wondering that also and why. It was one of the very questions she wanted to discuss.

Fulton ran his hand over his smooth scalp. "Either Geneck or the brotherhood."

"Yes, I agree. But which?" Edward said.

"More importantly, why? What purpose did it serve to move the bodies?" Jemima asked. Surely if they knew the why then they could discover the who.

"To put people off the scent," Fulton suggested. "If they left the bodies there then the police would concentrate on looking for Geneck in that neighbourhood. With Huntington's suggestion of somewhere dark, it would not take them long to go in the sewers. We were close to the lair. Geneck would be discovered if the police ventured there and could possibly dispatch him when he was weak during the day."

Fulton's reasoning was sound. "So you think it was Geneck? And the brotherhood?" Jemima asked.

"My money is on the brotherhood," Edward said. "They would not want supernatural events being spoken about."

Jemima blinked. "That is a reason. Not a strong one. I think Fulton has the more plausible reason, except that Geneck had not bothered to hide his work before."

"But it was not Geneck's work," Fulton said. "It was mine."

"Oh, quite so!" Jemima said. "He would not want his minions knowing of that carnage."

"Speaking of the brotherhood," Edward said. "Jemima, what were you doing talking to Mr White...your...Uncle Ferdy?"

Jemima waved a flippant hand. "I used to call him that when I was a small girl. No actual relation. He used to visit papa. I did not know he was from the brotherhood as a child, of course. And I only realised it when I was talking to him that he resembled one of the brotherhood that appeared in the square last night. I put two and two together. I did not recognise him fully, you understand. I only have vague recollections of him. But I was right. He was Uncle Ferdy."

Edward shook his head. "You had me going there. I did not know if you were bluffing or incredibly quick on the uptake. Mr White—Uncle

Ferdy—is indeed a member of the brotherhood and had come to demand the texts from me."

"They were not very helpful in the square, were they?" Jemima stated the obvious.

"No, they have their own agenda. I am not sure I am easy with it either. Not knowing and only suspecting part of it. The brotherhood want the texts, which I am prepared to give up if they help us with Geneck."

"But you said papa told you to keep them hidden."

"I know I did. I only know what he told me and not the whole story. Neither do you. It would be good to know it so I can feel easier in my choices."

Jemima stood up and went over to Edward, taking his hand in hers. "I trust you to make the right decision." Jemima was being sincere. If her husband was going to make a decision she was not happy with, she would do her best to change his mind—without him knowing, of course.

The tones of Aunt Prudence could be heard talking to the maid. It would not be long now before she invaded the parlour.

"There is one problem with our plan," Jemima said.

"And what is that?" Fulton asked, a touch of worry in his voice. Whether this was from what Jemima had said or the imminent arrival of the aunt, she did not know.

"We need another way of attacking Geneck," Edward said, beating Jemima to it. "He is too strong, even for you, Fulton."

"Will not those texts help you, dear?" Jemima asked hopefully.

"They might. I learned another spell, one more powerful again. However, if I use that spell, it will bring the brotherhood and it will certainly anger them. That visit this morning was a warning, a friendly warning."

"Oh?" She sat back in her chair. "That does make things interesting doesn't it?"

CHAPTER 11

On her way to Milly's room, Jemima passed Aunt Prudence on the landing as she headed downstairs to join Edward and Fulton. Aunt Prudence wore an elaborate lace shawl over the dark brown and black striped dress, combined with a voluminous lace cap over her tightly plaited and coiled grey hair. She was a sight to be seen, seeming a foot taller and a foot wider than she really was. Jemima grinned as she tapped lightly on Milly's door.

There being no direct answer but a muffled sob, Jemima went right in. It would not do to have Milly in tears and hiding in her room while Aunt Prudence was free to go wherever she liked in Milly's house. "Milly?" she said as she entered the darkened room. She expected Milly to be lying down upon the bed and had to check herself when that was not the case. Casting around the room, she found Milly standing at the window, partially obscured by the heavy curtains. "Oh Milly! I hope you have not let that abominable women upset you."

Milly cried harder, a real heartfelt sob, and Jemima went to her and held her close. "Oh Milly. Tell me about it. Why does it upset you so? It is only Aunt Prudence."

"You do not..." Milly began. "You do not understand. It hurts so much." Milly extracted herself from Jemima's embrace and paced in front of the small fireplace.

"Why? Please explain it to me," Jemima implored her.

Milly wrung her hands and shook her head.

Jemima lowered her voice in encouragement. "You can speak freely to me. I will not judge you."

Milly replied, "I know, but..." She shook her head. There was a small work table and two chairs. Jemima took one of the seats, folded her hands on her lap and waited expectantly.

Milly noticed this and nodded slowly. "Aunt Prudence took me in when I was orphaned," she began. "I was a wee thing. She had no children of her own and was not very well off. At first, we did not get on. She was afraid of me being so small. Yet she shared what little she had with me and we grew fond of one another."

Jemima grimaced. How anyone could be fond of Aunt Prudence, Jemima did not know. Well, she did grow on one, she supposed. A bit like living with a thorn in your thumb. "I thought Edward assisted you both. I hope that's not too indelicate of me to say so."

Milly wiped her eyes and blew her nose. "Later, he did," she replied in muffled tones, her voice thick from crying. "At first, he did not know of our predicament."

"That is very well of her, I suppose," Jemima admitted reluctantly. Taking a child in when one was in straightened circumstances was a large undertaking. Then again, the workhouse would have been Milly's lot if no other relative would provide assistance.

"In those early days, I was loved, Jemima. She was a mother to me in so many ways and I adored her. She is the only family I have known. My own mother I can barely remember."

Being an orphan, Jemima could sympathise, in part. "And?"

"We have had our ups and downs. Eventually, we accepted each other for who we were. At least that is what I thought. And now she is being so horrid, I feel crushed. I feel as if the past was a lie. How could she do this? How could she hurt me so?"

Milly burst into fresh sobs, standing there before the fire.

Jemima got up to lead Milly to sit opposite her. Holding Milly's hand across the table, she squeezed it gently. "I do not think she understands that she is hurting you, Milly. I am positive she would be mortified if she knew. It is just, and this is only my observation and opinion, that she is finding it hard to adjust. You have a husband now, who takes precedence over her. And you are expecting a child. Another person to come between you two."

Milly's eyes widened. "Are you saying she is jealous?"

"I would not use such a harsh term, but perhaps that her adjustment to the new arrangements makes it hard for her to know how to go on. So she grasps at little things that seem solid to her."

"But I tried to make her feel welcome. I agreed she should have the decoration of the nursery to help her find her place."

"I know...it is rather silly really and unfortunately excessively painful for you that your good deed has rebounded. You have felt it much more than it was meant, I am sure. Moreover, she, too, has overreacted because of all these other feelings she has. I did not realise you had been so close, so loving to one another, but it makes a perverted kind of sense."

"How so?"

"Well, that you were trying to be kind and she not really meaning to take up arms against you. It sort of blew up. If you do not mind my alluding to the military."

Milly smiled through her tears and squished up her very wet handkerchief. "You never liked her. Why do you care now?"

"Yes, I know I never have, not much leastways but she does grow on one. Sort of like a barnacle." She giggled and then stopped herself. "But I care for you and I hate to see you miserable."

"I will get over it," Milly said in a sad voice that pulled on Jemima's heart strings.

Jemima leaned in close and squeezed Milly's hand. "You know, I have not had the good fortune as you did of having a loving female relative. You and Aunt Prudence are the closest that I have come to a family. Edward does not quite equate to you, and Aunt Prudence, even though I must admit I find her odious at times, she does have some good points. You understand me. I do not need to explain myself. Whereas Edward needs an education."

Milly sniffed and then chuckled. "So," she said, "are you implying that I am taking this too much to heart?"

"Not at all. I am just trying to provide some context so that you can see, as I do, that this quarrel is not as bad as it at first seemed."

"Yes, you are quite right. Now that I look at it your way. I was feeling a hurt that was not intended. She has not stopped loving me."

"Quite the opposite," Jemima said. "She wants to be sure of your love."

Milly relinquished Jemima's hand, stood up from the table and walked to her bed where she fingered a blue-green pashmina draped over the coverlet. "I will have to find a way to talk to her about this."

Jemima squeezed her own hands together. Why anyone listened to her she did not know for she had no real experience with relationships, except at school where she was quite successful. Although some, Miss Blake, in particular, would have termed her behaviour manipulative. Jemima had always termed it insightful.

Jemima prayed that everything would work to plan. She was banking on Fulton having a quiet word to Aunt Prudence. That meant that Aunt Prudence should then bring up the topic of the nursery, in placating terms, of course, and Milly should take that opportunity to smooth things over. Jemima should keep her mouth shut and just watch from the sidelines. "Perhaps, Milly, Aunt Prudence will raise the issue and then you will be able to smooth things over."

Milly swung around. "I will not allow her to put that furniture in the nursery," Milly said quite savagely. "I have a duty to Ambrose."

"Certainly you do. But let us see how it goes on. Aunt Prudence may develop a liking for modern furniture after all." Jemima stood up and went to hug Milly. "Come on. Dry your eyes and come downstairs."

Milly frowned and bit her lip. "I have been so remiss. I have not spoken to the cook about dinner nor made proper arrangements with the housekeeper for Aunt Prudence's accommodation. I believe Edward is sharing with you."

"Yes, and that's fine. He moved his valet so that Aunt Prudence could have that room. It is a tight fit but with four bedrooms, we are nicely accommodated. Fulton's valet is up in the attics, sharing with Jakes and the footman, and Edward's valet is now in the dressing room. The scullery maid sleeps in the kitchen anyways and the housekeeper has a small room off the kitchen."

Milly gaped at her. "You know so much already about the running of the house."

"Why are you so surprised?" Jemima asked. "I am not completely ignorant of domestic concerns. And I was here a good two days or so before you ever set foot here."

"I am not surprised. Just feeling out of sorts because I am at a disadvantage. Of course, you are not ignorant. Forgive me, I never meant to imply."

Jemima laughed. "Now do not get missish. I took no offence. If you will excuse me I need to make some preparations."

"Preparations?" Milly asked, highly intrigued. "What for?"

"Oh, er...for what I am going to wear to dinner." That was a lie, but even though Fulton had revealed all to Milly, Jemima could not admit she was thinking about what she was going to wear after dinner.

Jemima escaped Milly's room and collapsed upon her own bed, the emotional highs and lows proving too much for her, and was soon asleep.

⚜

"Excuse me? Are you getting up, Mrs Huntington? You need to dress for dinner."

Beth bustled around the room, pouring hot water into the washbasin and pulling out a dress. Dinner? Jemima threw off the vagueness and her thoughts arrived one after the other: *Oh, yes! Aunt Prudence! Jemima! Must dress for dinner!* She yawned and then recollected that later she had to sneak out and kill a vampire. Her eyes focused and she rubbed the sleep out of them.

Catching sight of the dress her maid had chosen she sat bolt upright. "Not that one, Beth. I will wear the green one."

Without protest, Beth changed the dress over, placing the dark blue one back in the closet. "I am sorry, Mrs Huntington, I should have asked first. What shoes will you wear with the green gown?"

At the washbasin, Jemima wiped her face and shook her head. She was in no mood for dressing up. For the sake of her companions, she would make an effort. "I think the white slippers with the gold roses."

"That's a good choice. White stockings?" Beth asked, kneeling down to select the correct shoebox.

"Yes, of course." Jemima frowned. Was Beth teasing her? What else would she wear in the evenings with white slippers? Not black, surely.

After she was dressed, Beth fussed over her hair and added a pin just as the dinner gong sounded. Jemima's heart lurched. She hated it when it did that. She could not be scared of Aunt Prudence and a potential exchange of fire between Milly and her aunt. Everything would go to plan. She had to have faith. Aunt Prudence she could endure well enough for Milly's sake. She really did sympathise with Milly and her crushed heart. Jemima was certain that Aunt Prudence adored Milly and the tender affection Milly nursed for the old tyrant was returned.

"There you are dear child," Aunt Prudence said when Jemima entered the upstairs drawing room. "You look beautiful this evening. Like a new penny."

Jemima flashed a quick grin and then controlled it. "Why thank you, aunt. You look particularly resplendent this evening."

Aunt Prudence was lush with fabric. Great puffy sleeves, neckline overflowing with lace. It was as if she had spent her whole year's allowance on finery. The shoes peeking out from the hem of her dress were finely wrought and made from the same fabric as the dress. A jewelled brooch winked on her breast and bright rings adorned her fingers. Aunt Prudence preened. "Do you think so? I hoped to make an impression. I love being in London and much of my life you know was spent in retirement in the country."

"I did not think you had time to visit the warehouses on this visit, aunt," Jemima commented.

Aunt Prudence's face fell. "Oh no, I have not." She leaned in close, lifting her closed fan to her nose. "This was from our last sojourn. If you recall we did a lot of shopping in the warehouses."

Jemima's cheeks heated. Luckily, Milly came in and the aunt's attention was diverted.

Now that takes me back, Jemima thought. Their last sojourn was the shopping spree funded by her quarterly allowance and an abundance of lies. Perhaps the aunt meant to flaunt that in her face. Who knew what motivated that woman. Jemima quieted her mind, as she realised that she was over-estimating Aunt Prudence's ability to dissemble.

"Good evening, Aunt Prudence," Milly said politely with an absence of warmth that might very well have frozen Aunt Prudence to the spot. However, Fulton walked in and the aunt perked up, like a puppet on a string. "Fulton. How well you look!"

Fulton had spruced himself up nicely. A dark-blue coat, beige trousers, neat thin tie and clean white gloves. Jemima looked around for Edward. She hoped he was going to be there for dinner and had not sneaked off to his club to avoid the dreaded aunt and the potential for drama this evening portended. Not that she would blame him, but as she could not go to his club, it would be very unfair of him.

"Aunt Prudence, you look very well," Fulton said, returning the praise. His eyes latched onto Milly briefly. "May I pour you a drink? Sherry perhaps?"

The aunt agreed and Fulton cast a smile at Milly, who took a glass of cordial instead of wine. She looked peaky so it was for the best.

Footsteps forewarned them of Edward's approach. "Sorry to be late. I could not find my tie."

Jemima blinked. He had a valet and would not even know where his ties were kept. What had he been up to? Right then Jemima had an idea. Edward should cast a spell and make Milly and Aunt Prudence friends again and as much as she loved Milly's company, his spell should make them both want to pack up and go home to fix the nursery. If only they were alone, she could suggest it.

Fulton gazed at Milly from under lowered eyelids, his body tense. He was worried about her.

"Dinner is served," Jakes said as he opened the doors leading to the dining room.

Edward put out his arm. "You look very well, Jemima. Quite different from yesterday evening."

"Thank you, my love. You smell much better, too." Jemima grinned.

Edward tossed back his head and chortled. "Thank providence for lilac-scented soap. How did you get on with Milly?" he said quietly in her ear.

"It is all up to Fulton and Aunt Prudence now," she advised him.

Edward grimaced and pulled out her chair. "Oh dear."

"Precisely." Her heart warmed that they understood each other so well and were in so much accord.

The soup was served and sipped in silence. For once, Aunt Prudence did not feel the need to regale them with anecdotes about distant relatives and passing acquaintances or provide her opinion on what was wrong with the world.

So unnatural was this quiet that Jemima could not abide it and did her best to introduce some conversation. "Did you bring your needlework with you, aunt?" Jemima asked. She almost said "did you and Milly" but thought the better of it.

"Oh yes," Aunt Prudence said, placing her spoon in her empty bowl. "I have brought a project or two. However, I do not wish to impose my ways on your evening entertainments. Now that you are a married woman, I would not be so bold. What do you do here in Chelsea to amuse yourselves of an evening?" She smiled brightly at Jemima.

"We go to bed at an early hour," Jemima said before Edward could stop her.

The lady lost her smile. "How early?" Aunt Prudence asked, her jaw dropping.

Edward leaned forwards. "Not before ten-thirty I assure you. We read and talk mostly. Fulton might play for us if we ask nicely."

Fulton wiped his mouth on his napkin. "I will if you wish it."

"It must be Milly who decides," Jemima said. "She is the mistress of the house."

Edward kicked her under the table. A fulminating stare is what he got in return for that.

"What shall we do this evening?" Fulton asked Milly, his eyes taking on a dazzled expression as he gazed upon her.

Milly blushed. "I had not...I did not...please do what you desire. I will go to bed early."

Aunt Prudence's lips pursed. A look passed between Fulton and she. Jemima caught it. Milly did not as she was staring at her half-full bowl of soup.

The aunt sat up straighter and half-turned her torso so that she was facing Milly. "If you have brought your work with you, Millicent, I would happily sew with you."

Milly's breath caught and she looked up. "Really? I..." Her eyes darted that way and this.

"I have this very sweet design that I want to show you before I start embroidering it. For if you do not like it, I shall alter it to one of your liking."

Milly wavered, as if she was going to faint. "That is very kind of you," she said in a quiet voice. Then more loudly she said, "I am sure whatever you think is best will do."

"No, no. I will not hear of it. I need your opinion. You have such a good eye. Have I not always relied on you?"

Jemima started wishing for the next course because she was feeling queasy. How Aunt Prudence could pour on the syrup. Surely, Milly was going to figure it out, with Aunt Prudence being so overt about her overtures. She kicked Edward under the table and he glared at her. She jerked her head in the direction of the aunt and he gave her a puzzled look and then mouthed "oh".

"Aunt Prudence..." Edward began and trailed off.

"Yes, Edward, dear boy?"

Edward flushed and cleared his throat. "I was wondering—"

Jemima did her best to give an impression of calm. "What Edward means to say, aunt, is, would you play a game of cards with him this evening? You see when he plays me he always loses so he thinks he can have the upper hand over you."

Edward turned to her. "I do not lose."

Jemima laughed for Jakes heralded in the second course before she could respond.

"Why did you say that to Aunt Prudence? She will think I am an insipid fellow," he hissed in her ear.

"You were meant to divert her from letting on to Milly that she knows…" Jemima said by way of explanation.

"Knows?" He screwed up his face in puzzlement.

Jemima let out a sigh, tinged with impatience. "The furniture. The quarrel? That Fulton has spoken to her."

Edward nodded slowly. "Oh I see. Jemima your brain runs too hot. It will be all right. Fulton will see it to rights."

"Yes, certainly. But not if Milly gets wind of it."

Edward crossed his eyes and Jemima giggled.

"How did my life get so complicated?" he complained.

Jemima smiled wider. "Indeed."

"When do you think you will return to Hatfield, aunt?" Fulton asked.

Now that was taking her straight on. Jemima's ears pricked up.

"Well that depends on Milly. I cannot be there on my own in a house without a mistress. Besides, I am there to keep her company."

Milly chewed slowly, eyes flicking from Fulton to her aunt. She swallowed. "I am quite settled here in town with my husband."

Fulton put down his fork. "I am happy to see you, too. But you know it is not safe here."

Aunt Prudence frowned. "Not safe. Whatever do you mean?"

Obviously, Aunt Prudence did not read the newspapers or listen at keyholes.

"There have been some grievous murders here in London, aunt," Fulton explained. "Some quite close to Chelsea."

Aunt Prudence's generous chest rose on a deep inhale. "Oh dear me! How dreadful." She turned to Milly. "Please dear, do reconsider."

Milly's eyes glinted. The aunt and Fulton had perhaps crossed the line. Milly's face had a mulish cast. "I will not leave my husband."

"Of course you should not," Aunt Prudence said, barely drawing breath before she changed tack. "A husband cannot survive without a wife and you are the best of wives, dear. Fulton is blessed to have you."

"Oh god!" Jemima said under her breath. Edward kicked her again. "You will give me a bruise," she hissed out the side of her mouth.

"I have a headache," Edward said quietly in return and cut vigorously into a slice of beef. Then in a louder voice said, "Pass me those potatoes. And the gravy, if you please."

Jemima did. Her appetite was lost. She took a bread roll and lathed it with butter as the discussion at the end of the table continued. "I am getting depressed," she commented to Edward.

"Why?" he asked.

"I think Aunt Prudence may end up living with us."

A groan met that comment. There was no point intervening any further. There was a three-way argument going on about husbands, wives and aunts and the various merits of each both singly and combined.

"Dessert!" Jakes announced as he and the footman came in to remove the plates. Jemima giggled. The argument continued unabated.

Jemima spoke out of the side of her mouth. "When you go to drink port as I am sure you will do, tell Fulton to think up a better tactic."

Edward took his Apple Charlotte apart with vigour, his spoon cutting cake and custard in time to the words passing to and fro between Fulton, Aunt Prudence and Milly. "I will do my best if I have to hit him over the head," Edward muttered between swallows.

"Yes, that will be very productive." She glanced to the end of the table. Aunt Prudence was waving a spoon at Fulton and using it to make a point about how husbands had no business interfering in household matters. Milly looked ready to faint.

"Pray for me. I shall be stuck with those two, who love each other and will not admit it."

Milly stood up suddenly. "Aunt...Jemima...Let us remove to the drawing room and leave the men to their wine."

Fulton had his mouth open as if the words he was going to say had fallen from his mouth. He stood up. Edward just grunted with impatience as he too stood, kissing Jemima's hand as she swept away from the table.

Time was up. Jemima had so many ideas how to turn the situation that she could not decide which. Yet, she hoped there was a resolution before they headed out this evening. She could not bear the extra worry on her mind.

"Do not take long, dear husband," Jemima called after him. "Or I will not be responsible for my actions," she said to herself.

"Do control yourself, Jemima," Edward said sincerely.

Jemima rolled her eyes. He had really no idea what she was capable of, even though he had heard tales. *Poor man. Poor aunt.* Jemima grinned. *Poor everybody.*

"Jemima. Do bring your work," Aunt Prudence said.

Here we go again, Jemima thought and bit down on the very loud and robust refusal that was pushing its way up her throat. "Coming, aunt. I will join you and pour tea later." She joined the ladies at the table. "I am afraid I injured my finger," she said, lifting up a hastily bandaged finger. "Stuck a needle right through it. I had Edward quack me."

Aunt Prudence pulled out a pair of spectacles and positioned them on the end of her nose. "You never mentioned it before."

Jemima touched the bandage and winced.

"Do take care, Jemima. Puncture wounds can be quite dangerous." The aunt then flipped open a sewing case and diligently prodded the contents.

Jemima burst out laughing. Milly's eyes widened and Aunt Prudence drew back and levelled a quizzical look at her. "Are you feeling quite well, child?" Aunt Prudence asked. "Feverish perhaps?"

Jemima composed her face into a serene mask. "Do you forgive me? I am feeling quite well. I just had a stray thought." Jemima had the image of herself stabbing vampires through the heart with large sewing needles. It made perfect sense. If ripping out their hearts ended their lives then stakes would work too. She would have a word in private with Fulton about it. She suppressed her grin. Tempted to pull the novel she was reading out of her reticule, Jemima decided to ask Milly and Aunt Prudence what they were working on.

Jemima tried to ask Milly. Aunt Prudence got in first. She started explaining the layette she was working on for Milly and Fulton's child. Fine lawn with patches of exquisitely worked embroidery and hand-worked lace edging. Each piece was brought out and displayed in their various stages of completion. One item was complete and Aunt Prudence was using it as inspiration for the other pieces in the set.

Milly's eyes were round and there was something like hunger in her eyes. "Aunt, you have excelled here. Such beautiful work," Milly said and surprised herself as her eyes widened and a hand covered her mouth, too late to stop the unwilling praise.

"I know you appear surprised but I felt such delicacy was wasted on the poor and sewing for the poor is all we did in Kingsfold. Not that I believe the poor should not have nice things. Oh no, no, no! Do not reprove me. But the vicar's wife was so particular and the first time I sewed a little rose on a baby gown she upbraided me about it and said that I was putting on airs and instilling in the poor a desire for things above their station." Aunt Prudence touched the edge of her eyes with a lacy handkerchief one eye on Milly and the other god knew where.

Jemima had to hold her tongue lest she burst out laughing.

Milly reached out and clasped Aunt Prudence's hand. "It must have been hard for you all those years. You are so talented. I am glad you have free rein to sew whatever you like now."

To Jemima's surprise the aunt sniffed and wiped at some dampness around her eyes. Jemima would not own them to be tears. "Thank you my dear. I did what I could with what I had."

The aunt picked up her sewing again and then looked up and put out a hand to touch Milly's forearm. "Do you remember that old dress of mine I made over for you when you were but thirteen?"

"I do," Milly said. Her voice had taken on a soft, whimsical tone. "I loved it and I was very grateful."

"Grateful? You looked so fine. You shone those other village brats down."

Here Jemima was in unfamiliar country. While she was friends with Milly, she did not know all her past or her secrets. "What happened?" Jemima asked.

"It was nothing," Milly replied, a pink colour growing on her cheeks.

"Nothing? Those awful girls, farmers' daughters and tradespeople to the one, said that Milly was shabby. It broke her heart and mine. We fixed them up though."

Milly laughed. "We did. Now, aunt, if we do not start we will have to put things away before we have begun."

"No, we will not. I hear the men coming and as neither of them like to play cards we shall sew and if you can prevail upon him, your husband might play for us until the tea tray is brought in."

A light kindling in her eyes, Milly stood up to greet her husband and conveyed to him the evening's plans. Jemima considered that Milly and Aunt Prudence were back on the road to domestic harmony and stifled a yawn. How on earth was she to go on the hunt during the night? She was tired already.

CHAPTER 12

It took Aunt Prudence an absolute age to go to bed. Milly had gone up earlier, after spending a couple of hours with them. The aunt, though, was indefatigable, stitching away at seams to put together the previously embroidered pieces. Fulton played for an hour and then came to sit next to Aunt Prudence to watch her work. Jemima wondered how the old lady could not know about Fulton's passion for needlework. Surely she would work out that it was his needlework and not Jemima's that she had passed off in the past to satisfy the aunt's zest for industry.

Edward dozed at her side and she was tempted to elbow him. For her to nap in company would be frowned upon but he could do what he liked because he was a man and it would be overlooked. She kicked his foot and smiled when the aunt looked over, possibly distracted by the movement. Edward muttered and sat upright without opening his eyes.

Fulton did not bother to stifle his yawns, but the aunt was bent on her work and did not even notice.

Jemima stood up, disturbing Edward who had started to lean on her. "Do forgive me, Aunt Prudence. I must away to bed. My finger pains me so I think I should rest."

"Your finger?" Edward said. "What's wrong with your finger?"

"I hope it will be better tomorrow," Fulton said quickly.

Jemima had her bandaged hand hidden in her skirts and the meaningful look she sent Edward was totally misconstrued. "Are you ill?" Edward asked, coming forwards to hold her arms.

"I am quite well. Just a small injury that prevented me from sewing this evening," Jemima said under her breath. She showed him her finger. "Remember, you bandaged it for me."

"Oh, yes," he said. "How much you must have suffered in not being able to sew this evening," Edward said, finally understanding.

Aunt Prudence said with enthusiasm, "You can make it up tomorrow."

Jemima flashed a brief smile and retreated from the room. Upstairs she started to dress in her fighting clothes. Milly must have heard her moving about for she came in wearing a voluminous white nightdress that she half carried with her. At Jemima's quizzical look she explained. "A gift from Aunt Prudence. Fulton makes me take it off in bed though."

Jemima blushed at this additional information and tried to block out the picture. She coughed. "I am quite forward in my preparations but I do need assistance with the corset."

Milly did the deed. "The gorget?"

"A famous idea. We all said so."

"You are not wearing the leather trousers?" Milly asked.

"I did but we were in a sewer and they did not do quite so well. Not beyond repair but not dry enough to wear again."

Milly nodded and bit her lip. "I think I will order another pair made. You also need something for your head if you are running into sewers."

"I hope not to make a habit of that."

"What else happened to you?" Milly asked in a precise away.

"I spent most of my time protected by Edward's magical ward and then running. Fulton...I mean Ambrose was tossed about a bit and Edward I suppose is at risk that way too."

Milly's nostrils flared as she heard this. "Then they need additional protection in their battle gear."

Jemima reached for a straw bonnet among the pile she had sitting on a chair.

"Whatever are you wearing?" she asked.

Jemima paused. "I did not like to go without a hat and it kept me from brushing against the top of the sewer tunnels. Things hung down from them."

Milly snatched it from her and threw it into the fire. "You cannot wear it. Not only does it look silly, it does nothing."

Milly strode around the room stroking her chin. Jemima watched, fascinated by her decisive walk and animation. Not a half hour past, she had looked near to fainting. So this was the true Milly. No wonder Aunt Prudence was alarmed. Jemima was downright frightened by the change in her.

"I have it. Tonight you will wear a little hard hat and secure it with a number of hatpins. These you can draw out and use for defence if needed. They are long and sharp. I have at least two and you no doubt have even more."

Jemima had a drawer full of them. "I do. Which hat do you think will work best? I do not have any hard hats."

"Give me a moment," Milly said, then she went to the door, checked the corridor and slipped out.

In five minutes she was slipping back inside. "Aunt Prudence is still up. I can hear them talking."

Jemima checked the mantel clock. It was nearly time to leave. Milly presented her with a hat. It was covered in leather to match her corset, but a pattern had been carved into it. It had also been stiffened. Hidden in the decoration, a grouping of feathers, were two hatpins. There were black ribbons attached that would assist in securing it to her head. Jemima took it and went over to her drawer and inserted another five hatpins into the plumage. They slid easily into the hatband so as to not stick into her scalp.

"Sit down and I will arrange your hair," Milly said.

She unpinned Jemima's hair and refastened the bun lower down so that the hat would sit well on her head. "There. Perfect."

Jemima turned in her seat. "Thank you so much for helping...for understanding."

"Do not thank me! I am so envious. One day I shall help you fight all the bad things."

"All the bad things? But we seek only to fight this beast Geneck. I am not going to make a career out of it."

Milly stood back and shook her head. "I know you and I know Fulton and Edward as well. Now you have a means to fight wrong, you will not stop here. You enjoy it too much and are good at it."

"I hope you are wrong. I plan to retire to Willow Park and take long country walks and visit with you and Fulton and your countless children...except I will not like visiting the children so much."

Milly laughed again and then rubbed at her belly where her child grew. "You say that now but when you have some of your own..."

"No. We cannot have children of our own. Please do not mention it."

Milly grabbed her hand and squeezed it. "What do you mean? You do not want to or cannot?"

"I cannot...think about it. Please, it distresses me."

"I will do as you wish. I must go to bed. I shall see you in the morning and connive to hear about your adventures without Aunt Prudence listening in."

Jemima hugged Milly before she left. Sitting on the bed, she adjusted the laces of her boots while she waited for Edward to come up. She must have fallen asleep while waiting, for when she opened her eyes, Edward stood over her, fully clothed in his battle gear.

Jemima smiled at the name Milly had given their outfits. Battle gear was so appropriate.

"It is time," Edward said and pulled on the hand she lifted towards him.

"It is about time," Jemima said. According to the mantel clock it was half past midnight.

"New hat?" Edward asked.

Jemima smiled, pleased that he had noticed. Then squinted at him. "What are you wearing?"

"A bowler hat. Fulton has the same. Milly's idea. She thinks that later we can get them reinforced. For now though they are just bowler hats."

"Aunt Prudence?" she asked.

"Not quite asleep. We are to wait five more minutes then make our way outside. Fulton is seeing to the locking up so he has an excuse to be thumping about."

"Right then," Jemima said and stepped into Edward's embrace.

They held each other until the five minutes were done and then slipped from the room as quietly as the creaky floor boards allowed and joined Fulton in the street.

The public gardens of the Royal Hospital were not far away. It had been raining earlier in the evening, but by one in the morning a mist rising up from the river dropped like a cloak over the streets. When disturbed by their feet it rolled along as they walked.

Jemima breathed in the damp air. "I like working with you, Fulton. Your ability to rip out hearts and tear off limbs fills me with confidence."

"Jemima!" Edward chided.

"Jemima...I do not like hurting people," Fulton responded vehemently. "It is a terrible thing to say."

"It was a compliment," she replied. "And the truth."

"In very poor taste," Fulton answered and she could see by the set of his shoulders that he was actually upset with her.

"I was thinking, you know, when we were sewing—"

"You were not sewing," Fulton countered.

"I was not sewing," Jemima agreed. "But my story about why I could not sew gave me an idea."

Edward let out a sigh. "Really, not now. We need to concentrate."

Fulton lifted a hand. "No, let us hear her out."

Jemima curtseyed in Edward's direction. He bowed in return. There was to be no quarrelling while working. Jemima blinked. She had employment. Except she was not getting paid so maybe that did not count.

"You rip out hearts and the creature's minions die. Would not something like a needle in the heart do the same, or a stake for example?"

Edward leaned in closer, grasping her shoulders. "I read about corpses being stabbed through the heart!"

"I think it is a sound theory. Stabbing Geneck, though, would be a less certain proposition. He has magic now and is so strong. Something more is needed, I fear," Fulton said.

"I am working on theories," Edward replied.

"While you are doing that, do not even think of taking the blame for this," Jemima said. "You almost confessed to the police."

"I did not," Edward replied hotly.

Fulton piped up. "You had me worried. I thought you might."

The public gardens surrounded them. There was no place in London that was truly free of people. The homeless were scattered among the parks, the churchyards and alleyways. This particular park was emptier than the others. Still, there were dark forms hidden in shadows. People sleeping in the only place they could find.

"Edward, dear. You would not have a small spell that would make these people feel the need to move on, would you?"

Fulton raised an eyebrow. "Great idea, Jemima."

Edward did not bother answering and uttered a few words and waved his left hand in something of a figure eight while the other flicked and twisted. Again, Jemima felt something, a very subtle tug of awareness. How odd. From memory, she had not detected her father's magic so why was she suddenly, or maybe not quite so suddenly, detecting Edward's? Or maybe she was imagining it. She knew he was performing a magical spell so perhaps her mind invented a sensation. That was it. There had to be a logical explanation.

After a few minutes vagabonds, old men, some ragged children threw off their tatty covers and newspapers and wandered out into the streets, leaving their fragile abodes among the trees behind. Fulton turned full circle. "You best not tell the police about that one. They will have you working twenty-four hours a day, seven days a week. Very effective. You two are dangerous."

Edward tipped the brim of his bowler hat to acknowledge Fulton's comment. "Shall we take up positions?" Edward said, leading the way.

Jemima walked steadily behind him, even though her knees were shaking. The last thing she wanted to do was be the bait for Geneck. Even with Edward's ward preventing the beast from reaching her, the vile, putrid thoughts could not be blocked. When she opened her mind to lure him in, he poured the filth of his mind into hers.

Geneck had almost broken through the ward last time. The hand had come through, reaching for her. She might be showing a brave face to her husband and Fulton, but deep inside she was like a jelly mould quivering and ready to split apart.

Now that the park was empty of people, Jemima looked around, wary because there were so many places to take cover, so many places for evil to hide.

The wind picked up, shaking the branches of the trees and scattering leaf litter. The mist stirred and little whirls appeared where the wind sucked at it. The lapping of the river reached them. It was not that far. Sound grew flat with the thickening of the fog around them. It would be easy to lose one another.

"Stand here while I set up the wards. Do not move," Edward said and walked off. At first Jemima was to be unwarded so as to better attract Geneck. They considered that he would be wary this time and know it was a trap. Her being unwarded at first would be too much for him to resist. Once she made contact with Geneck's mind, she was to run to the first ward, which Edward would call into being. It was not far, a few steps. It was only a slight deviation from the last time.

Jemima watched him place the stones while her heart beat loudly in her ears. She had worn a blouse this time to better disguise the ruby glow of her heart machine. Still, she thought herself to be standing out. Too vulnerable. She had to quiet her mind. Edward would not let harm fall on her. Look how meticulous he was being about the warding stones. When he was happy with that one Edward returned and handed her a single warding stone. "You know what to do with this. But I am also going to use this tree as another ward. Just in case." He kissed her forehead as he went to a position behind the large oak on the edge of the park and Jemima sensed the magic growing there too. This time there were three lines of defence. A few steps to the first ward, then the tree or the stone, but she had to stand still to be in contact with the wards. That was the hardest thing to do as her first instinct was to run.

When he came back to her, he put his arm around her.

"Jemima...you are precious to me. Please be careful. As soon as you sense him, step into the first ward."

She leaned into him, liking the feel of his warmth as it surrounded her and taking comfort in the steady beat of his heart. "I know you care. I will be fine. We will do it this time. You will find a way."

Fulton called out. He was scanning the area, making sure no one remained. "Are you going to publicly exhibit all night or can we get started?"

"Ready?" Edward asked.

"Yes," she replied.

Edward stepped away from her, his long leather coat glistening with accumulated mist, and then he slipped away to take up his position. Of Fulton she could see no sign as he too had blended with the shadows.

Cool, damp air made her skin chill and she rubbed at her upper arms. Her heart beat steadily, prompted by the whir and spark of her ruby heart. Rather annoying, she thought, because she was scared out of her wits and now that Edward's comforting presence was gone she felt totally alone.

The previous time, Geneck's thoughts had clawed at her, the strength and the horror of them nearly shredding her sanity. The hunger in him, the rage, the sharp talons of spite ripping into her mind like someone hacking into a soft melon. Coercion thick as treacle had nearly smothered her, but she was able to fight it all. Right now she needed to do better, be stronger. Now she knew what she was up against, she could prepare. She had Edward's magic machine keeping her alive. She had Fulton close at hand. She had nothing to fear, she told herself.

Jemima let the night sounds of the park envelop her—the rattle of leaves as they rubbed against each other in the wind and the sound of the hull of a boat slapping against water in the river. These she used to calm her mind, centre herself. It was time to let go her mind, let her thoughts be seized by the monster Geneck.

With a large intake of breath, she closed her eyes and opened herself up the connection. Easily did she touch the thread of his thoughts, so close they seemed, he could be standing next to her. His thoughts were like a river of fire spouting into the dark of night.

Instead of being yellow or blue, the flames burned black and red. Her skin burned and her muscles tensed. *Come to me*, Jemima thought at him. *Come to me.*

A breeze tousled her hair. A warm breath brushed against her skin. She jerked around and screamed. Geneck was there.

He was not meant to be there. Not like this. So close. So dangerous. She had no warning. She was not in her ward. Before she could scream, he reached for her, skeletal hand bent like a claw.

Dodging away, she managed to scream this time before she stepped into the ward. Her screams cut off when he drove his thoughts like spikes into her head. She could not move. Her foot hovered over the ward but did not land. Her hand tried to throw the warding stone but was frozen.

This had been Geneck's trap, not theirs.

Frozen, muscles tight, breath caught, her lips curled in horror as he poured poisonous visions into her mind. Visions filled with fountains of blood, rending flesh and something even darker still. His thoughts sped through her mind, crashing and squashing all in their path.

Something unlocked, just a pause in his thoughts and Jemima fell backwards and through the maelstrom he caused in her mind. She heard whimpers. They were her own. She needed to move. She needed to get to the ward. It was so close.

Geneck fell back, hit by a blast of Edward's power. His mental assault lessened and Jemima fought her way free. She rolled clear, except when she opened her eyes she had moved further away from the ward. She drew up into a crouch, readying to dive when action exploded around her.

Fulton ran across the grass like a locomotive building up steam. He leaped, landing feet first on Geneck's chest and pushing him back to sprawl on the ground. Fulton used his chest as a platform to push off and away and then rolled into a standing position.

Edward threw magic, even while he built up a larger spell, one that made Jemima's teeth ache, made her hair rise on the skin of her arms and the nape of her neck. Fulton attacked again, keeping the beast distracted.

Geneck was very close to her. From being prone, he flipped over, dragging his body with his clawed hands, driving his fingers into the soft ground. He was coming for her. She needed to move. Quickly.

Jemima crouched, hands on the cool turf, rooted by fear to the spot. Then it dawned on her. Geneck was using her for cover. If he stayed close to her, Edward would not be able to loose the spell. If she broke for it and ran to the ward, he could grab her. Not if Fulton was harrying him.

"Fulton!" she called. "On three."

They had not practised this but she knew Fulton would understand. Fulton circled in. Geneck slavered and growled but stayed low and hidden from Edward by using Jemima for a shield. The ward was close. She could feel it. She wanted to be inside it.

Visions of him drinking from her ravaged neck overpowered her. Horror and gore and pain. He was using her mind against her. He knew what she was thinking and trying to divert her. She cast a glance in his direction. He was grinning.

Feelings of perverse pleasure filled her mind. She panted, trying to stay on task, trying to get into the right position so Fulton could attack. She needed to run to the ward. She needed to count to three. The vision Geneck spun in her mind grew, a picture of her long white neck. His jagged teeth descending. *No, no!* She tried to shut him out. He was undermining her, undoing her confidence.

Edward still worked on his incantation. His voice was soft on the breeze, soft but urgent.

"Jemima?" Fulton called out, hands clenched into fist. When she did not respond, Fulton drew in for another attack, trying to draw Geneck away from her.

Fulton tackled and tried to force him away. Somehow, she knew that Edward was ready. Jemima threw herself to the ground and rolled ready to avoid Edward's spell. The power that Edward amassed made her teeth ache and the air in her chest cavity vibrate in sympathy.

"Now," Fulton yelled.

Edward heaved the spell. She could not see its passage but she could sense the power of it as it washed over her. Peeking out sideways, she saw Geneck shudder, saw wisps of smoke issue from fissures that had split his skin. His roar of anguish echoed in her bones and her mind and he fell back with a thud.

Edward ran up, his hands outstretched. "Now, Fulton. The device. Rip it out while he is incapacitated."

Fulton glanced at Edward. "Are you sure?"

"Yes, quickly. Before he recovers."

Fulton kept his gaze fixed on Geneck. He did look incapacitated and his assault on her mind had quieted, yet she could not trust it. Geneck was powerful and clever. Jemima forgot to breathe and covered her chest with her hands. The glow from her ruby heart turned her fingers pink. She bunched her fists, not quite believing how close the spell had come to her.

Geneck lay immobile, agonised moaning leaking from his clenched mouth, incisors poking down to lie against his lower lips. Jemima had not seen him this close before, or his face so still before. There were traces of the man he once had been—powerful jaw, prominent forehead and deep-seated eyes. His body also showed signs of the man he had been, muscled, big arms that used to wield an axe.

Fulton was two steps away. Geneck jerked once, his arm pushing upwards. "Ed..." Fulton said.

"I still have him," Edward said, sounding as if he was straining. "But hurry. I will not be able to hold him long. Somehow, he is siphoning off my power. I cannot understand how he is doing it."

Fulton lunged, his augmented hand open and ready to snatch the emerald-powered heart from Geneck's chest. Jemima, still spellbound, had not run to safety within her ward. She should run. She must run.

Fulton's fingers contacted the device. It would be all right. But then an explosion ripped through them. Jemima was thrown up and back. Purple arcs of electricity snaked out to the trees, between Geneck and Fulton. Thrown back, Edward lost his control of the spell. Geneck was now free of it.

Jemima blinked, feeling stunned with the echo of pain in the back and legs. She could not form words to cry out a warning to Fulton.

Fulton and Geneck shuddered, their bodies twitching as the power played over their bodies. Fulton's hand released its hold on Geneck's heart and the power erupting from Geneck faded.

Jemima drew in a painful breath. Only the occasional flicker and spark played over Geneck's body, marking the place of contact.

Dazed, Jemima crawled, then climbed unsteadily to her feet. Shaking her head, her hair fell free of its bun so her braids brushed against her shoulders. Her hat was gone. Looking down, she saw her shirt was ripped, one sleeve hanging in tatters. Because the fabric irritated her, she tugged at it and tossed it to the ground. She should run to her ward and was about to when she caught sight of Edward.

Edward lay as still as death. Near to the fallen beast, Fulton breathed in a long shuddery breath but remained flat on the ground. Unconscious, Jemima realised.

Geneck lay still. The emerald glow from his mechanical heart flowed over the trees and the ground where he lay.

It was up to her to dispatch the creature. She had no idea what had happened. It could have been a confluence of magic from Edward and the mechanical device keeping the beast alive. Slowly, she approached the prone figure of the beast. She had nothing to dispatch him with. How she wished she had procured a stake to ram into his heart.

When she was within a few feet, Geneck's body jerked. Before she could even think or move, his eyes snapped open and riveted on her. She thought he was bunching his muscles to attack her, yet he did not. His dark glittering eyes watched her, though.

Caught, she stood still until a thought of his speared into her brain —a memory of a beautiful girl, with a smile to break hearts. Then a man's dark, calloused hands were on her, touching her. In the vision, Geneck held the girl, like a cat sinks its claws into a mouse, and molested her.

Jemima squirmed and she fought the lurid images. "Daughter," he said to her. "You are mine. Give yourself to me."

He spoke into her mind, crushing all her resistance. "Come! Give yourself to me."

Jemima writhed and struggled. She was not his daughter. She was not his to command. She had to remember that.

Jemima screamed as Geneck's thoughts focused on her. He wanted her to be his daughter. Together, they would never die. Together, they would feast on the flesh of lowly humans. Together, they would enjoy each other's bodies in sensual rapture.

The vividness of his vision made her retch. She fell to the ground and vomited onto the grass. She had to get away, had to run. Crawling backwards, she fought his hold on her.

Fulton jerked and Geneck's attention on her lessened. Jemima hardened her mind, surged to her feet and ran into the trees. Terror chased her down. She could not remember what Edward had told her, could not remember the location of the ward, either of them. She did not even remember her stone or whether she still carried it. Thoughts of safety and wards scattered. She ran and ran until her lungs burned. Then her strength gave out and she could run no more.

Bending over, she put her hands on her knees while she drew breaths down her dry throat and fought the sobs that wracked her body. Gradually, her breathing slowed and the night sounds of the park intruded.

She thought she had put distance between her and Geneck but she had actually put distance between herself and Fulton and Edward. She could see them there lying in the grass.

A snap of a twig and Jemima's head shot up. She turned full circle, seeing nothing. Someone was there. She jerked her head around, seeking Geneck where she had left him. But the mist rolled in and she saw nothing. No sign of Edward, Fulton or the beast.

A soft wash of air and the sound of fabric rustling alerted her to someone close. She turned. Her scream of fright was cut off by the hand that encircled her neck.

Geneck must have her.

A blackness enveloped her and she knew no more.

CHAPTER 13

A nudge to Edward's foot brought him to wakefulness. Another and he ignored it. He was sleeping. Sleeping was good. He was tired. It had been a difficult night.

Another more persistent nudge this time. He came to, blinking away grey light. Where was he? Feeling a dampness along his back and aches in all parts of his body, he began to collect that he was not in his bed. He moaned once and put a hand to his forehead. He had the most despicable headache.

"Mr Huntington?" the voice said, irritation evident in the piercing tone.

Edward touched his face, felt something sticky there and flinched when his finger stuck into a cut on his forehead. He had trouble remembering things. Like who and where he was.

Muffled footsteps sounded around his head. He heard another voice close by. "Mr Fulton, sir?"

A brush of fabric, the creak of knees as someone knelt next to him. A hand shook his shoulder. "Come on, Mr Huntington. Wake up."

The voice was familiar and irritating. Edward cracked open his eyes. All seemed grey around him. He blinked and Inspector Coleman came into focus. "Morning, sir. Pleasant dreams, I take it?" The detective spoke with a satirical air.

"Where...what...I..." Edward mumbled, trying to roll over and push himself up. Rather shaky, he did not mind the detective's help to get into a sitting position.

They were in a park. Fulton lay unconscious not far from him. The young policeman was trying to jolly him awake as well.

Edward sat up and looked around. A park? "What the devil am I doing here?" he said.

"I was hoping you would be able to tell me that," Coleman replied.

It was early morning and he was waking up in a park? He had been there quite a while as his clothes were wet. His clothes? He looked down and he was in a shirt, trousers and socks. His leather coat was gone. His protective vest and his gorget were gone too. He patted his pockets. His jacket was gone along with his wallet and fob watch. He stared at his hand. His signet ring was gone too. He looked at his other hand. His other ring was gone. He had been robbed.

Something else was missing, something important. He studied his surroundings, looked at the tree, the big oak tree where he remembered placing a ward. A ward for...

"Jemima?"

The detective lowered his eyelids. "Only you two here I am afraid."

Jemima must have gone home. By herself? But Edward's brain was scrambled and he latched onto the idea that Jemima was home safe. Had to be...

Inspector Coleman was speaking to him again. "I am sorry to say the pickpockets have been here before we found you. You have both been cleaned out. You will probably be needing a lift home as you look worse for wear." He turned his head and faced Fulton. "Your friend may be needing the hospital."

Panic made Edward shudder. "No, no. He has a physician." Edward tried to stand and Coleman helped steady him. "If you can help us get home. It is not far. I would be most grateful."

"What were you doing here, Mr Huntington?" Coleman said, narrowing his gaze. The uniformed constable had his notepad out.

"I honestly cannot say. I do not quite remember. That is extremely odd I know." He shook his head as if that would help clear his brain. "Is there a problem, Inspector?"

The inspector took a nice slow look around the park. Homeless people and urchins lurked on the fringes of the park, keeping clear of the law enforcement, Edward surmised. "No, none that I can see. No bodies here this morning, except yours. And as you are not quite dead, I cannot say there has been a crime. No point in chasing the thieves, they will be long gone by now. I hope nothing too significant to you has been stolen."

Edward looked down at his hand. "My wedding ring."

"Well, your missus will be having a complaint about that, I am sure."

"Yes. She will..."

Edward looked at his bare hand and then at the inspector. "Was Jemima at home?"

The inspector stared at him blankly. "We have not been to your house, sir, so I cannot say."

Jemima would be worried and he would quite rightly get a scalding for staying out all night. Had he and Fulton gone to the club? But they were near the river. He looked behind him. In the gardens of the Royal Hospital. Were they set upon on their way home? Edward shook his head. The club was in the other direction. He did not like the direction of his thoughts.

No, no. Not the club. Danger!

But for the life of him, Edward could not remember what it was. Just a gut full of dread. He needed to get home right away and see for himself that Jemima was there, safe and sound.

Fulton would not wake so the young policeman, the inspector and Edward managed to carry him to the policemen's carriage. It was rather cramped inside, but it was better than trying to walk home. Edward sat in the carriage and moved his body to the rock and sway and tried to pull his thoughts together.

"Mr Huntington?" Inspector Coleman enquired.

Edward turned his gaze to the policeman.

"We will be at your home soon. May I call on you later when you are feeling better? I have some questions to ask."

"Certainly," Edward replied automatically. "How did you find us if you did not go to the house to see we were not there?"

The inspector smiled slyly. "Well, sir, I was having you watched. It took a while to find you once you went into the park as my man had to call for back up. I am sorry I did not arrive sooner. It was a busy night."

"More attacks?" Edward's chest was tight. More deaths on his hands.

"No, just the usual. No more of those gruesome killings."

Edward sat back and relaxed into the chair. "Thank heaven for that."

Had not he and Fulton been going to fight the beast? Must have, because why was he missing his leather vest and gorget? He remembered their absence right enough. Is that what happened? Had they won? How could they have done that without Jemima? A feeling of dread grew in his gut and he was anxious to return home just to see her fast asleep in their bed.

Why was his memory so fudged? He licked his lips, tasted the tip of his tongue. Just a hint there, like the aftertaste of cinnamon. Magic.

"Are you certain, sir? No more attacks from the beast?"

"It is possible I suppose. But there were none that I have heard of this morning when I started my shift and I have been on the job since sunrise." He tugged out his fob watch and frowned at it, as if he had trouble seeing clearly. "It is now nearly ten."

A cold fist of fear tightened in Edward's chest. The lack of memory disguised some unfathomable terror. Fulton lay half sprawled on the floor of the carriage and half draped over the seat. Something bad had definitely happened.

"Here we are, Mr Huntington. Perhaps, if you ring the bell we can get some assistance to take Mr Fulton into the house."

The small frontage of Fulton's terraced house sat quiet and peaceful before him. Edward jumped down from the carriage, feeling his bones jar. It did not take long for Jakes to answer his frantic knocking.

Jakes fetched the footman and they came to carry Fulton to his bed.

As they hauled the still unconscious Fulton between them, Edward said urgently, "I will be in shortly. Make him comfortable. Do not upset the ladies. I will see to him, Jakes, and see if you can send someone to Heaton's practice, just in case we need him."

"Very well, sir." Jakes was at once curious and horrified at Fulton's state. Edward realised that he was injured and bloody as well. Not the kind of lark for a gentleman.

The inspector stood at the door, his eyes assessing as Fulton was carried up the stairs. "I will let you set things to right and call later, perhaps tomorrow if I cannot get away," he said, tipping his hat. "Please give my regards to Mrs Huntington."

Edward fell backwards. "Jemima?" He turned, rubbing his face vigorously. *Wake up, wake up.* Leaving the front door open, Edward hurried up the stairs and down the hall to their room.

"Jemima?" he said and pushed the bedroom door open. The bed was made. There was no sign of his wife. His stomach dropped and filled with leaden dread. He ran downstairs to the morning room, his eyes flicking to her spot in the corner. She was not there.

There was no sign of Milly and Aunt Prudence. He was not quite sure if that was a good or a bad thing. Surely if Jemima was with them, she would have come to greet them. Furthermore, she would not have left Edward and Fulton unconscious in a public park. "Oh my god, no!" he wailed as the full ramifications of the morning events unfurled in his mind.

Backing out of the morning room, he reversed his steps and headed to Fulton's room. Jakes was bathing Fulton's forehead with vinegar. Fulton was moaning but not conscious.

"Mrs Huntington? Have you seen her, Jakes?"

Jakes shook his head, his expression dour. "She did not return last night, sir. The maid said the bed was not slept in."

Edward fell back a step as if hit by a blow. He looked down at his bare hand. His wedding ring was gone and so was his wife. "Will you not help, sir? The master will not wake."

A loud wail disturbed Edward's train of thought. Milly had got word. They must be in the drawing room, sewing or some such.

Edward whirled. Bearing down on him was Aunt Prudence. "Edward Huntington," she began before she even reached him. "What is going on?" She came to an abrupt halt, feathers and lace and skirts whirling about her. "Where is your wife?"

Milly brushed past her and then him to dive to the floor by Fulton in the bed. She let out an anguished wail. Edward shut the door on that tumult and faced the aunt.

He fiddled with his collar and wondered why the lady terrified him so. He felt guilt enough already. "I do not know," Edward replied truthfully. "I was hoping she was safe at home."

Aunt Prudence narrowed her eyes at him, like he was some insect in a microscope. "Safe. At. Home! How could she be with you dragging her over the city? Do not think me ignorant of your tomfooleries and your ramshackle ways?"

"Now aunt..." Edward tried to respond but the aunt's glare got the better of him. "But...but..."

"Do not give me buts. You have taken that poor girl out and placed her in danger. You think I know nothing of what is going on. I tell you now I understand perfectly. I cannot live with that wife of yours and not suspect something underhand. I have too much exposure to her to remain ignorant. Not if I want to stay safe...and sane."

"It is not what you think," Edward began.

"It is everything I think and more," Aunt Prudence said. "And Fulton. Milly's beloved husband. What kind of shape is he in?"

Edward lifted both hands to prevent the old woman from entering Fulton's bedroom. "He will be fine. He is very robust and I am about to fetch a surgeon."

Aunt Prudence's normally pink complexion paled. "A surgeon?" She began to wail and fan herself as if she was going into a spasm.

He made shushing gestures that she ignored as she tried to get around him. "Let me through."

"Please, Aunt Prudence. It is nothing that serious. Heaton is a surgeon who is familiar with his condition, that is all."

Jemima. The thought of her was with him. He needed to rescue her. He needed Fulton. Jagged bits of memories from last night shifted into focus and then faded. It was unnatural this fugue he was in. He wanted to wail and cry himself but this was no time to fall to pieces. He had to move forwards, not think of the unthinkable.

"Aunt Prudence, I need your help. Please fetch some brandy and ask the housekeeper to bring hot water and clean towels."

Aunt Prudence hesitated for one moment, then a light glinted in her eye. She drew herself up to her full height and replied calmly, "Right away."

She turned in her finery and stampeded down the stairs.

He turned back to Fulton's room. Milly was blubbering all over Fulton. "There, there, that will not help things."

Milly lifted her face, red from weeping. "Will he die?" she said, her voice on the edge of hysteria.

"Not if I can help it."

Jakes had retreated to the corner, the contretemps a bit too overwhelming for the normally composed butler.

Milly hiccupped loudly then dissolved into tears all over again as she stared down at her inert husband. Edward knew exactly how she felt.

"Let us do something useful, shall we? Here, help me make him more comfortable."

Milly lifted her head again, wiping her tears. "Yes, of course," she said thickly and blew her nose. "I am terribly sorry. Fulton would be very angry with me and Jemima would have no patience with me at all."

Edward's heart hitched a beat at the mention of Jemima but barrelled on through. Jemima was not here and Fulton needed his assistance. "Not at all. He is very proud of you. Can you take off his shirt?" He let Milly take over and she ripped it down the centre of Fulton's chest and peeled away the sleeves. Then he turned to Jakes. "Here man, help me get him more centred on the bed." His boots and coat were gone.

Jakes was then joined by Fulton's valet and they succeeded in settling the unconscious man. "I say, Jakes, why do you not go downstairs and see where that hot water is?" Edward said.

Jakes darted off and the valet helped Milly and Edward get Fulton undressed and beneath the sheets. The valet was aware of Fulton's enhancements as was Milly, but the butler was not. There was no point in discombobulating the butler as they all depended on him. He sent the valet and Milly off to find a nightgown for Fulton in the dressing room.

While they were absent, Edward knelt by the bed and took Fulton's hand to inspect him for injuries. His arm mechanism looked to be in fine condition. He squinted at it and then used his thumbnail to loosen the screw of the housing to check the gem that powered it. The polished amber was not quite a gem but it did retain the power that Edward had spun into it. The gem gave off wan yellow light. As far as Edward could ascertain its power was diminished.

How? he wondered. He drew down the sheet to inspect Fulton's leg. There was some bleeding around the flesh where the thigh met the casing. It did not look severe. He studied the amber in the leg and it seemed diminished also. Something had drained the power from Fulton's artificial limbs.

Edward expected some decline in power over time. But he had inspected both of these last week and they had been fully charged. Edward thought he had invented perpetual motion but the visit from the brotherhood indicated otherwise. They said he had put magic into his devices. Imagine that. He thought his magic and his scientific work were entirely separate. Previously he had thought his charity work separate as well, but that had been self-deception. It had led him straight into Longhurst's trap.

Footsteps heralded the approach of the butler. The door to the dressing room began to open. Edward flicked the sheet over Fulton's leg and checked his eyes. Fulton was out cold.

Jakes came in with the maid following behind with a jug of water and towels. The butler held a tray with the brandy. "Thank you. Could you ask Beth for my wife's smelling salts?"

Not that Jemima ever used them. They were more for emergencies involving other females. *Oh Jemima, be safe. I will come for you soon.*

With a nod, Jakes retreated. Edward admired Jakes's fortitude. He was taking this in his stride. Perhaps he would tender his notice when Fulton awoke. He returned with the small vial.

Milly went to the basin and poured hot water in and tested the temperature. She was going to clean her husband.

Edward unstoppered the smelling salts and waved the bottle under Fulton's nostrils. He reacted, shifting his head away from the fumes.

"Here, let me," Milly said, putting her hands out for the smelling salts. She placed the basin on the floor and sat on the bed, waving the small bottle of pungent ammonia under her husband's nose. "Come on, Ambrose," Milly said. "Come back to us."

"Get out of my way," said a voice from the door.

Jakes was standing in the way of Aunt Prudence. Edward breathed slowly. "Aunt Prudence. Would you be so kind to stay by the front door in case Heaton knocks?"

"I am very happy to do so, but is not that the butler's job?" Her tone was matter-of-fact.

"Oh, quite right. Jakes, please show Heaton up as soon as he arrives," Edward said, while frantically thinking up ways to get rid of the aunt. Then he realised he did not need to. She was Fulton's responsibility, being part of his household. "Come in, Aunt Prudence."

Fulton's eyelids fluttered. Milly stoppered the smelling salts and handed them back to Edward who passed them to Aunt Prudence and she gripped them in a meaty hand while leaning over his shoulder to gaze upon Fulton.

"He will be fine in a while," Edward commented.

Milly glared at him. "How do you know he will be fine? He has not spoken a word," Milly said vehemently.

Edward jerked back and opened and shut his mouth, unable to respond to Milly's outburst. She had always been so quiet and shy.

Aunt Prudence leaned in, the lace on her shawl tickling the skin of his neck. "Oh, his colour is very bad."

Brushing her lace aside, Edward lifted his eyebrows at her, hoping she would take the hint, but she refused to. She moved next to him and nearly knocked him over with the bulk of her skirts.

"Ambrose?" Milly said. "Say something."

"Mmm..." Fulton said. "Mmmmpf."

Edward pursed his lips. Then an idea struck him. He leaned in close to Fulton's ear. "You are drooling in front of Milly, Fulton."

Fulton's eyes snapped open. "I was not drooling, I was dreaming...

Oh." He stared up at them gazing down on him and then winced. "Oh, my head hurts."

"Not surprising," Aunt Prudence said. "Whatever have you been doing with it?"

Fulton blinked. "Why is everyone in my room?" He turned his head. "Milly?"

She took his good hand and squeezed it. "You were injured, my love, and Edward brought you home."

A confused expression haunted Fulton. "We were out..."

Edward nodded and rubbed his chin. Fulton's memory was affected as well. It had to be unnatural means. A spell. Geneck? He would more likely drain them of life rather than memories. The brotherhood? Much more likely. Ah that confused things. Jemima was gone but which one of them had her?

Fulton cast his gaze in Edward's direction, eyebrows raised and mouth open to say something. Edward filled him in quickly with the details of how they had been found and brought home. As he was not too sure of the details that led to them being unconscious and he was not about to divulge all in front of his relatives, that was all he was willing to say. Fulton nodded, frowning and holding Milly's hand.

Aunt Prudence stood there brooding. There was an air of repressed violence about the old woman. It was buzzing around her head like one of her feathers.

Fulton looked at them in turn before asking, "Where is Jemima?"

"Not here," Edward said.

"She did not come home from your excursion," Milly informed him before Edward could stop her.

Aunt Prudence threw up her hands and wailed. Fulton tried to sit up but Edward pushed him back down again. "Wait for Heaton to see to you."

Fulton grasped Edward's forearm. "But Jemima?"

"I know," and there Edward's voice choked up. While he could not remember exactly what had happened, he could feel the loss and he knew Jemima was in trouble.

Edward poured some brandy and passed it to Fulton. Edward

poured himself a measure as well and downed it in one gulp. "Perhaps some privacy?" Fulton asked.

"Oh no, you shan't be rid of us that easy," Aunt Prudence said in a low voice. "Milly has as much right to know what is going on as Jemima does and as Jemima is not here, then I also have to know. Poor girl," she said, rolling the 'r'.

Fulton took two sips of the brandy and then flopped back on the pillows. Edward had the urge to drink straight from the bottle. Fulton shared a look with him and Edward nodded. What did it matter if they told all? Jemima was gone.

Edward peered over Aunt Prudence to the door to make sure no one else was listening and with the faint hope that Heaton would be there to interrupt and save him the telling. Although they would have to come up with a cover story for the servants because they would all know about Jemima's absence and the men's scandalous arrival with a police escort. Their conjecture and gossip would be far worse than reality. If such a thing was possible.

Edward outlined the current situation about the beast, Geneck, of which Aunt Prudence surprisingly knew a lot, making him do a double take. Edward shook his head, trying to shake off the surprise. Had he underestimated the old woman? He had underestimated Jemima so perhaps he had erred there as well.

"As Jemima's blood was used in the revival of the beast, she has a connection to him...it. An unholy connection and yet it proved useful."

"You used her as bait?" Milly said in a hard tone.

Fulton sat up straight, bristling with the unvoiced accusation.

"Fulton was against it," Edward said.

"And you were not?" Aunt Prudence concluded. "Your own wife. Your former ward?"

Edward sagged under the weight of those accusations. They were true and he was not sure the mitigating circumstances would exonerate him. There was, of course, Jemima's own audacity and refusal to stay out it. "I was desperate. It was Jemima's idea. People are dying. Innocent people. If I could stop this, if Jemima could help me, then I had to try."

"Yes," Fulton said. "We had a duty. These enhancements that

Edward has given me make me strong. I can fight these minions and this beast. At least I thought I could. But something went wrong... Geneck knew it was a trap. He sprang it on us instead."

Edward folded his arms and stared into the fireplace, watching flames leap and dance.

"There were other complications. Another party interfered with our plans. I think they attacked us also. I tremble at the thought that they might have Jemima. Although surely they are better than the beast."

"Then this beast does not have her?" Aunt Prudence demanded.

Edward looked up and met her steely gaze. "I do not know, but I am going to find out. Just as soon as Fulton here gets the all-clear from Heaton."

The sound of the doorknocker reached them and then voices echoed in the vestibule. Soon feet thumped on the staircase and along the hall. With a sharp knock, Heaton entered the room.

"Huntington! What the devil has happened here? Why is this room so full of...fe...people?" He smiled and even Edward could see it was fake.

Aunt Prudence nodded to Milly. Milly stood and then stooped to land a kiss on Fulton's brow and then she left the room with her aunt. Edward shut the door behind him and then sagged against it and met Heaton's quizzical look.

"Is this more of your hocus pocus adventures, Huntington?" Heaton asked as his gaze narrowed on Fulton. Edward was dishevelled and possibly bruised and there was dried blood in his hair and on his face. There was no point in trying to deny it.

He gave Heaton a brief outline of the morning's events. "Knocked unconscious, was he?" Heaton shook his head. "I wish you two would take up the gentlemanly arts of study and repose or producing children. Quite a lot safer than sleeping in parks and being robbed. Beasts! If I did not already know what you were capable of I would have you put away, Huntington." He clucked and approached Fulton. "Let me look at you." He visually checked Fulton's head and pressed against the bone. When Fulton flinched, Heaton looked more closely.

"That's a nasty bruise," Heaton said as he lifted the hair at the back of Fulton's neck.

Edward blinked. He had not thought to look there. At Edward's sound of surprise, Heaton glanced over his shoulder. "He should not come to too much harm. Do not go anywhere. I will check you over as well."

Fulton moaned as Heaton prodded him. "Follow my finger," Heaton said. "And how many am I holding up?"

"Too many," Fulton replied.

Heaton chuckled at his response. "Still full of bravado, I see."

Heaton then asked Fulton for permission to inspect his body for other wounds. Fulton gritted his teeth and said yes. When Fulton was rolled over, a large brown stain on the sheet was revealed from a large scrape where Fulton had skidded along the ground. However, after Heaton used some saline solution to clean the skin it looked to be a claw mark with an ugly ridge of ripped skin. Edward swallowed and the memory from last night came rushing back into his brain. He had been so hellbent on spell casting he had not realised how close the fight had come between Geneck and Fulton.

"Is it serious?" Fulton asked.

Heaton shook his head. "I will put a dressing on it. Hold on as this might sting." He dabbed on some cleaning solution. Fulton winced but remained stoic. Heaton peered closer. "I do not think it will need stitching but it will leave a scar. You must keep it dry and clean. It might hurt if you move too quickly. Get your wife to change the bandage daily. Call me if there is any fever or festering."

Fulton's jaw clenched. "I will not have my wife change my bandages. She cannot know," he said fiercely.

Heaton blew some air through his lips. "Stay still while I bandage this up. Huntington, will you see to the proper care of Fulton's wounds?"

"Of course."

Keeping himself busy while Heaton worked, Edward picked up a dropped tie and put it on the dresser. Tossing a scoop of coal on the fire, he stoked up the embers, hoping to warm the room. He still felt chilled to his bones.

Heaton examined the appliances in Fulton's arm and leg and then checked him over once again, checking the movement of fingers, toes, ankles and elbows. He had Fulton grip his hand and squeeze. Satisfied, he then prodded Fulton in the ribcage, which elicited a wince that made him growl. All in all, a thorough examination. "You have definitely been in the wars." Heaton sat back and cast a glance in Edward's direction. "He will live. I am not so sure about you." He got up out of his seat. "Sit here, Huntington. I need to check you over, too."

Edward was going to argue but caught the tight expression on Heaton's face. His medical friend was worried so he suffered himself to be examined. After removing his shirt, Heaton pointed to eight fist-size bruises on his torso. No wonder he felt as if he had been trampled by a herd of elephants.

He had no recollection of receiving them or engaging in hand-to-hand combat. He had been wielding magic, not fist fighting. Bewildered, he sat while Heaton packed up his things. "I suppose I am wasting my breath warning you to be careful. Whatever it is you are up to, I am sure it is for a good cause. However, Fulton should spend a day, perhaps two in bed. Call me if he is difficult to wake or has any blurred vision or weakness in his arms or legs."

Edward had not apprised Heaton of the business with Geneck. He had invited him to the wedding, but Heaton and Sylvia could not attend due to Heaton's busy London medical practice. Heaton held out his hand and Edward shook it. Yet Heaton knew about Edward's work through Fulton's various injuries and operations. It had been Heaton who approached him for assistance all those years ago. Heaton suspected something unusual and he was a smart man.

"I have yet to felicitate with you on your marriage. Is Mrs Huntington here? I would like to share good tidings of her with my wife."

Edward's stomach sank and he sat back in the chair, feeling an urge to throw up. "She is not here at the moment."

Heaton dropped down beside him. "Good god, man. Are you all right?" He began lifting Edward's head.

Edward shook the doctor off. "No, I am fine, I tell you." He got to his feet, pulled on his shirt. "I will see you out. Jemima is sure to pay a visit to Mrs Heaton as soon as it can be arranged."

Heaton frowned as he studied Edward's face. "Very well. I know you are keeping things from me. I do not have time to pester you about it." He turned to leave, case in hand and paused. "Remember Huntington...Edward. We are friends and I will help you if I can."

Edward took the hand that was held out to him and shook it. "I know, old chap. I swear I will come to you if I need help."

He led Heaton out and saw him off into the street. Then he shut the door, rested his head on the wood panel while he garnered his strength and resolve. It took effort because he was drowning in fear and despair. He had lost Jemima.

On returning to his friend's room, Edward tottered over to the chair next to Fulton's bed and sagged down into it.

Fulton edged further up the bed and frowned. "You look terrible. Do you remember what happened?"

Edward shook his head, tears threatening. "Something terrible, Fulton. Jemima is missing."

Fulton threw off his bed covers. "We must go after her."

Edward put out his hand and pushed Fulton back. "No, you cannot."

"I feel fine. Come on, we must be quick."

Edward shook his head, a sob escaping him as he put the heel of his hand to his forehead. "That's the problem. Do you not see? We were found by the police insensible in the park. We had been battered, robbed."

Fulton clenched the sheet in his fist and his face was set in stone. "And?" He sat back in the bed, the neck of his nightgown peeping out of the covers.

"We fought Geneck last night that much I know, even if I cannot remember the details myself. I have flashes of memory. I think perhaps the brotherhood were there..."

Fulton let out an expletive.

Edward nodded, agreeing with the sentiment. "There was no sign of him this morning. No sign of Jemima! I thought she had run home. I hoped it would be so, but when we returned she had not been here."

Fulton's features grew thoughtful and he bit his bottom lip. "She would not leave us like that—alone and vulnerable. She is too loyal. Loyal and brave."

Edward realised then that his friend knew his wife better than he did. A little stab of jealousy entered his heart, but he dismissed it. Instead, he was grateful for what information Fulton could provide. He should know that much about her himself. Had she not put herself in a trap to rescue him? "Ambrose. I...I...I do not want to think of her with him. I have killed her. I have killed my wife!"

Fulton slid out of the bed and pushed to his feet. "Stop that right now. Wailing over her loss will not help her. We have to act now."

Edward threw back his head, tears in his eyes. "How? I do not know who has her."

"I thought Geneck." Fulton faltered and then sat back on the edge of the bed. "If not Geneck, then who?"

"The brotherhood were there. I am sure of it. Why else can we both not remember what happened? It is not normal."

Eyes wide, Fulton said, "We have been hexed?" He leaned back on the edge of the bed, rubbing his bald pate. "I would have to wonder why. And why take Jemima?"

"I do not know. To extort the texts from me, perhaps."

Fulton sat on his bed with head bowed, rocking back and forth. Edward sat wiping tears from his eyes and fishing in his empty pockets for a handkerchief, which appeared to have been stolen along with his other personal items.

A knock on the door made them start. Edward called out. "Who is it?" He hastily wiped his eyes with his shirt sleeve.

He did not think he could cope with another encounter with Aunt Prudence. To be mentally and physically pummelled was not something he could bear. It was probably Milly coming back to tend her husband. Edward lurched to his feet.

The door opened and Jakes put his head in. His eyes widened at the sight of his master sitting up awake. "Excuse me, sirs. Mr Brown and Mr White to see you."

"Speaking of the devil," Fulton said. "I will join you shortly. Jakes fetch my valet, will you?"

"Yes, sir." Jakes went to shut the door.

"Wait," Edward said. "I have a better idea." Edward stood up and went to the window, not wanting the butler to see him overset. He parted the curtains with his hand and peered out to the mews below. "Tell them we are indisposed." He could not help the harsh tones in his voice. He wanted to fall down and wail and despair but that would mean he had given up. Jemima was out there somewhere. He reined in the anguish by telling himself that she was safe. He had to go find her, but for that he needed to understand what had happened the previous night. He turned his head, taking in Fulton looking pale and weak on the bed. Right now, Fulton needed him.

Jakes hesitated, lowering his eyes before raising them again. "I already advised the gentlemen that you were not at home." He looked slightly scandalised. "They informed me that they know perfectly well that you are at home, because they saw you arrive with the police."

Edward's gorge rose. How dare they! He had no time for the brotherhood. They had been there last night. He was certain. And they had not assisted in the fight. Because of that Fulton was badly hurt, he was too and Jemima was gone. If they had Jemima, then his gamble would not endanger her. If Geneck had her then time was running out and he had plans to make to get her back. He walked up to Jakes. "Then they know we are indisposed. Tell them I said go away." Edward said, quite out of patience. He turned back to the window, thinking the butler had gone.

Jakes cleared his throat. "Do I have to, sir?"

Edward turned at the fear in the man's voice. Remembering the chaos of the last visit, how Jakes had been overset by some spell or other heinous act by the two magicians, he took pity on the man.

"Ed...they may know something about Jemima."

Edward started at the sound of Fulton's voice. He had completely forgotten his friend was in the room. He really was beside himself.

"Let us hear what they have to say before we make judgement," Fulton suggested.

Either they already had Jemima or they could help retrieve her.

Fulton continued speaking in fragile tones. "Show them up to my room here, Jakes. There's a good fellow. They will have to cope with the informality of being entertained in a sick room. Seeing they are so pushy, they deserve to be discommoded. Oh, and keep the women folk away if you can. I suggest you take Aunt Prudence and Mrs Fulton morning tea—the best the cook can provide."

Jakes turned his gaze to Edward, who after examining Fulton with a critical eye, gave a confirming nod. Jakes still looked uncertain. "Yes, yes, quite right, Fulton. While neither of us is fit to entertain, you may bring them up, Jakes. I will make sure your master is not overtaxed."

"Very well, sir." Jakes shut the door.

Edward squared his shoulders and faced Fulton. "It is your house, do what you will, but do give me leave to at least change my shirt."

"No, stay where you are. There is no point putting a gloss on things. You may not think I am very strategic, but follow me on this one. Seeing you so low, they will reveal their hand.

"For me, though, I will have my robe and a cravat," Fulton said, positioning himself on the bed. Edward stood gaping until Fulton pointed. Edward turned in the direction of a small closet and stepped up to open it. Edward was currently in possession of Fulton's dressing room, he realised, and wondered how Fulton could bear to be inconvenienced by such a small wardrobe to store his things. The dark-red quilted robe hung on a hook behind the closet door. A box of cravats sat on the shelf. Edward lifted the top one, saw it was a dull brown and then swapped it for a dark blue one. Then after presenting these items for Fulton's inspection, Edward assisted his friend to don the robe. Fulton managed the cravat quite well by himself while Edward held a mirror for him.

Fulton lifted an eyebrow, a silent request for comment.

"You will do, Fulton. You'll do."

Fulton then sat on the bed and put his covers over his knees. The sound of footsteps approached.

CHAPTER 14

Jemima woke in a dark room. She was cold, devastatingly hungry and very, very angry. Of Edward and Fulton there was no sign. She had no idea whether they were alive or dead and worst of all she hated the feeling of despair their absence created.

Having been imprisoned before she knew the drill. She tested out the confines of the room. Bare walls, slightly damp. A door that shuddered when she pulled on the handle. A small window that let in pale light. She inhaled and tasted dust and damp on her tongue. Being in London she could be anywhere within the city limits. It was a small, cramped city with many hiding places.

Her last memory had been of running in the park, away from Geneck and his awful visions. Was it him that now held her prisoner? Was it one of his minions who had captured her and brought her here to await his master's pleasure? Jemima rubbed at her upper arms, but the chill that thought evoked could not be warmed away. Not by physical warmth.

Jemima listened at the door and at the window. There was no glass, only a rusty grate. She hoped to get some clue as to who her captors were before starting to call out. The thought of Geneck, his monstrous body anywhere near her, made her hyperventilate. When the sun went down he would come for her, make her his daughter in the flesh as well as in mind. She wanted to scream for help, to call for Edward and Fulton. But they were not there. Not in the cells with her. She would have heard them by now. She was on her own.

Shuddering, she pushed the thoughts away. It could not end this way. "It must not end this way," she said in a whisper to the dark corners of the room. Edward had saved her life for a reason. He had given her life and she believed she would not lose it in some stupid, mindless way. She would not permit it. In the darkness, the light of the ruby powering her heart leaked through the fabric of her blouse. Her corset held her ribs tight. Oh how she wished she had stuck some hatpins in there instead of the hat, which she had lost.

Closing her eyes, she tried to doze against a metal pole. A drip, dripping of water hitting a puddle or a bucket kept her from rest. Was she back in the sewers? That thought made her shudder because she thought of Geneck and how he could totally own that space. Damp, dark, rat-infested corridors beneath the earth. Light dribbled in through the window. It was not quite sunny, more like a grey haze. Could it be somewhere under the surface?

Ramming her eyes shut, she muttered to herself. "Must not think of him. Must not let him make a connection. Must. Not. Think. You do not want to draw him to you. You do not want to have his vile thoughts in you." She kicked at the wall and tried to think of something else, something that would not lead to thoughts of Geneck.

Edward came to mind, his vivid blue eyes in his olive skin. The way his hair curled around his collar. The way he looked at her in their intimate moments. That would not do. Thoughts of Edward made tears flow down her cheeks. *Where are you?* Another awful thought came. What if he was dead? Perhaps Fulton too. Neither of them would have let her be taken if they could help it. Both would have given their lives to save her. She knew that. Unfortunately, that thought did not give her any comfort and only provided more fuel for her despair. Had they been killed in that terrible explosion of power?

She recalled running and looking back and seeing their bodies jerk. Her mind was full of flight. Had Edward and Fulton been insensible and unmoving afterwards? She could not remember clearly what happened then. It just grew dark and her body fell and fell and she did not recall landing.

A sound like a pebble dropping silenced her thoughts. She sniffed and listened. Someone was approaching. The light from the window had faded to a paler patch of dark. The room was becoming a black box, stifling in its closeness. Impenetrable in its gloom.

My ruby light. Jemima tugged at her blouse, opening her corset so that the rose-coloured glow escaped from her clothing. A shape loomed over her. Hands touched hers. She jerked back, taken by surprise. "Who are you?" she demanded, her voice verging on hysterical.

No answer. What felt like a lump of bread was pressed into her hand. She nearly dropped it when a body drew close to her, so close she could feel the warmth radiating over her. A breath rasped in her ear. "Who...who are you?" she asked again.

No answer. The rim of a metal cup was pressed to her lips. She sniffed. Water. She grabbed the mug and took a long drink. Then she took a bite of bread, trying hard to chew without choking, then moistened her mouth with a sip of water. Her hunger was powerful. The bread would help. She took another bite.

She swallowed a mouthful, sipped water and then stared out into the darkness. "Where am I?" she asked.

Again, no answer. Had they left? She had not heard the door open. But now there were no sounds of someone breathing, no scent of someone. Had she been that distracted by the food and the sudden appearance of her captor that she did not notice their departure?

She was alone. She took two deep breaths and stretched out with her senses. Nothing. No one. Once she was convinced her visitor had indeed left and was not returning, she relaxed a little. Having some stranger near her while she was this vulnerable irked her. She ate the bread, grateful for something to sate her hunger and eager to keep up her strength because she was not giving up. She was going to fight.

Some hours after, the pressure on her bladder woke her from a doze. "Hello?" There was no sound. She patted around the floor of the cell, hoping to find a bucket. Her ruby light eventually revealed the outlines of a small pail. Guessing its purpose, she went over to inspect it, using her foot to prod it. It was empty. Grateful for the dark as she undid her trousers. She sighed in relief as her bladder emptied.

Once she was comfortable and dressed again, she made for the door. It was time to find out where she was and who her captor was. Better still, it was time to break out.

With a thump on the door, she let out a yell. "Let me out!" Then she took a deep breath and put everything into the next bellow. "Let. Me. Out! Help!"

When that roused no one, she thumped on the door until her hands became bruised and sore. She wailed. She cursed in English and French. She described all the things she was going to do to her captors then rethought that tactic as that would not likely induce them to free her. After a long drawn-out wail, she threw herself to the floor. Let them deal with that.

She waited, quiet and still.

The tell-tale signs of footsteps approached, slowing as they neared her cell. She lay very still, but alert, as a key turned the well-oiled lock. She braced herself, ready to kick out. The door swung open and a light blinded her. She threw up her hands, surprised and unable to move.

CHAPTER 15

Mr White stepped into Fulton's bedroom, his dark eyes taking them in. His face registered surprise on seeing Fulton still reclining in his bed. His gaze passed over Edward, now resident in an easy chair. Mr Brown did not accompany him.

As there was no chair to offer him, none was offered. He had forced this interview, after all. The man's impertinence obviated the need for normal politeness. Mr White seemed to agree, for without any greeting or enquiry, he stated, "I understand you fought Geneck last night and lost."

Edward blinked, his memories still rather hazy. "Yes," Edward said, hoping that the other magician would enlighten them. He was soon disappointed and had to ask, "How do you know that?"

Mr White cocked his head as he considered Edward, then diverted his gaze to Fulton. "I cannot reveal how I know, only that you are watched by more than one party. Certain energies you use in your magic advertise your presence."

"I used a forbidden spell. That should have summoned you."

Mr White stood there with a neutral expression on his face.

Edward surged out of his chair, hardly restraining his anger. "You and your so-called brotherhood could not be bothered helping me fight the beast. You sit there, thinking yourself safe, but I wager you are not. When he finishes in London, his sphere of influence will expand, the number of his minions will grow and he will be a plague on all the kingdom."

"It is a beast of your creation," Mr White said, unruffled by Edward's tirade. "Thus your responsibility to deal with."

"I told you they gave me no choice. They threatened Jemima. What do you expect me to do then?"

Here there was a flicker in Mr White's eyelids. "Your wife is not at home." It was a statement, not a question.

Fulton started, Edward noticed. He decided to provide a minimal response.

"No, she is not."

"Pity," Mr White said and shrugged and looked around the room. "I would have liked to talk old times with her."

Edward said nothing, but watched him. Did the old bastard know something? His heart rate had ramped up. Mr White was confusing him and also filling him with dread. If he was asking after Jemima, then the brotherhood did not have her and that meant...and he could not even consider that.

"When will she return to the house?"

Edward frowned and stared at the floor. He could not bring himself to speak. Fulton spoke from the bed, his voice weak. "We do not know."

Mr White's head shot up, his gaze arrowing between them both. "Taken?" he said and paled.

Edward stalked to the window, trying to suppress the emotion that boiled within.

"Yes," Fulton supplied. "We thought you had her."

Edward swung around, ready to hurl accusations, but Mr White had gone.

"What the devil? Where did he go?"

It could mean only one thing. Edward was nearly toppled by the level of anxiety, guilt and fear that punched up through his gut.

"We have to go after her." Fulton tried to get up but fell back against the pillows. Edward came over and pressed down on his shoulder to prevent him rising again. Fulton had gone grey and his skin was clammy. His friend was not well.

"Does this mean Geneck has her and not the brotherhood?" Edward's voice was faint. He was afraid of the answer, afraid of what the brotherhood's magician might mean.

"Yes, it must," Fulton replied. "For he was genuinely shocked."

Edward nodded, his heart heavy. "Yes, I thought that also." He had been nursing a secret hope that the brotherhood had taken her and that they would keep her safe until he surrendered the texts. The texts, however, had not been mentioned.

"We must act now before the night comes," Fulton said. "Help me to get up."

"But where do we start?" Edward said, clutching Fulton's shoulder.

Fulton snarled. "I do not know. Anywhere. The park. We can backtrack from there." Fulton did not move, though. Edward wondered at that. Fulton was always quick and action-oriented.

Edward nodded, feeling calm descending now they were starting to formulate plans. "I think Mr White knows something, even though his surprise was real and not feigned."

Edward kept his gaze fixed on the door where the old magician had stood.

Fulton grasped Edward's hands. "It's not too late. Geneck must have been weakened as we are weakened. She may not be dead. She may not be defiled. We have time. Consider, it is daylight, he is dormant. We must make plans. Oh goddamn, why do I feel so weak? What happened to me?"

Yes, Edward thought. *Why is Fulton weak and becoming weaker? Even fading before my eyes.* He locked gazes with Fulton. "What do you remember from last night?" Edward asked, hoping that Fulton would be able to fill in the holes in his memory.

"I remember the fight and the blood. You were working some great spell by the look of it. I kept Geneck and his minions occupied." Fulton sagged against his pillows as if the effort to speak was draining him.

The details started to form in Edward's mind. "Yes, now I recollect.

A powerful spell that should have demolished Geneck and brought the brotherhood running to our sides. No wonder my memory is wiped. Some of the power must have rebounded on me. But why? There is something I am not seeing."

"That I cannot answer. I remember you yelling at me, urging me to rip out the heart device while the vampire was immobilised. But when I touched it, something happened. Electricity arced between us. It was as if we were conductors."

A light sweat gathered on Fulton's brow and his skin grew pale.

"Interesting." Edward scratched his chin, feeling the stubble there. He had not shaved or washed and he felt very dishevelled. He noted changes in Fulton as they spoke but could not quite account for them so he continued on. "So, Geneck's power reacted to you for some reason. The power of the mechanisms were drawn each to the other." He stood and paced, again tugging the curtain aside, hoping to see Jemima sneaking along the mews in her leather garments in an attempt not to be noticed. That sentimental thought brought tears to his eyes. *Oh Jemima, how I have let you down.*

There was no point being mired in sentimental misery. That would not save Jemima. Turning away, his ideas began to move, getting over the lethargy that had been plaguing him. "Before casting that spell I checked all the ramifications in the texts. None talked of such as these. Then again, none have made such machines as mine." His head jerked up. "That is it! My machines are the differentiating factor."

"And does that help us?" Fulton asked, his voice raspy.

Edward was still thinking, and put up a finger to ask for a moment to think. Fulton's eyes closed and his friend seemed to be asleep. Very odd. "Fulton, what is the matter?"

Fulton's eyes fluttered open. "I...I feel so tired and heavy. Drained of strength."

Edward stared and then moved to the bed. "Fulton!" His friend did not move and only sighed. "I need to check something, Fulton."

No reply. Edward waited and when no further response was forthcoming, he sat on the edge of the bed.

"I am going to check your arm and then the leg again. I know

Heaton examined you earlier but..." Fulton did not object and Edward worked quickly as his friend seemed to be fading in front of his eyes.

Fulton opened his eyes with difficulty. "My arm feels very heavy," he mumbled. "I can hardly move it."

Edward's eyebrows rose. "Really? That is rather strange. It looks to be in working order. I will check the power source." Edward inspected the housing for the gem, removing the polished amber he had used as part of the mechanism. Edward's brows drew together as he studied it.

Fulton's mouth turned down.

"What is it?" Edward asked.

Fulton reached over and grasped his artificial arm with his other hand. "It feels strange, lifeless and heavy without the gem to power it. Worse than before when the gem was still inside. I thought it would still be responsive."

Edward rubbed the shiny piece of amber between his palms, like he had done to initiate the spark more than a year ago. Now he used a machine for this purpose but he always rubbed the gem first and stood nearby. Somehow that spinning machine was able to draw on his magic to infuse the gem. It was done in such a small amount that he did not notice. Edward had not tried to measure his power. Wilbur's writing never mentioned such a thing. But now that he thought about Mr White, he realised there was something there, a kind of itch and that could mean he was detecting the other man's magic. The brothers had said they detected his magic in the mechanisms in Geneck, Fulton and Jemima so he must have placed a lot of power in them.

In the park, a lot of magic had been present. From his spell, from Geneck and the other person behind the tree. He thought that had been Mr White, only now that did not seem to be the case. Another person from the brotherhood? Or a rogue like Longhurst? A possibility to be sure. He tried to recall his feel for Longhurst, and recalled he was more like a sour taste on the tongue than an itch.

The gem glowed brighter, sending out pale yellow light. As Edward held it, he could both visually and with his other sense that its power had been restored. So that was what captured magic felt like. He needed to jot down his observations.

Thinking about last night, something about the explosion of power could have drained Fulton's gem. His spell should not have affected the gem though. The powers and symbols he used just could not have done that. If it was not the spell then it was Geneck. That beast was not inherently magical. The heart device was though. If Geneck did not deliberately drain the power then it was accidental or coincidental. There was something important here he was not seeing. It was disappointing to realise that after his years of study, he knew so little about magic. He was certain the brotherhood would know more. Unfortunately, they were not likely to share and right then Edward had no idea how to change this fact.

While he looked on, Fulton's cheeks sagged and his breathing grew shallow. He was fading before Edward's eyes. Hastily, he replaced the gem in the arm mechanism.

Fulton's visage improved noticeably after a few deep breaths, his eyes glittered with health and his cheeks even developed a pale pink hue. Edward did his best to hide his surprise. He glanced at the leg. "The leg now."

Revealing the leg by folding back the sheet, Edward checked the casing again, opening it to reveal the gem. It, too, was emitting rather a dim light. A larger amber gem, its inner glow had almost faded. After Edward's re-priming, it sent out bright shards of light. He slotted it back in, bitting his lower lip as he did so. He was afraid of what was going to happen.

Edward sat there for a while, just studying Fulton as he grew healthier, as his colour returned to normal and his energy level increased. Fulton sat up and then rang the bell. He was hungry.

The charge in the crystals should have no effect on Fulton's general wellbeing. He could not quite bring himself to explain his concerns to his friend but he knew if he did not attempt to explain it, Fulton would leap to conclusions. Edward stood up, flicking the sheet over Fulton's leg construct, seeing the damaged flesh already improving.

"Excellent idea, Fulton. Food will help."

Fulton sat up, using his elbows to raise himself higher. "Yes, I thought so. I feel very hungry, just now. Let me see...what can an invalid extract from the kitchen at this time of day? One of cook's omelettes would go down well. A couple of muffins, a few slices of that excellent ham we had yesterday. Make sure the coffee is brewed too."

Jakes arrived in time to hear the order.

"For two?" he asked.

"Yes, thank you," Edward replied.

Fulton frowned after Jakes closed the door. "Tell me, my dear friend. What just happened? One moment I felt near to death and now I am my normal energetic self."

Edward had to be quick. News of the food order was bound to bring Milly and Aunt Prudence.

"It was never my intention...I do not even know how this has occurred."

"What?"

"I think my magic. The power in the gems, which you know I thought was perpetual energy, is part of me and it appears that somehow it is fused with your life force."

Fulton sat up and furrowed his forehead. "I do not know what you mean. However, I suspect I do not like it."

Edward rubbed his mouth before speaking, as if trying to form the words. "The two devices which give you strength and sometimes unnatural speed and agility are keeping you alive. Or maybe not, but there is a syncing there and when the energy in the gem waned so did your life force."

"So I am never to be free of them if I want to live?" Fulton asked.

Edward stared. He had had no idea that Fulton imagined a time when he would not have them.

Fulton shrugged. "An idle fancy of mine. That science would progress enough to give me back my limbs as they were."

"Oh, I am sorry, Fulton. I am glad that you live."

Fulton raised a hand. "Do not continue. I am content. It was but an idle fancy and I have achieved more than I ever expected, even when I had all my own limbs."

"Ambrose?" Milly said, after knocking on the door. "Oh? You are looking so much better. Jakes said you ordered food. May I come and sit with you?"

"Of course, my dear. I am sorry to make you worry." Milly went over and picked up Fulton's hand, staring adoringly at him. Edward's heart thumped awkwardly because the sight of his friend and his wife holding hands made him think of his own erstwhile wife and whether he would ever get to see her again and whether she would ever look at him like that again.

The butler arrived and Fulton propped himself up on the bed in anticipation of food, with Milly plumping his pillows.

Edward stood up. "It is time I took myself off to wash and change. I shall rest up. What time do you think?"

"Around six."

"There is some for you, sir," the butler said, indicating the footman who also held a tray.

"Quite so, I will take it in my room. I shall be needing hot water and my valet."

Jakes placed the tray over Fulton's legs and stood erect, turning slightly to face Edward. "It shall be as you desire."

Milly's mood lightened on seeing her husband brandishing his knife and fork and tucking into an omelette. "Thank you, Edward," she said as he reached the door.

Milly's words were so heartfelt that Edward could feel tears forming and his throat closing. He bowed his head and left. He did not deserve such gratitude. He had much to think about.

CHAPTER 16

Ferdinand De Blanc materialised in his room at the brotherhood's converted monastery. Ancient stone walls surrounded him, but they did not offer comfort. His heart beat frantically. Jemima Hardcastle had been taken by the beast. If she was not already dead, she soon would be. He had to do something. He had to get his brothers to fight the beast, to liberate the girl at least. Some of them recalled Wilbur Hardcastle, some of them loved him and perhaps some sense of decency would make them band together to help the girl.

They had a chance, too, to recruit Huntington. With his talents and insights into magic they could progress to great things instead of dwelling in fear of progress. Change could not be averted. It came upon you whether you wanted it or not. He opened the door and strode out into the hall. He had to see Benedict, their revered leader. It was the first course of action at least. Not all the brotherhood lived in the old abbey, but most visited frequently. As Ferdinand had no family living, it was a natural place for him to reside and pursue his study of magic and ethics.

The Revered's secretary, Brother Malcom, sat at the desk outside of Benedict's office. "Brother Ferdinand Le Blanc, how may I assist you?"

"I have an urgent need to speak to the Revered. Is there any chance I can see him?"

Brother Malcom ran his finger down the page of the appointment diary. "He is currently in a meeting and is due back shortly. You may wait, of course, brother."

Ferdinand bowed. "Thank you."

Ferdinand stood, for there were no chairs, and lapsed into a light trance, the better to order his thoughts. He needed to formulate his arguments and counter-arguments. Huntington looked way out of his depth and Fulton was in some kind of dire straits as his life had been fading in front of Ferdinand's eyes. Obviously, they were no match for Geneck. That should be argument enough just there. The brotherhood did have a philosophy of non-interference but letting people be slaughtered was not something that should be allowed. It ought to be enough of a stimulus.

Benedict, the Revered, came into the reception room with a quick stride, his bulky form dressed in his formal robes of rich, dark-blue velvet with a fur mantle over the shoulders. He acknowledged Ferdinand with a slight incline of the head as Ferdinand bowed. "Revered," Ferdinand said.

"Brother, you wish to speak with me?" Benedict was physically intimidating and his booming voice equally so. More shocking was that Ferdinand jerked when Benedict spoke, even though the Revered was endeavouring to speak quietly.

"Yes, I..." He stopped as Brother Winston came up into the room. The tall, gaunt Mr Brown, otherwise known as the Executioner, bowed.

"Ah, you wish to speak to me too?" Benedict said without humour.

Brother Winston inclined his head deferentially to both the Revered and Ferdinand. "I can guess what brings Brother Ferdinand for it is a topic on my mind also."

Ferdinand narrowed his eyes. The subject of Huntington was something he did not agree on with Brother Winston.

"Come in, then," he said and walked into his office.

Brother Winston motioned Ferdinand to go first with a graceful wave of his hand. Ferdinand chewed his lips, wondering what was going to happen next. To say he did not trust Brother Winston was an understatement. The man loved his work as Executioner too much and the fear of him within the brotherhood gave him power.

They took a seat and Benedict sat at his large ornately carved desk. "Well, brothers, what is on your mind?"

Ferdinand got in quickly. "I wish to appeal to the brotherhood on the matter of the beast Geneck."

Revered Benedict did not move a facial muscle and his eyes oh so briefly flicked to Winston. "I thought we were staying out of that business."

"It was decided, yes, initially. But I have new information."

Winston tensed, eyebrows high. "A new development. Pray enlighten us."

Ferdinand bit back on his irritation. This was meant to be his interview with the leader, not with Winston, who was of equal rank.

"Huntington and his creation Fulton fought Geneck last night and were defeated. Jemima Hardcastle was captured and is currently missing, probably in the hands of the beast at this very moment."

Benedict put his elbows on the table and made a bridge with his hands. "Why should we act in this matter?"

"It is obvious they cannot deal with the beast. All will be in danger," Ferdinand burst out before Brother Winston could speak.

"And?"

"They have Brother Wilbur's daughter."

"Brother Wilbur was executed lawfully for being a renegade and for theft," the Revered said without emotion.

"Yes, I know...but his daughter is still part of us." Ferdinand made an exasperated sound. "We owe it to her to rescue her."

Winston scoffed. "A female? A small talent. Not worth the effort."

Benedict lifted an eyebrow at Ferdinand, silently inviting him to respond.

Ferdinand half turned in his seat so that he was addressing Brother Winston as well as the Revered. "Yes, she is guilty of being a female and not very talented in magic." He tapped his chest. "She is also a bearer of one of Huntington's machines."

Benedict frowned as he peered over the bridge of his fingers. "So you think she is worth saving because she could be of use in study?"

"No, I think she deserves to be rescued for herself alone." He leaned forwards and met Benedict's almost dark eyes. "The rest is just inducement for those among us who have an interest in studying Huntington's inventions. However, it would be better to have him join us and share his knowledge. This we could encourage if we helped him fight the beast and saved his wife. It would show him that we have courage and conviction. He is a philanthropist and enjoys helping others."

Benedict dropped his hands and sat back, eyelids lowered. Winston breathed quietly next to him, but said nothing. "Some of what you say has merit. But mounting a rescue would put brothers in danger. They may not be willing to take the risk, particularly if Huntington and this Fulton were so unsuccessful. Huntington did use a high-powered spell."

"I know, I felt it," Ferdinand said.

"I know because I saw it," Brother Winston said.

Ferdinand jerked in his seat. Brother Winston had been there? All kinds of suspicions arose and he had to fight to keep them from showing in his expression.

"And what is your opinion, Brother Winston?" the Revered asked.

"Huntington has a great natural talent but he is untutored. I gather Wilbur left him advice. If that's the case it was poor advice. The man hardly understands what he does."

Ferdinand broke in. "All the more reason to bring him into the fold. Tutor him. Learn from him. He could be a great magician."

"Or a great disaster," Brother Winston replied.

Benedict blew out his breath. "There is a meeting of the brotherhood within the hour. It is mostly resident magicians with a few visitors popping in for the meeting. I shall canvass your request with them. Will you abide by the consensus?"

"Of course, I must." Ferdinand said, but squeezed his hands into fists. He did not like his chances.

Benedict shifted his dark, glittering gaze to Brother Winston. "And you, Brother Winston, will you also abide?"

"Most certainly."

They were dismissed. Ferdinand stood, bowed to the Revered before he swept from the room, his own plain brown robes flowing out behind him. There was some exchange between Benedict and Winston that Ferdinand did not quite understand. Brother Winston did not take his leave. Ferdinand did not like it. That was because he did not like Brother Winston and did not trust him at all. He was the official Executioner and that being said, he knew of no one who actually liked him. And Winston had been there. He had witnessed the magical battle that had weakened Fulton, injured Huntington and resulted in Jemima being captured. Surely the man had no heart at all. How could he witness that and not provide assistance?

FERDINAND HAD TO SIT THROUGH ALL THE GENERAL BUSINESS OF THE meeting before the topic of Huntington and Geneck was introduced. He was not invited to speak, which was annoying to say the least. The Revered put the case to the assembled brothers. It was not that their leader did not put the facts of the case properly. He did them justice. There was an absence of emotion in the presentation that Ferdinand felt hindered the argument. Brothers were the same as other humans and could often be swayed by appeals to their emotions, to their better natures.

Brother Elliot stood, gathering his robes around him. He had transported there for the meeting and did not live there except for a few weeks at a time when he wanted to work on a project. "I see no need as yet to provide assistance. Has Huntington asked for it?"

Revered Benedict looked to Ferdinand. "Has he, Brother Ferdinand?"

"Yes. He said that if Geneck is not stopped all will suffer, including us. For the beast would be as a plague across the kingdom. He used the forbidden spell to force us into action."

"Why ever did he raise the creature then?" yelled Brother Jerome. "It is his problem. Let him deal with it."

"There is the matter of his wife, Jemima. Wilbur Hardcastle's daughter."

"The renegade? What do we owe him? Nothing!" added Brother Winston.

A general argument broke out then. Ferdinand thought there were a number of brothers who sided with him. But the loud ones seemed to have the majority. The vote was close but was still a no.

"Would anyone object to individual members providing assistance?" Ferdinand asked.

A few voices called it "Yes", but here the leader intervened. "If a brother or brothers wish to aid Huntington in this matter, then they may by all means do so. Do not, however, expect assistance and do not bring harm or exposure to the brotherhood. This is our abode, our safe haven. Do nothing to jeopardise that."

"Thank you," Ferdinand said with a bow. "I am truly grateful."

After the meeting he would speak with those who had spoken in favour of his proposition. Small help was better than none at all.

Ferdinand found only two other brothers who were willing to help him—Brother Algernon and Brother Nestor. Without the backing of the conclave of the brotherhood, none of the others wanted to risk being outside the consensus.

"I was a friend of Brother Wilbur, as you know," Brother Algernon said. "But I did not agree with what he did. He married that woman and abandoned us."

Ferdinand nodded. He did not mention the other things that Wilbur had done as they were not widely known. Ferdinand had met Elinor, Wilbur's wife, and completely understood Wilbur's decision. The woman was like a goddess, lovely to look upon, beautiful in nature. Her every movement was a melody. Of course Wilbur was smitten.

After a long life alone, he had found love and it gave him new direction, new life. He managed only a few years before she died. Her illness was tragic and Wilbur had mourned for a long time, bringing up his child most unnaturally and reclusively. At least he had let Ferdinand visit. He smiled at the memory of their times together. They often sat up late at night in front of the fire, debating and talking about the past, about the brotherhood. Wilbur had criticisms, of course. No organisation was perfect. Ferdinand had often encouraged him to return but Wilbur was stubborn to the last.

"Will you contact this Huntington and tell him of our aid?" Brother Nestor asked, with his youthful enthusiasm. He was one of the youngest members of the brotherhood.

Ferdinand checked the time. "I fear it is a little late for that. We will go to where he is and see what we can do."

"A bit of a gamble," Brother Algernon said. "We might get in the way."

But the sun would set soon and Huntington would already be on the hunt. "We will head to London, near Chelsea so we can be at hand. If Huntington uses a powerful spell we will know exactly where he is and go to his aid."

Nestor nodded reluctantly, setting his long brown curls wobbling. With pale skin and pink cheeks he looked even younger than his twenty-one years.

"Very well," Brother Algernon said. He was old and wiry, but a steady fellow. "I will meet you there. I have a few things to prepare."

"I thank you for your assistance. May we win through."

"May we win through: shadow and stealth," they both replied. It was a motto of the brotherhood of sorts.

Born of discrimination and fear, the brotherhood had remained hidden since the early days when their numbers were decimated and their members hunted. Magic was feared in the past and feared now. Brothers needed to stick together.

⊗⊗⊗

EDWARD WENT TO GET DRESSED FOR THEIR EXCURSION, TELLING Aunt Prudence he was attending his club later that evening and would not be home until late. He walked carefully, nursing the bruising in his torso. The bruises throbbed with greater and greater intensity as the day progressed.

The old lady only glared at him and went back to her sewing. He envied her the ability to lose herself in her craft. If only Edward could relax enough to do something other than fret about Jemima and the threat of Geneck.

At least Fulton had made satisfactory progress during the day, once Edward had recharged the gems. In front of his mirror, Edward paused in tying his gorget. His original one had been stolen, but Milly had had more than one manufactured so was able to supply another from the chest that Fulton had delivered. He never suspected his young relative of being so practical, clever and organised. Then again, he had not taken much notice of her at all. With a touch of guilt, he knew that to be entirely his own fault.

He resumed adjusting his neck protection and studied his reflection. He really did look quite odd. A scarf should help disguise it. However, that was not important. Saving Jemima was important and killing that beast. Damn, he had never thought his magic would cause him so much trouble. His cousin Wilbur had counselled him in his journals to use his gift wisely. Edward had always tried to do so. He had used it unwittingly in his inventions. Hopefully the repercussions would not be severe. If only Jemima had not been used against him. If only he had not kissed her at Primrose Manor. If only...

No. That would not do. He loved her and could never regret being with her.

"Are you ready?" Fulton called from his room down the hall. There was no preventing Fulton joining in this desperate search for Jemima. Indeed, Edward would be lost without him. Fulton was good in a fight. Edward had a lot more to learn about engaging with the enemy and using his magic and his muscles for hand-to-hand combat. It was not gentlemanly, he supposed, but neither was being a magician. One did not admit to using magic in polite society. Not that he cared that his friends and acquaintances would cut him. In theory, though, it being widely known would be inconvenient.

"Just a moment," Edward called back.

As he adjusted the scarf, he thought more on the gems in Fulton's appliances. It seemed to Edward that his magic and Fulton's life force were inextricably linked. Fulton could not exist without Edward's magic. That fact had been brought home to him that morning while watching the life fade from his good friend when the gems had been removed for recharging.

It was so strange though. Fulton could exist without an arm and leg but not without the gems. How could that be? Now that Edward had polluted him with magic, the poor fellow could not live. He frowned over that puzzle. Was it his magic that had saved more than Fulton's limbs? Had it indeed saved his life? Perhaps he would never know the answer to that.

He thought of the consequences for Jemima. Was it the same for her too? Her apparatus was more critical as it powered her heart. Would his magic flow through her too? And what changes would it bring?

The poor girl had not asked for such a fate. Edward checked his image in the mirror and made sure his vest was buttoned up tight. When he thought of Fulton's agility and power, the infusion of magic to enhance his natural talents made sense. In a way, Edward had created a sort of super soldier. Fulton, of course, would not like it to be termed that way. He was desirous of being normal. Everything he tried to do, he did because he wanted to be a normal man. He was a normal man, just one with extraordinary abilities.

Fulton tapped on his door and opened it. He was dressed for their outing. "Are you ready?" Fulton asked as if the weight of the world was on his shoulders.

Edward ran his hands down his clothes and reached for his coat. His new leather one had been stolen so he had to use his normal one. "Just now. I say, Fulton, your powers of healing are amazing. The bruising on your face has almost faded."

Fulton nodded and frowned. "Yes, very good ol' chap. You best hurry. There's trouble."

Edward jerked his head back, his body getting ready to fight. "The brotherhood?"

Fulton's lips turned down and he shook his head. "Worse. Aunt Prudence."

Edward picked up the rucksack that held the lantern and some candles and matches.

Edward was no less perturbed. Aunt Prudence was as annoying as the brotherhood and possibly slightly more dangerous. She could damage a man's sanity if he was left exposed to her rants for any period of time. "Damn that woman!"

When he went downstairs, Milly and Aunt Prudence were standing in the hall blocking the way to the front door. Thankfully, Jakes was nowhere to be seen. The butler probably guessed there was a fight brewing and had strategically absented himself.

Milly stood a little to the side, near a tall sculpture. She was dressed in a navy blue coat and held a dark, plain-looking bonnet in her hand. Aunt Prudence barred the exit with her bulk, assisted by an elaborate dress, also dark in tones, and a plumed hat. Her coat was draped over her arm as if she was ready to depart on an outing.

"What it heaven's name is going on here?" Edward said in a commanding tone. "Why are you standing there?"

Aunt Prudence's eyes flashed. "You are not leaving without us." Aunt Prudence drew herself to her full height, which was up to Edward's shoulder, and glared at him with ferocity. Her girth was an impressive obstacle and Edward was quite taken aback.

He lowered his eyebrows and effected a bored voice. "I have no idea why you are making a fuss. We are going to the club. It is a gentlemen's club. I often go there," Edward said.

He reached up to his neck and realised his scarf had come undone and his gorget was in plain sight. He coughed and hoped the heat in his face did not betray a blush. "I am a gentleman and it is my prerogative to go to the club when I will."

Something like a growl escaped from the old woman.

Edward blinked, shocked to hear such a sound. He was not mistaken either.

"I never thought I would have to scold you, nephew, but you are lying to me. Shame on you." She turned a terrifying look in Fulton's direction. "You too? How could you?"

"We are not lying," Edward said, feeling his cheeks burn. "We are going out on gentlemen's business. It is no concern of yours."

"Balderdash!" Aunt Prudence said.

Milly sucked in a surprised breath, her dark eyes widening. "Aunt you should not speak so to Edward."

"Why ever not? I am sick of them treating us as if we were stupid. We know what is going on. I worked it out myself. You, my dear, were informed. There stands the difference between us." She rounded on Edward and Fulton and drew out her index finger, straight and accusing. "How dare you lie to me! If your mother were alive she would box your ears for you. Your father being a dissembler himself would probably not have noticed. I do notice, however."

Edward shook his head, flabbergasted by the old woman's audacity. She could not possibly know all. She might have guessed something, especially after he and Fulton were escorted home by the police and Jemima being missing. "If you know what we are about," he began, "why are you blocking the door? We are in a hurry."

"Where else would we be if not here?" she asked. Milly nodded and folded her arms and regarded them with a militant glint in her eyes.

"You should be in the drawing room sewing," Edward pointed out and gripped the rucksack tighter.

Aunt Prudence lifted her chin. "No. We have both tried that and it does not work." She exchanged a look with Milly and then smiled. "We wish to help."

"Help?" Edward said in a shocked voice, which ran counter to Fulton's angry response.

"Absolutely not!" Fulton raged. "My wife is with child. Are you out of your senses?"

Milly winced but Aunt Prudence bore the verbal assault quite well. She merely met Fulton's hot gaze with a cool society stare. "We can be useful. I am not saying that we will be fighting...creatures like you do, but we can keep look out. Can shout warnings and can call for help if you need it."

Denial sat on Edward's lips and Fulton's fury was palpable. Yet, it was not in his mind to refuse the old woman. Milly was entirely Fulton's call. For Aunt Prudence, they both shared the responsibility. She had been such a thorn in his side, he realised he had not truly seen who she was. She had been the annoying old relative—someone to pity and give charity to. There, it seemed, he had erred. He had seen what he wanted to see: an annoyance, a silly old woman. Now, there was something else. Audacity, intelligence and even bravery.

Before he could respond himself, Fulton had rounded on the aunt, voice fit to rattle the rafters. "I absolutely forbid it!"

Aunt Prudence lifted her Roman nose. "I may reside with you, Fulton, by choice and under your sufferance, but that does not give you dominion over me." She shot a look at Edward and lifted a warning finger. "Nor does it give you a say over me either, nephew. No matter how grateful I am for your financial support all these years, you do not own me.

"Since my father died, I have been in control of myself. I have no husband to order me about or restrict my movements. I have been my own woman too long to start kowtowing to you just because you think you know more than I do."

With Fulton dead against it, Edward had to toe the line. He tried another tactic. "You could do us a great service by staying here and caring for Milly," Edward began.

"Yes," Fulton said. "I rely on you to look after her."

Aunt Prudence smiled, but it was a knowing smile. She knew they were trying to pull the wool over her eyes and keep her out of the way.

"No." To Fulton she said, "You may order Milly about as she is your wife. I do recommend against it though because such high-handed tactics are not good for cordial marital relations. Me, however, you cannot command. Just recognise that I can be useful. I am an old woman. I am someone who will be overlooked in a crowd. I can go places you cannot. I can act like a silly old woman with ease." Here she lifted an eyebrow. "I will also be believed if I call for help. And more importantly, you are wasting time."

"Get out of the way, then," Fulton said, his face reddening and making his bruises darken. He looked ready to manhandle her out of the way.

"No, wait," Edward said. "She's right. If she knows what is going on then it makes sense to use her. We will have another set of eyes."

Fulton turned on him, fist clenched. So much rage in those normally placid eyes. "Are you out of your senses then? Who will stay with Milly?"

"No one," Milly replied. "I am coming, too. We will stay out of your way and monitor the situation." She lifted her bonnet and put it on her head.

"No!" Fulton said, changing his tone. "Please, do not ask this of me."

Milly laid her hand on his fist, massaging it until he relaxed. "I must ask it of you. If you truly respect me as a person you will honour my wishes."

Fulton bowed over and placed his forehead on her hand. "You will tear my heart out."

"Not deliberately. Aunt Prudence will keep me safe. You will be there to protect me, too."

Fulton shook his head. "Madness." He breathed deep and closed his eyes. Then suddenly he said, "But we cannot delay further." He looked to the window. They had so little daylight left. "We must go now before we are too late."

Aunt Prudence snatched up her umbrella and Milly collected hers. It was not forecast for rain but it was London and the weather was changeable so Edward thought nothing of it. He had no mind to ponder his inexplicable female relatives. He had a job to do.

They exited the house to walk down to the public gardens, that being their reference point for starting their search. It was where Fulton and Edward had been found in the morning and it was where Jemima was last seen running away.

Milly had her hand on Fulton's forearm. The aunt strode without her customary wobble, though her clothing did appear to have a life of its own. Edward frowned. Had he been a dupe all this time? Was Aunt Prudence something other than he had always thought? There was no trace of decrepitude about her. Yet she always complained of some ailment. Or had he imagined that, expected it even?

They arrived at the park but this time Edward did not bother using a spell to disperse the homeless. Being early evening, not many had made their beds for the night and his priority was looking for Geneck. The beast was not in the park but beneath the ground somewhere. Dark shadows lengthened as the sun dipped behind the buildings. "We must find the entry quickly before the light fades," Edward said while scanning for signs.

Fulton placed Milly's hand on her aunt's arm and started a wide sweep of the area, walking in an apparently casual manner, but the intent was there in the set of his shoulders and the angle of his jaw to those who knew him.

Not long after, a shout came from Fulton. "You two wait here," Edward said and sprinted off in the direction of Fulton's call.

Near the entry to the private parklands that bordered the public gardens, Fulton had come upon a grate. Sounds of water sloshing beneath their feet reached the street level. "Here," Fulton said.

Edward closed his eyes, trying to see paths of magic. It was not something he had tried before, but it was necessary to test his theory. If the brotherhood could track him, he should be able to track others. He was learning so much more about magic and his ability daily. The pathways were confused. All he could sense was the water. "Nothing of use. We should enter here."

With a tug, Fulton lifted the grate and jumped down. "All clear," he called.

Edward, not as agile, sat on the edge of the opening and lowered himself down. Fulton had him by the legs and assisted his descent. Once down, they were standing on a small platform, a square of concrete. In both directions was a narrow ledge along the wall, barely wide enough for a person to walk. Fulton called over the sound of the water. "Which way?"

Edward had to think hard about this. He was not used to sensing out magic, not his own at least. But Jemima must have his magic infused in her body and that meant there must be some tie to him. There had to be. Edward studied both directions using his eyes and his senses. One had to call to him more than the other. He focused on Fulton and detected a faint buzz. Not just the sound of Fulton's devices, something more—a hum along the nerves. That must be his magic's signature.

Edward closed his eyes, blocked out the sound of the water, the pressure of the land above and Fulton. There was something. Yes, away from the river. That made sense. "That way," he said and indicated in the inland direction. "It is not far."

The tunnel here contained runoff and was close to the river Westborne that had been contained and built over. It ran towards the Thames so they must go in the opposite direction.

"Hoy!" came a call from above. "What are you doing down there?"

Edward squinted upwards and made out a familiar face. "Coleman?" He covered his eyes for the light was behind the policeman. "What are you doing here?"

"The same as you, I expect. Make way, I am coming down."

Coleman dropped beside them and he moved over so that his constable could do likewise. Edward was not sure how this would work. "I...er..." He was not about to nursemaid the police and hide his magic from them. There was too much at stake.

"Never mind trying to explain. Your female relatives directed us here so I know what you are about. I have left a few men up there on patrol." He rubbed his hands together. "Which way then, gentlemen?"

Edward shook out his body, trying to get rid of the annoyance he felt. "Follow me and keep the noise down."

Edward removed a small lantern from his rucksack and lit it. It cast a yellow glow and with the remaining daylight that filtered in from overhead, he could see well enough. He thought of conjuring a magically powered light but decided against it. His magic was not infinite and he did not wish to advertise himself to the police or to their quarry.

Fulton stepped in behind him as he led the way on the narrow ledge. Soon they came upon a metal stair. He lifted the lantern, using a slight spell to enhance the light in a subtle way. Overhead was a kind of junction. Red bricks, neatly joined together, arched overhead and allowed tunnels to intersect. Rain water runoff and sewage met. Edward scrunched up his face and he heard Coleman exclaim over the stench. Yet, from previous experience, he knew the smell would lessen quickly as their noses adjusted.

They went up a level and into a large round tunnel. The flow of liquid was middling and Edward did not care to look too closely at what was passing by his feet. It was dark in there and growing darker.

Yet that sensation he felt was growing stronger. This gave him hope. Jemima depended on him. He enhanced the lantern further and it revealed the outlines of the tunnel for about ten to fifteen feet ahead. Fine growths hung from the round ceiling and Edward ducked to avoid them, not quite able to repress a shiver.

Not five minutes later, Fulton squeezed his elbow and Edward paused. The echo of their steps died away and only the sound of water trickling could be heard. "Dim your light," Fulton whispered. This Edward did. A heartbeat or two passed before their eyes adjusted.

A pinprick of light glowed up ahead. His heart raced, his breathing quickened. They hurried closer until Edward was in range. Halting the others, he straddled the stream of waste and raised his fist, squeezing it tight to summon a spell. A simple one that let out a concussive wave. He let it fly ahead of them along the tunnel. Not deadly but it should knock out whoever was there.

"Hurry!" Edward said and started to run, lowering his body down into a crouch as the ceiling was invisible. Being knocked out by a jutting brick or change in tunnel height was not part of his plan. Fulton it appeared followed his example and Edward had no idea about the policemen. He hoped they followed his example for he had no time to stop and revive a concussed law enforcer.

They entered a wider space—some kind of work space. There was equipment stacked in corners: pumps, cement bags, tools. Three men lay sprawled unconscious in the centre of the room. A table was overturned and spilled dark liquid surrounded some mugs.

Fulton knelt down and examined one, checking the unconscious man's neck. The tell-tale bite mark was clearly visible. "Minions."

Edward let go a breath. At least he had not knocked out innocent workmen and they were on the right trail. Minions meant Geneck was near.

The police crept around inspecting the unconscious men. Coleman met his eye. Surprise was etched into every line on his face. "How did…"

"I have no time for explanations Inspector. We must hurry on."

Edward checked the room for another passageway or a cell. Somewhere Jemima could be held captive. When he found nothing, he pulled up short. He had to use his talent again. They were on the right track. He had to believe that. Had to.

He pointed in the direction where he thought Jemima was. A narrow gap in the wall, enough to fit through if they turned sideways. Fulton knocked Edward out of the way so he could go first. Faint yellow light filtered through the small space. Edward wanted to shove Fulton out of the way but Fulton had already started to squeeze himself along. Edward had to get there. He handed the lantern to Coleman and passed over the matches to light it. Not that they needed it just now. It was better to have both hands free, he found, as he slid in behind Fulton and did a stiff-legged side walk to get himself through to the other side. Sounds reached him and he had to hold his breath to be certain. Voices! Shouting!

"Fulton?" he said.

"I hear it," Fulton replied.

They spilled out into the space and chaos was already in progress. Stunned, Edward gaped trying to assess what was happening. The minions were fighting. But fighting who? Edward could not make sense of it before he had to duck a blow and then kick the person out of his way. Fulton was there, punching and kicking just to keep his position. Coleman came through behind them with a grunt. He swore and then started yelling something about the police, but no one heeded him. He was wasting his breath. Soon he, too, was drawn into the fray.

Edward caught sight of him hitting a minion across the head with the lantern and then forgot about Coleman as another man came at him with fist raised, eyed wide and unheeding. He flicked a spell and the man's knees gave out and he skidded to the floor and flopped on his face. Edward stepped over him and tried to work out where the centre of the battle was and what and who was fighting.

In the confusion, Edward had trouble identifying the other party engaged with the minions. Then he saw Mr White or someone who looked like Mr White. It was but a fleeting glimpse. That meant the brotherhood. The brotherhood were here fighting? For Jemima or to kill Geneck? Geneck was not here yet. So it must be for Jemima. Hope soared in his heart at this unlooked for boon. Assistance at last!

Trying to assess the room while the fight was in progress was difficult. So much action was distracting and there was magic too, stray strands of it getting in the way of his focus on Jemima.

One of a group of minions attacking Mr White moved to the side and Edward could see something at last. On the other side of the room was a door guarded by two minions. The brotherhood magicians were aiming there and that is where the fighting was thickest. That had to be it.

"Jemima!" he called out. "Jemima!"

He had to let her know he was close. The shouts and yells and screams drowned him out though. Searching around him for his friend, Edward called out. "Fulton! Over there." He pointed to the guarded door.

Fulton raised a bloody hand to signal he understood. He then started in that direction. Another group of people, their dark robes swirling as they lashed about with their hands, sent minions flying, screaming or falling to the floor as they fought along the edges. They seemed to be aiming for the door.

Edward squinted and saw that a tall, gaunt man looked to be closest, with two others trailing behind. He turned to study Mr White, who was further away.

A whistle sounded. It was the constable now through to this side. He blew again.

Distracted, Edward missed what happened next. Fulton was still cutting a path through the minions, tossing bodies to either side. Screams and cries filled the small space. The light went out suddenly. Edward had not noticed that there had been an artificial light.

Out of the darkness, Jemima's voice called. "Edward."

"Jemima!" Edward responded and was about to cast a spell to light his way, when a ball of hot white light blazed above their heads. Edward blinked, dazzled in the extreme. He could not see. He stumbled over the bodies that lay strewn around him.

"Jemima?" he called in the sudden silence. She did not answer. He knew she was gone.

He blinked and sheltered his eyes from the light that was waning slowly above their heads. Groans echoed in the space. He blinked and wiped at his eyes. He saw Fulton who stood at the now open door.

Finally, Edward's vision cleared. The brotherhood were gone, except for Mr White who stood next to Fulton by the now-open door. The door that had kept Jemima prisoner.

Like a wave breaking on the shore, the remaining minions escaped through another tunnel, with Coleman in pursuit. The constable ran after them, blowing his little whistle for all he was worth.

"No, no," Edward moaned out the words as he stepped over the injured and the dying to reach the room.

He had to see for himself that the room was empty. "Jemima!" Edward cried and pushed into the small cell. There was a residue of Jemima there—a faint taste of lavender and power. He swung around and faced up to the brother. "Who took her?" he demanded.

Mr White paled and he opened his mouth to speak and then shook his head. "I do not know. We were so close to rescuing her."

Edward let out a wail of frustration and pain. "Jemima!" His voice echoed into the tunnels.

Then Fulton slapped him on the back and Edward pulled himself together and squared up to the old magician. "It was you and your brotherhood."

"No. It cannot be," Mr White said. "We three volunteered to help you recover her. Why would we then steal her away?"

Edward was moved by the man's obvious distress. "I saw another group. They had the look of the brotherhood."

Mr White blanched at the accusation.

Fulton's face was a picture of frustration. He thumped the door so hard it bounced back against the wall with a great thud.

Coleman ran up, diverting Edward's attention. "Lost them. We nearly had them, nearly had the beast."

"Not the beast," Edward said, shaking his head. "It was just his human servants we were fighting. We nearly had her back."

"Your wife? I am sorry, Huntington." Coleman looked around. "Where is that other gentleman?"

Edward looked up from where he had slumped. Mr White was gone. "What other gentleman?"

Coleman's mouth hardened into a thin line. "Come now, Huntington. We are in this together." He walked about and indicated the shadows. "Who was that man—or men, for there were a number of them?"

Edward nodded, barely controlling his anger and his shame. They had lost Jemima again. "All I can say is they are representatives of a mysterious group of people who have an interest in this affair."

"And?" Coleman prompted.

Edward tried to stand upright. Fatigue and the bitter taste of defeat weighed him down. "I do not know who they really are or where they reside." He rubbed his face, trying to focus. He met Coleman's suspicious look. "That is the honest truth. If I knew I would be headed there right this moment." Tears welled then. He had lost her again. Fulton grabbed him around the shoulders and squeezed.

"We will find her. We will try again." Fulton said softly in his ear.

The inspector nodded as he watched them. "Very well, we should make our way back," Coleman said. "You are no use to us here blubbering like a child. We have a beast to hunt."

Edward rallied. He looked in the direction of where the minions had fled. There was a knot of something. A sensation that was distinctive and alien and stronger than it had ever been before. A tight ball of gloating, laced with anger. It was Geneck he was sure.

Edward pointed in its direction. "He is that way. I do not recommend you fight him on your own. Not if you value your life and the lives of your men."

"Oh, do you now? I don't have the luxury of being squeamish. My job is to protect the people of London. How about you come along then and wave your hands about and do your hocus pocus whatchamacallit?"

Sadness near overwhelmed Edward. He was to blame. If Coleman died it would be on him. "There is no point. We cannot win."

Coleman bristled. "He has your wife, man. You cannot give in so easily."

"It is by no means certain that he has my wife, sir. He had her but now someone else has taken her."

Coleman studied him. "Have it your way. I will come back with you and retrieve my men. Perhaps you can come up with a means to fight this creature."

Edward shuffled along with the support of Fulton. "I think of nothing else, believe me."

After many twists and turns, they backtracked and then exited the tunnels in the place where they first had entered. Milly was there, leaning down into the hole, a lantern in her hand. "Did you find her?"

Fulton mumbled to her and she retreated from the opening while he and Edward climbed out. Again, she peered down the hole where Coleman was climbing up. "She is not with you?"

"No, unfortunately, Mrs Huntington was taken," Coleman said, standing up straight as he finished brushing the dust off his hands. His constable came up behind him.

Milly stepped back, obviously not quite understanding. "But... but..."

Fulton shook his head at her and Milly covered her mouth and stifled a cry.

Aunt Prudence stood a distance off, her eyes searching the grounds. "It is very dark now. I see shapes moving beyond the trees." She took a few backwards steps to be near them. "I do not like how they move."

Edward frowned, but he did not dismiss the aunt's observations. He also looked to the perimeter. In among the trees, minions gathered. A second passed and then he realised.

"Attack!" Edward called.

The police reinforcements who had been loitering about the park sprang into action. Calls leaped across the park. Coleman shouted orders. Batons were raised and uniformed men formed lines. Fulton shook his head and ran into the throng, shoving between the police to get in front of them and meet the attack head on.

Edward glanced about him. What if their womenfolk were hurt? "Run back to the house. Lock yourselves in."

Milly moved next to Aunt Prudence. "Do not worry about us," the aunt said. "We came prepared."

They lifted up their umbrellas, brandishing them like swords.

There was no time now to worry about them. Edward had to help in the fight. He knelt, summoning a spell, closing his mind off from the noise and the emotional pain of losing Jemima. He had to believe he could save her. Just do this and then you can go find her.

Bodies flew through the air at Fulton's charge. Edward shot down three minions in a single spell. One got behind him. He heard a screech and a thump. When he turned to investigate, Aunt Prudence was extracting the point of her umbrella from a fallen minion's gut. Milly was being pressed by another minion who successfully dodged the point of her make shift weapon. She fell back and landed on her rear and ended up dropping her umbrella. Aunt Prudence fished around in her bonnet. Edward was ready to send a spell, but was too late.

Aunt Prudence flicked her wrist and the minion went down. Edward raced over to Milly and pulled her up. "Stay by me," he said.

He glanced down at the twitching minion who had a long hatpin sticking out from his throat. With an assessing glance at Aunt Prudence, Edward re-thought all of the arguments he had ever had with the old woman. She could have killed him with her hat many times. He suddenly admired her forbearance for he had been terribly condescending at times.

Geneck's presence drew closer and then hovered there on the fringes. He did not attack. Edward puzzled at this. He seemed to be surveying them, searching for something. Could it be that he was looking for Jemima? A few more moments passed as the fighting continued.

Like a breath exhaled, the minions disengaged, retreated.

The sound of the word 'daughter' floated on the thin mist that embraced the park. It was Geneck calling for his daughter. Fulton had killed her and now he searched for a replacement. Was Jemima to be the replacement?

Edward went to give chase but held back. It was unusual behaviour. Geneck had the advantage in numbers and growing magic. Why pull back?

Coleman ran up to him. "Do we pursue?"

Edward shook his head. "I have not thought of a way to kill it yet. You would spend your men's lives unnecessarily. We should be grateful that it has chosen to withdraw."

"But I thought you had a plan. You came here. Did you not come to kill him?"

Edward shook his head. "No," he said almost choking on grief. "I came to get my wife. It was still daylight then. Now the beast is awake and powerful."

"Ah yes. For a moment Mrs Huntington slipped my mind. It must have been all the innocent lives at stake." He bared his teeth.

Fulton came up, covered in blood and gore. His normally white gloves were wet and red.

"I am sorry," Edward said to the police inspector.

"Damn you and your sorry!" Coleman stormed off, swearing up a storm.

Aunt Prudence started remonstrating with him for speaking so in front of ladies.

"Unnatural females," Coleman bellowed and went off with his men, apparently to follow on Geneck's heels and not listening to anything Edward had said.

Fulton went to his wife. "Milly? Are you hurt?"

"No, not at all." Her bonnet was askew and her umbrella was bent. "I am exceedingly well."

Fulton growled. The male companions appeared to be doing a lot of growling. The womenfolk were really bringing out the best in them.

Fulton queried Edward with a flick of his brows. "They acquitted themselves well," Edward said with a bow towards Aunt Prudence and Milly.

Fulton let out an exasperated sound. "I am all for self-determination for yourself, Milly. But you cannot take our child into danger. It will not do."

"But I need to know how to defend myself. What if you or Edward are not there when we are attacked? Edward admitted we acquitted ourselves well so why can you not accept that? Aunt Prudence dispatched two of these devils by herself. We may not have your strength but we certainly have agility of mind."

Fulton hunched his shoulders and glowered but said nothing more.

"Indeed." Edward was in no mood to argue. Jemima had an excellent mind. He wished she was there at that moment. He wished he would never be parted from her ever again. Yet he had to push those feelings and regrets down so he could focus and plan.

Geneck's behaviour firmed up the suspicion that he no longer had Jemima and was now actively searching for her. That meant that the brotherhood had snatched her. Why though? What possible interest could she be to them? Geneck wanted her, wanted a replacement for his daughter. He already had a blood tie to her. If only he could think of a way to destroy the creature so that Jemima was no longer in danger.

"Let us go home. There is nothing more we can do here," Edward said.

❦

JEMIMA SCREAMED. THE BRIGHT LIGHT DAZZLED HER AND THERE WAS confusion all around. "Master wants you," said a voice that loomed out of the glare.

"No. No. No," Jemima cried and then kicked out blindly. She was not going down without a fight. Her foot connected and she kicked again. A hand grabbed for her arm and she bit and clawed until that hand went away.

Screams erupted and Jemima stopped resisting. *What was that?* Those that were trying to haul her out of her cell were distracted too.

"What's that?" asked one.

"Somink," replied another.

Jemima felt rescue was at hand and started to fight again, kicking and punching to make her way to the door. Her eyes adjusted now. She had four assailants standing. Two were on the floor. Outside she could see minions swirling about and other figures. "Edward?"

Lights glared overhead. Dark-robed figures engaged with the minions. Bodies flew through the air in a way that reminded her of Fulton. "Fulton!" she cried but her voice was drowned out by the heightened screams. The minions who had tried to wrestle with her fled. She tried to follow but the door shut before she could get there. "Let me out!" she screamed and banged her fists.

Thumps rebounded on the door, likely bodies being thrown. *Stay cool and calm. Edward is here. He will find you.*

The door rattled not long after. Jemima stepped away, readying herself for friend or foe. A tall thin robed figure stood there. Fighting continued behind him. "Come. I must take you to safety."

"Edward?"

He nodded. She took his hand and was tugged away out of her prison. "First you must sleep."

"No, no," she said, catching sight of men who looked like Edward and Fulton and realising her mistake. "Take me there, take me..."

All went dark. She was aware but not able to open her eyes. Hands carried her and then came a sensation that made her sick and faint. For a while she did not know what had happened or where she was.

She woke up in a dark place. It smelled like her previous cell, except this time her hands and feet were tied. Her head rested on a pillow. She had swapped one prison for another. Edward would not know where to look for her. *Oh Edward. I am so sorry.*

She kicked and wriggled but to no avail. "Let me out. Let me out!" she called out. She kept that up for quite a while without result. The air was damp and musty. She was underground again. Had Geneck recaptured her? Panic leaped into her mind. *No, no, no!*

❧

DEJECTED, THEY WALKED HOME. FULTON SAID NOTHING BUT WAVES of anger seemed to fall from him. Aunt Prudence walked with head high, her umbrella at the ready. Milly walked beside her husband, whispering to him. Her words had no effect in easing Fulton's tension. Edward began to think of a plan—not to kill Geneck—that stumped him still—but to get Jemima back. She was in less mortal danger with the brotherhood he hoped, expected.

New battle lines had been drawn around him. He would respond in kind. Yes, the brotherhood had meddled where they should not. They had acted for their own gains. Pity, for he had expected better of Mr White.

The brotherhood would be an interesting foe. They were magicians but they were also men and easier to kill or subdue than the beast Geneck. Edward shuddered at the direction of his thoughts. He was a gentleman magician and one such as he did not kill. But a gentleman should protect his wife, give his life for hers. How to reconcile these opposites was beyond him at that moment.

When they arrived back at Fulton's house the front door was ajar. The flickering of a street light made shadows jump.

Fulton stepped in front of him. "Let me go first."

"But where is Jakes?" Milly asked.

Fulton lifted a hand for silence and stepped up to the stoop. Edward stood in front of Milly and Aunt Prudence, who huffed. "Wait, please," Edward said to them both.

Fulton was gone for some five minutes, putting Edward's nerves on edge. Had he found the domestic staff murdered? Was Geneck sitting on the sofa waiting for them?

Fulton came back to the door, his expression not at all comforting. "You best come in. Morning room."

Edward could not relax. Something was definitely wrong. He pushed open the door and there was no sign of Jakes or a footman or a maid. Candles burned in candelabras, their light flickering over the carpet and walls. He was tempted to call out a hello but refrained.

The floorboards creaked ominously as he stepped into the hall. Milly was close behind, with Aunt Prudence billowing her skirts over the stoop. He pushed open the door to the morning room, the downstairs parlour, expecting a blood bath. The fire was unlit, but stacked with kindling and a bucket of coals stood at the side of the hearth. Fulton stood there, shoulders tense, glaring at someone sitting in one of the wing chairs.

"The devil take you, White!" Edward said coming into the room. "What have you done? Where are the servants?"

Mr White put down the sherry he was sipping, sliding it on to a side table. He looked up at them both, apparently unconcerned. He was wearing a suit, rather than the robes he had been wearing the last time they had met. He peered around Edward. "Ladies. Do come in."

Mr White picked up his sherry and peered up at them, expectant or weary, Edward could not tell. He squeezed his fist, wanting to slap that drink right out of White's hand.

Milly and Aunt Prudence took seats, casting glances at Fulton and Edward.

Putting the wine down again, Mr White sighed. "Oh do sit down. I have not harmed your servants. They are asleep in the kitchen. I thought it best considering the circumstances."

Edward thought about the open door but before he could articulate that thought, Mr White spoke again. "Never fear, your house and your possessions are perfectly safe."

Edward shared a look with Fulton and together they backed up to sit on the sofa, not taking their eyes from the magician.

"Now is not that better? I have come to talk to you about Jemima."

Edward surged up again, fists clenched. "So you have taken her!"

"No, I have not taken her. I do not know who has taken her."

"It is not Geneck," Edward said in a flat voice.

"I agree. There is another party."

"Bleeding hell," Fulton growled. "Who else would take her? We know why Geneck wants her but..."

Edward sat back, all the air flying out of him. Mr White nodded. "Yes, you have guessed right. It is your work that is of interest."

"My fault," Edward said.

"Nonsense. The pretty little thing would be dead without your intervention."

Edward's eyes lifted and centred on the magician from the brotherhood. "Who?"

Mr White shook his head. "I know it is a member of the brotherhood. I do not know for certain. I have suspicions only at this time. I must investigate further."

"Is she in danger?" Milly asked, surprising Edward. He had forgotten she was there.

"I do not think so. I cannot be sure, you understand. There is a ruthlessness to this abduction that surprised me."

"It is cruel to take her from her family and loved ones," Aunt Prudence interjected. "Do you and your lot have no respect for families?"

Mr White stared at Aunt Prudence. "Yes, I agree with you, good woman. We do respect families and strive to protect them. Jemima was protected from harm previously because of our respect for families, regardless of the crimes of the member of our order."

"Well, bring her back!" Aunt Prudence bit back.

"I will do my best." He smiled kindly at Aunt Prudence and then returned his attention to Edward.

"I wanted you to know that I am on your side. I cannot overtly help you for you are not a member of the brotherhood. However, Jemima is protected under the oaths exchanged with Wilbur Hardcastle. Who, as you know, was my friend."

"So they did kill Wilbur Hardcastle."

Mr White opened his hands in a kind of shrug. "I cannot comment." The man pushed himself up to a standing position. "I will leave you now. I will try to send word to you if I find anything. Meanwhile, continue your own endeavours."

With that he stepped out of the room and into the hall. Fulton went after him and came back straight away. "He is gone." Edward stood and began to pace.

Noises issued from the kitchen. Very soon Jakes's voice sounded and there was a knock at the door. He put his head in and then came into the room. "Forgive me..." He glanced around, clearly not remembering how they had got in. "Shall I bring the tea things?"

Aunt Prudence lifted her hand. "Yes, please, Jakes. And I think we need something a little more substantial. Bread and butter if you please."

Jakes bowed his head. "The cook has made scones."

"Oh, that will do then. Thank you." Aunt Prudence approved and then settled her skirts and lifting her face studied them all with a serious expression.

Jakes retreated. Milly covered her mouth to stifle a laugh. What she found amusing Edward did not know. "Milly!" Fulton said from his place by the unlit fire place.

"I am sorry. It was the look on his face. On top of us standing at the door, thinking the worst when it was only that nice Mr White."

"Nice Mr White? Are you out of your senses?" Fulton said, his voice as excited as Edward had ever heard it.

"Not at all. It was very good of him to tell us that he supports us and that Jemima has some protection."

"Good thought, Milly. Sensible girl," Aunt Prudence added. "I thought he was a very nice gentleman."

Edward sat down heavily. Fulton joined him. The brotherhood were an unknown quantity. Mr White, or whatever his name was, had been helpful. But he had not explained himself or why he had been there fighting Geneck's minions.

Jakes came in about an hour later pushing a trolley. He still looked rather rattled and blushed as he organised the food. The cook had outdone himself. Not only was there scones, jam, cream, butter and slices of ham, he had made little pastries filled with spiced meat and fruit.

"Thank you, Jakes. Very well done," Fulton said.

Jakes stood upright, blushing profusely. "I strive to do my best, sir."

"Indeed," Edward said, taking a plate with a scone on it from Aunt Prudence. "Perhaps you should have an early night. Get the footman to lock up."

"Sir! That would not do at all." Jakes lifted his chin and made his mouth turn down at the sides. Then he exited the room with upmost dignity, leaving them with their food. The poor man knew something was amiss and blamed himself. Pity there was no way to disabuse him of that notion without risking them all and general exposure. The servants had enough to talk about. It was a wonder they were not the scandal of London already. They probably were in the servant circles and soon that would spread to the middle and upper classes. With a sigh and another bite of scone, Edward decided he was beyond caring.

CHAPTER 17

Ferdinand De Blanc strode through the halls of the priory, his mind deep in thought. Something was not right in the world, something was out of kilter. He frowned as he walked through the corridors, wishing the rain would cease so he could walk down to the pond and out along the garden walk where he could think more clearly. He had suspicions but he needed more to tackle the problem.

The conclave had voted not to assist Huntington in destroying the beast he had created. Ferdinand considered that decision to be wrong. They had, however, let him and some volunteers attempt a rescue of Jemima Hardcastle. Unfortunately, that had gone terribly wrong too. That wrongness he suspected came from within the brotherhood itself. Someone was working against him and it was more than just political machinations.

He had seen Huntington and Fulton in the aftermath of Jemima's first abduction. Huntington's emotions were raw. He told the truth when he said he did not know where his wife was. However, he soon figured out that Geneck had been responsible rather than the brotherhood. Now, though, the brotherhood were under suspicion and not without cause.

Ferdinand feared Edward would work out where she was and why.

Yet in acting precipitously, he could endanger his wife further. Ferdinand had to do something and he would have to tread carefully to free her, to save her life, for Jemima indicated danger for the brotherhood on many levels: ethical, moral and physical.

He turned the corner and pulled up short, surprised by the taller, younger brother. "Brother Winston? G...good morning."

Brother Winston inclined his head slightly, the briefest of acknowledgements. "Brother Ferdinand. Looking for something?"

Ferdinand's eyes went to an old wooden door. Shut, it led to basement storage rooms. They were as old as the priory, perhaps even older if some of the Roman arches in the supports were original to the site. "I thought some wine would be good to go with dinner, seeing so many of the brotherhood have stayed after the conclave. I had a couple of Spanish reds tucked away in a private corner."

"No need. I saw Hamish, not ten minutes ago taking a whole cask up to the dining room."

Ferdinand smiled and feigned surprise. "Did you? Well, Hamish has the best nose and I am sure my selection would be nothing to it."

He went to walk on but Winston stood in the way, his robe billowing slightly from his breathing. He crossed his arms, eyebrow raised. "Anything else I can help you with? I have a small experiment fermenting below and am keen that it not be disturbed."

Ferdinand's instincts went on high alert. While the rules of the brotherhood were fairly equalitarian, Winston had the leader's ear and no question a certain amount of influence. Ferdinand could find himself running foul of the Revered. "No. I was heading to the end of the corridor as I was hoping that the rain would clear so I could take in a tour of the gardens. The weather in Kent is usually so mild at this time of year."

Winston did not blink and his countenance showed no interest and he still did not move. As the Executioner he had an outward appearance of calm most of the time and was difficult to prick to anger.

Ferdinand took the hint. "I shall head this way then and leave you to your experiments. Forgive my intrusion." With a short nod to his fellow magician, he exited by the nearest exterior door. The light rain was not an impediment to his turn around the garden. He needed somewhere quiet to think so he continued along the curved walk, past the ducklings gambolling along the lawn, past the edges of the lake where water birds fed among the bulrushes and down to the bank of the river where the fronds of a willow dampened his robe.

There he let his thoughts expand and let his conclusions converge. Either Winston was involved in some secret experimentation, which was likely, as he was always experimenting and being secretive about it. Or Winston had Jemima. Ferdinand leaned towards the latter. It did not give him any good feelings about Jemima's welfare. Winston was not known for being sensitive to other humans and for him females were particularly distasteful. He was certainly ruthless enough. When he thought back, it was Winston who had argued that Huntington should be ended, but his creations studied. But who was pulling Winston's lead?

It was not like him to act alone. Unless Ferdinand had been completely mistaken about him. He had considered Winston previously when looking for intrigues, trying to track down who had promoted a particular nasty action. Winston had not taken on a leadership role in the past, usually just subtle prods to promote intrigue. Could that be a disguise in itself? Ferdinand shook his head. Winston had little imagination to be the instigator of such an outrage himself. He followed orders. That was what Ferdinand considered, but still there was doubt.

A magician's family was sacrosanct. One did not prey on wives and children of the brotherhood. Or mothers, sisters, parents or even cousins. Nothing Huntington had done had warranted such a blatant disregard of his most basic rights as a magician. He was not a member of the brotherhood to be sure, but he would qualify if he were to apply for membership. If only they had reached out to him instead of trying to bully him into handing over the texts. And now this.

When he thought of Huntington, he realised that the young, self-taught magician was ignorant of the order and the rules. Winston would not have failed to exploit that. Only the uniqueness of Huntington's work had swayed the conclave to vote against termination. That and his naivety. How could he be judged by the brotherhood when he was not even a member and was ignorant of the rules?

Leaving the river behind him, he continued along the gravel path to the old dovecote. The building was empty and clean, used as it was as a place of meditation. He cast a spell on the door so that his brothers knew the building was occupied. Then he folded himself onto a bench and began to chant, stretching his awareness to the land around him. He came upon the main building of the priory and then threaded his power through his probe so he could reach into the basement.

Within a minute, he was gasping and cold. His mind had been shoved rudely away and his own power rushed back at him like the snap of a tender branch released too quickly.

Panting, he opened his eyes and found himself on the floor of the dovecote. His head hurt where he had hit it. That had been a powerful repulsion spell. He climbed to his feet, a few aches and pains reminding him that he was no longer young. His dizziness settled quickly. The head injury was not so bad.

Rubbing his arms vigorously, he calmed his racing heart. What he had found confirmed his worst conclusions. The basement rooms where Winston worked had an enchantment on them. The taste of the spell was strange. Ferdinand did his best to shake free of the sticky web of power, trying to clear the vestiges and to savour them at the same time. The power derived from Winston and from someone else. This had to be the silent and elusive partner.

It was the first piece of evidence he had found and it was heart-wrenching. Was this the source of the rot Wilbur had told him about? All those years and Ferdinand thought his friend was slightly addled, not quite returning to normal after the loss of his wife. There had been anger and rage, too, when he asked for assistance in saving his wife and was refused. Wilbur's grief had been great indeed and now his daughter was at the mercy of the same forces that had manipulated him all those years ago.

Ferdinand could not help but think that the refusal had been the right thing to do. It was not their way to interfere with nature and the process of death. Until Huntington came along and saved the daughter from the same ailment. There had been no repercussions from that. Not for Jemima, at least, but the monster? Yes, terrible repercussions.

Ferdinand did not know the details of Huntington's invention, but the ruby heart could not be hidden from any magician with the sight. The invention had caused a stir and a reinvigoration in the efforts to retrieve the texts. What Huntington had achieved was not in any texts. No, Huntington had invented that amalgam of magic and machine himself, of that Ferdinand was certain.

But the texts held something powerful, something more powerful than victory of life over death as found in Huntington's devices. Ferdinand had not read them in their entirety, but Wilbur had given him an account of the contents. Some only vague hints. Too terrible to even speak about Wilbur had said, lest they corrupt the listener. There were powerful forces in the universe and the texts could unleash them, unpredictable as they may be. In the wrong hands, existence could be threatened.

Ferdinand swept his gaze around the dovecote and then headed for the door. If Wilbur was right then there was good reason to keep the texts out of the brotherhood's hands. He could not stand back and be idle. He had to act.

The sunlight blinded him for a moment and he wavered where he stood. How could he report his suspicions? Who among his allies would support him against such a powerful opponent? Ferdinand shook his head and then continued down the path, teeth clenched. He had a difficult choice to make for one who could influence the estimable role of Executioner must be a powerful adversary.

Ferdinand paused as it came to him. There was one hope. While Winston functioned as the Executioner, he did not wield the powers of his role every day, because a ritual was needed to confer the power of the conclave on him. Ferdinand considered and took a few more steps along the path. Yet, on his own Winston was still a formidable enemy.

A honk of a goose startled him and he realised he had been standing on the path looking like a stupid old fool and he hurried on.

Ferdinand needed help to liberate Jemima, to rescue her before Winston and his secretive ally had a chance to harm her in their search for Huntington's secrets. If Huntington had achieved even half of what the brotherhood had expected, then that discovery had the potential to be great indeed. He could take his place as the greatest magician of modern times.

Ferdinand shook his head, mumbling to himself as he neared the main building, taking the long walk up the drive past the priory gates. The priory was isolated, long ago shunned due to its bloody past. Many Catholic monks had died during the dissolution. The brotherhood had been in possession for many hundreds of years since that time, using their magic to maintain the superstition surrounding the buildings and the extensive grounds. It was easy to enhance the locals' aversion to the place to maintain their isolation.

As he trod up to the main gates and pushed the heavy doors open, he thought of Jemima, of how she'd been when still a child—precocious, loving and Wilbur's whole world. Although estranged from the brotherhood, Wilbur still allowed Ferdinand to visit. Their friendship had transcended Wilbur's break from the order. Ferdinand's loyalty to Wilbur was known among the brothers. For Wilbur's friendship he would fight for the daughter, no matter what it cost him. He would fight for Jemima as a matter of honour.

Once inside, he made his choice and stormed down the corridor with renewed purpose.

CHAPTER 18

They kept the room where Jemima was confined dark. It was cold and a trifle damp. Jemima coughed, afraid she was going to come down with some horrible influenza if she stayed any longer. She really wanted to get out of there.

When they came for her, though, she screamed. The touch of their hands was sudden and their skin icy. They grabbed her bound feet and her bound hands. She could not even fight them because she could not discern them from the general gloom. They wore black and kept their faces covered.

They could see her without the aid of a candle or a lantern. That was troubling. Who had her? There were two of them who carried her, stopping before leaving the room to put a sack over her head, which they tugged tightly around her throat with string. She screamed out some more but they did not appear worried about the sound she made. Jemima had to stop to husband her breathing.

A rustle of the fabric of their clothes. It was a lot of cloth, like a rough skirt or cloak. Their movements were quick and coordinated, unlike Geneck's minions. If Geneck did not have her, then that left the brotherhood. "Uncle Ferdy?" she rasped out.

"Yes, dear. Be still." The voice that responded was quiet. She chewed her lips. It was not Uncle Ferdy, she was certain. He would not harm her, of that she was pretty sure. Had she made a mistake in calling out to him?

Who had her then and why? How dare they grab her, keep her locked up in the dark and then put her bag over her head and manhandle her. She found that she could not restrain her outrage. It was better than cowering in fear.

"How dare you touch me! I demand you unhand me this minute!" Saying this with a bag over her head and struggling for breath did not come out as authoritatively as she would have liked.

"What did she say?" another voice, croaky and weak sounding, said. The one pretending to be Uncle Ferdy laughed. "The bag is muffling what she is saying but I think you are hearing the blathering of her temper."

"Should we shut her up then? I do not like women who are noisy." It was the older croaky sounding voice.

"No need. As long as she cannot see what we are doing then there is no problem."

They placed Jemima on a metal table. Flashbacks to being held by Longhurst rushed at her. *No that was stone, this is metal. Think, think. What are metal tables used for? Examinations! Autopsy! Vivisection?*

Gathering her resolve, she panted, but before she could twist herself off the table she was held down. Heavy straps passed over her shoulders, stomach, hips and legs and they left little room to move. The sacking over her face prevented her from seeing even though there was now diffuse light reaching her.

"No!"

"Please focus the light more." People moved around her. Their robes swished. It was definitely the brotherhood. No wonder her father had hated them and never talked of them. They were doing the unspeakable to her.

"Now let us see what Huntington has done here." She felt cold fingers as they tugged at her corset, unclipping the busk at the top. She screamed.

"Oh do shut up, woman," an older man's voice said.

She screamed again and thrashed her head from side to side. Hands gripped the side of her head. "Stop or I will cuff you one."

Gritting her teeth, she took the threat seriously. The other man laughed softly. "You do have a way with women. I never knew. A handy trait."

"Phah! Young whelp. Move aside so I can inspect this machine you told me about. Ahhh. Intriguing."

Hot, helpless tears bathed her cheeks as her chest was exposed so that they could get better access to her ruby heart. How humiliating. She wanted to slap them soundly and put out their eyes. Yet, she knew they were not interested in her as a person or as a woman. They were not staring at her exposed breasts. She was just a thing holding a mechanism they were interested in, something that Edward had made.

The hatch on her heart was opening. Both of them gasped. "What an amazing amalgamation. See the machine, how it spins."

"Yes, and it uses the power of the gem, which is actually full of his essence."

"Not a useful device if one must keep it fuelled with one's magical essence. You would be depleted after a while."

There was a pause as someone touched the skin around the machine. "True. From what I understand he does not need to replenish it. Something in this device keeps the essence and grows it so that it is sustained."

The hands fell away. "Bring the magnifying glass."

Some movement, a click and clink of equipment. Not unfamiliar sounds to her as she had spent a lot of her childhood in her father's laboratory. "I see...mmm. Very intricate work. Huntington has a fine hand. This device could have multiple applications." This was the older man and there was a hint in his voice of reluctant admiration.

"Yes, limited only by our imagination and our skill." This was the slightly younger sounding voice. Jemima was chilled, not only because her flesh was exposed but how they talked about her heart, her ruby heart, without emotion. Just with greed.

"If only we could duplicate it," the older man said, breathing heavily, or was that because he was leaning over her?

"Can we not dismantle it and then see if we can build it again?" the younger man suggested.

A pause and hands that were touching her lifted away. "It would kill her. Her heart is dependent on the device."

"So? She is only a female. Who cares what happens to her? This is for our future, for the future of magic."

There was a sound at the door.

The light went out. "What was that?" the older man asked.

"A problem. I will deal with it. Keep her here and keep her quiet." She heard footsteps and the door open.

A hand pressed down on her face, squishing her eyes and nose. She struggled and bit. A hand thumped her across the head. She tried to scream Edward's name, but a heavy cloth was put over her face and weight put behind it. She could not breathe. Could not scream. She struggled and struggled but to no avail. Her lungs burned. *Not like this. Not like this.* She tried to relax, hoping that she could survive longer if she did not fight. She passed out.

⚜

SHE WOKE TO VOICES TALKING OVER HER. "PROBLEM?" THE OLDER man asked.

Jemima drew in a huge breath and another. The suffocating fabric was gone. "You nearly killed her," the younger man said.

"No such thing. She was going to scream. I had to do something." It was the older man.

"Very well. But please be careful. Until we have extracted the device we need her alive."

"What was that noise all about?"

"Nothing that cannot be handled. We will have to put her back now though."

"Why?"

"Because someone suspects what I am up to. The ward has been detected, tested and measured. Someone seeks to know what is going on in here. I predict you will be consulted soon and asked to act against me. You must be ready."

206

"Not Brother Ferdinand again? Meddlesome fool. Just like that Wilbur." The older man spat the name out.

"Just so," the younger man responded.

Hastily, they put the casing back on her heart and roughly tried to reclip the corset together. Then without any ceremony or discussion they carried her back to her dark, damp cell. The door whined as they opened it and then they swung her and dumped her onto the floor, which was covered by sacks and loose materials. Jemima wailed as she was thrown and then let out an *oomph* when she landed and rolled. If only her hands were not tied. She could have saved herself a bump on the head where she hit the edge of the bunk.

It took a while and a great deal of manipulation but she finally climbed onto the bed. It was better than the cold floor and the scratchy sacking. Jemima sat there and thought hard on what had just occurred.

On one hand she was relieved she was not at the mercy of Geneck. On the other, she had no idea what kind of trouble she was in, except she did not hold with being abducted, manhandled like baggage and then tossed back on her derriere in a cold damp cell. She did not have to use her imagination to consider the situation sinister—it was, and not just for her: she worried for Edward as well. If they took out her heart device, she would die. Then they would go after Edward to learn his secrets. She was positive they could not replicate his work. Edward was special and they were not, otherwise they would have discovered how to make a device just from hearing about the idea. Was not some inventor always building on other people's ideas? They were idiots. Dangerous idiots unfortunately. How was Edward ever going to find out she was here? She began to fret and then comforted herself. Edward was clever. He would work it out.

She found a comfortable spot on the bed, tried to think warm thoughts and dozed. What else was one supposed to do when locked in a cell? Her lips were dry and her throat parched. They had not left her any food or water. Another reason to nap. She needed to conserve her strength. She had a feeling she was going to need it. She was getting out of there. She just wasn't sure when.

Her eyes closed and she blocked out the musty smell and the cold by clutching her bound hands to her chest and soon was asleep.

⚜

Benedict, the Revered, listened to Ferdinand, his face creasing with worry. Encouraged, Ferdinand revealed all that he knew and all that he suspected. He had gone too far to hold anything back.

Benedict's bushy brows had lowered over his black eyes until the weight of knowledge almost closed his eyes. "Ferdinand. Tread carefully. This is a foul conspiracy of which you speak. Even if the girl is here, Brother Winston will be able to explain it away. It will not prove anything. Let alone a larger conspiracy."

Ferdinand bowed his head, acknowledging his master's words, then raised his head to meet that dark gaze. "I know, Revered, but it will help Jemima. I fear for her life. And I think it will prevent an insuperable breach with Huntington. Surely it is best to bring one such as he into the order so that his great discovery can be explored and shared."

Benedict fiddled with a leather-bound tome on his desk, righting it so that it was square with the corner. He glanced up at Ferdinand. "I have sympathy with your argument." He then stared down at the desk, then reached for his fountain pen and rolled it in his fingers. "However," he said and coughed a phlegmy cough, "you forget he has our texts and is now blatantly using them."

Ferdinand clenched his jaw. "I have not forgotten. Indeed, I think about it all the time. He has them and has used them, yes. He has not used them for evil. When he has used the spells that we can detect, he does it to gain our attention, to seek our help. He has asked me several times now for our help to destroy Geneck. He told me also that he was forewarned by Wilbur Hardcastle that the use of the spells in the texts would alert us. Huntington is desperate. He does not know how to stop the beast. Indeed, I think he is unaware of the significance of his inventions and the great potential for good they have and the serious risk of harm if used for ill."

Benedict waved his hand like he was shooing away a fly. "Yes, yes, but what does Brother Winston and his supporter or supporters hope to gain?" He pushed up from his chair and strode over to the window, his robes swirling at his feet. He was a large man, but getting older. Ferdinand noticed that his gait was slightly off, that he had some problem with the knee. Ferdinand himself suffered from arthritis on occasion so could sympathise.

Ferdinand followed behind him. "I do not know. Perhaps if we force their hand with Jemima, we will know more."

Benedict turned, the lines on his face deep around his cheeks and between his eyebrows. "Very well. I will convene the conclave again. I warn you it will annoy many to have another meeting called so close to the previous one."

"Thank you." Ferdinand bowed, his heart feeling lighter already.

"You may thank me now. Be ready for anything."

Ferdinand stepped back, bowing again at the door. "I thank you again. For the sake of the brotherhood."

"Go now. I will see you at the conclave."

Ferdinand shut the door, his heart beating double time.

CHAPTER 19

Ferdinand watched as the members of the conclave gathered in the converted chapel, now ringed with benches to create a small amphitheatre. He hurried to his seat, the last ally hastily whispered to in the corridor. How he hated calling in old debts and requesting the return of favours. He preferred that rational debate ruled the order. But now he knew for certain that it did not. Influence and manipulation were like treacle in the air. Shivering, he could not hide the trepidation he felt.

He acknowledged other brothers who came into the room and took their seats. Many were still in residence after the last conclave, which swelled the numbers. Most brothers only came to the priory for meetings and to study, many living out in the community as normal people. Many had families and business concerns of their own. He hoped Huntington's situation would create sympathy among these brothers. Surely empathy, too.

The brothers talked among themselves as they waited for the seats to fill. The Revered would enter last. Ferdinand caught sight of Winston and he tracked the Executioner to his seat at the left hand of the Revered. Ferdinand could see no particular acquaintances acknowledged. It was as if the man had no friends among the brotherhood at all. That could not be right though. A tactic?

Winston directed his stare at Ferdinand and a shiver ran up his spine. Winston knew who had instigated the meeting. Winston knew what Ferdinand was up to. His only hope lay in the fact that he had acted quickly and that Winston would not have had time to prepare a counter-offensive.

A hush overcame the room. The Revered had begun his walk from the old vestry. He wore a rich red robe overlaid with an apron embroidered with gold that glinted in the light streaming in from the windows. The brotherhood were not much for ceremony, but they liked their leader to look the part. Benedict was much esteemed within the brotherhood. He was known for his wisdom and the beauty and depth of his power.

Benedict's secretary, Brother Malcom, thumped the floor with his staff. The meeting was called to order. "The *Societas Magicas* calls Brother Winston Gabriel to answer questions concerning his actions," Brother Malcom Bremer, the Revered's secretary announced, his voice booming up to the high-vaulted ceiling and all around the chamber.

Winston stood and walked to the centre so that all the tiers of brethren could see him. "I will answer questions of the brotherhood. Ask," he said, bowing with a flourish.

Ferdinand thought that implied nonchalance and complete disrespect for authority. Did the Executioner truly believe that he could not be called to account? Who was his supporter?

The secretary read from a document. "Have you taken Jemima Hardcastle Huntington into your custody?" His commanding voice echoed throughout the room.

Ferdinand shifted. They had worked hard on the wording of the question. If they had asked "did you take Huntington's wife from him", he could answer no. If they asked "do you have Jemima Hardcastle Huntington secreted in the priory basements" he could also answer no by removing her to another place.

Winston's eyes narrowed, his fist clenched. "Yes."

A ripple of whispers flowed through the gathering. Heads turned to neighbours and brothers shifted in chairs.

The next question was read out. "On what basis did you perform such an act without the sanction of the conclave?"

Winston rolled his shoulders back, his gaze raking the brotherhood that surrounded him. "For protection."

The speaker's head jerked up. The prepared questions and possible answers did not cover this response. The speaker inclined his head to Benedict.

Benedict sat forwards. All eyes were on him. "Whose protection?"

Winston bowed to the Revered. "Hers and...ours."

"Nonsense!" a voice called from the audience.

"Liar!" called another. Shouts erupted along the back tier. Ferdinand could not see who had called out. They were not allies of his. He frowned, wondering what was going on.

Winston responded to the insults hurled at him. It was his right. "I do not lie. Her husband is a danger to her. I sought only to protect."

Ferdinand's head jerked back in surprise. Then anger. "By what right do you seek to protect a wife from her husband? Even the law of this kingdom does not do that."

Winston levelled his gaze at him, an insouciant smile playing about his lips "The same right as you to defend him. Interest."

Brothers turned to one another, perplexed by the answer. Winston claimed to have an interest in the wife of a fellow magician, had accused the husband of being a danger. This was unprecedented. While they did not follow common law and a number of brothers did not legally marry their spouses, there was no rule to prevent a brother trying to lure away another's wife. Surely this was not the case. Winston hated women.

It had to be a ruse, but not one easily uncovered. He thought back to when they had met with the Huntingtons. Winston showed no particular interest in Huntington or Jemima. It was only the texts that were of interest to him. From memory he had not even acknowledged her presence. Then again, when she had called Ferdinand "Uncle Ferdy" Winston had started, surprised by the intimate connection. Ferdinand rubbed his chin. His role in maintaining a clandestine friendship with Wilbur all through the years was exposed in that one innocent exclamation. Messy.

Yet, put in another light, it was he, Ferdinand, who had greater interest.

After conferring hastily with Benedict, the speaker pressed on. "You will present her to the conclave immediately so we may decide her fate. Her safety is important to the brotherhood. Respecting family of brothers, both former and current, is important to our code. We would have no harm come to her while in our custody."

Winston's eyes glittered and his gaze passed over the assembled brothers. If there was aid from a secret ally, it was not forthcoming. He inclined his head and grinned. There was nothing of merriment in that grin, more like the baring of teeth. "If you insist."

Winston closed his eyes. Ferdinand tensed. Magic. Winston dared to bring forth magic within the conclave itself. Power surged out over them all. He had not even sought permission to use such power. He was that confident.

Ferdinand's eyes darted to Benedict. The Revered did not act. He sat calmly. The secretary, though, held to his staff, wrath written on his features.

Ferdinand looked about the room. A lot of the display—fog and lightening—was for show, merely tricks. The main doors burst open. A small whirlwind spun into the room. Robes flared and flapped in the wind. A couple of pebbles from the floor flew up and ricocheted against the wall. Candles guttered and then reflamed. The wind grew in strength, flinging dust. Many of the brothers lifted their hands to shelter their eyes, not willing to use magic to deflect the wind without express permission. Ferdinand squinted and could feel the tension rising around him.

Anger, surprise and chagrin wove together, changing the atmosphere. A loud retort sounded. An explosion and a puff of fire and smoke. It cleared somewhat and Jemima appeared, squatting on the ground, hands over her head. She peeked out through her hands, curious. Her eyes glittered, but something like rage touched her expression.

As she stood, it was revealed she was dressed all in leather from the long boots to which breeches had been tucked, to a leather corset with ties loosely holding it together over a ripped white blouse. He saw immediately she had been restrained because her delicate white wrists bore red welts. At her ankles, he saw where the leather boots had been chafed by rope. Winston had tied her. Outrage boiled his blood. How dare he do that to her. A young, harmless woman.

⬱

Jemima stood up straight and she glared over the bunch of men in robes who ogled her. This was not Geneck at least. This must be the secret brotherhood to which her father had belonged. They had dared abduct her? Then she saw him. "Uncle Ferdy! What in hell's name is going on here? Why have you taken me from my husband?"

Furore erupted around them. Gazes and words centred on Ferdinand. She liked that her words had such an effect on the audience.

"It was not I!" Ferdinand said quickly. Then he gaped at the men who were leaning down and yelling at him. "Tell them it was not me," Ferdinand said, hands imploring.

Jemima creased her forehead. "If not you, then who?" She turned around and saw Winston. "You!" she said, pointing decisively. "It was Mr Brown."

"Order. We will have order." The voice boomed around the room and the speaker thumped his staff and the occupants of the room quieted down. He stood next to a big man in opulent robes.

The man in the robes bowed to her. "I am Benedict, the leader of the brotherhood. I am known as the Revered." Then drawing himself up to his full height he asked, "Tell me, can you identify your abductor?"

Jemima squinted, looked to the sea of faces and then back to Mr Brown. "There were two of them, maybe three."

"And can you confirm it was Brother Winston?" he asked, voice having a decided crack to it.

Jemima bit her lip. How could she be certain? "Mr Brown would need to speak further before I can confirm the sound of his voice. They put a sack over my head. I did not see. Only heard their voices."

"Brother Winston, will you speak to this woman? You have already confessed to taking her for her own protection. However, now that suspicion has been cast on Brother Ferdinand, you can act to exonerate him."

"I did not take her," Uncle Ferdy expostulated, turning a nasty shade of red.

The Revered lifted his hand and Uncle Ferdy shut his mouth.

Mr Brown grinned and it was not nice. Even Jemima could see that. "Why would I do that? It is as much his fault as anyone else's."

Jemima stared at him, her mouth opening. "It was you. You threatened to—"

"You were taken into custody by Brother Winston without our permission," the Revered intoned, interrupting her.

Jemima was annoyed at not being able to finish her sentence and condemn that nasty Brother Winston with his own words and deeds.

Ferdinand appeared annoyed as well. "I demand that you clarify that I did not have any involvement in the abduction of Jemima Hardcastle."

"Huntington," Jemima corrected. Uncle Ferdy acknowledged her.

Winston sneered at both of them, for Uncle Ferdy had come up closer to her. "You soft-hearted pile of jelly," Mr Brown said with a growl. "You encouraged Wilbur as you have coddled this girl. Look at her. Look what you have made."

"What has he made?" Jemima asked but was drowned out by Ferdinand's outrage. She had no idea what he meant.

"I did nothing a brother would not do for another. The poor girl was left all alone in the world. Yes, I have taken an interest in her. Huntington loves her. He risked everything to save her."

"Enough," Benedict said. "This is a diversion. We must deal with what is at hand."

Winston closed his expression and Ferdinand bowed. Jemima lifted her eyebrows and regarded the Revered, not quite understanding what was going on.

The speaker banged his staff again, picked up a document and started to read. "We vow we will restore you to your husband."

Jemima grinned. That was good news indeed.

"No, not yet," Winston said.

Jemima went to open her mouth, but Uncle Ferdy shook his head and she understood she was to keep quiet.

Brother Winston turned to his audience, hands in front, pleading. "We must study her. You know she is kept alive by that mechanism, that ruby heart. By seeing what Huntington has done with this creature, we may understand it better."

Jemima rounded on him. "I'm not a creature. You are!"

CHAPTER 20

E dward paced the drawing room. He knew that Fulton had been dressed and ready to go by six o'clock. However, raised voices from his room indicated that there was a domestic discussion in progress. He continued to pace while waiting for him to come in and share a light meal before they ventured out to rescue Jemima. The door opened and Edward swung around, expecting Fulton and then halting suddenly when Aunt Prudence came into the room. "I thought to join you for dinner."

Edward acknowledged the aunt and passed her some sherry when she took a seat. The occasional raised voice reached them. Aunt Prudence smiled in a knowing way. Edward would not be surprised if she had put Milly up to it. After years of suppressing the girl's spirit, she was now encouraging her to disobey her husband.

With that thought, his cheeks grew hot with annoyance and confusion. Jemima had never obeyed him and he was beginning to think he liked it that way. How miserable would his existence be if Jemima said "yes, whatever you say, dear" every time he opened his mouth.

The sun was close to setting and Edward found he could not stop pacing, could not sit still. "Where do you think you will seek Jemima?" Aunt Prudence asked.

Edward stopped his pacing and turned to face her. "I do not know yet."

"Dinner is served," Jakes announced.

Aunt Prudence led the way into the dining room, her feathers and lace seeming alive as they moved and gyrated as she walked. Jakes took the covers off the meal, which was laid out on the table for them to serve themselves as they had requested a small and informal meal.

Steam wafted off the roast beef and the aroma of horseradish made his nose twitch. Next to that was roast potatoes and creamed spinach. His stomach lurched. Despite the logic of setting out with a full belly, there was no way he could eat. It was a battle of wills. He knew he needed to keep up his strength if they were to find Jemima and fight the brotherhood.

The sound of the front door knocker startled him. Aunt Prudence scooped some spinach onto her plate and then a generous portion of roast potatoes. The cook had sliced the roast beef thinly, the inside so red it was in stark contrast to the dark brown of its crust. A number of these she slid onto her plate. She lavished gravy over the whole and put a tiny speck of horseradish on the side near the meat.

Jakes went to open the door.

Aunt Prudence shifted in her chair to stare at the entry to the dining room. Not that it would allow her to see any better. "I wonder who that could be?" she said.

Edward frowned, wishing that Fulton would hurry up. "I have no idea, nor time for idle social interactions. I should have told Jakes to turn them away."

Feet sounded on the stairs, louder than the butler alone. Jakes knocked and then opened the door. He did not bother to announce the detective and his young, pimply-faced sidekick who brushed passed him on their way through. "Mr Huntington? Perhaps you have time now to talk."

Coleman turned, catching sight of Aunt Prudence. He bowed. "Madam. Pleased to see you again."

Aunt Prudence smiled, really smiled and put out her hand. "The pleasure is mine."

Edward's stomach turned at the thought of those two flirting, but it seemed obvious to him that is what was happening. Admiration at least. Aunt Prudence had to be at least fifty if she was a day. He frowned. He actually did not know how old his spinster aunt was. Something in his memory but so far back it was an echo of nothing at all. Later he would think on that puzzle.

Jakes caught his eye. "I will inform Mr Fulton of the detective's arrival, sir."

"Yes, thank you Jakes," Edward replied.

Edward spread his hand gesturing at the settee. "Take a seat, if you please."

"Oh yes, do join us at table. As you see there is plenty of roast beef," Aunt Prudence said. "My father always said that a medium rare roast was the best thing for the nerves. Do you not agree, Inspector?"

Edward stood by the fireplace, a dainty candle snuffer twirling about his fingers. He was not eager for this interview. He just wanted to get on with it and have his wife back. Geneck ended, of course, and maybe a nice dinner afterwards. He was too full of anxiety to do justice to a meal right now.

The detective took up a seat opposite Aunt Prudence. "Thank you for the kind invitation but I have already eaten."

Edward swallowed, his throat thick with grief. They had failed to save Jemima and Coleman visiting just made it all so much more real.

"Now, Huntington, no more prevaricating if you please. We went to rescue your wife last night. I would like to know more about the people who you think stole her away just as we were about to win through."

Edward turned. "I do not know—"

He could not reveal the brotherhood's existence to the police—a secret brotherhood was a secret brotherhood. You just did not shout their address to the wind and not expect some retribution. Not that he knew the address anyway. At the moment, Edward had had enough of purgatory and dead people piling up and now a missing wife. Speaking of the brotherhood would bring the mother of all hexes down on his head and on all the following generations of his line. It was not something he was keen on. He really just wanted to get out of there and find Jemima.

"Now, don't you try to gammon me." The inspector rocked forwards on his chair.

"I speak truly. I do not know the particulars of these people. I fear they have my wife and she is in terrible danger. I am waiting for Fulton and then we will be off." His voice broke at the last.

"Then you know where they are..." Coleman narrowed his gaze.

Edward shook his head. "I do not know."

Fulton came in looking about him, as if he was ready to fight, all energy and action. "What is going on, Huntington?"

The inspector half-turned in his seat so he could see Fulton by the door. "That is exactly what I want to know. Perhaps you'll join us, sir."

Fulton looked around him, his breath hitching when he saw Aunt Prudence. She arched her eyebrow at him.

Fulton glowered and then came up beside Edward.

"Well?" the inspector said, his eyes moving between them.

Edward put down the ornament he'd been twiddling in his fingers and stood up straight. "Well what? Did you manage to kill the beast, Inspector?"

Coleman sat up straight, his chair falling back. "No."

"And how many men did you lose in the pursuit?" Fulton asked.

Coleman's skin became tinged with pink. "Too many."

"I think you should leave Geneck to us," Edward said, lifting his chin a little higher.

"But you said you didn't know how to kill it."

"I will find a way," Edward returned. "I must."

"You can kill as many of the minions as you want," Fulton said to the inspector.

Coleman bolted out of his seat. "Just see here. You are trying to pull the wool over my eyes. You know what's going on and you aren't saying."

"No, we are going to seek Jemima and..." Edward began.

"We are not sure of our success," Fulton finished for him.

"But your gentle wife?" Coleman said. "You took her into danger in the first place. How could you?"

Edward put his elbow on the mantelpiece, his gaze staring into the distance. He tried not to think about Jemima and what she must have suffered and what she must still be suffering.

Fulton *harrumphed*. "Mrs Huntington is not that gentle nor so fragile. I thought you might have noticed. Consider the most unnatural female you have ever imagined and you might come close. The truth is that we had no choice but to take her because she threatened to hunt for Geneck by herself and would have done so if we had not permitted her to accompany us. She has a tie to him, you see."

"Tie?" The inspector's gaze kept going to Edward, who wanted to rant and rave and was doing his upmost to keep his composure. Nothing but blame and blame and blame again went round his head. It was all his fault. He should never have tried to use science once he knew about magic. Merging them had caused all this. If it hadn't been for Fulton's arm and leg constructions, Longhurst would never have targeted him. Now he had to conceal what he suspected from Fulton and he didn't know if he could...or should.

Fulton continued because even though he paused for Edward to continue the explanation, he had not done so. "Yes, I'm sure you are not aware, sir, that some of these black magic cults use blood and sacrifice in their rituals. If you will humour me for a moment."

The inspector raised a hand to protest.

"If you believe that such a creature as this Geneck exists then I am afraid we will have to prevail upon your intellect a tad further. Jemima's blood was taken from her when she was still a maid. This blood, which was forcibly taken, was used in the ritual to raise Geneck. Somehow this has formed a bond between them. She can feel his mind and in turn he can feel hers."

Edward turned suddenly, dropping his hand by his side. "We used her to lure him out of the tunnels. Going down into the sewers proved to be hazardous. He was able to attack us. We thought the park would serve, not realising what would happen."

"And what did happen, Mr Huntington?"

Edward could not meet Fulton's gaze. He turned and walked to the window. "A strange interaction of power," he said under his breath.

"What did you say? I did not quite catch that."

He turned. "Something unexpected."

A soft crackle of the fire was the only sound in the room. Fulton gaped at him and so did the inspector. The policeman stood upright and hurried to the fireplace, with the uniformed man behind.

Milly came in then, looking defiant. Fulton went up to her and showed her to a chair. Edward thought Fulton was being overly deferential. Had Milly won the argument?

Then Edward heard the words, "Huntington! You must come now!"

Edward jerked as if he had been slapped. Had he imagined that? He stared at the empty air around him.

Fulton looked about him and so did the policemen. "What the blazes!" This from the inspector who spun around, looking for the source of the voice. "What sort of game are you playing at?"

Edward glanced about him. "It is not me! I am no stage act."

The voice was familiar. He stood still, hoping it would sound again, though the desperation in the voice frightened him.

He cleared his mind. "Where?" he asked the air in front of him.

"Kent. Priory. Hurry."

Fulton came over to him, grabbed him by the shoulder. "Was that Mr White?"

Edward studied his face while thinking it through. "Yes, I believe it was. He must have found her."

"Yes, yes." Fulton raced to the door. "Jakes. Jakes."

"Yes, sir," the butler's voice echoed from down the hall.

"Get my carriage ready. We are going to Kent. Quick as you can."

"Yes, sir."

Aunt Prudence stood. "We must pack, Milly, dear."

"Oh no you will not," Fulton said in no uncertain terms. "You Aunt Prudence are going to care for Milly. She is feeling poorly."

"Only because you shouted at her."

Fulton blustered. "I did not shout," he shouted.

"Please, aunt," Milly said, placing her hand on the aunt's forearm. "I think we must let them go alone to Kent."

Fulton left the room to see about organising things for the trip.

Aunt Prudence shifted her position. She had polished off her meal as if nothing untoward had been going on around her. "Very well. I will stay with you. I imagine this Geneck is in Kent, too."

"What?" Edward and Coleman said.

She turned and looked at them in turn as if they were simpletons. "It makes sense. Surely your Mr White is afraid of Geneck. If they had the power to rid us of this Geneck they would have before now. It is their moral and ethical duty. It seems to me that they are as powerless as you to stop him."

"You mean..." Fulton said.

Aunt Prudence shifted her gaze to him. "They do not know how to kill him either."

Edward raised his head from staring down at the aunt, feeling queasy. "Yes, and if that is the case and Geneck followed Jemima..."

Coleman faced Edward. "I take it by the look on your face that you concur with Miss Wainwright's deduction?"

"I do," Edward said, swallowing bile. He was going to be sick.

"This is outrageous. So you do know who has Jemima?"

Edward shook his head. "Maybe...I do not know for sure. Mr White...the voice...he says Kent." He was reeling from the casual observation from the aunt that had eluded him. That was why the brotherhood would not assist. They did not know what to do. That left everything up to him. Unless Aunt Prudence knew how to fix it. While she might have excellent powers of deduction, he doubted she knew anything about magic.

Edward went up to the drinks cabinet and found some brandy and shakily poured some into a glass. He took a hasty sip and poured another glass.

He handed a glass of brandy to the detective who was white as a sheet. The young policeman was sitting in the chair by the table with his head between his knees, his notebook and pencil fallen to the rug near his feet. The policeman had been overset by hearing a voice not belonging to anyone in the room and then Aunt Prudence's announcement, which would have unhinged anyone. Edward had almost lost his composure.

Edward did sympathise. Considering the supernatural even on an intellectual level was a bit of a leap: being frightened out of your wits by the unexpected had the capacity to overset one's mind.

He took comfort in the fact that the inspector was able to drink two snifters of brandy in close succession, even while his hands shook.

After a few minutes, the inspector was able to utter a feeble thank you. He stood up and nodded to his young companion. "I shall leave you then. Madam, Mrs Fulton," Coleman said with a bow. The young policeman got up to follow him out, the boy having refused a shot of brandy to steady his nerves. His legs looked a little shaky but his back was straight.

Edward nodded to Fulton, giving the all-clear for him to address the detective. "Continue to scour the sewers and graveyard crypts for the vampire's supporters. They can be out in daylight too and may function close to normal. You will know them by this." He held out the medallion he had taken from a dead minion and placed it in the inspector's unmoving hands. "And most likely by bite marks on their necks." Fulton pointed to points on the neck where he had seen the bites. "They may seem to be bewildered or slow, but that is Geneck's hold on them."

"We will double our efforts. Please finish this business, sirs."

"We will do our upmost. And if you could keep an eye on Aunt Prudence and Mrs Fulton we would be most obliged." Edward shook Coleman's hand. The man was finally growing on him. Not nearly as much a knucklehead as he had first thought.

Coleman inclined his head and left the room.

Fulton squared his shoulders. "We are for Kent."

"But first you should eat. I believe dinner is growing cold," Aunt Prudence said.

Edward considered this. Now he knew where they were headed, he was not as anxious and felt able to eat. "We may as well partake. We could be on the road for a couple of hours or so and the carriage is not ready yet."

CHAPTER 21

Winston glared at Jemima, dark menace in his eyes. Ferdinand quailed. Such a look would have frozen his innards. Winston was the Executioner and it was a role he enjoyed by all accounts. Yet Jemima Hardcastle stood up to him. After all that she had been through.

Benedict sat still, arms folded, eyes hooded. Silence fell over the conclave. He glanced sideways at the speaker and nodded. The speaker lifted the document. "We vow to restore you to your husband once we understand why you were brought here."

"No!" Jemima shouted. "I will not consent to this." She lifted an arm, finger pointed directly at Winston. "He wants to take out my ruby heart to examine it and copy Edward's work." She turned in a circle and glared at them all in turn. Ferdinand was half proud and half intimidated by that glare. "Do you know what that means?"

Benedict leaned forwards, his frown making his dark eyes disappear into the folds of flesh around his eyes. "What does it mean?" he said gruffly. Ferdinand could see he was nearly out of patience.

Jemima turned to face the Revered. "It means he wishes to murder me. He knows full well that my heart is dependent on the machine. He does not care about that. He only wants its secrets. He would rather do that than ask my husband about his work."

Benedict sat back, dark eyes once again visible as they centred on Winston. "Is this true?"

Winston strutted around Jemima. "You would believe this ignorant girl over me? I have no intention of harming her. Although I do intend to learn the mysteries of Huntington's device."

"Huntington's device is my heart," Jemima said. "And I am not ignorant. My father saw to that."

At the mention of her father, there was a murmur among the gathered brothers. Ferdinand's gaze raked the gathered men, wondering who would support the girl. It was heartening to know that Wilbur had some supporters. That they remembered him.

"You know nothing of magic matters," Winston said, standing over her with a sneer on his face.

"I do know a little," Jemima said, seemingly unafraid. "I know that Geneck can find me wherever I am. We have a blood tie."

"Geneck is in London," Winston said, stepping back, some doubt now showing on his features. He looked left and right as if checking if there was anything behind him.

Jemima closed her eyes. "I do not think he is..."

Ferdinand shivered. Murmurs broke out among the members of the conclave. "She is lying," one called out. Ferdinand did not see who spoke and could not identify the voice.

Jemima stood up straight and blinked. "I am not lying. How do you think Geneck captured me in the first place? I was the bait and he took me. Do you think my husband would willingly place me into danger? Of course he did not. He had no choice. The monster is drawn to me. It knows my blood. My blood calls to him."

Winston's face had lost all smugness. He apparently believed Jemima. "He is fixated on you?" The question was a mere whisper and his eyebrows were so high he looked comical instead of fearful. "In what way?"

Jemima narrowed her eyes. "Well, lately he thinks I am his long-lost daughter. Fulton and Edward killed her reincarnation or whatever you call it and now he calls me daughter."

Winston took another step back, mouth dropped open and fingers twitching nervously.

The Revered spoke again. "What is she saying?"

Winston looked to Benedict and back to Jemima. "I...er...think she means that Geneck is coming here."

Ferdinand's heart lurched. That could not be possible. Even as he thought that, he knew it must be true. Did not Geneck send a severed head into Jemima's bedroom at Willow Park? Sussex was not that far from London. Kent was just as near. Ferdinand's eyes darted over the room, looking in dark corners, looking for a sign. They had hoped to pass unnoticed by the beast for he had confounded them. The reluctance to assist Huntington came not from pride but from fear. They did not know what to do, did not know how to kill the beast.

A roar sounded. It made the stained glass windows tinkle in their lead. A thump was felt beneath Ferdinand's feet. "What is that?" he said, knees atremble. He knew. He suspected. He wondered if any of the others knew.

Jemima let out a squeak. "It is him. He is here. He is here."

"Shut up," Winston said, nearly charging her. "You lie. It is a trick."

She turned to face him, fists tight. "Why I would never..."

A scream sounded from the corridor. A human scream locked in terror. A collective gasp filled the room. Benedict's dark eyes were wide now and he sat on the edge of his seat.

Jemima stepped back, hand over her mouth, her eyes large blue orbs of fear.

A thump sounded. The large oak door shuddered. Heads turned towards the door. Another thump and Ferdinand could see the wood jump and the lock rattle. If it was Geneck it would not keep the beast out for long.

Ferdinand let out an inward cry to Huntington. "Huntington! You must come now." Huntington heard him and asked where, so Ferdinand told him.

Another force hit the door and it flew open and smashed against the stone wall. Nothing was there. How could that be? Ferdinand narrowed his gaze, hardly able to hear anything over the loud pumping of his heart and his hastily sucked-in breath.

A collective gasp alerted him that something had happened behind him. Impossibly, his heart beat harder in his chest, making it tight and painful. He turned slowly, fearing what he would see. The beast ready to strike him down, his death written in the beast's eyes. Yet nothing was directly behind him. His gaze travelled further to where Jemima and Winston had stood.

Towering over them was the beast. Ferdinand stepped back instinctively. It was tall, nearly seven feet, thick boned. Almost whole-looking skin now clothed its naked dead form. Green light shone from the dark orbs of its eyes and a matching green glow came from the device implanted in its chest.

Winston made a gesture, a spell, but Geneck swiped at him, extinguishing the spell, and Winston fell to the ground apparently lifeless.

Geneck took a step, gathering Jemima to him, her fragile neck in his raw-boned hand. He loomed over them and let out an inhuman growl. The sound vibrated in Ferdinand's bones. He almost lost control of his bladder, but was able to control his fear. Jemima needed him strong. Needed him alive.

It was quiet for just a moment. Geneck poised there—the conclave caught in a moment of inaction. Ferdinand moved only his eyes, afraid that any movement would trigger the beast to move. Then, in the next breath, screams and shouts erupted and filled the room as the members of the conclave reacted to the beast in their presence. Unbridled fear permeated the room. It was difficult to stand against it. Ferdinand looked into Jemima's frightened eyes, then he dropped his gaze as Geneck kicked something away from him.

Winston's body rolled a short distance, limbs flopping about and landing at odd angles. He was probably dead. Ferdinand considered that death had not been part of the Executioner's plan. Not for himself at least.

Now the threat was everywhere. Screams echoed and Ferdinand tried to ignore them and focus on Jemima, who needed him right now.

Ferdinand stood close to the beast and he had never felt so alone in his life before. This was a great test for him. He was likely going to die but he could not let Jemima die without a fight to save her. If only they had taught Huntington how to transport himself with magic. He would be with them right now.

Jemima shivered in fright. Indeed many of the brothers began jumping from their seats to the floor in their haste to leave. Ferdinand's gaze was riveted to Jemima. The beast used his other hand to rip the ties holding the top of her corset. A pale rose glow emitted around a small metal plate in the centre of her chest. Her ruby heart!

He traced a finger along her breast bone and she shuddered, her limbs jerking. His tongue extended from his mouth, long and wet; he licked almost touching the flesh between her breasts. Jemima let out a sound that made his innards curdle, a moan of such horror he thought she was surely to lose her mind from the horror of it.

Finally, the cowardice of his brethren got to him. "For god's sake," he cried, fists clenched at his sides. "Stand and fight."

A few looked over their shoulders at him. Some hesitated. "Use your magical defences," he urged. "Hurry."

A spell shot out from somewhere near the Revered's door. The taste of it was like that of the speaker, a sizeable talent. It had no effect on Geneck, except to make him roar and change direction.

Saliva flicked, hitting a brother in the face. He wiped at it hastily using his sleeve. It left a red mark and blisters arose. Trust the beast to have acid saliva.

Another mighty spell impacted on Geneck and the beast fell back, forcing Jemima back with him. She passed out from the spell. Geneck staggered, shook his head, and the spell fell away. Jemima was like a rag doll in his hand. That spell had to have been Benedict's. Geneck roared and his glowing green gaze sought out the magicians who were hexing him.

Ferdinand stood still and waited, hoping for a chance to snatch Jemima from Geneck.

Quicker than he anticipated, the beast dropped her and leaped onto the seats, ripping the throat out of one young magician before the lad could even flinch. The young man had fallen in his haste, his robe caught on the edge of a bench.

Ferdinand begged silent pardon when he began weaving the spell. When it impacted, part of the seating stand erupted in splinters, but

Geneck had leaped again, heading it seemed to the Revered and the speaker, who threw magic from the upper doorway. Protected for the most part, they could retreat quickly if needs be into the Revered's inner sanctum. Whether that would be an ultimate safe haven, Ferdinand did not know. He thought there was perhaps a secret way out of the priory from the Revered's rooms.

Ferdinand cast his eyes around, saw he had a chance to run to Jemima. If only the magicians would keep fighting they would divert the beast's attention.

"Jemima!" he hissed urgently in her ear, kneeling by her side. He dared not call out in case he alerted the beast. Her head flopped back. He patted her cheeks, then slapped them. "Come on, Jemima. Wake."

He contemplated a rousing spell. He cast a look around at the noise of benches being shredded and wood and splinters flying. He sheltered Jemima with his body, crouching over her still form. Her skin was pale. The ruby heart, though, still beat and he could see the pulse at her neck. She was alive. Just knocked out by Benedict's spell.

A shrill scream made him look around. The speaker's body dangled from Geneck's fist, human blood covered the beast's torso like an apron. The speaker's head hung by a thread of tendon, his neck having been ripped out. The speaker's feet twitched as the beast chomped down again. Chunks of flesh dropped from his roaring mouth. The bodily remains were thrown and landed across three intact benches, breaking them into pieces. That roar again and the beast was off.

Ferdinand turned back to Jemima, his throat suddenly dry. "Jemima. Get up. We need to run."

Magic was not going to stop the beast. The beast seemed to absorb the spells rather than his skin repelling the magic as might be expected. Ferdinand thought that it was an important observation. One that should be shared with his magical brethren. They had to change what they were doing. No wonder Huntington had not been able to dispatch it. The beast must be increasing in power from the magic. *No. Not possible!*

That thought made him freeze, momentarily. Then, breaking free from that paralysis, Ferdinand began to argue with himself. The beast absorbed it. That did not mean it was growing stronger. Or did it?

Whatever was happening they needed to rethink their approach and develop a concerted effort to defeat the beast. He needed to get his remaining brethren together, consult with them about the problem and mount an attack, combine their strength. If only Huntington could get there to assist them. If only they had reached out to Huntington and helped him learn magic earlier.

Jemima let out a low moan. He stared down at her and then slapped her cheeks harder, leaving pink marks on her skin. "Hurry!"

A scream echoed around the room. Another brother caught. Ferdinand winced as the man was violated by the beast. He looked down at Jemima, eyes fluttering open. Dare he distract the beast for a moment so the brother could escape? He closed his eyes and concentrated. Yes, if he directed fire from there. Another scream interrupted his concentration, but he refocused. A fireball coalesced in the corner of the room, far from where Ferdinand crouched, vulnerable with Jemima. He launched it.

Geneck let the brother go. Tearing the remains of his robe away, the man fled naked through a side door. Geneck was surrounded in flame and Ferdinand's breath hitched. Would it work?

Then Geneck shrugged and the flame dropped from him as he roared out his anger. His gaze raked the room, looking for prey. Ferdinand stayed perfectly still. The glowing green gaze settled on him.

Dear heaven. No!

A scrambling sound grew loud. Another brother not quick enough to escape. Geneck's head jerked in the hapless brother's direction. Geneck leaped. Ferdinand winced as the beast struck.

"Uncle Ferdy?" Jemima said in a quiet voice. Her eyes flickered and she opened them wide, breathing deep and hard as her gaze focused. The sound of the brother been torn apart filled the air. "Oh god," she said. "It is not a dream."

Ferdinand shook his head. The door was so close. "Can you get to your feet?" he asked.

She glanced to the door and nodded. He helped her up by the hand. He could dematerialise but he did not think he could dematerialise her at the same time. Huntington's magical signature was on her and it interfered with his own.

Jemima was up and together they launched themselves at the door. It was a temporary save as Geneck would only come after them. He had come for Jemima after all. The magical brothers were just too tasty to ignore, Ferdinand suspected.

He kept moving, had to. He could not leave Jemima there to be defiled or fed upon by the beast. A worse thought assailed him—of Jemima converted into a beast, reincarnated into Geneck's daughter, with Jemima's soul lost to torment.

With the magic within Jemima and the heart, too, she would be unstoppable. Jemima had magic? Yes. A small talent. Not trained in any way. Unacknowledged by her and everyone who should know these things. There was something else about her, also, something he could not put his finger on. She was healthy but that was not quite it.

Jemima held tight to his hand as they half staggered, half ran to the door. Ferdinand tripped and Jemima pulled him to his feet with an amazing show of strength.

"Thank you," he said.

She shook her head, frowning at him. "If not for you I would be dead."

Their feet slapped against the stone as they ran into the corridor. Beyond was another door, the one that led to the chapel wing. They headed for it. He could see movement there. The remaining brotherhood gathering. Hope soared in his heart. They were going to fight instead of running. United they stood a chance. If Huntington arrived, they might be able to beat this monster. The door began to shut.

They bolted through just before the heavy door slammed shut. Tall and wide, it was made of oak and iron straps and was reinforced with magic. Unfortunately, this main door to the wing had been standing open while the conclave was in session, with only the inner door shut. A custom they would need to revisit in future. If there ever was a future.

They stood beyond the door as the brothers gathered behind it. A sense of relief washed through him. There would be a counter-attack. Jemima wriggled her hand, silently begging for release.

He let go and turned to her. "I'm sorry. I did not want to lose you."

She rubbed her hands together and gave a worried look at the brothers at the door. "What are they doing?"

"They are readying for a counter-attack. Excuse me, I must consult with them. Stay here. I will be back in a moment."

Ferdinand sought out a brother who he thought was sympathetic and intelligent enough to listen to him. Augustus Finch loomed ahead and Ferdinand trotted up. "Brother Augustus! I must speak to you."

Augustus did not move from his position. "Can it wait?" he replied without breaking concentration.

"No. Listen. The creature absorbs our magic I think to use himself. You throw a spell at him, he only grows stronger. You need to think of a different way to attack him. Use a different type of magic."

Augustus frowned and turned to stare at him. "Another type of magic? Are you mad?"

"No, just observant. It is the only way."

Augustus returned to the joint spell, picking up the thread of it as if he had not been interrupted. "I will need to consider this but I will spread the word. Scant as the brotherhood now are. Our losses have been many."

Ferdinand thought of the Revered. He had not seen him die. His secretary had perished but maybe the wily old man had escaped.

Geneck let out a howl. The beast was on the hunt again. A crash sounded. Wood splintered. Glass shattered. Jemima cringed and shared a look with Ferdinand.

A thump against the old oak door sent a few of the brothers stumbling back. They were reinforcing a good strong ward. Ferdinand could almost taste it. A thump sounded again. The brothers who had fallen back surged forwards to push against the door again.

Ferdinand did not like their chances. He began backing away, taking Jemima by the hand. "Come."

Augustus called out to him, his face seamed with strain. "Help us, brother."

Ferdinand sped up, dragging Jemima with him. The door rattled again and looking back, he saw some of the brothers fall to the ground, senseless, their magic spent. Geneck was going to break through.

"Faster," he said to Jemima again. "He is coming."

Jemima sped up but managed to get out between pants. "But he can...go through the windows...Why does he...not?"

Ferdinand glanced over his shoulder. She was right. Geneck did not have to come through that door. "The magic. He must be drawn to the magic."

"We can run but he will come for me in the end. He knows where I am. I cannot escape."

"I will stay with you. Protect you."

Jemima shook her head as he led her down a darkened corridor. "No. You cannot protect me." They slowed down and Ferdinand listened for signs that Geneck was behind them. "Tell me where I can go in the hope that he follows me." She stopped and looked behind them. "Before he kills everyone or turns them into minions."

Ferdinand stopped walking and turned to her. "Minions?"

"Yes, his servants. They do as he wishes."

Ferdinand gaped at her, shocked. "I had not thought of that possibility." He had thought death the ultimate degradation, but to become a mindless servant was worse. Jemima was right—he was only delaying the inevitable.

Looking at her, though, he could not give up. He could not leave her to fight on her own. There was hope of escape until the very end. Many things could happen. And Huntington. He could show up and turn the tide.

"Let us get moving again," he said, taking her hand and turning to continue down the corridor. Out of the gloom, Geneck emerged, barring their way.

Jemima let out a shriek. Ferdinand felt piss dribble down his leg.

Standing erect, Geneck's bloodstained body had runnels of blood running into and out of the seamed flesh. The heart device emitted sickly green light and a barely perceptible buzz tickled Ferdinand's senses. The beast roared at them, but then his head jerked higher and focused behind them. Ferdinand could hardly think, then he remembered the magicians who worked on the door.

Ferdinand swung around and Jemima called out in a shrieking voice. "Beware! The beast is here!" Together they ran to reverse their steps. The sticky thump of Geneck's feet on the floor following only made them run faster. They rounded the corner into the vestibule filled with yellow lamp light.

"He is coming!" Ferdinand yelled.

A few brothers turned and screamed at the looming shape that came after them. The door was abandoned, like ants leaving a nest. Now brothers sought to get through to the other side now Geneck was here on this side. The door was unmagicked and brothers scrambled to pull it open.

Geneck gathered himself for a leap. Ferdinand was out of time.

He tipped Jemima over by putting his knee behind hers. "What?" she said before toppling. Luckily she did not fight him as once on the ground he rolled onto Jemima and kept on rolling calling on his spells and praying that her own inherent magic did not interfere with his own.

They dematerialised. They were in a moment of non-existence and then they found form again, just as cold and wet swallowed them. Sitting up spluttering, he looked around. They had landed in the pond outside. Ducks protested their sudden appearance and Jemima sat up, hands trailing pond slime and marsh fronds.

In the panic, the pond was the only place he had been able to picture and it was fresh in his mind from his walk and he only had enough power to move both of them a short distance. "What did you do?" she asked. "He will kill them now."

Ferdinand shook his head. "They were already doomed. If he wanted them, they were there for the taking and us being there was not going to change that. We would have to witness it."

Jemima grew pale and then crossed her arms. The water was cold. Tears tracked down her cheeks. "They were wrong to take me but I do not think they deserved this end."

"I agree. We must keep moving. Your husband is on his way."

She sniffled. "Really? Poor Edward. He must be out of his mind with worry."

"Rightly so. You are precious to him."

"It is not just me. All these innocent people dying. It eats at him. He blames himself, you see."

It was evening and the light was fading. They best get moving. He made a small glow in the palm of his hand. "Come out of there. We are safe for the moment." Geneck's howls could be heard from the grounds. Screams, too, soul-curdling screams. Ferdinand had to shut it out. Geneck sounded rabid and very angry. Each screech sent chills up Ferdinand's spine.

She took his hand. "There is no use trying to sugar coat the situation. I am not safe while he lives. It is not just my mortal form that is in jeopardy, but my very soul."

He patted her hand. "Now, now, do not let hysteria take you."

She tugged her hand back. "You do not understand. I am doomed unless you can stop him. He wants to make me his daughter. Do you know what he did to his daughter? Do you?"

Ferdinand did not have to imagine. He had read the reports.

"And then he will make me like him. A vampire. Then I will start killing." She slapped her chest. "With this ruby heart, I will keep on killing just like him until someone, somewhere finds a way to stop me and this thing in my chest. This could be the end of the world as we know it."

Ferdinand stood up straight and his mouth dropped open. She was perfectly right and that just made the situation worse. A howl filled the darkness. Was Geneck now in the grounds?

Her composure crumbled and she began to cry, helpless angry tears. Ferdinand reached for her and drew her into his embrace. If what she said was true, she might well be doomed.

A long eerie scream caused him to involuntarily shudder and he knew that Geneck was on the hunt.

CHAPTER 22

Edward and Fulton were on the road within half an hour, lumbering up to Kent in the old coach on the way to Kent. It was slow going as there was so much traffic: carriages, Hansom cabs, hackney coaches, carts full of produce and pedestrians. "So where in Kent do we travel?" Fulton leaned over to ask. "It is a pity we missed the train as it would have been faster."

"Perhaps, Fulton. But the carriage gives us a bit of leeway. White said a priory. I have looked up the directory and it is here." He pointed to a spot near Maidstone.

Fulton leaned out the window and yelled to the coachman. "Make for Maidstone. Hurry!"

Edward had been staring out at the houses, the gaslights illumining the streets. It would not be long before the gaslights faded to give way to rural scenes lit only by the light of a gibbous moon. "I hope we are there in time." Edward tried to keep up his spirits. "His request did seem very urgent."

"It must have been for him to call out like that."

"Perhaps he was excited by finding Jemima."

Fulton rubbed his hand over his head and grimaced. "It could be something worse. This will not do. You will have to try another method to find out what is going on."

Edward frowned. "What other method?"

The carriage lurched and Edward grabbed onto the handhold. Jemima was right. This carriage was abominable.

"Obviously White was able to reach out to you and send his voice. They have also disappeared on occasion." He clicked his fingers, making a snap sound. "Can you not use your magic to contact him?"

Edward sat back suddenly, clutching onto the hand strap to stop him lurching to the side. "I have not tried it, but it makes sense, as much as any of this makes sense. Give me some time and quiet if you can."

Edward tried to shut out the various noises in the carriage. The rattle of the wheels on the dry road, the beat of the horses' hooves and the call of the driver as he cracked his whip. These Edward acknowledged and pushed back. He thought of Mr White, Uncle Ferdy as Jemima had acknowledged him. "Ferdy?" He called out with his mind. Not that he expected a response.

He tried again, assembling the image of the man in his mind, then he thrust his consciousness into it, the part of him that resonated with magic.

He considered what Ferdy stood for. Then it came to him. "Ferdinand?" he said aloud, but also using his mind, his magic to push the word out. There was no verbal response, yet there was something. Fear. Tremendous fear and urgency and the picture of Jemima as he had last seen her, wearing her leather corset. "Jemima!"

He snapped open his eyes to find Fulton staring at him. One eyebrow lifted. "I cannot be certain. I detected something but it could be wishful thinking on my part." Yet as he sat there being rocked by the carriage, that feeling of whimsy died away. If that was Ferdinand, then he had not seen Jemima in the corset, not in the visits to the house, so he must be seeing her now. He tried to recall the detail of Jemima's face. She was scared out of her wits.

"How long before we reach Kent?" he asked Fulton.

"Not for two hours at least with this confounded traffic."

"I cannot wait that long," Edward stated in a no-nonsense tone.

"What choice do you have?" Fulton's response was worried.

"I must have some choice. I am going to find out." He turned to face Fulton. "Now, if I suddenly disappear do not be alarmed as it is my intention to will myself to this place."

"Will yourself. What place? This priory that you guessed at?" Fulton could not keep the incredulity from his expression.

Edward shook his head. "Where would a brotherhood of magicians hide in Kent?"

Fulton gaped at him and gave a shrug. "I have no idea. You know of this place. I am not well acquainted with Kent. But I do know there is a large number of castles and places like that in the county."

"The one that I mentioned is quite famous and by the river. I have a feeling that is the place. If I do succeed, head for it."

Fulton squeezed Edward's forearm. "What am I supposed to do if you take yourself off to this priory like a puff of smoke? You will have no protection."

Edward grinned. "I have learned a lot from you, old chap. Besides, it is full of these magical brothers. What more help do I require?"

"They are not your friends. I am afraid for you. If they are in trouble it is probably Geneck." He screwed up his eyebrows as he reconsidered this. "Or Jemima, come to think of it. She would put any right-thinking mind quite out of their senses."

"That is my wife you are talking about."

"I know."

Edward thumped Fulton lightly on the arm. "When we are through with this terrible episode I am going to tell Jemima what you said."

Fulton chuckled. "Edward, I hope you do. Please, please be careful."

Edward rolled his eyes. "I have not gone anywhere yet."

"Hurry up then. The suspense is killing me."

"I will send you word if it is not the priory."

"I count on it."

Edward closed his eyes and tried to follow a trail.

THE SCREAMS AND SHRIEKS OF HORROR AND PAIN ECHOED AROUND the priory grounds. Ferdinand stayed close to Jemima, his desperation raging. He had no idea if he could defend the girl if the beast chose to strike and he could not bear to hear his fellow brothers slaughtered. Someone needed to rally them, organise them, amalgamate their power. Where was the Revered? Had he been the first to die? His memory flashed to the scene in the hall. The Revered had been there and then gone. Ferdinand thought he might have sought safety but now he was not so sure. Surely their leader would fight to save the brotherhood.

A long, piercing wail and Ferdinand shuddered. This would not do. They needed help. He sent a desperate call to Huntington. Then the large stained glass window smashed in the refectory and made his steps falter. He could not see how, but sensed the life of a fellow brother extinguish. His nerves were so on edge. It had been his intention to take refuge by the river in the dovecote but now he hesitated, looking between the priory and the river.

"Uncle?" Jemima's voice no longer quavered. "Leave me here. Go help them. I cannot bear to hear the screams."

He turned to her, reached out and squeezed her hand before shaking his head. "I cannot leave you here undefended. I could not forgive myself if anything happened."

"But if you do not leave me you will not be able stop him. He is growing stronger the more he feeds. Can you not feel it? He is sucking in their magic as well as their lives."

"Oh," he said, realising that was what he had been feeling. The magic being sucked out of his fellows. He faced her, still holding her hand. "But you said yourself that he will come for you."

"He will. I have no choice in that. I could stay here and hope that I can distract him. Or I could go with you now and have him take you before my eyes and every last one of you. Then he will be so powerful there will be no stopping him and I will suffer a fate worse than death. Best you go to help your friends while you still can."

Ferdinand looked at her shadowed silhouette and then back to the dark, towering mass of the priory's main building. "You make a well-reasoned point."

"I am full of surprises. Besides I am not defenceless."

Ferdinand gaped at her, at the soft rose-coloured glow on the white skin of her face. Her eyes were dark hollows and her hair a tangle falling to her shoulders. That is what he had been missing. She was strong. Physically strong. It was something in Huntington's invention. Fulton had it, too. He had thought it was deliberate but maybe it was an accident, a side effect. He could not imagine Huntington deliberately making his wife into a fighting machine. It would make conjugal relations a bit too interesting. It set his mind at rest. She was right. His brothers were better served with him trying to help them. He had done his best for Jemima. "Very well, then. God keep you from harm, child." He kissed her forehead. "Keep moving. Keep him confused."

"I will," she said as she embraced him.

Ferdinand left her there, not far from the pond, and ran back to the priory building. Ducks squawked, disturbed by the rush of his feet and the flutter of his robes. A swan honked at him and tried to peck.

He headed for the library, which adjoined the dormitory buildings via a long corridor. It was there he hoped to find some alive among his fellows that would assist in making a stand against the creature. He increased his pace when he heard the creature growling not far away, its voice carrying through the shattered remains of the windows.

Furniture smashed. Glass broke. Voices choked off and the dull thump of bodies hitting walls and floors made his footsteps falter.

Lights flickered in the hallway as he ran along, sending a mental summons to meet in the library. Some responses were tinged with fear, others anger. There were some brothers remaining. That was a relief. He was not totally alone.

"Pio?" Ferdinand whispered when he entered the library, calling for the librarian. A small bald man peeped up from under the desk. "Ferdinand? What is happening?"

"A vicious vampire is loose. Who else is here with you?" At the sound of the door opening, two other brothers entered. The elderly Foster Smythe and the middle-aged Harry Pilkington.

"Ah good. Four is not a great number but sufficient." Pio slid his eyes to the left. Ferdinand saw Godfrey Guest and Rene D'Larvve come out from behind a bookcase.

"Come forwards."

The frightened men stumbled to meet him. They were not the cream of the brotherhood. Old, not very talented, Godfrey had a bad leg, Foster a tic. However, they were better than nothing at all. Without the great leader, there was no one to organise a defence. "Come, come," he encouraged them, waving at them encouragingly. When they were close he leaned in. "Now this is what I propose."

CHAPTER 23

Jemima squatted in the bird hide that was nestled in the bulrushes by the pond. She knew it provided little real safety but found the close walls and the low roof comforting. Also, she could peer out over the pond to the building beyond. Not that she could see anything. A few windows of the building were suffused with a golden glow. The occasional scream from some wretch who was being fed upon and howl of the beast set her shivering in her boots. "Really, Jemima. Not a good showing at all. Quaking in your boots like some girl. You are better than that. You can think of something...just do it quickly."

If she had been in a better frame of mind, she might have asked herself if she was out of her mind talking to herself in the grounds of a priory. Considering what she had been through, she thought all eccentricities were justified.

She turned and looked outside the doorway. She could make out the path through the bulrushes. Her gaze flowed over the woods. *A stake is what you need. Something with which to strike, thrust or hit.* She ground her teeth as she imagined herself wielding a weapon. She had trained for it with Fulton and Edward. Edward had even trained which surprised her. It was not gentlemanly to go around killing people with a stake. It certainly was not something a gentlewoman should do.

"Pah!" she scoffed to the damp night air. There was no point in being ladylike. She was not going to save herself by offering Geneck a well-poured cup of tea and a cucumber sandwich. Although, she paused, it might be a good distraction.

Ah well, you will probably perish, but you will go down fighting. She nodded at the thought and edged around to climb down and out of the little hide. Enough of feeling safe.

Finding an appropriate piece of wood proved to be time-consuming in the dark, particularly with the sounds echoing around the grounds of the priory. It struck her as odd that Geneck had not come for her straight away. Then again, he could find her when he liked and he had all that prey so close at hand. She wondered if magicians' blood tasted better than normal people's. The magic he was ingesting—would that make him too powerful for Edward to destroy? Edward was already struggling to find a way. She prayed that he was whole and not too worried about her. Uncle Ferdy said he was on his way. Well, that was brilliant. What was taking him so long?"

⚜

"You're still here," Fulton observed, when Edward opened his eyes.

Edward growled low in his throat. "Interesting observation, friend. Perhaps you can think of a way."

Fulton rubbed a hand over his scalp. "Me?" He shrugged. "I have no idea what you are trying to do, but it looks dammed annoying. All that creasing of brow and grinding of teeth."

Wrath filled Edward. "That is not helpful." He shooed Fulton back. "Look away if I bother you."

Fulton sat back, his body rocking in time to the movement of the carriage. "If such a thing were possible, even within the realms of possibility, I cannot for the life of me understand why you did not whisk yourself away to Jemima's side the minute she went missing."

Edward's anger grew. How dare Fulton blame him, find fault with

246

him. "You take that...wait." A kernel of an idea formed. He wagged his finger at Fulton and then rested it against his chin. "I think you may have something."

"What?" Fulton's face was full of frown.

Edward smiled a little, his heart warming with the idea. He leaned in closer so Fulton could hear him over the sound of the horses and carriage. "Well, as you say, if it were possible, then I would have done it. But I have not been thinking with my heart, with the part of me that really counts." He slapped his chest. "In other words, my will, my soul, my heart. I have been trying to use my intellect." He tapped the side of his head. "Therein lies the issue. I am connected to Jemima by love, not intellect."

Fulton coughed lightly, eyes widening in expectation. "And?"

"I am not certain yet. It is an idea."

"Well, do not let me keep you."

Edward sat back. "Oh do shut up and give me leave to experiment in peace."

Fulton spread his hands as if inviting him to continue.

Closing his eyes, Edward focused inwardly to where his passion dwelled. He loved his experiments and he loved Jemima. He focused on her, on what he felt for her. The feeling of loss when he had looked down at her still form and how he felt when she came to life, when she held him, demanded that he marry her. The joy of making love to her. Yes, that was it. He followed along the passion, brought in that part of him that he used in his experiments to ignite the stone, to throw spells. He thought of transporting himself, of the little information he had gleaned from White, a certain movement of the hand, a movement in the mind. Something changed. He gasped as cold flame engulfed him. His yell was smothered by flame. Then he was ready to throw up the meal he had eaten as the world altered around him.

"Huntington!"

After much yelling and arguing, Ferdinand got the group of magicians co-operating and out of the library. The arguments were long. They considered themselves safe surrounded by books, as if those weighty tomes were a kind of shield. They did not like it when he explained what was happening to the rest of the brotherhood while they quaked in their sandalled feet.

In the long corridor that connected the library to the dormitory they could hear Geneck ahead of them, smashing his way through the dormitory, rooting out the tasty morsels of men who hid there. Ferdinand knew he faced his own death. Luck had been with him so far. The thought of Huntington provided some hope, but where was the man? Not there. Not helping.

Ferdinand shut his eyes and tried to use his magical senses. His brothers did the same. "Can you feel it?" he asked.

Rene spoke from behind. "It is a magical force—a large one, dynamic."

Godfrey screwed up his face. "It is the monster. It is as you say. He is devouring their magic as well as their souls."

Ferdinand's heart lurched at the confirmation of his own thoughts and feelings. What would Geneck become when he had taken all the magic? Besides unstoppable? Ferdinand could not imagine. Pio, the librarian might know but as he was a quivering, non-speaking member of this group, cowering at the back there was no point in asking. If they survived then later they could discuss it.

If they survived.

Another long drawn-out scream reached them. It echoed long around the corridor. They could all sense the creature now as he appeared to emanate power like a magician wielding powerful spells. Ferdinand wondered at this. How could the foul beast be absorbing magic? The history of the beast did not mention it and his original rampage had been well documented. Vampires have their own dark magic—able to spell people, raise more vampires and so on. But this was different and transgressive. They would have to be careful.

The tall doors crashed open, unhinging one. Geneck stood there slavering. His flesh was fissured as if health and life had been sucked from it. Ferdinand took note of this. His appearance was declining but his power was increasing. Was the power itself harming him?

The light from his mechanical heart beamed strongly, perceptible more so than previously. His eyes were beacons illuminating the air around him a vivid sick green. Ferdinand shook his head, trying to control his fear, his visceral reaction. Giving into despair was not going to help them. He had to remain strong. "Concentrate, old fellow," he said under his breath.

Geneck shrieked that bone-numbing shriek. Ferdinand detected a tremor running through Brother Godfrey next to him and movement behind. "Keep calm. Keep to the plan," he advised his fellows.

Geneck leaped. They divided as he landed, keeping out of the way, except for Pio, who was snatched up in those clawed hands, his neck breaking under Geneck's jaws.

"Quick, form up," Ferdinand commanded, trying not to see the light die in Pio's face. He never would get an answer to the question he wanted to ask. The sound of slurping and bones crunching made Ferdinand's stomach roil. "Now!"

They began the incantation. Ferdinand noticed something—a wall of violet growing around the beast. They had to be careful to envelop the space so he could not leap free. Unfortunately, Geneck noticed it too. He dropped Pio's limp corpse and threw himself at the barrier. Power began to draw away, like he was a magnet. In less than a minute he was able to bend it, pushing a clawed finger through, not quite breaking out.

Ferdinand saw the danger. "Change it! Make it neutral by reversing the flow. He can tap into it. Draw it like a sponge. Make it a mosaic."

The tempo of the spell changed, the violet sheen turned crimson. Geneck threw himself again. This time he rebounded. No more power was leached away.

That was it. "Change it, pattern it."

The crimson became like a waffle, green and pink inside a dark red square. Then those shapes changed to circles. "Randomise it."

The shapes changed in structure and in colour. Ferdinand could not see a pattern. The snarl of the beast reached them. He picked up Pio's head and threw it at them. Godfrey cried out, but maintained his flow of magic.

"What now?" called Brother Rene. "We cannot hold him all night."

"Hold steady. Help is coming." He sent out his mind, desperation making his reach stronger than he believed possible. *Huntington. Come quickly. We cannot contain him long.*

He detected something, like a lock turning. He called out as something grabbed him, something so cold it burned. He yelled gutturally, as if all his force was wrenched from him. His part of the spell began to falter. Shoring it up quickly, he glanced around him. Had he just connected with Huntington?

Geneck's rage was boundless. He threw himself against the barrier. When that did not work, he menaced individual brothers. The barrier protected them but his visage was awful. Mouth opening wide to show his sharp fangs, then opening impossibly wider with the crack of bone as his jaws disconnected like some exotic snake. He waved his blood-stained penis at them, then let his tongue roll out for them to see.

Ferdinand squinted, trying to get a better view of Huntington's contraption. In the back of his mind was the thought that as long as they held him, Jemima was safe. Could they hold him to sunrise? What would happen if it did? Was it enough to vanquish the beast?

As Ferdinand assessed Geneck, the beast continued to rage against his captors, and he doubted they could last till dawn. Something was vibrant within the beast. Using his magic senses, he thought it centred on Huntington's heart and the emerald spinning within, energy barely contained within it. It was ripe with magic, more magic than Ferdinand have ever seen in one place.

CHAPTER 24

The crack of a branch had Jemima swinging around, brandishing her stake, which she had found by the edge of the pond. Someone had been using it to dig holes in the soft earth as it had a nice pointy end. It was too dark to see.

Nothing was there. She was jumping at shadows. She heard the sound again.

"Uncle?" she called out, certain that Geneck would not be so shy as to creep around. He was likely to come raging out of the dark at her.

Another footstep to her right.

With a harsh intake of breath, she pivoted in that direction. "Uncle?" She waited a beat, frowning. "Hello?"

Jemima's breathing sounded noisy to her ears. The whir of her heart machine made it difficult to pick out the sounds in the night-shrouded garden. There was someone there, she was sure. The evil Winston was dead. It confused her that this person did not identify themselves. Surely with all that was going on in the priory all should work together. Another creak sounded, like the squeak of leather in a shoe. The situation made her think of that dark cell where that magician Winston had kept her. It was that kind of feeling of being observed by something unsavoury.

"Jemima!" Edward's voice echoed in the distance. Her head turned in that direction. Too far away to be Edward who was watching her. She shifted her grip on the stake, tempted to ferret out whoever it was that silently stalked her.

Another desperate call from Edward. "Here! Coming!" she called and tucked the stake into her belt. As if the moon had slid behind a cloud she had to feel her way carefully along the path and follow the direction of his voice rather than sprint. She wanted so much to be with him, hold him. But twisting an ankle in a rabbit hole or on a rock would not do. Damp branches smeared her face with dew and sharp twigs scratched her face and tangled in her hair as she made her way towards her husband. "Edward," she called again tentatively to be certain of the direction. She was not even sure he had heard her. There was silence. Had he gone away already?

Soon the flickering lights from the windows provided more illumination. She looked behind and was certain that whoever had been there was not following. The bushes remained still, no tell-tale waving indicating that someone was moving behind her.

Coming further out into the open, but still within the shelter of trees, she tried to summon her husband again. "Edward." Her voice rang out.

"Jemima? Where are you?"

She sighed with relief, not realising how tense she was just trying to make contact with him. "I am here." She thought about where his voice came from.

His voice came out of the darkness. "I think to your right, further down the path."

With better light, she was able to quicken her steps, her boots clicking on the stone path. She passed under a huge oak, her hand trailing on the thick trunk "Edward?"

The branches rustled above. Her head shot up. Something was in the tree. A shadow moved. She sucked in a breath thinking it was Geneck, but then realised it was not when there was a very human groan and some cursing. Edward.

"What on earth are you doing up there?" She looked up at him, trying to move closer to the trunk but not getting very far as the roots were in the way.

He hung upside down and she saw his face. His hair was ruffled and there were leaves hanging from his ears. "Jemima? Thank god you are alive." He pulled himself upright. "Now if only you could help me get down. I appear to be snagged on a branch."

Jemima pulled in her chin, slightly bewildered. Obviously, her husband was not a tree climber. That did, however, beg the question of why he was in the tree. A growl from the priory building echoed across the grounds. Now was not the time to be asking questions.

Lucky for Edward she was a tree climber from way back and as she was dressed in pants instead of a silly skirt, she was in a position to assist. She placed her stake against the trunk and felt along for a nodule, something for her to gain a foothold on. Slapping the tree when she found it, she stepped back and leaped, her foot finding purchase. With her hands outstretched, she was able to find the first branch and pull herself up. She progressed past two thicker limbs, circling the trunk. Edward was higher still. With some light coming from the windows, she could see his dark shape looming above her. He was caught up around the rear of the tree on one of the flimsier branches. Quite high up, she was not sure it would end well if he fell out. How he had managed to flip himself down to see her, she did not know. He could have broken his head or something and that would have landed them all in a right pickle.

Working her way up, she grunted with effort, grateful she was still wearing the leather clothes Milly had made. Given all the excitement she had been experiencing she was thinking better of needlework. There was a good reason for it after all, besides whiling away the hours and trying to outshine all other women present. That smacked of bitterness and she put that thought aside. The sound of fabric ripping made her stop. "Edward?"

"It is fine, really." Another rip.

"For god's sake hold on and stop moving. You will fall." Pressing her lips together in effort, she reached up and managed to get her fingers around the top of the next branch. "I am getting closer. Hold on." He was close now. She had to edge out onto the branch. It bent slightly with her weight.

He caught sight of her. "Damn it, Jemima. I was meant to rescue you."

Jemima was two steps onto the branch and was not enjoying the sensation of the bough bending. The words to a lullaby came to her... *when they bough breaks the cradle will fall*..."Don't get tetchy with me," she exclaimed. "Whatever took you so long?"

"I did not know you were here."

She nodded and withheld the "typical" comment that came straight to her lips. She bit down. Then easing out a breath she said by way of boosting his spirits at having to be rescued by her, "There is still plenty of rescuing to do. Geneck is still in the priory. I believe there are many dead magicians littering the halls."

"Dear heaven," he wailed. "I am too late."

Edward and his damned guilt. She wanted to strangle it out of him. However, that would not be very ladylike and would possibly not be a suitable thing to do to one's spouse. "I believe there are some alive in need of rescue. All is not lost. And then there is me."

She could not quite make out the curse that he muttered to the night air. "Hold on. Nearly there."

The light was not good. She had to stand on tip toes to de-snag him from the outer branches. His twisting and turning had only made it worse. The hem of his coat was easy to unhook. He was only half in that. The elbow of his shirt took some work as it was firmly ensnared by several branches. She just ripped the fabric of his shirt. "Better?" she asked.

Edward was cursing. "Of all the damn, stupid, imbecile, idiot, godforsaken..."

"Dearest, you will find you are disentangled now from this end. Can you work the rest of yourself free?" Jemima started to edge back along the bough for she thought it would not stand both their weights and Edward needed to step onto it to dismount from his perch.

A grunt. He moved his arm. The branches *shushed* a bit as he tugged, apparently to free his foot.

His movements were very vigorous and angry. "Do not forget to hold on," she said, grabbing a safe hold of the main trunk.

She saw his feet reach the bough she had been on a few seconds before.

"Whaaaat?" He waved his arms and with a look of consternation, he fell. There was an *oomph, blah, grunt* before Edward was able to arrest his fall. Jemima scrambled down to the next level, lucky not have been taken down when Edward fell.

For a very clever man he had no idea about tree climbing. Carefully, she picked her way down the tree, sliding the last bit with her legs around the trunk until her rear reached the lower branch. She looked beneath her. "Edward?" She was certain he had not landed on the ground, but he was no longer in the tree.

She lifted her leg off the branch and got ready to make the final descent. She lowered her foot, feeling for her foothold. Her ankle was grasped. "Edward?"

"Drop!" a voice ordered.

Jemima pushed away, dropping down. Edward's arms caught her around the thighs. He let her glide down him, turning her until she was face to face with him. "Oh Edward. It is—"

She did not get a chance to finish her sentence as Edward's mouth came down as he proceeded to kiss her soundly.

The frustrated screech of Geneck from within the priory broke them apart. "Geneck!" Edward exclaimed as if coming to himself. "Stay here. Stay safe," he said with a pat on her rear and then bolted off, the white of his linen shirt showing in the dark of night. Looking down, she saw the coat he had been wearing discarded. It had leaves coming out of the pocket.

She put her hands on her hips and shook her head. "I have just rescued you and you tell me to stay put?" She let out a breath. "Men."

Deciding there was no point staying outside in the dark, she sped off, hot on the heels of her husband.

EDWARD FOCUSED ON THE NOISE AS HE ENTERED A LONG CORRIDOR. Turning right he saw the group of men with a coruscating crimson wall in front of them. He could feel the power emanating from it. They were magicians then. More of the brotherhood whom he had never met.

Part of him reeled with what he could sense. It was as if travelling as he had through the ether (he could think of no other name for it) had opened up all his senses, as if some great connection between his heart, soul and mind had exploded into being. He could feel the others' magic as if it was his own.

The crimson wall shuddered and trace lines of weakness began to fray the edges of the shield. The magicians refocused and the barrier was restored. Edward studied the shield of magic and noticed that it was less strong than previously. The magicians were weakening. That drew his attention back to the moment. He narrowed his eyes, seeing through the wall of power. It was Geneck on the other side.

Even through the magical barrier, he could feel Geneck's life force. It pulsed like a throbbing headache behind his eyes and the beast's power had grown so vast he could not get the measure of it. What had been happening here? How had Geneck got so powerful, so fully loaded with magic? It was more than the magic he had drawn from the gem fuelling Fulton's devices. Edward had thought that had been an accident, a clash of devices, but if it was not then...then Geneck was drawing power from the magicians. "Dear heaven," he exclaimed as the ramifications came tumbling through his mind. Geneck would be unstoppable.

The barrier held but the brothers were weakening fast. He sought out Ferdinand. The mind that had called to him in such desperation. Circling the group of men, he found the brother. Sweat poured off the older man's face; his pale eyes were wide and his jaw clenched as his lips quivered a chant between them. Edward checked the nearest brother and he was the same. Focused and chanting.

Edward touched Ferdinand's shoulder. "Ferdinand? It is Edward Huntington. What can I do?"

Ferdinand continued on as before. After a minute his voice roared inside Edward's head. "Cannot defeat him only contain him. He draws our power. You cannot fight him with power. He takes it and it makes him stronger. Be warned."

"But how do we fight?" Edward responded.

Ferdinand's presence slid away. Edward walked up and down around the brothers trying to figure out what to do. He checked his watch but it had stopped at 1.30. He tried to estimate how much time to sunrise. Then at least the beast would need to seek shelter. He studied the place, the priory and realised there were plenty of spaces for the beast to hide in the dark. Then come nightfall he would be free to roam and destroy.

He put his hand back on Ferdinand's shoulder. "Can you keep him contained until sunrise? The sun will weaken him." It was a paltry option, he knew. It did not address the real issue. What to do with the beast.

"Do. Not. Know."

Behind him, Edward heard footsteps and turned and saw Jemima. He walked swiftly in her direction, body tight with tension and anger filling his gut. "I told you to stay. It is too dangerous here."

Her bright blue eyes were defiant, her pale skin a glow, with pink blushing her cheekbones. "It is just as dangerous out there as it is in here."

He frowned at her. In response, she smiled, eyes twinkling. Edward wanted to kiss her and smack her at the same time. Had she no idea of the danger? Had she no sense of decorum?

Geneck threw himself at the barrier again, this time almost breaking through.

Jemima gasped with her hand over her mouth, her eyes widening. "Is that all that is left of the brotherhood?"

"I do not know," Edward said. "I could add my power, but that barrier is not going to stop the beast."

"What will stop it, then?" she asked.

Edward stared at Geneck fighting to break through. "I have not thought of a way yet. Fulton trying to rip out the heart device did not work." He turned to face her. "He nearly died for the touch set up a connection which drained Fulton's device."

Jemima touched her chest, her fingers splayed over her heart device. "Drained it?"

Edward drew her close. "Yes, drained it." He rubbed her back. "What did you mean it was dangerous out there? What has been going on?"

"I was abducted by this evil-looking brother who wanted to know about your device. He was going to take it out of me and pull it apart. He did not care if I died in the process." She stood back and indicated with a jerk of her head to the gardens. "Just now someone was following me. The evil guy is dead but I think he had an accomplice. They might still be after your secrets, even with Geneck peddling death at their door."

Conflicted feelings came over Edward. That someone would hurt Jemima to steal his secrets. He would be willing to share with the brotherhood if he felt their motives were good and they only had to ask. A sudden anger flared up within him. They had taken her and were prepared to kill her. Had they no respect for life? He watched the brothers fighting. Did they deserve his help?

Jemima reached out and squeezed his forearm and then stepped closer, removing a leaf from his hair. "Do not dwell on it. Geneck's arrival is more than punishment enough." She closed her eyes, steadying her breath. "You can imagine the carnage. They did not consider his link to me. Did not think of the risk to them."

He nodded, understanding and grateful that she understood something of what he was feeling. He took her hand and squeezed it. "Keep close to me. Do what I say."

Jemima nodded, a timid smile creating a dimple in her left cheek. Edward returned to the circle of brothers and found Ferdinand again and mind-spoke to him. "How can I help you?"

"Give power. Small amount," Ferdinand said.

"How?" Edward said, frowning at the barrier and trying to make sense of the interconnected threads of magic. He had never worked in concert with another magician before.

"See how we feed the barrier? Give some to all. It will help. Touch us one by one and share."

Edward was concerned about the suggestion of touching a

magician for there was a risk of breaking their thread. Edward studied the barrier to determine how they were channelling their power into it. He thought he saw how it was done, looping around and then feeding back through each magician and out again. He could feed a little in here and there without disturbing the balance. He returned to Ferdinand to let him know what he was going to do.

He touched him on the shoulder. "It is Huntington. I can give you all strength to keep going. We need to keep him contained until dawn."

Ferdinand groaned through his clenched jaw. Edward closed his eyes to better sense the other magician's power. When he located it, he pushed some of his own in. He stood back and could see that his solution worked.

Before moving to the next magician, he touched Ferdinand's shoulder. "Better?"

"Don't...do not continue...I have second thoughts."

Edward stood stock still. "Second thoughts?"

Ferdinand sweated. "Yes. I realise you need all your strength to fight the beast. We cannot hold him much longer. My brothers cannot stand for so long. It will kill them before the beast does. He is very powerful and his power is increasing. Do not expend your might this way."

"But I cannot defeat him." Even his mind voice was full of despair.

Ferdinand shuddered and screwed up his face as if the effort of mind speaking was difficult. "You...are...the...only...one...who...can."

Edward dropped his arm and gaped, his stunned gaze travelling from Ferdinand to the other magicians and to the pulsing crimson barrier. There he could see it was beginning to falter and fade. All the brothers were sweating profusely and he could see the tremors in their limbs. And as he watched one fell to the ground.

The barrier faltered. Geneck's hand came through, claws grabbing at air. Then the barrier closed but it would not be long until it folded completely.

He did not have much time to find a way to defeat the beast once it broke through. All these lives depended on him. If he did not find a means they would be ripped apart in front of him. And Jemima? Geneck wanted her.

Edward stepped back, putting distance between him and the brothers.

Jemima came up to him, touched his elbow lightly. "What is it?"

He turned to her, looking down into her eyes, afraid of speaking the inevitable.

Her blue gaze stared up at him with such trust, some admiration. He glanced back at Ferdinand. "They cannot hold him much longer. Not until dawn where he must flee the light. I must...I must fight him."

Jemima's expression changed. Her brows drew down, her lips grew firm and her posture straightened. "How will you fight him?"

"I do not know...yet."

❦

JEMIMA WAS DONE WITH FEAR. SHE WAS IN SOME PLACE MENTALLY that was beyond terror. She had had enough. When Edward said he did not know how to stop the beast, all hope died. Just in that one moment. There was no point in depressing Edward's spirits with her negativity. He had sufficient already.

She had trusted that he would find a way. Or it was not meant to be. He had saved her life, married her and she had been happy with that life. In that place beyond fear, there was no emotion, just fierce thought. She had to think of a way to save herself. She had to be willing to go beyond what she thought possible.

Glancing at Geneck, she knew she would rather die than become his creature. She had to be content with what she had had. She had to die. If Geneck got to her it would not end in oblivion. She would not rest. No. Geneck would take her soul and warp it, replacing it with a semblance of his daughter. He would use her body too and make her kill people. He would pollute Jemima like sewage pollutes a river.

She stood there gazing at Geneck, feeling the awful sense of him oozing into her mind. He was calling to her, begging her to come to him. It was relentless.

"Jemima come away," Edward said.

Jemima rubbed her arms. "Why? It makes no difference where I stand. He can reach me here or there with his mind."

Edward frowned and clenched his fist. What was the point of his futile anger? It was not going to help. "When he breaks through," she said, "he will take me. He will use my body, fill it with the foul essence of his daughter. I will have no will. I will witness it all. If you cannot stop him I am doomed."

"No. Jemima!" Edward's voice was pleading. He did not want to hear the truth.

Walking up to him, she dropped her arms that crossed her chest. "Better to rip this contraption from my body now than let me live another minute." She pointed to it even though he knew what she was referring to.

"No," Edward said with a sob. "No. You must hold on to hope."

"Swear to me that you will do it. If you cannot stop him. Swear you will rip this device from me."

"No!"

"Yes...Please, Edward," she said as she stepped up to him and gazed into his beloved face. "Please...If you love me you will do it."

Tears tracked down his cheeks as he shook his head. "I cannot destroy you."

She could not bear to look upon Edward's shocked and devastated face. "Think of something then. Use me to lure him where you can kill him. If you will not take this out of me, then make me useless to him, make this ruby heart useless to me."

※

Dawn was at least an hour away. During the hours, another brother had fallen. Despite Ferdinand's advice, Edward had shared his magic with the men and the barrier still held, although it was weakened and the remaining five brothers were almost spent. Edward sat on the stone floor, back resting against the wall. He looked to the ceiling, going over in his head what he must do but nothing he thought about made any sense. A soft murmur sounded nearby—Jemima curled up asleep in the corner. He looked at her sweet face, wondering how she could sleep through all that was going on around her. Then he recollected she had probably not had much rest at all. The soft glow of the ruby heart bathed the lower half of her face. He could not regret that machine and the gem that powered it, not like he regretted the one in Geneck's body.

The only reason the barrier was still working was that Geneck had stopped trying to get through. The beast waited.

Edward was deep in thought. A smash against the barrier and Edward jumped. Jemima startled awake, her eyes wide.

After being quiescent for a time, Geneck had renewed his attack on the barrier. Fatigue and loss of magic affected the remaining brothers. Geneck could probably sense their growing weakness. He and Jemima had removed the two fallen brothers. One had passed on. The other was sleeping, too weary to wake.

No other magicians came to help and Edward grew concerned that Geneck had so decimated their number. Yet he did not know their number truly. More could still be there in hiding, waiting, despairing.

Edward checked his watch, praying that Fulton would arrive in time to help him but he despaired of that. The beast must be tackled by Edward himself. He stared at the barrier, tempted to tell them to drop it so he could get it over and done with. But failure meant they would all die. And Jemima? Edward would fail if he did not come up with something other than throwing power at the creature. Reinforcing the brethren's shield would achieve nothing.

He paused, his head jerking up. If throwing power at it did not work, what about drawing it off? How could such a thing be accomplished? He knew how to infuse objects with power, but had not tried to do the opposite. He sat up straighter, trying to get his mind to follow the thought. Yes, and draining the gem. Fulton. Remember Fulton. His gem had been drained. What if Edward could draw the power away in a similar fashion? *Think, man. Think!*

Something Jemima said. Make her useless. Drain her gem...

There had to be a way to save Jemima. He could take her away but Geneck would only follow and he would have no help. Here, there were some magicians and the priory was isolated so other innocents would not be drawn in. Just the thought of Jemima with Geneck...

Would Geneck turn her into his daughter as Jemima predicted? Edward shuddered at the thought.

Better to rip her heart from her chest and let her die than come to that fate. Jemima had said these words to him and he could not bear thinking of such a deed. Yet there was wisdom in her words. Timing. It was all about timing. If Geneck dispatched him then he could not protect Jemima, could not end it for her as she wished. Chewing his knuckles, he agonised over what he was to do.

"Edward?"

It was Jemima. She ran her hands through his hair.

"Jemima?"

"I hate to see you like this, so tortured."

Edward's heart lurched. She worried for him, when it was her life that was at risk, her soul? "I wish there was something I could do to ease your burden, some comfort I could give you."

He took her hands in his. "I worry that I will fail you." A sudden flare within the crimson barrier drew him to his feet. He urged Jemima behind him. Another brother had fallen. Only four remained. Geneck's hand reached through, dragging the fallen magician through. The magicians stepped around closing the gap with the barrier contracting as a result. The muffled screams of the dying man made gooseflesh rise on the skin of Edward's arms.

Jemima's hand shook as it slid into his elbow. Her eyes were wide, her expression frozen in shock. "Edward. Can you turn off this heart of mine? Can you do it now before the end? Reach out with your magic..."

Edward staggered. "Turn off?"

Jemima stood her ground.

"No. It was meant to beat for a very long time, to help you live."

"I know," she said softly, stepping up to him, running her hands through his hair and brushing a kiss against his mouth. "I cannot be his daughter. I saw what he did to her. He shared the memory with me. If you love me. If you care for me, you will do as I ask. Before the end, I must die."

Edward trembled. "We could all be dead by then."

Jemima shook her head. "No. You would have an end. You would be dead. Me? I would live a half-life in torture, living as that creature's whore."

"Jemima?" He sucked in a breath, hearing such a harsh word from her lips, even though he knew it to be true.

Jemima shrugged. "I know it is not polite to say so but you must hear the awful truth of it." She picked up his hand and placed it on her heart. "Take the power from it and let it end."

Edward tried to pull his hand away. "I cannot." He drew back from her, shaking his head.

Her brow furrowed. "Cannot or will not?"

Edward shrugged. Then he stared at the barrier a kernel of an idea forming. He held Jemima's hand and squeezed. When Fulton had tried to pull out Geneck's heart in the park there had been an explosive reaction. Then later Fulton's gems were depleted. While this was rather startling and disturbing for Fulton in the long term, there was a thought. What if he could control this effect? What if he could draw the power from Geneck's emerald as Fulton's gem was drained. He shook his head. The plan was too feeble. It did not take into account how Geneck could enhance his power, how the magicians found their power sucked up by Geneck.

What did it matter? He had no choice. It was the only logical thing to do. Yet, his promise to Jemima?

Another magician fell. He watched in horror as the barrier faltered, as the magician was dragged by the legs inside the barrier. The scream less muffled than before. The barrier contracted once again. He had to act if he was to preserve any other lives.

"Jemima?" She looked up, her face full of hope and fear mingled together.

"Come. I have a plan." Taking her hand, he led her down the corridor into the large hall there.

"You will do it?" she asked, voice strangely flat.

"Yes."

On entering the hall, straight away he saw the destruction and the carnage among the tiers of benches. Geneck had been in here already. Lamps still shone from the walls, flicking shadows here and there. It had been a teaching room. The floor angled up, with benches for observers. Below was a table, an altar perhaps. He checked his step, wishing immediately to find somewhere else. He turned and realised that the hall had once been a chapel. One of the many that the priory contained, he supposed.

A trio of stained glass windows loomed over the altar, which was built from the same fabric as the chapel. "Come," he said, tugging her hand gently.

She forced her gaze away from the scenes of carnage. A torso at an odd angle on the step that held the benches where students had once listened to a lecture. A bloodied hand flung to land on a bench. A spray of grey matter up the wall.

While she did not quake in fear, he saw the horror etched on her face and wished he had found a better place. Her last thoughts would be of this place, the last smells of death, the last feelings of fear and loss. She deserved so much better.

They walked to the altar. She paused and gazed up at him, her eyes questioning. He nodded and they continued to walk. In the distance, he heard a cry, another magician down perhaps, but he would not hurry Jemima's last moments.

Lifting her under the legs and shoulders he hoisted her onto the bare altar, kissing her as he laid her down. She clung to him, deepening the kiss. He wished there was time for more. Breaking the kiss, he eased her back down. "Relax. It will not hurt."

Tucked into her belt was a wooden stake. She rolled a little and took it out. "Take this. It might help."

Silently he took the stake and pushed it into the back pocket of his trousers.

He brushed his fingers through her hair. She nodded and closed her eyes. The catch on her ruby heart opened with a slight click. There within the gem spun sending out rose-coloured light. This was not the same as Fulton's construction. Jemima depended on the machine and she would die without his power. He stared at the ruby, taking his time to consider what he should do. He could not bring himself to end it. He had too much hope for that. He could leave her with a thread of life, a semblance of death.

A crash sounded in the corridor. A shout. A scream. Was Geneck loose already? Was Edward so out of time?

Jemima touched his hand. "What are you waiting for?" she asked him, eyes closed, her breathing calm.

"Jemima?" he whispered, not able to hide the pain of losing her. So much was unknown, experimental. He could lose her.

Her eyelids fluttered open, a smile ghosting her lips. "I am ready, Edward. I have had more life than god had decreed. I had my life with you, short as it was."

Tears tracked down his cheeks. He licked his lip, his tongue too thick to speak. "Thank you for loving me," he finally managed to say.

Tears glistened in the corner of her eyes. "Good bye," she whispered.

Edward moved his finger to the top of the gem, feeling the energy pulsing. He had put more energy into Fulton's gems so he focused on drawing it out. At first nothing happened. Pulling his finger back he chewed his lip, considering his options. He was reluctant to pull the gem out because that would surely kill her outright.

Trying again, he placed his finger on the spinning gem. The rotations began to slow. He felt the power flow back into him. The rose light faded until there was a warm core of light. The rotation of the gem slowed once and once again and then slower still. Jemima did not move. Her face was still, like one sleeping. Her chest rose slowly; her nostrils flared slightly as she inhaled. She lived but she was on the verge of death. He kissed her cool lips, felt like weeping when she did not respond. If he did not survive the confrontation with Geneck, she would be useless to the vampire. Her life span was a matter of minutes once the remainder of the magic within the gem dissipated. There was only a slight thread of power that might give her more.

He arranged her limbs and crossed her arms over her chest, leaving the ruby heart exposed. Then he arranged her hair, tangled and dirty like it had been when he first met her, around her shoulders, clearing her face of stray strands so that she could repose in comfort.

The sound of another body impacting the floor reached him. He looked up to the stained glass windows. There was a light outside. A false dawn, perhaps. The sun was not going to aid him.

Facing the door, Edward ran, jumping over shattered benches and a corpse. He kept on running until he reached the circle of magicians. So few remained.

"Huntington!" Fulton's voice reached him. His compact frame was wearing breeches, boots and a shirt. "God blind me. You made it. When you disappeared I thought I had lost my mind."

"Fulton! Ware, the beast is about to get through." Edward recollected the stake and tugged it free. "Take this."

Fulton drew out a similar thing from his back. "Keep it. You will need it." He cast a glance around him. "Jemima?"

"Safe for now." Edward did not wish to explain. He did not wish to argue with Fulton, who would only throw in his own arguments. *Do not think of her now. Deal with the moment.*

Fulton grinned and stood slightly hunched as if readying himself for a tackle. "I am ready."

Edward went up to Ferdinand, who had fallen to his knees, his chin resting on his chest. The man appeared to be on his last legs. Reaching out he mind spoke to him. "I am ready. Count to twenty and then drop the barrier. Tell your companion."

Ferdinand gave but a flicker of recognition, a mental nod.

"Then run. Seek safety."

The count went through Edward's brain. The barrier dropped. Ferdinand lay sprawled in the corridor, holding onto one of his brethren. No help coming from that quarter. At least they were alive.

"Geneck!" he called, willing the beast's attention to himself to allow the others time to flee. He dared not look at them, dared not see how they fared but kept his attention on Geneck as his eerie green-glowing eyes centred on him. A growl and a clawed hand rose.

Edward stayed still, waiting. "Jemima is dead."

Geneck lunged, his head moving from one side to the other as if examining some strange specimen. As if he was smelling, trying to pick up a scent. A growl emitted from his fetid lips.

Edward held his ground, even though every part of him screamed for him to run.

Edward's gaze dropped to the heart so close now. Could he reach out and...

Geneck guessed his move and surged backwards in one fluid movement. Edward stood still, offering himself as the perfect bait. Geneck ventured closer. Edward gripped the stake, waiting, waiting for the moment. Geneck moved. Edward struck. The stake ate flesh. A roar and Edward felt the impact, caught a glimpse of the world spinning around him and landed, sliding along the floor until he hit the wall.

"To me!" Fulton shouted, waving his stake menacingly as he ducked and weaved, so swift was he that Edward could not focus. Or perhaps he was affected by the blow. Edward tried to get to his feet and fell back down.

Geneck sniffed the air. His head turned towards the teaching room, to Jemima. No! Edward thought. The creature could not possibly feel her, so close to death. Her mind must still be active. Before he could say anything, Geneck dashed away, half climbing the walls to get around Fulton before skidding into the doorway of the teaching room.

Edward screamed. "Geneck! No! Take me! Geneck!"

Fulton came up to him. "What is going on?"

"It's Jemima. He is gone after her...but..."

"What? What has happened to Jemima?" Fulton asked, voice with a hard edge.

"I drained her heart of power." Edward nodded, seeing Fulton's expression. Fulton knew what would happen.

"No. You could not."

"She demanded that I do it. Her logic was sound. It was the only way." Edward's voice hitched. "Come on. Hurry."

Fulton turned and sprinted in front of him.

"You must destroy him," Ferdinand called out. "Save the world from him."

Edward heard the words in his mind and ears. He bit his lips and ran after Fulton. Edward skidded on some blood as he raced through the broken set of doors. Geneck was prowling among the debris as if searching. How had he missed seeing Jemima where she was laid to rest?

Fulton yelled at the creature and threw broken bits of furniture at him with no effect. The beast was sniffing the air again.

Why? Edward's gaze darted to the altar. Jemima was gone. "Jemima?"

Fulton called out. "What is going on? I thought you said Jemima was in here."

"She was!" She could not have possibly moved by herself. "Someone has taken her." It was impossible. Who would be alive to do such a thing with the beast on the loose and brothers dying? Jemima had said someone had followed her. Had they stood by all this time, waiting for an opportunity to grab her? Edward could not account for it. Such single-minded malice. But surely they understood that the beast would find them.

"Fulton," he called out. "Let him go. He will lead us to Jemima. She has not got much time."

Fulton stepped back, eyes ever watchful, and was soon standing with Edward. They stood very still.

Geneck howled like the beast that he was, lashing out at furniture, sending wood and chairs flying. Edward flinched as some debris headed for him. Fulton knocked it away with a flick of his hand and it broke into splinters.

The beast raked the walls with his claws, gouging ridges in the marble. Edward picked up a piece of wood and threw it, hoping to catch his attention, meanwhile he was frantic, thinking about what had happened to his wife.

Geneck turned his head as the wood struck a glancing blow on his shoulder. Edward picked up another piece and threw it, hoping Geneck would face him and the beast did. The green light shone out of his chest brighter than Edward had ever seen. The beast had taken in more energy, had probably been feeding off the barrier all this while. Edward had an idea. "Find Jemima. Quickly."

Lips crept over fangs as the creature gave a warning growl. Yet the intelligence that was Geneck seemed to understand. He shifted his head, circling it around and then stopped, focusing on a small door that was hidden in the shadows by a section of wall that jutted out to create an alcove.

Edward squinted at him, at the pulsating heart. That was his own magic, sourced from within. There had to be a way for him to take it back inside him. He had managed to drain Jemima's heart. If he could get close enough, if the beast was quiescent, he could do the same. Surely he could. The possibility of Geneck staying still long enough for that to happen, though, was very low.

Regret was something he did not have time for. A sense of calm came over him as he watched Geneck run rampant through the building looking for Jemima. He shoved the altar and when it did not move he smashed it with his fists, growling in frustration. Then he approached the door.

"He has found her?" Fulton asked.

"I think so. But that door. It is too small for him."

"Wait for it," Fulton said just as Geneck punched through the door and ripped it off its hinges. Then with fists he smashed at the surrounding doorway to make it larger.

"Can we get around him? Can we get there first?" Edward asked.

A sound at the door drew their attention. It was Ferdinand. "I cannot help you," he said weakly as Edward and Fulton approached. "I have no power left."

Edward knelt. "Someone has taken Jemima. Where does that small door lead?"

Ferdinand licked cracked lips. He scrunched up his brow. "Taken? Again? Below. They have taken her below."

"Damn it to hell," Fulton said. "They have taken her into darkness. The beast will be safe from the day. He will be able to function."

Edward squeezed Ferdinand's shoulder. "Rest if you can. We will go after him." To Fulton he said, "We best hurry then. If he can still sense where Jemima is, she still lives. While she lives she is in danger of being corrupted by the beast."

Fulton's eyes narrowed and he nodded before turning to the door. "We may as well follow, then, if he can find her."

"We will have but a short time to act," Edward said.

"I understand."

They left Ferdinand who was now unconscious and raced after Geneck. He was easy to follow now that he was through the door. They were careful not to stumble on parts of masonry that had fallen after Geneck's passage. They turned a corner and Geneck was nowhere to be seen. Evidence of his passage was everywhere: robed bodies, partially dismembered.

Edward could not afford to be distracted. He needed to keep up with Geneck and trust that Fulton would keep him safe. He let the relaxation flow through him, finding a place of calm within himself, even as destruction and anger whirled around him.

He could taste Geneck in the air. The vibration of the beast's power washed over him. Edward stood still, letting it fill his mind. The reek, the stench of the corrupted magic nearly overwhelmed him and then he detected the cords of magic bound together and began to unbraid them, separating out the essence of himself.

"Huntington? What are you doing?" Fulton asked as he grabbed him by the elbow and steered him through the debris field.

"Tracking him. Understanding him," he said in whisper.

With wonder, he found the part of Geneck that was him. There he could compare that essence, that flavour to what he remembered of Fulton and even Jemima. That was him? That was how he tasted and felt?

A loud crash and then instinct warned him to move. Geneck leaped, landing where Edward had just stood. Fulton had jerked him sideways and tossed him out of the way. He felt the displacement of air from his passage as he rolled coming to a stop against the smashed remains of a lower bench.

Geneck whirled, advancing on him.

Fulton stood, legs spread in front of Edward. "Find Jemima!"

Geneck raised an arm ready to swipe Fulton away, clearing a path to Edward. Shakily, Edward climbed to his feet. "Jemima..."

With a roar, Geneck turned and dove down a stairwell. "Hurry," Fulton said, grabbing at his arm.

Edward stumbled along, fighting the light-headedness. Had Geneck sensed a connection as well, recognised what Edward had been doing?

Fulton stopped and shook him. "Pay attention or you will break your bloody neck. Stairs now. Stairs."

Edward acknowledged him, putting his hand on the banister as he followed Fulton into the dark depths below. Although he could taste his power in Geneck, he had no idea how to draw it back in and he dared not fight with that power. Who knew what the consequences could be? Geneck already had too much.

Geneck came at them in the darkness. It was like being hit by a train. A blunt force shoving him up. Before he could blink he was in the air, not able to breathe. His mind screamed for Fulton. Edward had just enough presence of mind to slow his fall. He fell hard, his arm hitting against something firm. Rock or wall. He shuddered as the pain hit. He had broken his left arm.

Shaking his head, he used his back against the wall and his legs to lever himself up while he clutched his arm to his side. Breathing through the pain, he shook his head to clear it. Something was not right. Why did not Geneck attack him? He had the opportunity but he had not tried to drain him, to feed on him. "Fulton!" he called out.

Geneck roared at him. He felt the hunger in him, the need. He wanted his daughter back. He wanted Jemima and now she was gone he could not have her. Edward turned his head on the side, trying to work out a way forwards.

Surrounding Geneck was an aura of green light, a kind of emerald halo, emerald fire. Edward reached out to touch it, fascinated by the part of it that originated in him. His gaze dropped to the emerald spinning in the mechanism. He slowed his breathing, feeling every pulse of power the gem emitted. He was in that gem. He could take that power back if only...

Suddenly, Edward could not breathe. Geneck had him by the throat and had lifted him up into the air. That close the beast's thought hammered into Edward's mind, nail points of demand.

Geneck brought his face close, breathed the stench of death straight into Edward's lungs. Before he lost him, he had to try. If he could just stretch out a hand. He reached for his power and drew it back, welcomed it back. Edward clung to the thread of power, bringing more of it into himself. Unfortunately, the amount must have been small, because Geneck did not appear to notice.

Then Geneck let go with a deafening roar. Edward dropped and rolled, crying out as he jarred his broken arm, seeing red-tinged lights.

Fulton was there, moving so quickly that all Edward could sense was the movement in the damp, heavy air.

"He has lost her," was all he could get out through his bruised throat. "I nearly had the thread of power. I could have..."

A light filtered in from a dark corridor as a door opened and shut with a thud. Geneck stilled.

Fulton desisted.

"Jemima!" Edward said, trying to move.

Geneck leaped, his claws scratching against the stone of the walls and ceiling as he scrambled like a spider to the source of light.

"Help me, Fulton."

Fulton was there, arm under his and helped him walk. "We are close. I am sure."

Through his pain-filled gaze, he saw Geneck turn his head as if he had heard something. With the green eyes glowing, his movement was easy to track. Geneck cried out and started to savage the doorway. It was a struggle for Edward to stay on his feet.

Fulton eased him down. "Stay here," Fulton said.

Edward must have passed out because next he knew Ferdinand was there shaking his shoulder. Edward opened his eyes to see Ferdinand's haggard countenance, his hands shaky, but the brother was able to help Edward to his feet.

Edward was amazed the older magician lived. "How...I..."

"The beast has run off," Ferdinand said. "Your friend is in pursuit."

"He's looking for Jemima," Edward said, not quite able to bring his mind into focus.

"Has he found her yet?" Ferdinand asked.

Edward coughed and clutched his broken arm to his body. "I think she is in there, just down the hall. Those who stole her from the altar... they might be able to stop him."

Ferdinand clenched his mouth, then fixed Edward with his pale eyes. "Winston's co-conspirator."

"Who is Winston?"

Ferdinand assisted Edward along the corridor. It was hard to place his feet in a straight line. Perhaps he had broken more than his arm.

"Mr Brown. You met him at the house in Chelsea." Ferdinand panted as he shuffled along, bringing Edward with him. He had not recovered and it was amazing that he had come this far to follow them.

"I do not know who he is in league with. But he is the one that abducted your wife in the first place."

Edward cursed. "Wilbur was right not to trust your brotherhood."

"No. Yes. Maybe..." Ferdinand paused and readjusted his hold on Edward and then continued on. The door was closer. "Our rules forbid harming a magician's family. He had no right to take her and no leave to do so. There is something rotten in the brotherhood, that is what Wilbur discovered, why he left us. I should have believed him."

"Where are we?"

Ferdinand made a small light and cast a look around the destruction around him, blinking as if waking from a dream. "We are close to where Winston had rooms in the basements. That door is quite near to the cellar."

A distant thundering crash and then a raw scream echoed. "Is it Fulton or Geneck? We should hurry." Edward peered down the gloomy corridor. He tried to extricate himself from the magician's hold. "I will be fine now. Find safety, Ferdinand. You cannot help us now."

"Wait, let me," Ferdinand said in a gentle voice.

Edward stopped fighting and nodded.

"Some of us," the old man began, "have special gifts. Mine is healing small hurts." He stroked a shaking finger down the length of Edward's forearm. Edward let out a gasp as heat flowed into him. Before he could protest, the old magician had twisted the wrist, making the bones fall into place.

Edward felt weak at the knees and broke out into a fine sweat. Ferdinand patted his hand and fell back to use the wall for support. "Go, young man. I fear that you are right. I am too weak to help you. Find Jemima. Stop the beast."

CHAPTER 25

Jemima was aware. She felt herself being lifted and detected the scent of the man carrying her. It definitely was not her husband. The chill night air caressed her skin. She wished that she had had a chance to bathe and change into a nice nightgown before she died. That had been her thought last time she was close to death. She had no such hope of reprieve. Edward was not about to fashion her a new heart. Not this time.

Her abductors had not covered her face. She could not move but through slitted eyes she recognised one of the men by his voice. It was the old one.

She shivered, though it was a long drawn-out shiver, slowed down in time like the beating of her heart. A thread of her life was letting go. Death was coming for her.

Another man was with the old one. She did not know him by smell or sight. Her ears though picked up the swish of robes, so she guessed he was one of the brotherhood. Why were they taking her when their brethren were being slaughtered? Perhaps they did not care what was happening around them.

Of course they did not care.

Her brain was slow but the thought arrived. They did not care to share the secret of her with anyone else.

"Is she dead?" the older magician asked. Wine-tainted breath spilled over her face and up her nose. She could not draw away. Could not react.

"No, no yet," the other one said. "Let's look at what he has done, perhaps we can learn from the difference." He rummaged around. "I will take more notes."

They were rough as they tugged her corset apart and opened the casing on her ruby heart. Shadows obscured the light as they leaned over her.

"Ahhh, see it spins slower, the light is less," the older man said excitedly. "He has drained it."

There was an intake of breath. "Why would he do that?" The shadows moved. "It is his wife. She will die."

The old man cackled. "No matter. She was a troublesome creature I expect. That is a good enough reason to be sure. Could never abide females."

The younger man let out a sigh. "No, I do not think he did it for that reason. Huntington would not do that even if she was annoying." There was a pause. "Mmm. I am thinking he did it to protect her though I cannot...unless?"

"What? No wait. I think I know," the older man replied. "When she was summoned to the conclave...the beast came to her straight away, came for her."

The young brother said, "Yes, yes, the sun had set. The beast was free to move about. Perhaps it even followed her here when Winston stole her from Huntington and the beast's minions."

"Perhaps it had been lying here in wait."

"No, no," the younger one said. "He would have struck straight away as it was still dark. No he followed afterwards and he moved swiftly."

"Yes, yes, very quickly. Faster than any contraption could deliver him."

"So if we think back and consider that Huntington knew the creature could sense her..." There was a loud exhale of breath. "Yes, that is it. That is why he used her for bait. The beast can find her. He has done this to protect her."

"By killing her?" The old man's voice was harsh and Jemima found it grating on her nerves, what nerves that remained. She felt no fear. No bodily reaction to danger.

"We could try to revive her? Add some essence perhaps?"

"If we did it would be for our own purposes. To see that our magic could be infused in the gem. She is already doomed. She is as good as dead."

Jemima could not react. She wanted to. Her ears could hear and her mind could think, though her legs were heavy and her arms, too. And it was cold. Not a shivering cold. Just a numb kind of cold. Dying was not very amusing, particularly when two evil magicians plotted right over the top of your nearly dead body.

They could kill her, she supposed. Had not she already volunteered to die? Better dead than Geneck's pawn. But these underhand dealings by the brotherhood angered her. They were trying to steal something from Edward and they had no regard for her or for Edward or for what Geneck was doing to their fellow magicians. These two were evil, treacherous, and had to be stopped. Perhaps she could use her strength. She tried to move but there was not enough energy inside her to manage it. No instructions were reaching her limbs. Her vision faded somewhat. She could no longer make out the magicians. Just a flickering yellow light.

They peered into the device and tried different things, making groans and tsking sounds.

"You do not think the beast will find her down here?" the younger brother asked.

"With her dead—almost dead—I doubt it. Look at her. A corpse just waiting to stiffen."

There was movement. A sound in her chest. Then something happened.

"What did you do?" asked the older man.

"I stopped the gem from spinning."

"Why?" the older man asked.

The voices were growing distant.

"I did not mean for it to stop. I just touched it."

"Well, now it has stopped glowing. I thought we were trying to make it spin faster, not stop it."

The young man's voice pleaded. "I apologise. I know what we intended. The gem reacted when I drew near, the remaining energy discharging. I could not know..."

A pause that seemed to drag on forever. "So she is dying? Now?"

"Yes." It was but a faint sound, echoing into the distance. "Not long now."

Not only was her hearing fading, Jemima's mind closed off also, and there just in range of her senses was a mind so terrible, she shied away from it. But she knew its scent. Knew when it latched onto her.

Jemima screamed silently in her mind, the last vestiges of her consciousness filled with fear of the beast's ravenous need. Breathing was a memory. Warmth a distant thrill. Cold seized her toes and crept up her legs. Soon it would reach her heart. Her ruby heart.

⁜

A ROAR. JEMIMA'S EYES SNAPPED OPEN. A SUDDEN SURGE OF LIFE within. Another roar filled the air before the door shattered with pieces of wood flying in all directions. Jemima saw it clearly though her heart beat limply in her chest. That surprised her because her ruby heart no longer shone. How? What gift of life was this? She could not move. The numbing cold still crept along her body inexorably.

The two magicians recoiled. One of them screamed throatily. The other leaked a sharp smell of urine that tickled the back of Jemima's throat.

The older man gathered his wits and threw bolts of power at Geneck. He flinched but they had no impact. The beast lunged for the old man and held him nose to nose. "Please," the old man began as he cried. "Please, I can give you whatever you want."

Geneck's head turned to Jemima. She could feel the heat of his look, feel his need of her.

"Take her. Leave us in peace. But take her. She is yours. We will not stop you."

Jemima heard a whimper. Her heart beat another beat, her chest rose as a breath slid into her. She should be dead and was not...yet.

Geneck lowered the old man somewhat gently and he angled his body to study the younger man. He sniffed as if smelling something familiar. Jemima knew the young magician did have a strange scent, like he ate a particular herb, something sickly sweet in his sweat.

Geneck reached down, grabbing the magician by the hair. The older man stepped sideways, seeking to sneak away unseen. Jemima wanted to point at him, wanted Geneck to see. She wanted them both punished. Why was she alive? Her finger pointed and her hand lifted, straight armed and true. It was enough to attract Geneck's attention before it flopped back lifeless on the table where she lay.

Darkness gathered at the edge of her perception. Her heart beat once again, slower, less forcefully. Her chest rose less higher than before.

Geneck stalked behind the old man. As Geneck's clawed hand penetrated through his spine the old man squeaked, then slid indecorously into a heap of his own blood. Geneck did not bother to feed. Then he turned his attention to the younger magician whose crooked nose bled and his close-together eyes appeared crossed as they stared in horror at his approaching doom. The swipe from Geneck took off his head. Jemima smelt the blood, heard it spurt. She did not need to lift her head to look. She saw the head travel into her line of vision. Now the magicians were dealt with there was only her left. Death was closer now. She willed it to come to her faster. *Come to me now death. Before he takes me to a dark place where I can never escape.*

A rush of air and Geneck was there. She could see herself through his eyes. The cold filled her gut. Only her hands were warm and pliable, though she dared not try to move, to even see if she could.

Thoughts cascaded—Geneck's thoughts, and Jemima could not shut him out. He stepped almost reverently up to the table. His emerald eyes glowing, his jaw unlocking as he opened his mouth. He lifted his hand to shoulder height and then opened it, talons displayed.

Jemima sucked in a last terrified breath.

"Stop!" Edward shouted.

The beast turned. Fulton came in so quickly Edward only caught a flash of his movement out of the corner of his eyes. Geneck was gone.

Edward spun around. It was a closed-in space. Fulton moved again and Edward ducked as Fulton leaped in his direction. He needed to get to Jemima. Jemima who lay dying. Jemima who could be saved if only they could defeat the beast. He cast a glance at her. Leaching the power from her ruby heart had not saved her. Geneck had still found her.

A sob exploded out of him. He had failed. Failed to stop Geneck. Failed to save Jemima. Was she right to say that she had had extra time, time to be with him? Yes, by heaven she was right. And when he thought of the slaughter he understood what she meant. The terrible guilt had overshadowed them. What kind of life was it when you lived in fear, lived with that beast's thoughts in your mind?

"Fulton?" Edward cried.

Fulton leaped and Geneck just appeared and swept him off course to smash into the wall. Fulton hit with a sickening crunch. Edward winced. Geneck stalked up to Edward. For a moment Edward faltered, did not know what to do or how to react. He pulled the magician's trick and transported. He materialised near the door and grabbed onto the jamb to steady himself. He had not mastered the art of it. He wavered. He was going to throw up.

Fulton shook his head, rolled his shoulders and then steam-rollered into Geneck. Geneck fell back. Fulton punched and punctured Geneck's torso. The beast screamed and roared. Fulton was thrown back.

Edward tried to get around the two as they battled it out. Fulton had blood leaking down the side of his face from a small cut in his head. His hand where he had mangled the beast was dripping gore. Edward stood on his toes to peer at Jemima. The light in her ruby heart was faded. Yet he detected a slow breath. She was still alive.

He either had to save her and bring her back to life or take the last of her life force before Geneck took her. Edward's foot slipped and he saw that blood was congealing on the stone floor. A body lay close by. He still did not know what he would do. He thought he had the courage to let Jemima die as she desired, but found he could not, did not want that.

A cry came from Fulton and Edward turned around, searching the room. It was a blur of movement as Geneck and Fulton fought. Edward crouched, readying a magical blow. He had to devise it so that it took power rather than used it. Fulton landed a blow that shattered one of Geneck's teeth.

"Now!" Edward called. Fulton ducked to the ground and rolled away.

Edward released the spell. Geneck turned to him and walked towards him but experienced resistance from the spell. Geneck faltered but pushed against the invisible barrier until he smacked Edward across the head. Stars flew out of Edward's darkened vision and he had the sensation of flying. The spell blew apart and Edward caught the recoil. He vomited on the ground where he landed and struggled to his feet, using the table to steady himself. Wiping blood from his chin he stood, he realised he was next to the table. "Jemima?"

She was unharmed despite her ordeal. The ruby heart had just a faint blush. Edward realised it was his presence that generated it for when he had touched Jemima it let out a pale pink glow and when he removed his hand it had died away. Residual magic?

"End it," Jemima whispered so softly that he barely heard her. It was like he could tell in his heart.

"Oh Jemima!"

The sound of the fight continued. He reached out. He would remove the ruby. That was the best way. She would die then, no residual magic to keep her alive.

"Agh!" Fulton cried.

Edward swung around. Geneck had him. His heart thumped. "Fulton?"

He thought his friend was up for anything. He was meant to keep the beast occupied so that he could...he could...kill Jemima.

Geneck slavered and changing his hold on Fulton, ripped his leg off and threw his body against the wall.

"No!" Edward shouted. Blood spurted freely from Fulton's thigh. He would die quickly without help.

"I am sorry, Jemima."

Edward raced to where Fulton lay, coming in and out of consciousness. Geneck growled but did not attack. He sauntered back to Jemima, taking his time.

Edward closed his eyes, praying for useless forgiveness from Jemima. If Geneck turned her, she would have to be killed like Geneck must be, but would be just as unstoppable. Damn Longhurst for forcing him. Damn his heart for loving her.

He ripped up Fulton's shirt and tied a tourniquet around the wound. He used magic to stem the flow of blood, temporarily sealing the wound. He would not travel well but it would prevent his life leaking away from him. Edward turned back to Jemima. The beast hovered there as if savouring the sight of her.

Fulton's hand come up and landed on his. "Save her."

Fulton could not be left. Not right at this minute. Edward shook his head. "I cannot. Both of you will die."

He bent to examine the wound and realised that it was a clean wound, the beast tearing off the device from Fulton's leg. If he could find the leg, he could reattach it.

"No, no, no," Fulton cried. "Save her."

Edward shook his head. "I have done all that I can. It is up to Jemima. She can will herself to die. The beast hesitates."

Fulton grabbed his hand. "Please. Leave me." They shared a look. Edward's heart lurched. He was set to lose the two most important people in his life. Fulton was going to be a father. He could save him. He was not so sure that he could save Jemima. He had to trust her. Alive or dead, strange as that seemed.

The beast moved. Edward and Fulton were no longer important to him. Jemima's chest stopped moving. Edward held his own breath. Then he saw where Fulton's leg was. Seeing that Fulton was lying pale as a sheet and panting, with eyes closed but lips moving in some kind of prayer, Edward moved, sliding across the floor on his rear.

The beast turned and looked over its shoulder. Edward thought it was going to come for him, but it turned back. Jemima raised her right hand.

Edward started and swallowed. How was she doing that? She was beckoning the beast closer. Edward reached for the leg device, which was heavy, and he held it to his chest as he quietly slid back to Fulton.

He could not start work on it but he nestled it next to Fulton's other leg and wished he had thought to bring his stasis stones. The pain would be easier for Fulton if he was in stasis. He caught the glitter of Fulton's eyes. He was watching the beast. It moved slowly, nearly leaning over Jemima's form. Her fingers brushed the flesh of the beast's chest and Edward sucked in another breath. Her eyes were shut, that much he could see.

The beast put a taloned finger on her chest. There was a lascivious, dripping-with-desire expression on its face, in its glowing green orbs. Edward revolted at it. Jemima's eyes opened and she blinked. An odd smile touched her lips. Edward wondered if that was the corruption of the beast already possessing her. The taloned finger dipped into her ruby heart.

Her body jerked, straining as if in a seizure. Her feet hammered against the surface of the table and her jaw was in a rictus grin. Edward wept as he looked on, tears trailing down his cheek.

"Jemima!" he said softly, intensely. "Oh Jemima."

Then he noticed something. Her ruby heart glowed hotly and then electricity arced out of it. Her hand moved, her fingers touched Geneck's heart. The beast looked down, a surprised look on its face. She did not have the strength to harm it. She was not trying to rip the device out of Geneck's chest as Fulton had done. Her touch was almost gentle, sensual even. The beast stood there and did not move away, did not break contact.

Green arcs of power looped around the beast, crackling and sizzling. It was like the encounter with Fulton, except more controlled. The green power covered Jemima's body, little forks of green tinged lightning and emerald fire climbing all over her. Her eyes glowed with a sick light. Was he losing her? Was this the end? The beast consuming her mind?

He wiped at his tears and the wet of his nose with a sleeve. "Jemima." He wept her name.

"Watch," Fulton wheezed out.

Edward once again studied the tableau before him. Something

strange was happening. The beast was jerking around now as Jemima stilled. Her chest rose and she inhaled. More of the power was running into her. Her ruby heart shone so bright he had to cover his eyes. Her hand pulled back and power arced between it and the beast. Geneck let out a cry—a weak cry.

"Weak?" He voiced his thought. "How?"

He studied Jemima and he could see it now, a vortex inside her gem. It had been empty, devoid of magic. She had not died, though, as she should have. She was hungry for life. Her gem was hungry for power.

Fulton pushed himself up higher. "She is doing it. Killing the beast!"

Edward nodded, not quite sure he was believing what he was seeing, but it looked that way. Jemima sat up.

Geneck fell to his knees, power arcing and contacting the walls. Edward's hair stood on end at the static discharge. Jemima's eyes now held the emerald fire, her fingers, too. Geneck's form lost its robustness, his torso thinned, the skin fissured and dried up. He collapsed, his head hitting the edge of the table, then he fell to the ground.

Jemima sat up, haloed in green flame. Edward could taste the power on his tongue. He dared not breathe. Was she still his Jemima?

The power display continued for a few minutes more and Jemima sat there unseeing. She sucked in another breath and another, almost coughing. She wiped her mouth with the back of her hand and focused on him. The flare of power in her irises died. The emerald fire dimmed, but still sat there beneath the surface of her skin.

"Did it work? Did I kill him?"

Edward hovered, wanting to go to her, but hesitant, afraid. He was not sure it was her. His Jemima.

She cocked her head in a way that was so Jemima. "Edward? What is wrong with you? Why do you not answer me?"

"I...er..." His gaze flicked from her to the body of the beast.

"What happened to Fulton?" she asked, looking around him to Fulton, prone on the floor.

She turned her body so she could slide off the table and lower herself to the ground. She glanced down at her bodice and tried to tie it together. Then she noticed the green glow on her finger tips. She held them in front of her face, wonderingly staring at them. "What is this?"

Edward swallowed. He was sure it was Jemima, but he needed to take precautions in case it was the beast in possession of her.

"We need to burn the body," Edward said, indicating with a nod to the husk of Geneck.

"In here?" She looked up and around. "You might set fire to the building."

Edward nodded. Her logic was still intact. "Yes, we will need to take it outside."

She frowned at him. He had not moved. "Edward, what on earth is wrong with you? I expected a hug perhaps, a kiss and a smile. Some screams of delight that I am alive." She stood up straight and her eyes widened. "Why am I alive?"

ༀ

JEMIMA'S BLOOD BURNED BUT IT WAS NOT AN UNPLEASANT FEELING. Not after finding her body struggling for every breath and feeling the cold crept up until it almost stole into her heart and mind. Why was Edward looking at her strangely?

Her empty heart had taken the power from Geneck. She had not known her ruby heart would react that way. However, it had and she could understand why. Edward had drained it unnaturally. A part of Edward was in her, remained in her. It made sense. The magic in the gem was the essence of him. He loved her. He did not want her to die. This was why she lingered. His essence refused to let her go. He would understand this if he put his mind to it.

If Edward's magic was in her, it enhanced her own. She had some 'small talent' if she had overheard Brother Winston correctly. She interpreted that to mean magic. She did not really want to die either, but felt it incumbent on her to die to save the world from Geneck. She was puzzling this out while Edward stood there like a nincompoop and blathered about burning Geneck's body.

She rolled her eyes and put her hands on her hips. "Really. If that is the best you can do, take care of Fulton while I take this thing—" she kicked Geneck's dried shell, "—outside and burn it."

Fulton groaned and Edward turned away from her. She shook her head. When was she ever going to understand her husband? When was he ever going to understand her? For surely he was out of his senses. She guessed this was with worry. She hoped it was worry over her. But first things first. She picked up Geneck by the hand and dragged the corpse towards the door. Unfortunately, the brittle thing broke off. She tossed it onto the torso of the thing and leaned down to grab the corpse by the neck. Geneck was surprisingly light but given he was a kind of mummy thing it made some sort of perverted sense. He was a being of magic and had been drained of magic.

She paused on the threshold and glanced back at Edward working on Fulton, who let out intermittent hisses and scrunched up his face.

She took another long look at the remains of the beast. It had been full of magic. That magic, logic told her, had gone into her. She gave another tug and the body moved in the direction she wished to go. She walked along, dragging the remains of Geneck behind her, searching for a staircase to lead outside. Everywhere were signs of violence and death. Geneck had done that.

You could do that, she thought. She shook her head. *No. I would not do that.* Then instances where she might tear a place apart if required came to mind. To fight for Edward she would do anything. But kill?

She shook her head. *No. Dear heaven, I hope to god I never have to make that choice.* Mindless minions of this beast, yes. Why was she worried? Why was Edward too afeared to come near her? Did he think she was now a killer?

Locating the staircase, she dragged the body. Sickly daylight crept in through a window, illuminating dark stains on the whitewashed walls. She kept stepping up. Her nose twitched. There were other smells here, not pleasant ones. This was what death smelt like: blood and guts and excrement. When that thought hit her she bent over and vomited in a corner.

She wiped her mouth on her sleeve, the remains of her blouse somehow remaining on her body. Stepping over some glistening dark glob of something, she continued up and found the door leading to the garden.

It surprised her that Geneck weighed nothing. She found an open spot of ground and dumped him there. Certain that he was truly dead, she looked around for kindling. The ground was damp. It must have showered sometime early this morning. Indeed, white-grey clouds obscured the sun. She located a wood pile and brought some over, tucking pieces under the body. She stood up and considered it. There really was not enough time to do this the conventional way.

Her hands glowed green and tingled. Power. Could she use it to burn the beast? She was about to and then thought better of it. What if she inadvertently reanimated the creature? It still had its heart device.

Dropping to her knees, she flipped the body over so that the chest faced the sky. She hesitated before touching the device, remembering what had happened. She searched around for something and could find nothing that would suit her purpose. She rose and went back into the building. There had to be tools in there somewhere. She went in search of things, hands over her nose for the smell was rising.

The sound of carriages approaching had her head jerking up. Who could this be? The police? Minions? Surely the minions would expire once the host was dead. She found a long metal rod, with a sharp end. She had no idea what kind of tool it was but it was surely suited to her purpose.

Walking back outside, she ignored the calls of "Hello, anybody there?" and kept to her purpose. She could not afford to be distracted and this had to be done. She shoved the edge of the tool into the beast's chest and levered up the end of the device. She did this two or three times and then flicked the device as far as possible from the body.

She chucked the tool away and it landed with a thump. More carriages arrived. Through the trees she could see that it was the police. She faced Geneck's corpse. "You shall never rise again."

Then she lifted her hands and power shot out of them. She wanted heat and flame and she got exactly that. The brittle, dry corpse caught. At first it smoked and then flamed when the few pieces of wood under it caught. Licks of fire poked up through the eye sockets and through the wound in the chest. She stepped back as, all at once, it caught with explosive force.

"Mrs Huntington?" a voice said.

Jemima turned, hiding her hands behind her back. "Yes, Inspector Coleman."

He looked at her with wide eyes. She looked down at her clothes, covering the glow in her chest with a hand while she brushed some dirt off her breeches. "I do apologise for my appearance. I am surely most indecent."

He took off his coat. "Nevermind your attire, Mrs Huntington. Are you quite all right?" He covered her shoulders with his coat.

"Oh, yes, thank you, quite fine." She snuggled into the warm, wool fabric.

He leaned to one side to peer around her. "And what is that burning there?"

Jemima turned around and peered at the fire. It was well alight and not much could be seen of Geneck. She doubted the policeman would believe her. "It is the beast, Inspector. It is dead. Well and truly dead and it will not come back again."

He coughed and there was a slight smile on his face as if he was humouring a child. "I see. We shall certainly be glad of that. Perhaps you can tell me where your husband is."

She pointed to the building. "Down there, one floor down. Fulton is badly hurt, I am afraid."

He tipped his hat. "Thank you. I shall consult with him." He took a step and paused. "May I say how happy I am to see you well, Mrs Huntington. We all held grave fears for your safety."

"Entirely well justified." She smiled, a touch sad though. "Do be prepared, Inspector Coleman, as there are a lot of dead people in there. The beast was at its worst."

He nodded and walked away. Not far away was a bench and now that Geneck was almost ash, she thought she should sit down for she was suddenly faint.

There were yells and cries of horror as the police discovered the bodies. Apart from Edward and Fulton, Jemima did not know who was alive. After a while she grew tired. She had no wish to find a bed or to enter the buildings where so many bad things occurred so she stretched out on the bench. She might have slept, she was not sure. Only she was woken by a familiar voice.

"There you are, dear child," Uncle Ferdy said to her.

With a start she sat up. "Oh you!" She stood up and impulsively hugged him.

He patted her back. "There, there, I am pleased to see you. I did not think I would see daylight again. And here you are, hale and hearty, enjoying these gardens."

He released her and held her at arm's length. "Something is different about you."

With pursed lips, he studied her, looking into her perhaps, and then his eyes widened. "Dear god. You are full of power."

She nodded. "Yes, apparently I sucked it all out of…the beast."

"What?" He reached out and touched a loose lock of hair. Nothing happened. He cupped her head, patting her. "My dear child, you must tell me what happened?"

She stepped back, forcing him to drop his hand. "I cannot. You will have to ask Edward for a technical explanation."

"I will certainly, but what do you think happened, child?"

"My ruby heart was hungry for power, for life, so when Geneck came, it took it."

Uncle Ferdy lowered himself to the bench. "And you, Jemima? Were you hungry for life?"

She sat down next to him and looked up into the tress. "Yes, I love my life. I love my husband. I did not want to leave it, really. I was willing to sacrifice myself, though. Is that wrong of me? To want this life?"

Ferdinand sat back and closed his eyes. "No, my dear Jemima. Self-preservation is second nature to us. Sometimes we act for our self-protection when we are not even aware." He opened his eyes again and met her gaze. "That is why we value heroism. Because it is so against our nature."

More carriages pulled up. These had flat tops and she could see that bundled forms were being laid upon them. They were gathering up the dead. "I see. Yes, I suppose you really have to try hard to be a hero." She thought about it some more. "Or be totally out of your mind."

Uncle Ferdy chuckled. It was a sad sound. "I am glad I am alive," he said by way of explanation. "There are but a few of us left."

"I fear Edward may need help saving Fulton. He was badly wounded."

Uncle Ferdy widened his eyes. He was so weary that his wrinkles seemed more pronounced than ever. "What can I do that your husband cannot?"

"Send for Heaton. The doctor that helped him with Fulton before."

"A non-magician?" he asked, askance.

"Well, yes. He has scientific knowledge and, as you know, Edward is good at marrying magic and science."

"I will do so then. I have his direction as we have studied him for a while now." He rose to his feet with a groan. "I will do that now. Give Huntington my thanks for dispatching the beast. I had given in to despair for he did not know how it was to be achieved."

Jemima grinned, her gaze on the smouldering ash. "I will certainly pass on your thanks."

CHAPTER 26

Inspector Coleman escorted Jemima directly home to Chelsea. She did not mind being separated from Edward so much. He had not come near her and she was at a loss to know how to heal the breach that had opened between them. She had thought it through and she could not decipher the logic of his apparent distaste for her, for that is what it seemed to her.

Fulton was in a bad way and it was best that she return home to assure Milly and Aunt Prudence that all that could be done was being done. Heaton had been sent for.

Inspector Coleman was not an ideal travelling companion. He prodded her with questions and then asked the same questions again slightly differently. "So you were unconscious most of the time?"

"Yes, that is what I said. I woke up and the beast was dead."

"And you have no idea how?"

"Not really, no. I think you will have to apply to my husband for a technical explanation. He was there."

"Yes, I know he was, but he is otherwise engaged with saving Fulton."

Jemima looked out and saw that they were near the house. She rubbed her forehead as she had a terrible headache. The sun blinded her and she hid her eyes with her hand. This questioning had persisted for hours.

"Here we are," Inspector Coleman said as the carriage pulled up. "I will see you indoors."

Jemima decided that being a helpless female was a good pose to adopt with the policeman. She wore a cloak over her attire, one that Coleman had fetched for her. The sight of a woman in breeches had scandalised all the males she had encountered and Coleman thought it was best.

He then rested her hand on his forearm and supported her inside. The door flung open before they reached the stop. "Ambrose?" Milly exclaimed, handkerchief already held tightly in her clenched white hands.

"Alive," Jemima said.

Milly nodded, her face pale. She let Aunt Prudence draw her back inside. "See, child. I told you he was strong."

Aunt Prudence looked directly at Jemima. "Do come in. It is so good to see you. You, too, Inspector."

Jemima looked sideways at the inspector who had taken off his hat and inclined his head in acknowledgement. Aunt Prudence had used a tone of voice when talking to the inspector that Jemima had not heard before. She studied the policeman and then went inside. She wanted a bath and bed and food. But most of all she wanted her husband with her, his arms around her and him telling her how much he loved her. At that moment, she despaired of ever having such again. For she had become a monster. That was what the problem was. Edward thought she was Geneck or at least as evil as that beast.

Yes, she replayed that moment in the basement, Geneck dead on the floor and Edward staring at her, half in horror, half in despair.

"Come into the morning room," Aunt Prudence said. "We have a fresh pot of tea. Jakes!" she called down the hall. "Refreshments, if you please."

Jemima allowed herself to be steered into the morning room. The place where she sat with the tea things in the corner was still set up. The kettle blew steam from its place by the fire. Milly spoke. "I am pleased to see you are safe, Jemima."

Jemima grimaced. "Fulton will be fine. Edward is with him and Heaton too. You will see him soon as good as he was before."

Milly nodded gravely. "I wish I had gone with them."

Jemima's eyes widened. "I think not. It was horrible, Milly."

"Jemima speaks true," Aunt Prudence said as she poured water in the tea pot. "Take some tea."

Aunt Prudence handed Milly a cup of tea and then gave one to Jemima with a pat on the head. Jemima felt a bit teary then. For Aunt Prudence that gesture was akin to a declaration of undying love.

Jakes came in with a trolley. Jemima perked up. There were chicken sandwiches, neatly trimmed, and hot scones with jam and fresh cream. Bread rolls and butter. Inspector Coleman sat upright too, his eyes as keen on the trolley as Jemima. Milly had a slight smile as she watched them. They shared a look and Jemima grinned at Milly. Aunt Prudence was doing the ministrations and they had to wait for her to pile up a plate and hand it to them.

Jemima sipped her tea, hot though it was, and then took her plate. She could not decide what to eat first but was so suddenly empty that she did not care what. She took a bite of a chicken sandwich and her eyes rolled up in the back of her head. She then bit into a hot bread roll with melted butter and then a bite of scone. Perhaps the scone was the best—soft and light and buttery, with fluffy cream to offset the delicious tartness of the strawberry jam that dripped onto her plate.

Aunt Prudence chuckled and lifted a plate to her lap. "It is good to see you have an appetite. Indeed, nothing seems to faze you."

Jemima swallowed. "Forgive me. I have not eaten for days. I am dirty and tired and I do beg to be excused."

"I have ordered a bath prepared for you, Jemima," Milly said. "I shall come up and help you myself."

Jemima shuffled the last of the sandwich into her mouth, ready to wash it down with the last of her tea.

"You must be exhausted, dear girl. Go along with Milly. I saw Beth taking up a pail of water to your room." She leaned sideways. "Make that two...oh here comes the footman with another pail."

Jemima drank off the tea. "Thank you, Aunt." She stood up,

clutched the cloak around her. "Do forgive me, Inspector. I am done for."

He stood up. "I am sure we will speak later."

Milly took her arm and walked companionably to her room.

In her room they found a steaming bath. Milly wasted no time in helping Jemima remove her dirty clothes and Jemima gave no more thought to Inspector Coleman or Aunt Prudence. She did, however, burst into tears thinking about Edward and the look on his face. She lifted her hand and the green power was there at her command.

"Jemima?" Milly asked with a frown. "What is that?"

Jemima looked up. "A long story. Edward will have to explain."

As she wiped the tears, she lay in the warm water, trying to understand. Milly put soap in her hair and rubbed her scalp. Jemima wept with the joy of it.

"I am fine now, Milly."

Milly stood up. "Ring if you need anything. I will go back downstairs and wait for news of Ambrose."

After the door closed behind her friend, she thought more about her current situation. She had more magic than Edward. Entirely accidentally. She had no expectations about being a magician. Then the idea came to her as she scrubbed her hair. Perhaps it would fade away. Yes, it would disappear. Or maybe it could be drained from her.

As she dried herself off, she put on a nightgown, although it was barely past noon. She was exhausted both in mind and in body. There was no point being miserable. Misery would come later when she spoke to her husband who would no longer want her because she was a distempered freak with magic powers.

When she woke from her nap about half-past seven in the evening there was a note on a tray on her bedside table. It was from Edward. She held it in her hand and breathed a few times to calm down.

She opened the note.

Dear Jemima.

I am glad you are at home and safe now. I am still with Fulton. It has been touch and go but he is doing much better. His leg has been re-attached and he is beginning to heal nicely. Heaton thinks he may return home tomorrow or maybe after that.

Please assure Milly that he is out of danger and will be restored to her shortly.

Your loving husband

Edward

Jemima studied this note, looking for clues. Only the "your loving husband" gave her any comfort. He had not attempted to explain that look. She would have to wait.

A knock at the door and Aunt Prudence opened it. "Oh, you are awake. I have held dinner back on the off chance you may join us. Mr White is waiting to speak to you, too."

"Edward?" she asked, throwing her legs over the side of the bed.

"Only that note, my dear. Shall I help you dress?"

"Yes, thank you." For the next half hour, Aunt Prudence assisted in the tying of corsets and piling up of hair. Jemima had never appreciated her so well before then.

"Shall we then? I can smell the dinner. Can you?" Aunt Prudence asked.

"I surely can."

Together they walked down the hall to the dining room. Mr White stood when they entered. "Mrs Huntington?"

"Oh hello Uncle Ferdy. Thank you for waiting."

"Mr White is joining us for dinner," Aunt Prudence said with a glint in her eye. Something about Mr White joining them for dinner excited the old lady.

Jemima looked askance at Aunt Prudence. Milly was sitting by the fire, staring into the flames. "Oh Milly. Fulton should be home tomorrow. He is doing very well. I had it from Edward just now."

Milly smiled. "Thank you, Jemima. I had a note also." She held up a letter. "Edward is remaining with Ambrose then?" she asked.

Jemima sighed. "I do believe he is."

Mr White drew her to a corner of the room while Aunt Prudence fussed over Milly and helped her to the table.

"Are you well, child?" he asked.

Several questions were burning in her chest. "Yes, I am fine now that I have had a nap. But pray tell me and no shilly shallying if you please. Am I a magician?"

Mr White's eyebrows climbed nearly to his hair line. "A magician? Why no, child. You are a female. A small talent if any."

Jemima was at once relieved and then puzzled. "Then why sir, if you please, can I do this?" She lifted a hand and let the green glow show.

He swallowed once and glanced at her. "Oh," he said and licked his lips. "We may have a problem."

"Oh? What problem?" she asked.

"I fear you have a lot of magic and must learn how to use it."

"Why is that a problem? I am happy to study."

He shook his head. "Women are not magicians..."

"But you just said."

"I said you have magic...that is not the same thing. The title is reserved for men."

Jemima was starting to understand and it revolted her sense of pride as well as making her understand the degree of prejudice against her sex, which she could not help as she had no choice in the matter. It also made her think of Edward and his expression. Was that the reason?

Jakes called her back to the task at hand. "Dinner, Mrs Huntington."

Mr White offered his arm and they walked into the dining room. The soup was being ladled into her bowl as she sat. "Forgive me for making you wait."

❦

SOMETIME IN THE NIGHT, THE MATTRESS MOVED AS A BODY CLIMBED into it. She was awake instantly. "Edward?" she whispered.

"Yes," he whispered back and gathered her into his arms.

She thought the meeting would be awkward. She nuzzled her head against his shoulder. "Are you all right? How is Fulton?"

"I am well, just tired. Fulton is doing very well. Heaton is going to deliver him tomorrow." He kissed the top of her head. "Thank heaven you are safe."

"I am safe because of you."

"No. In spite of me."

Jemima jerked up. "What on earth do you mean? I am alive."

"Yes, you live," he said and brushed a finger against her cheek. He had built up the fire and there was a faint glow that allowed her to see his eyes glittering in the light. "I was so afraid. I thought I had lost you. I thought I had said goodbye to you. When Fulton was injured and you were almost dead, I was in a dilemma."

"Dilemma?" she asked, slightly awed. This conversation was not taking place at the time or place she had imagined it and nor was the content of the conversation anything like she expected either.

"Try to save you from Geneck or stop Fulton from dying. I hope you will forgive me for choosing Fulton."

"You had already saved me from Geneck by draining my heart. Do you now understand what happened?"

He urged her to lie against him and stroked his hand along her arm. "In part. I had seen something similar when Fulton tried to rip out Geneck's heart. A loop of some kind, a connection that drained Fulton and Geneck took the power."

"I did not want to die. I think my ruby heart knew that. You see, you are in my ruby heart—the essence of you. When Geneck came for me with all that power, the ruby heart reached for it, drew it in."

"You think you have my essence in you?" he asked, sounding rather astounded.

"Yes, your magic. You put it in the gem, did you not?"

"Yes, belatedly I did realise that. But that is not my essence."

"I think it is. I think this magic you have is part of you and takes after your character."

"An interesting suggestion. One that will keep many a magician pondering for years to come."

"So, Edward. What about the magic I have in me? It is not just you anymore. It is from Geneck and the magicians he killed."

Edward nodded and ummed and ahed.

"Well? Are you stalling?"

Edward coughed lightly, stifling a laugh she expected. "No, not stalling. Just speechless."

She sat up and glared down at him. "Speechless? I tell you, sir, that

that is not good enough. I want answers, not silence. Mr White is most dismayed. He says that magicians are men but agreed I had magic."

"Yes, you do. Always did have some. Now you are fair burning with it. I can feel it throbbing beneath your skin."

"I did? But you never said. Now what am I supposed to do?"

"Learn to control it, dearest wife."

"But Mr White said..."

"I will teach you and I will continue to learn. Mr White will come around. The brotherhood are sadly depleted. They will need you and me if they are going to continue."

"Then you do not find me repulsive?" she asked hesitantly.

"Why no! Why ever would you think that?"

"Just the look on your face, sort of horror, revulsion..."

"I was amazed and horrified but not at you—at what had happened. I could barely think straight, and Fulton was bleeding, and you were alive and I nearly fainted but could not because Fulton needed me. Did you think I...I did not love you anymore?"

Jemima sniffed. "Why yes, that is exactly what I thought."

"Dearest, Jemima. We have our whole lives ahead of us. Something I thought I would not have when you demanded I drain your ruby heart and let you die. Through the highs and lows I will love you. Through your escapades and adventures, I will be there. You may yell at me and think me dull, but I will never stop loving you. You are my life."

"Ohhhh!" she said and snuggled into him again, kissing the tip of his chin. "Edward, you say the loveliest things."

"You say that now. Wait until you start your lessons. You have ten times more power than me, my love. You will be a force to be reckoned with. I am not sure who to pity more; me for having to teach you or the brotherhood when they find out that they have a woman magician in their midst."

Jemima chuckled. "But can you now drain this power from me?"

"No, I think not. You drew it into yourself and now it is part of you. You just have to learn to use it responsibly."

"Oh, Edward. Are you sure? Will it not offend your masculine pride to have a wife who is more powerful than you?"

"No," he said and kissed her forehead. "No, because I will be right beside you on this, our next journey."

"When do we start?" she asked, closing her eyes with a sigh of contentment. Edward's arms and warmth surrounded her.

"In the morning, but first we have something else to do."

He lifted her chin and kissed her lips.

"Oh, I see. A very important undertaking."

And then she did not speak for quite a while.

The End

ACKNOWLEDGMENTS

I wish to thank my readers for their support. I am so glad you enjoy my stories. I hope you keep on reading and enjoying them.

I would also like to thank Maxine McArthur for being so supportive of the Cry Havoc series and for encouraging me to keep writing, more and more. It was great to work with you Max.

Many thanks to Jason Nahrung for fantastic proofreading. Nobody does it better...

I have some great writing buddies and I'd like to give them a shout out: Nicole, Kylie, Russell, Cat, Rob, Shauna, Kim, Rob 2, Ian and Joanne.

I couldn't do this writing gig without the support of my family: my partner Matthew Farrer and my kids and grandkids. You give me the energy and the excitement to keep going.

I dedicated this book to Bridget, Matthew's mother, who passed away not long after I finished the draft of this story. It was a pleasure to get to know you Bridget and also to take care of you at the end. I hope there are many books where you are.

I had such fun writing this story. In my heart I think I like it better than Ruby Heart. Maybe that's because I know the characters better, or because I've let them leap out of the holes I had them in.

Do let me know what you think, dear reader. I hope you have as much fun reading *Emerald Fire* as I did writing it.

Donna Maree Hanson

February 2019

ABOUT THE AUTHOR

Donna Maree Hanson is a traditionally and independently published author of fantasy, science fiction and horror. She also writes paranormal romance under the pseudonym of Dani Kristoff. Her dark fantasy series (which some reviewers have called "grim dark"), Dragon Wine, was first published by Momentum Books (Pan Macmillan digital imprint) in 2014. *Shatterwing*: Part One, and *Skywatcher*: Part Two, are now re-published independently in digital and print-on-demand formats. The next two instalments of Dragon Wine, *Deathwings* and *Bloodstorm*, were published in 2017. The final instalments in the Dragon Wine series, *Skyfire* and *Moonfall,* were published in 2018.

In April 2015, Donna was awarded the A. Bertram Chandler Award for "Outstanding Achievement in Australian Science Fiction" for her work in running science fiction conventions, publishing and broader SF community contributions. Donna also writes science fiction romance/space opera, with *Rayessa and the Space Pirates* and *Rae and Essa's Space Adventures* out with Escape Publishing. *Opi Battles the Space Pirates* was published independently in 2017. In 2016, Donna commenced her PhD candidature researching feminism in popular romance at the University of Canberra. Also available is her epic fantasy series The Silverlands: *Argenterra, Oathbound* and *Ungiven Land.*

The Cry Havoc series is a steampunk-themed fantasy, with romantic elements, starting with *Ruby Heart* and *Emerald Fire*. It is based in Victorian England and features magicians and a very precocious Jemima Hardcastle. Another book, *Amber Rose*, is planned in the series.

Donna lives in Canberra with her partner and fellow writer, Matthew Farrer.

ALSO BY DONNA MAREE HANSON

Cry Havoc Series (steampunk fantasy)

Ruby Heart, Cry Havoc Book One

Emerald Fire, Cry Havoc Book Two

Silverlands Series (Epic Fantasy)

Oathbound:Silverlands Book Two

Ungiven Land: Silverlands Book Three

Dragon Wine Series (Dark Fantasy)

Shatterwing: Dragon Wine Part One

Skywatcher: Dragon Wine Part Two

Deathwings: Dragon Wine Part Three

Bloodstorm: Dragon Wine Part Four

Skyfire: Dragon Wine Part Five

Moonfall: Dragon Wine Part Six

Love and Space Pirates (Science Fiction Romance-Sweet level)

Rayessa and the Space Pirates

Rae and Essa's Space Adventures

Opi Battles the Space Pirates

Short story collections

Beneath the Floating City: Short science fiction stories

Through These Eyes: Tales of Magic Realism and Fantasy

www.ingramcontent.com/pod-product-compliance
Lightning Source LLC
Chambersburg PA
CBHW021408110726
47901CB00008B/2110